my cat LOKI

Volume 2

Story and Art by
Bettina M. Kurkoski

TOKYOPOP®

HAMBURG // LONDON // LOS ANGELES // TOKYO

My Cat Loki Vol. 2
Created by Bettina M. Kurkoski

Lettering - Star Print Brokers
Production Artist - Lucas Rivera
Cover Design - Anne Marie Horne

Editor - Lillian Diaz-Przybyl
Digital Imaging Manager - Chris Buford
Pre-Production Supervisor - Erika Terriquez
Art Director - Anne Marie Horne
Production Manager - Elisabeth Brizzi
Managing Editor - Vy Nguyen
VP of Production - Ron Klamert
Editor-in-Chief - Rob Tokar
Publisher - Mike Kiley
President and C.O.O. - John Parker
C.E.O. and Chief Creative Officer - Stuart Levy

A **TOKYOPOP** Manga

TOKYOPOP and 🐾 are trademarks or registered trademarks of TOKYOPOP Inc.

TOKYOPOP Inc.
5900 Wilshire Blvd. Suite 2000
Los Angeles, CA 90036

E-mail: info@TOKYOPOP.com
Come visit us online at www.TOKYOPOP.com

ISBN: 978-1-59816-732-0

First TOKYOPOP printing: August 2007
10 9 8 7 6 5 4 3 2 1
Printed in the USA

TABLE OF CONTENTS

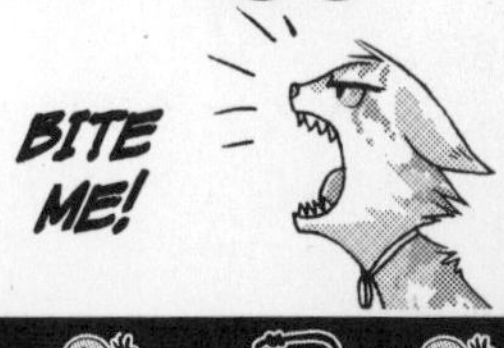
BITE ME!

CHAPTER 1

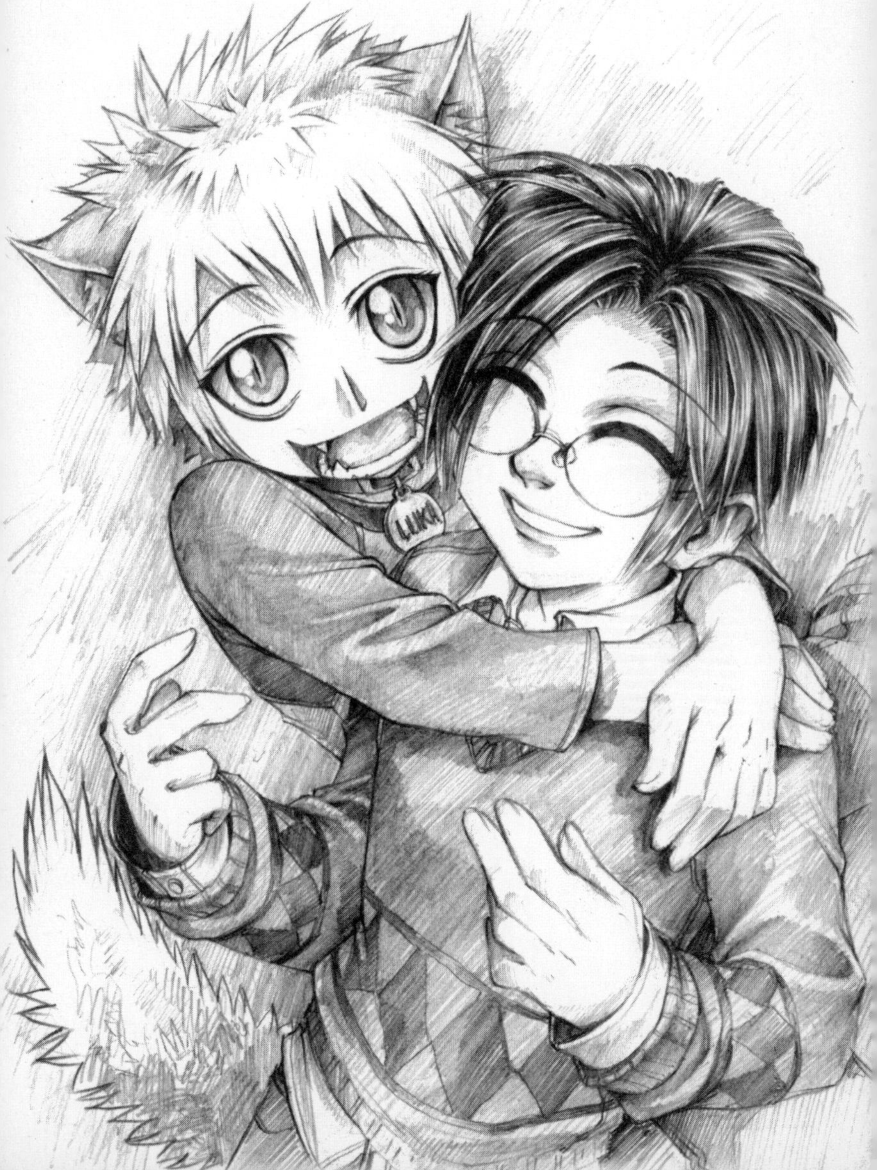

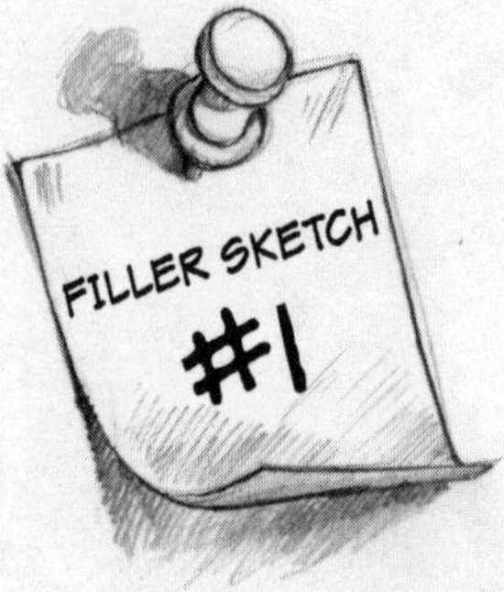
FILLER SKETCH
#1

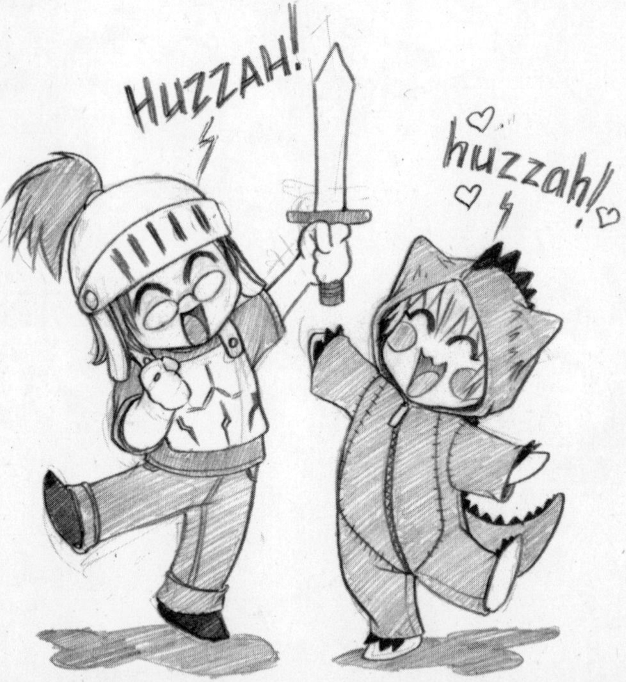
HUZZAH!
huzzah!

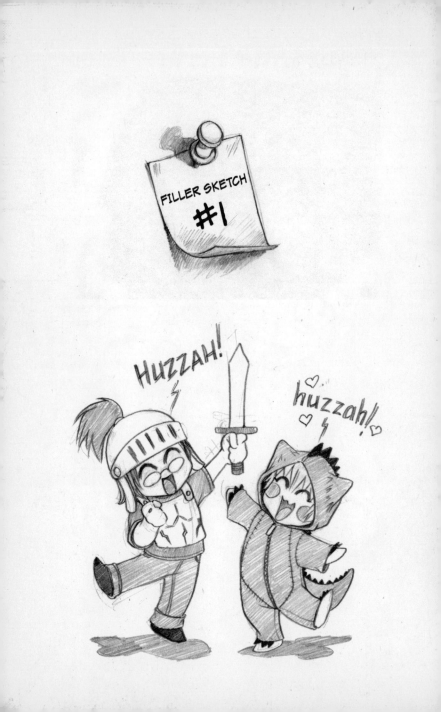

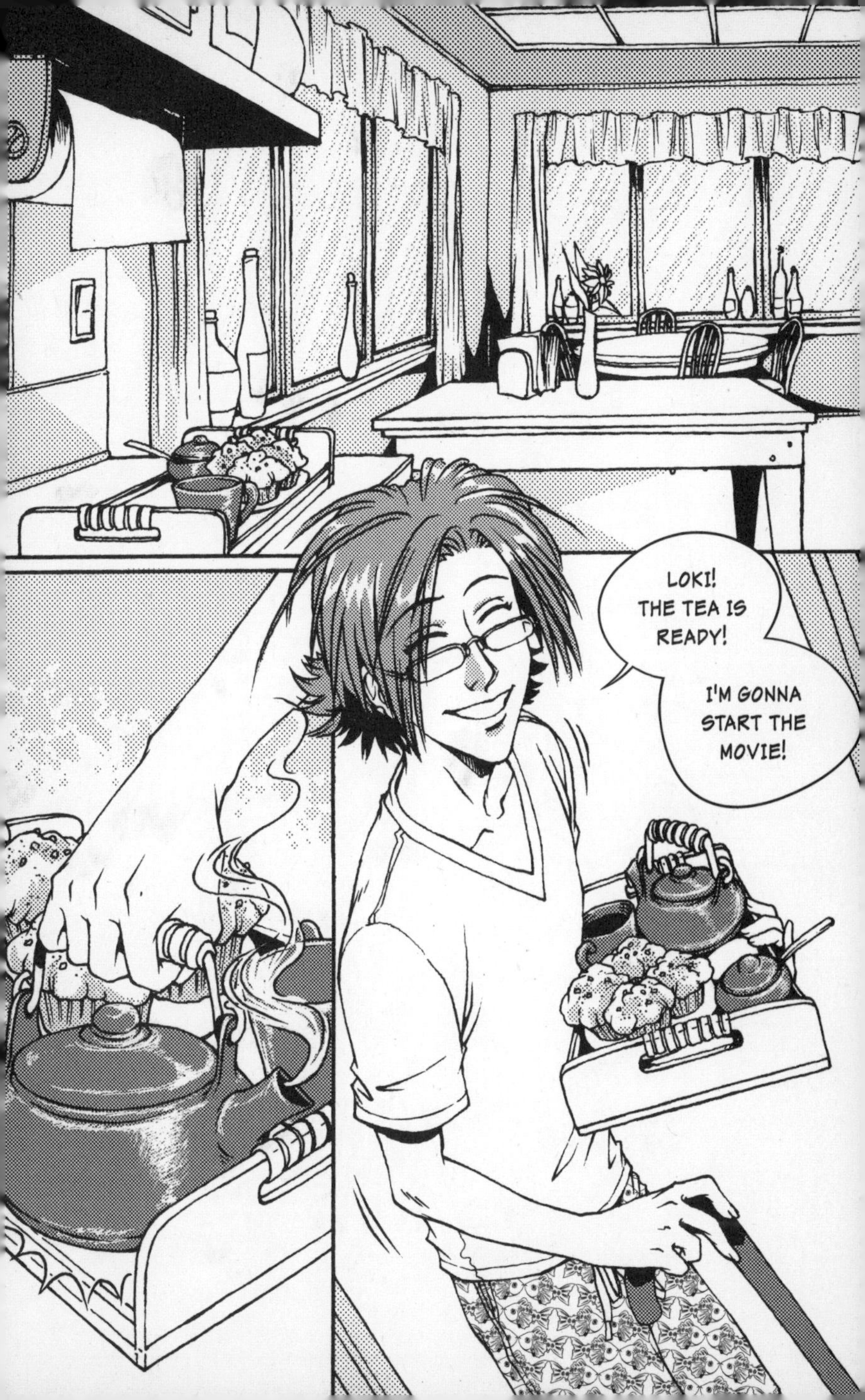
LOKI! THE TEA IS READY!
I'M GONNA START THE MOVIE!

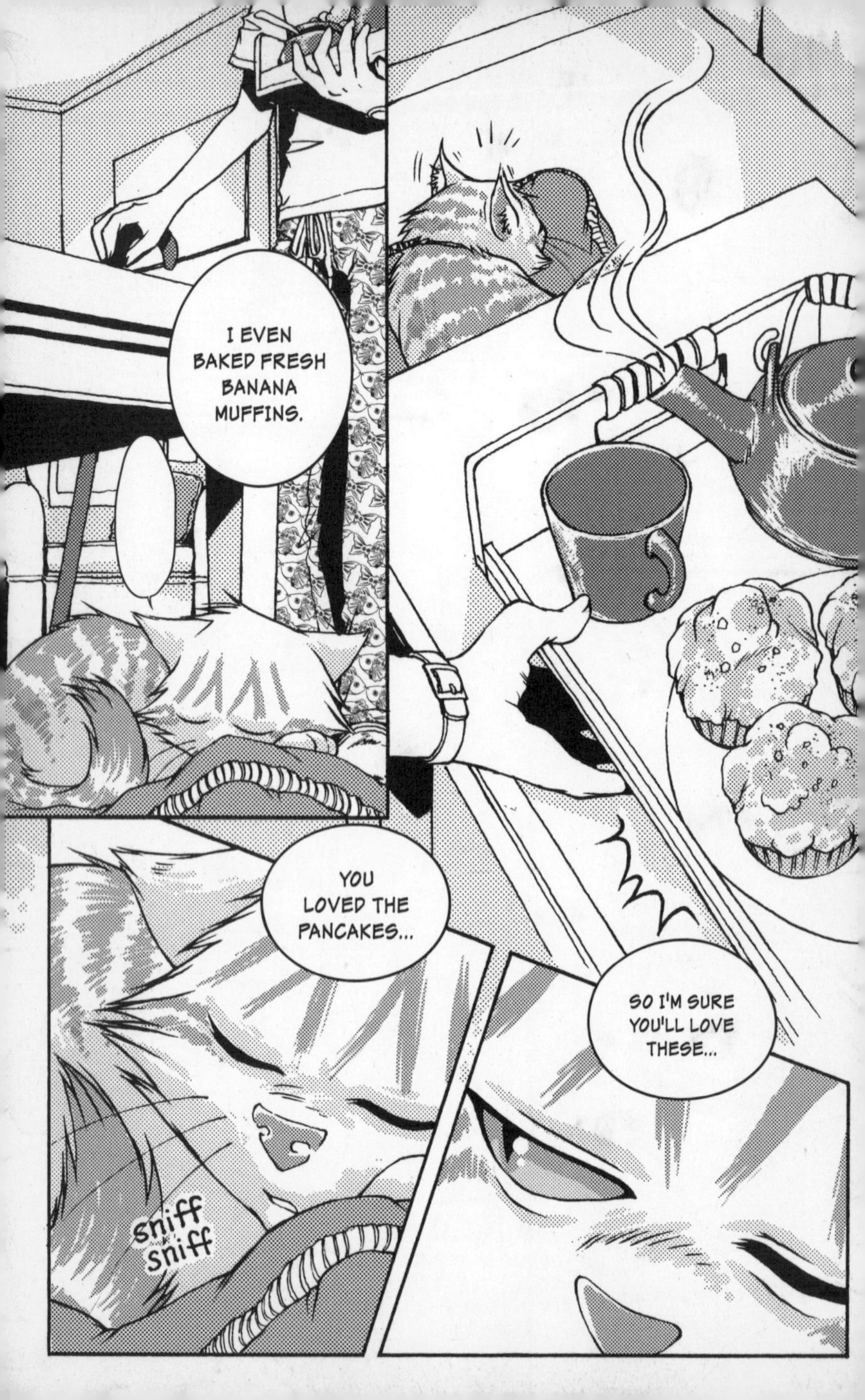
I EVEN BAKED FRESH BANANA MUFFINS.
YOU LOVED THE PANCAKES...
sniff sniff
SO I'M SURE YOU'LL LOVE THESE...

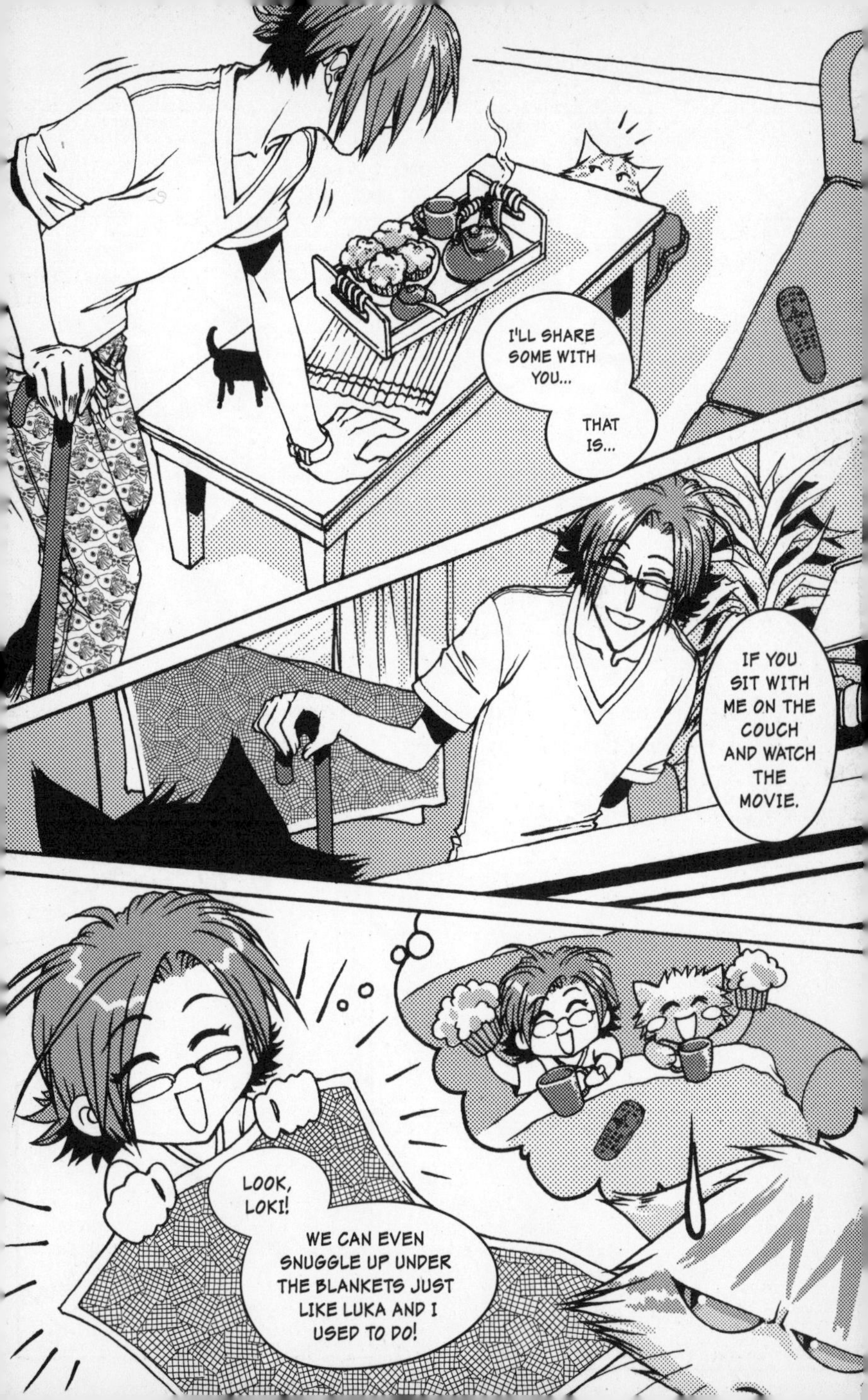
I'LL SHARE SOME WITH YOU...
THAT IS...
IF YOU SIT WITH ME ON THE COUCH AND WATCH THE MOVIE.
LOOK, LOKI!
WE CAN EVEN SNUGGLE UP UNDER THE BLANKETS JUST LIKE LUKA AND I USED TO DO!

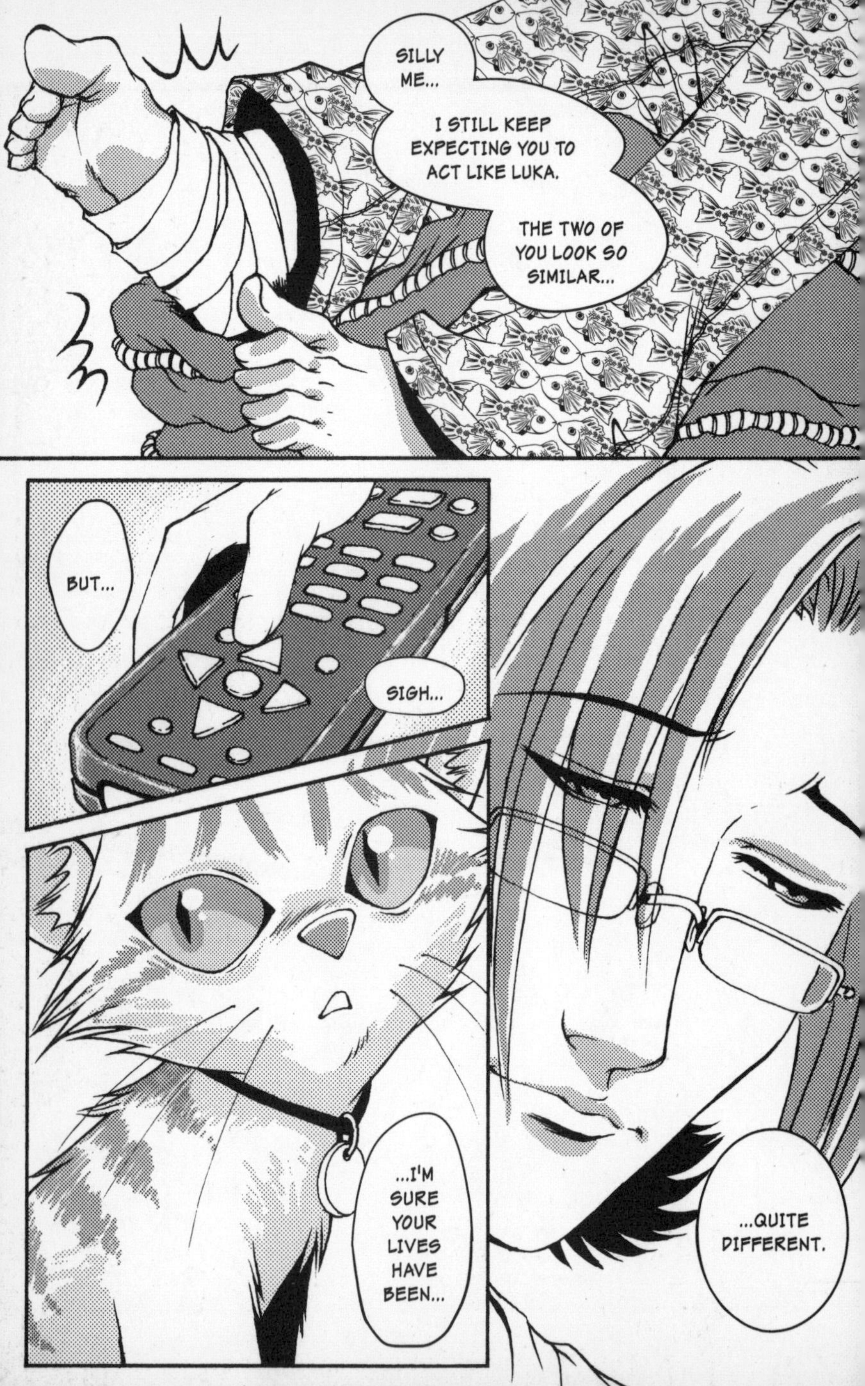
SILLY ME...
I STILL KEEP EXPECTING YOU TO ACT LIKE LUKA.
THE TWO OF YOU LOOK SO SIMILAR...
BUT...
SIGH...
...I'M SURE YOUR LIVES HAVE BEEN...
...QUITE DIFFERENT.

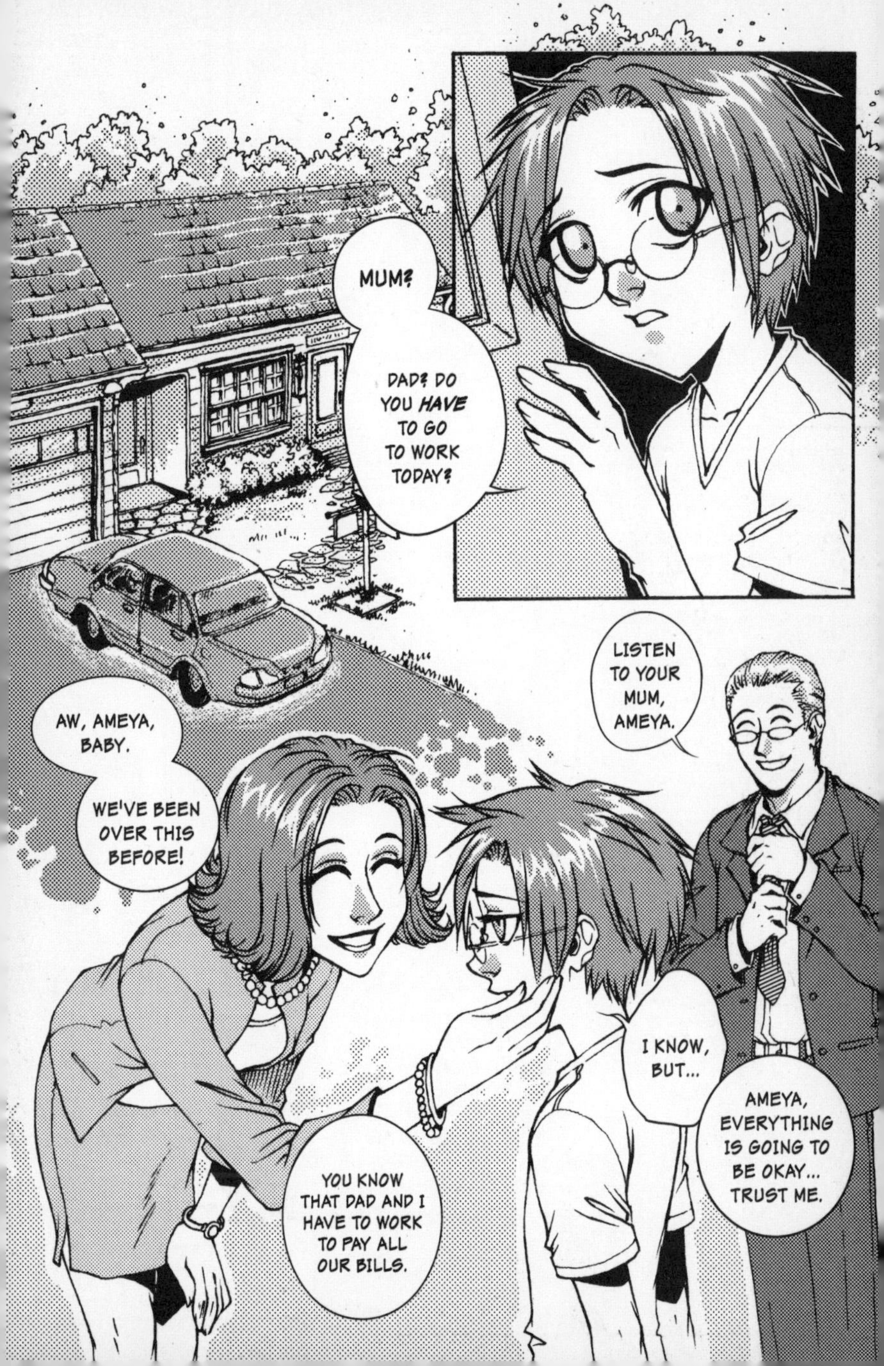
MUM?
DAD? DO YOU *HAVE* TO GO TO WORK TODAY?
AW, AMEYA, BABY.
WE'VE BEEN OVER THIS BEFORE!
YOU KNOW THAT DAD AND I HAVE TO WORK TO PAY ALL OUR BILLS.
I KNOW, BUT...
LISTEN TO YOUR MUM, AMEYA.
AMEYA, EVERYTHING IS GOING TO BE OKAY... TRUST ME.

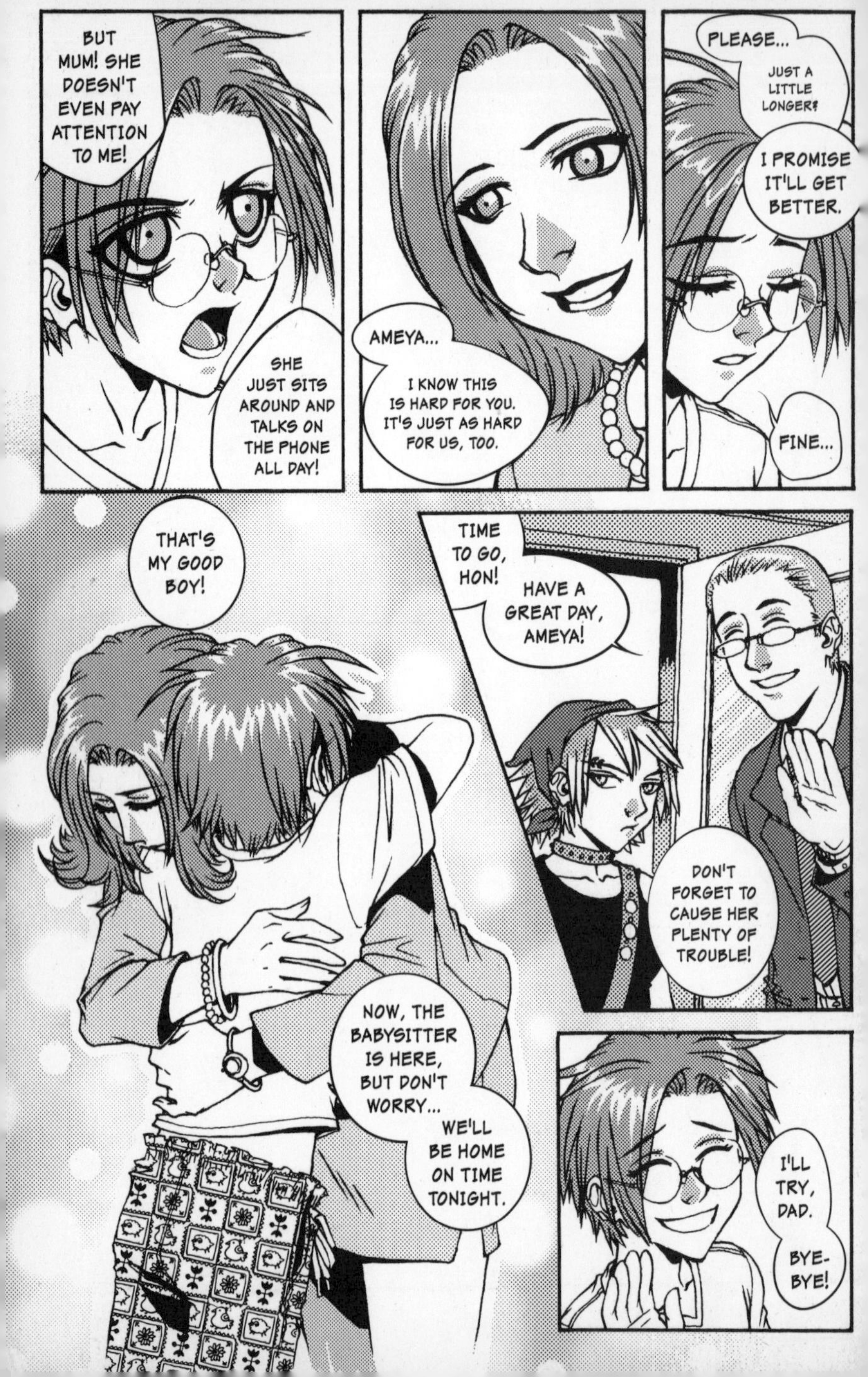
BUT MUM! SHE DOESN'T EVEN PAY ATTENTION TO ME!
SHE JUST SITS AROUND AND TALKS ON THE PHONE ALL DAY!
AMEYA...
I KNOW THIS IS HARD FOR YOU. IT'S JUST AS HARD FOR US, TOO.
PLEASE...
JUST A LITTLE LONGER?
I PROMISE IT'LL GET BETTER.
FINE...
THAT'S MY GOOD BOY!
NOW, THE BABYSITTER IS HERE, BUT DON'T WORRY...
WE'LL BE HOME ON TIME TONIGHT.
TIME TO GO, HON!
HAVE A GREAT DAY, AMEYA!
DON'T FORGET TO CAUSE HER PLENTY OF TROUBLE!
I'LL TRY, DAD.
BYE-BYE!

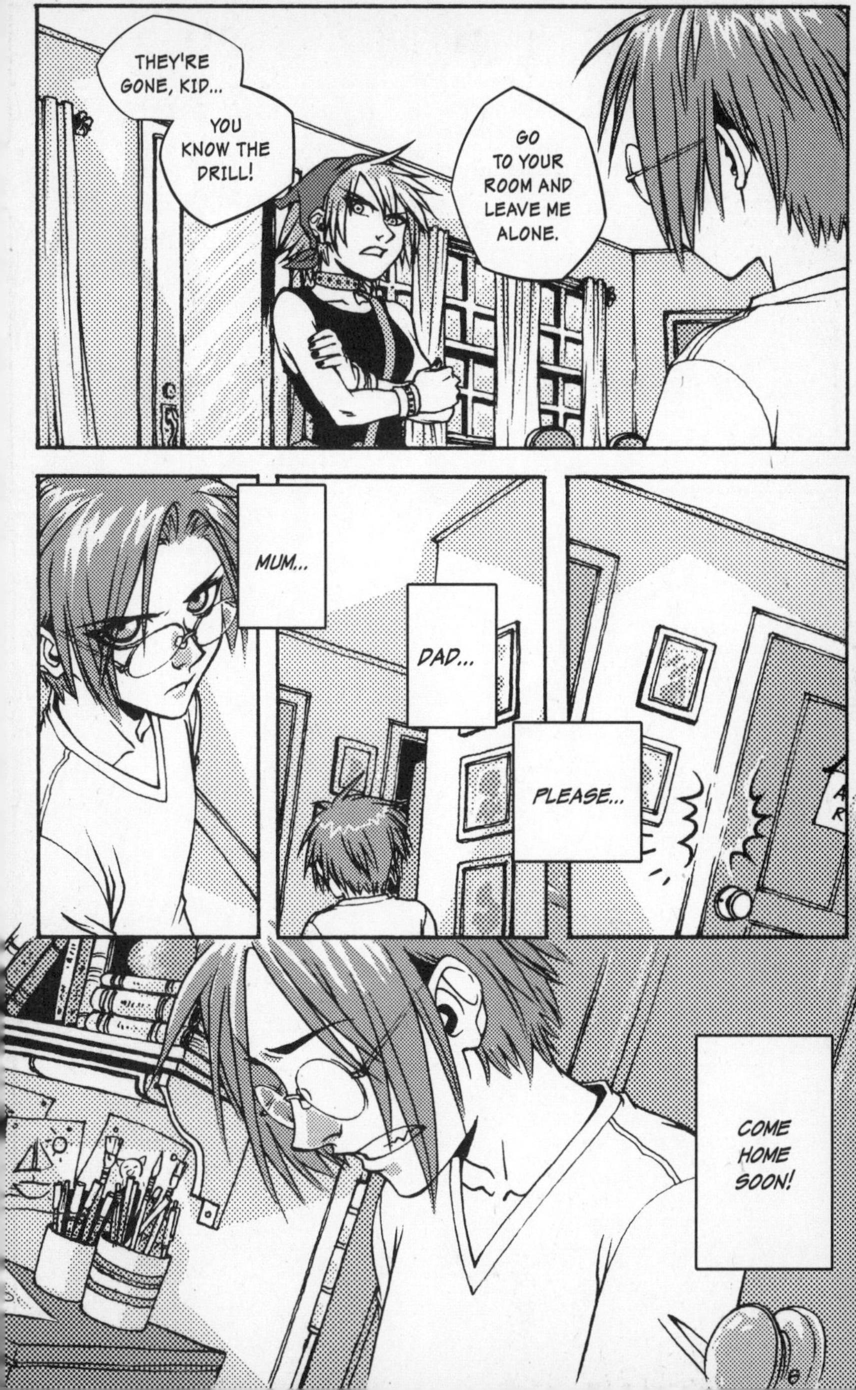
THEY'RE GONE, KID...
YOU KNOW THE DRILL!
GO TO YOUR ROOM AND LEAVE ME ALONE.
MUM...
DAD...
PLEASE...
COME HOME SOON!

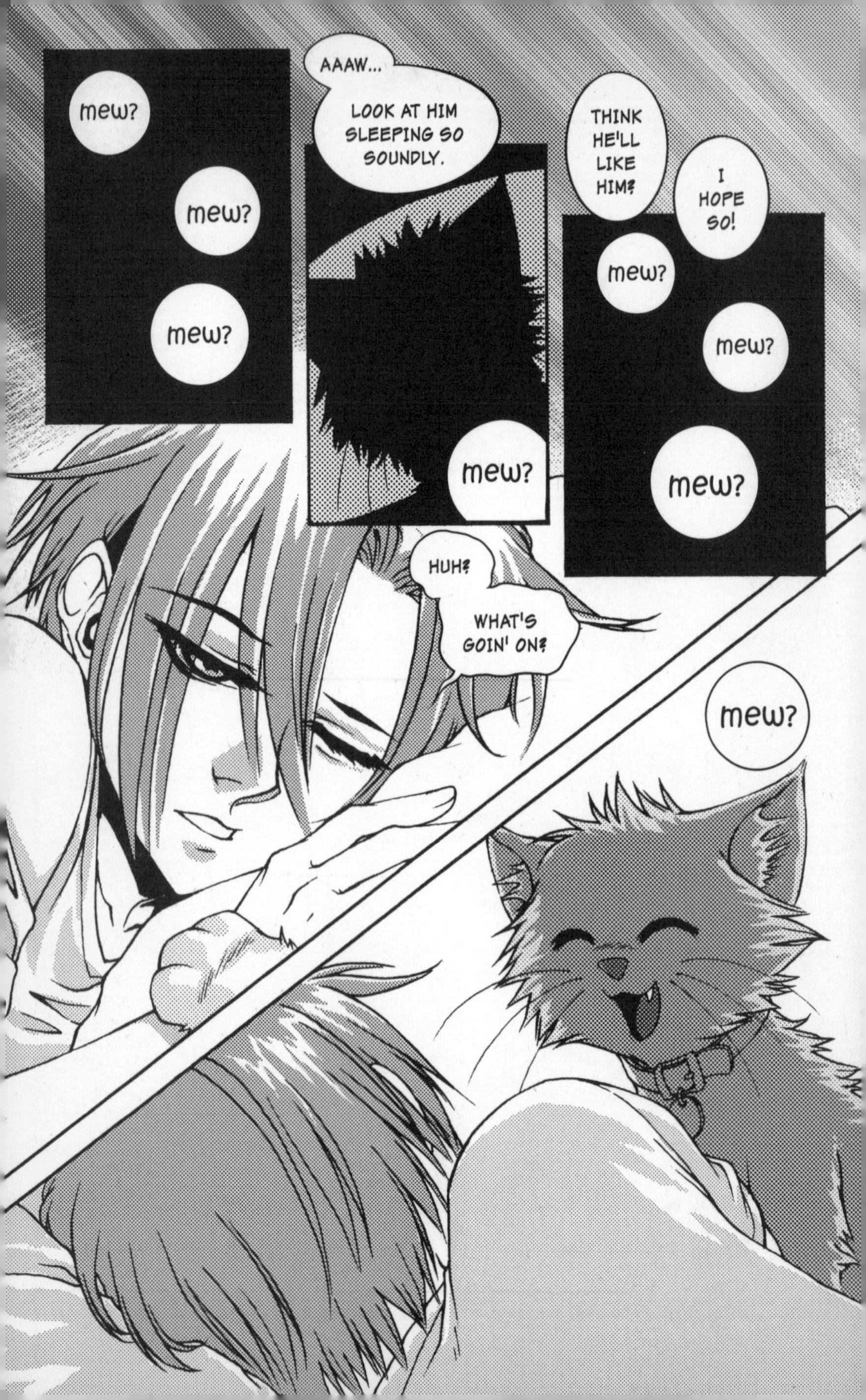
mew?
mew?
mew?
AAAW...
LOOK AT HIM SLEEPING SO SOUNDLY.
mew?
THINK HE'LL LIKE HIM?
I HOPE SO!
mew?
mew?
mew?
HUH?
WHAT'S GOIN' ON?
mew?

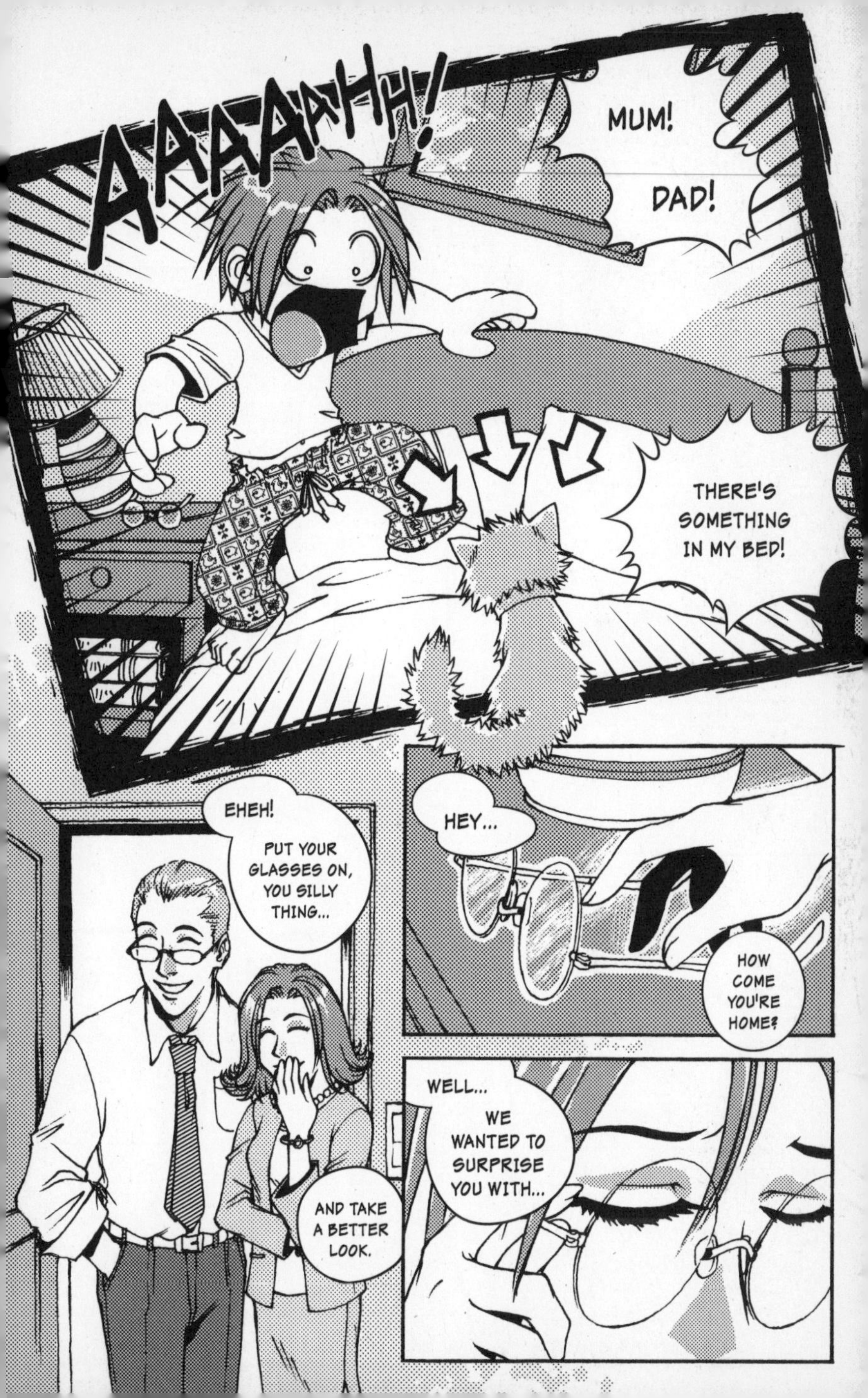
AAAAAHH!
MUM!
DAD!
THERE'S SOMETHING IN MY BED!
EHEH!
PUT YOUR GLASSES ON, YOU SILLY THING...
AND TAKE A BETTER LOOK.
HEY...
HOW COME YOU'RE HOME?
WELL...
WE WANTED TO SURPRISE YOU WITH...

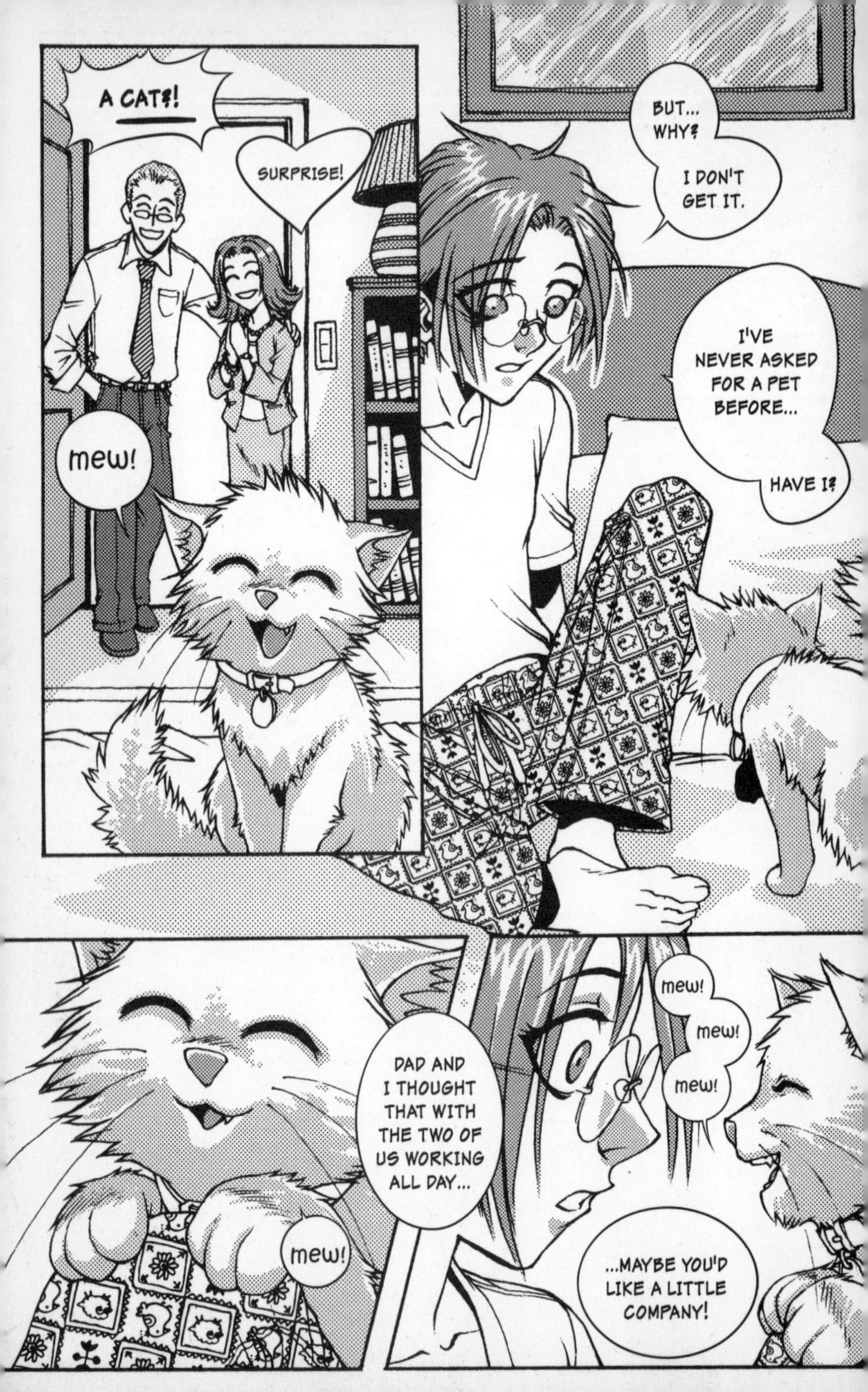
A CAT?!
SURPRISE!
mew!
BUT... WHY?
I DON'T GET IT.
I'VE NEVER ASKED FOR A PET BEFORE...
HAVE I?
DAD AND I THOUGHT THAT WITH THE TWO OF US WORKING ALL DAY...
mew!
mew!
mew!
mew!
...MAYBE YOU'D LIKE A LITTLE COMPANY!

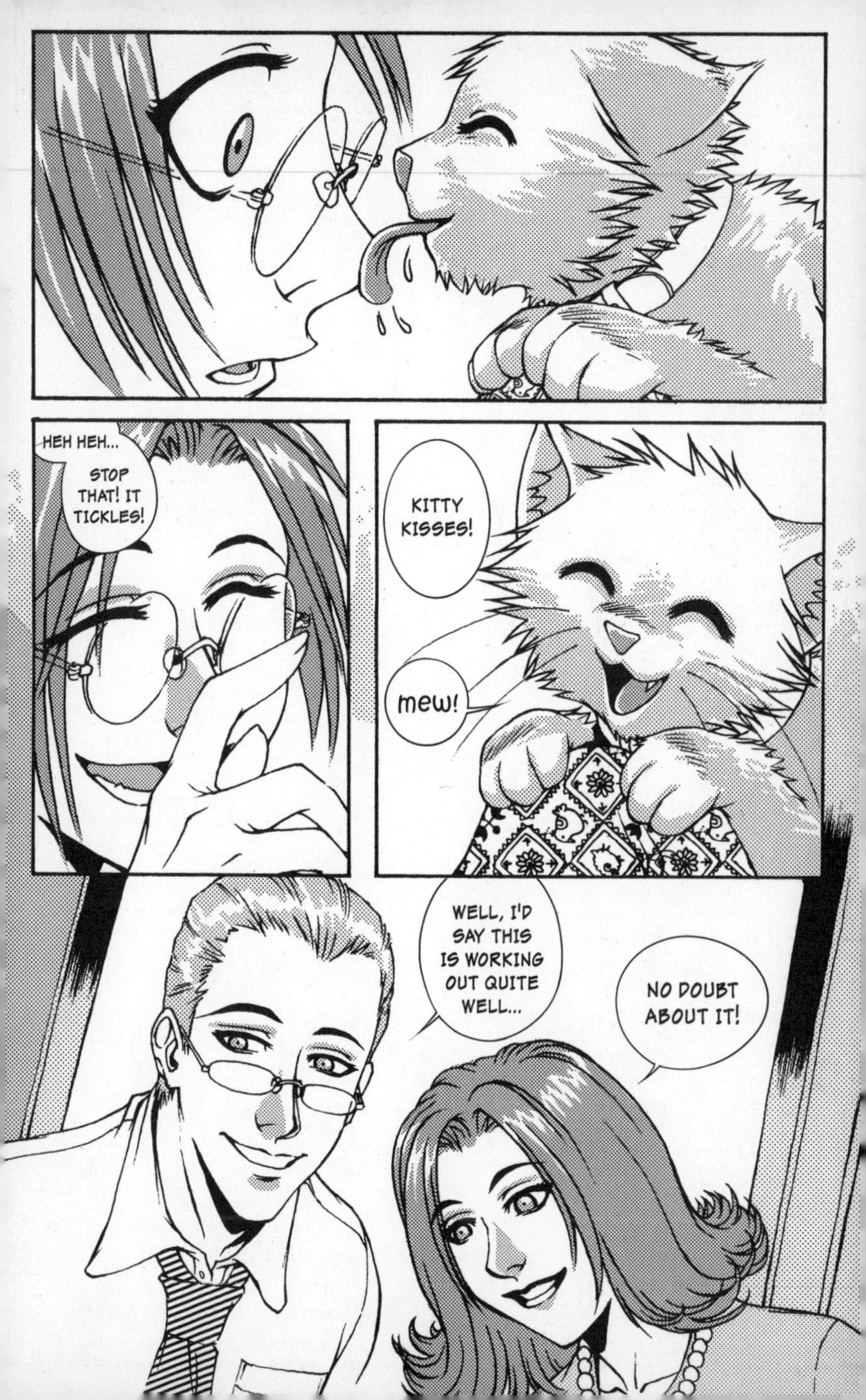
HEH HEH...
STOP THAT! IT TICKLES!
KITTY KISSES!
mew!
WELL, I'D SAY THIS IS WORKING OUT QUITE WELL...
NO DOUBT ABOUT IT!

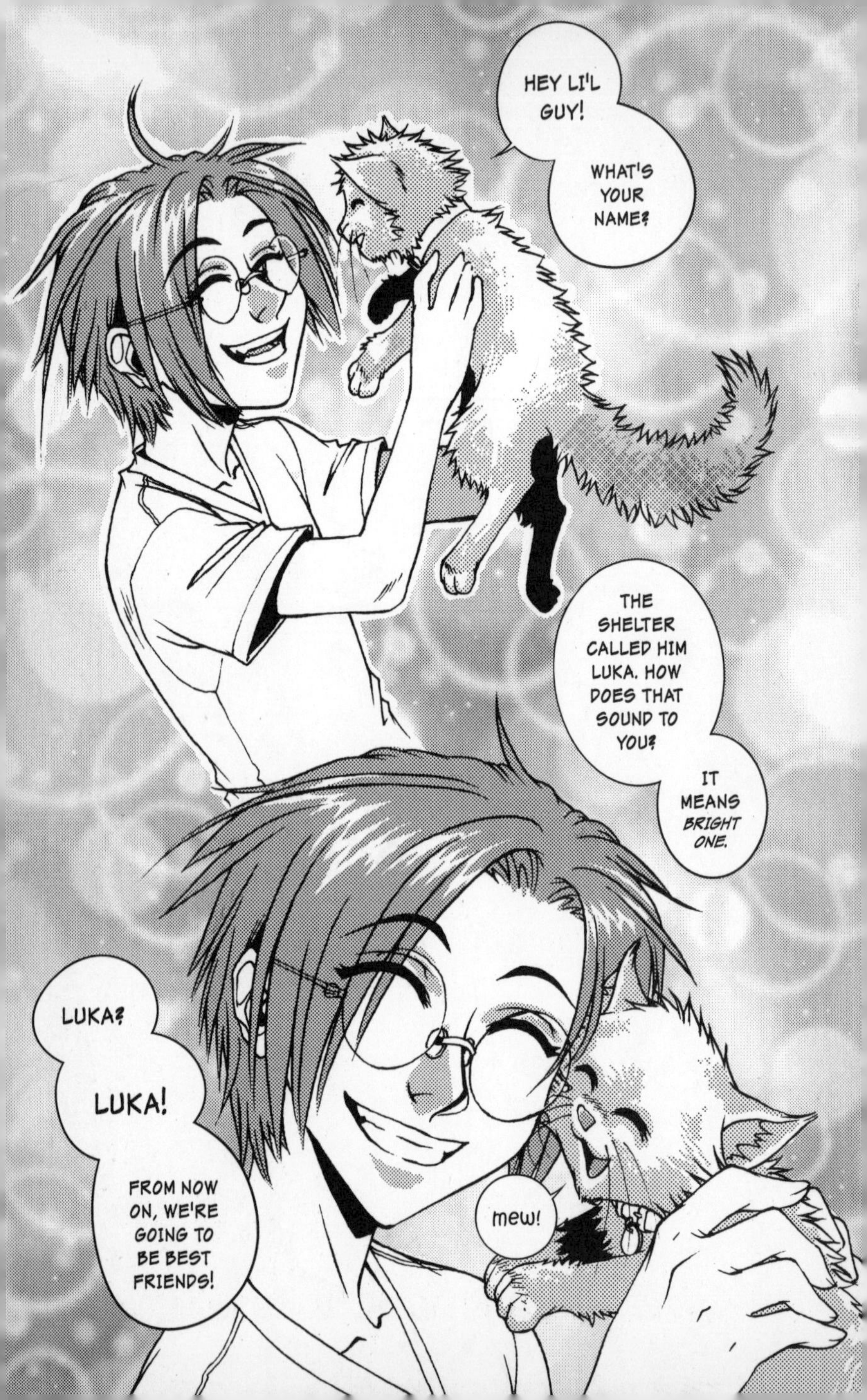
HEY LI'L GUY!
WHAT'S YOUR NAME?
THE SHELTER CALLED HIM LUKA. HOW DOES THAT SOUND TO YOU?
IT MEANS *BRIGHT ONE.*
LUKA?
LUKA!
FROM NOW ON, WE'RE GOING TO BE BEST FRIENDS!
mew!

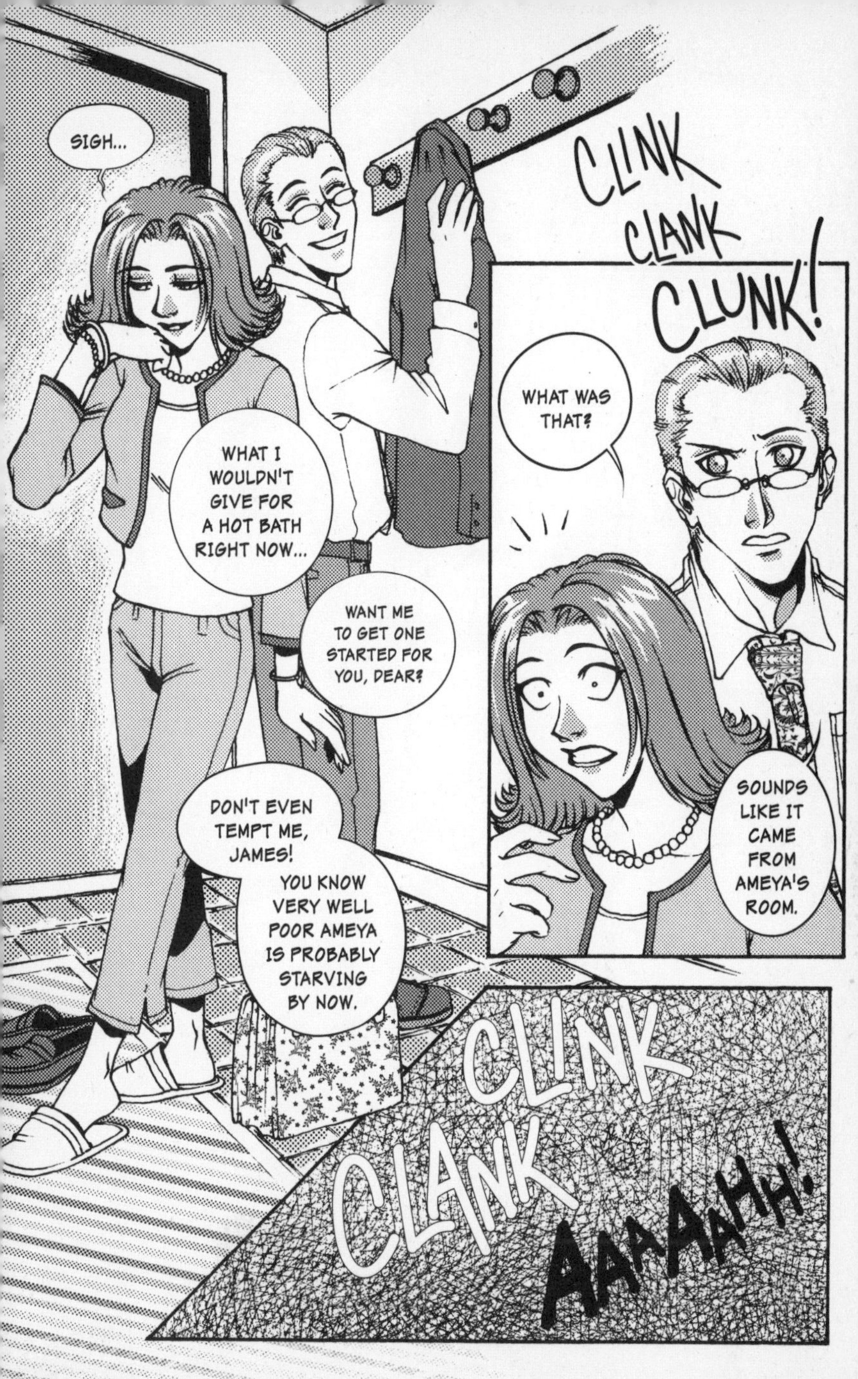
SIGH...
WHAT I WOULDN'T GIVE FOR A HOT BATH RIGHT NOW...
WANT ME TO GET ONE STARTED FOR YOU, DEAR?
DON'T EVEN TEMPT ME, JAMES!
YOU KNOW VERY WELL POOR AMEYA IS PROBABLY STARVING BY NOW.
CLINK
CLANK
CLUNK!
WHAT WAS THAT?
SOUNDS LIKE IT CAME FROM AMEYA'S ROOM.
CLINK
CLANK
AAAAHH!

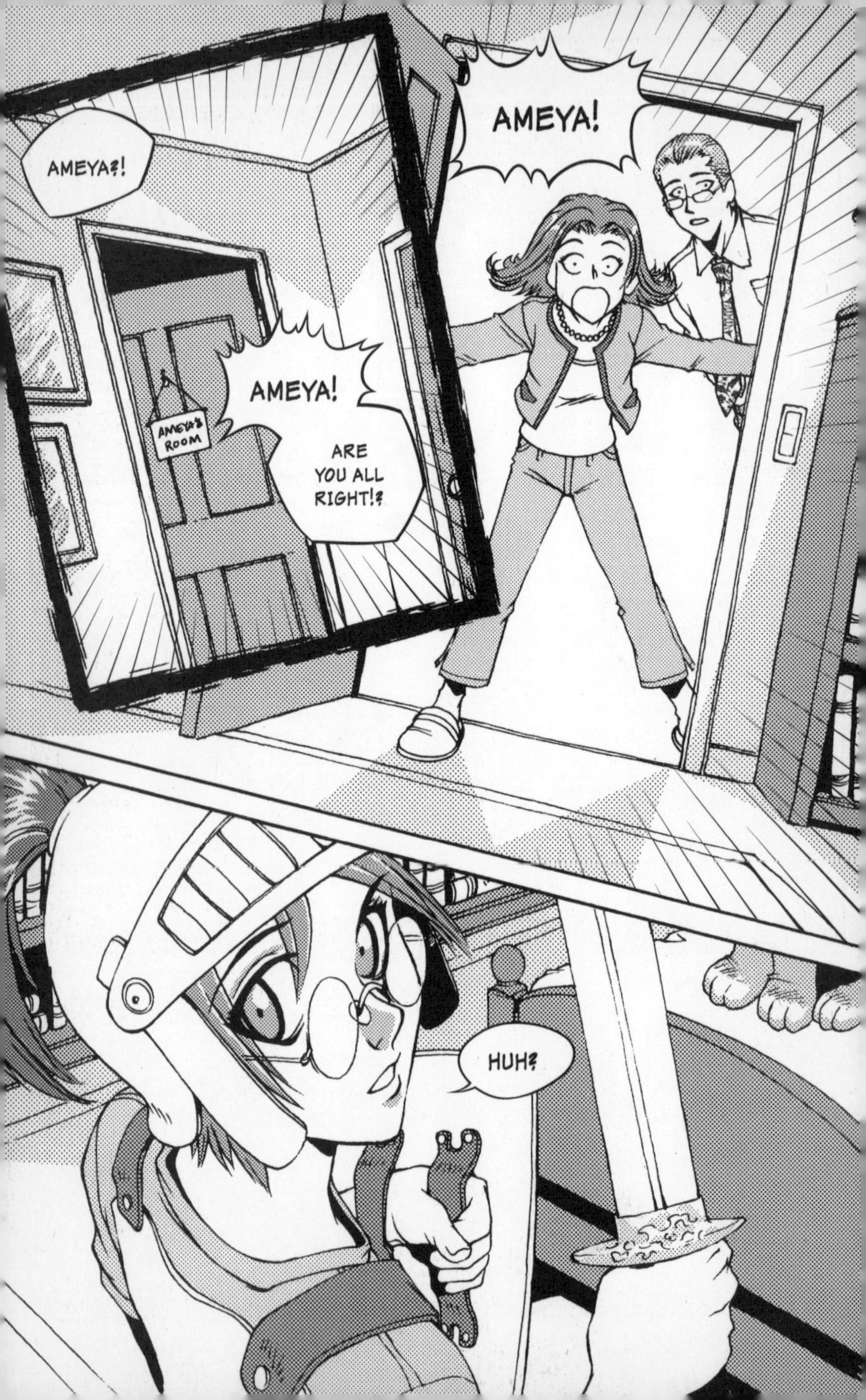
AMEYA?!
AMEYA'S ROOM
AMEYA!
ARE YOU ALL RIGHT!?
AMEYA!
HUH?

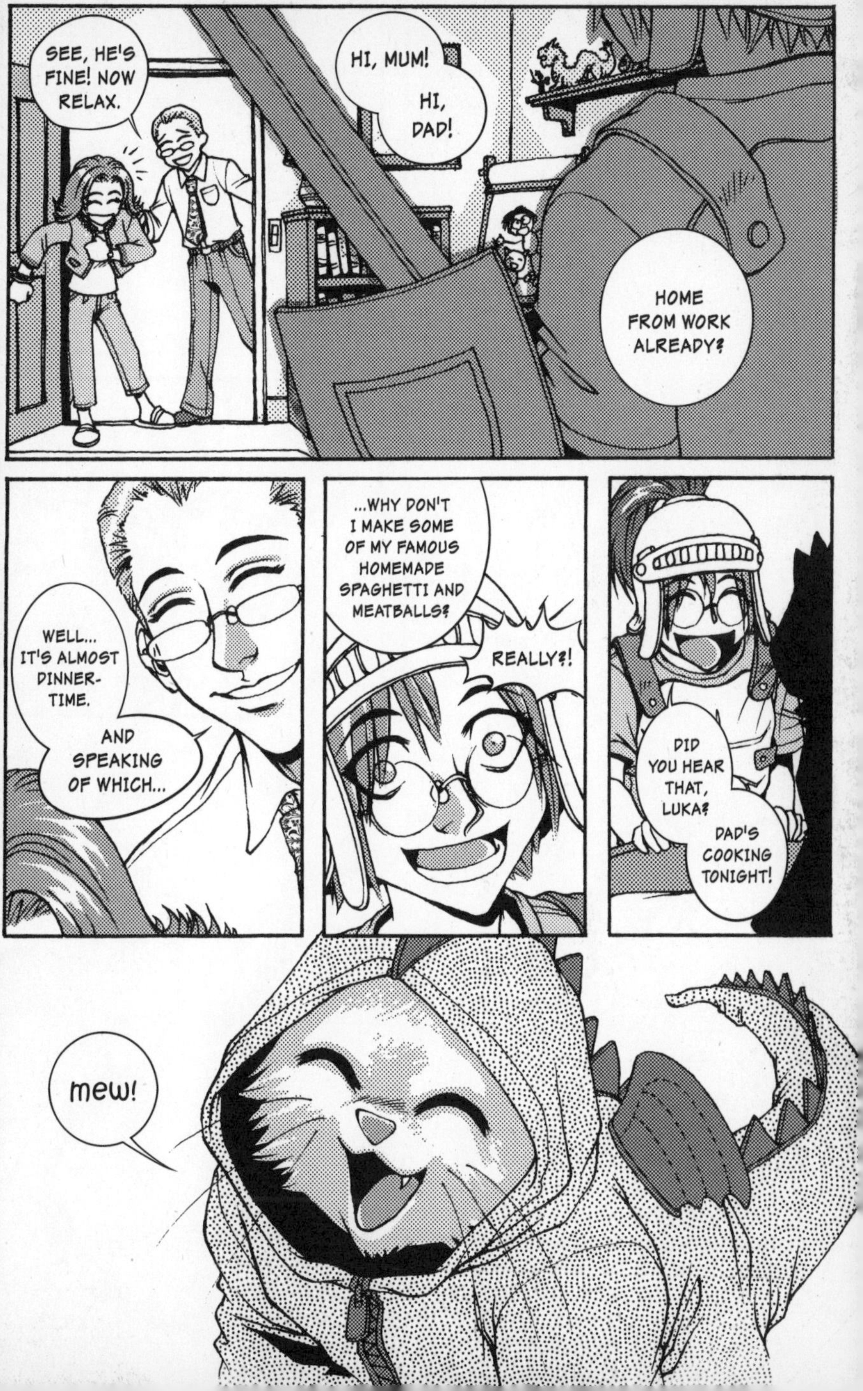
SEE, HE'S FINE! NOW RELAX.
HI, MUM!
HI, DAD!
HOME FROM WORK ALREADY?
WELL... IT'S ALMOST DINNER-TIME.
AND SPEAKING OF WHICH...
...WHY DON'T I MAKE SOME OF MY FAMOUS HOMEMADE SPAGHETTI AND MEATBALLS?
REALLY?!
DID YOU HEAR THAT, LUKA?
DAD'S COOKING TONIGHT!
mew!

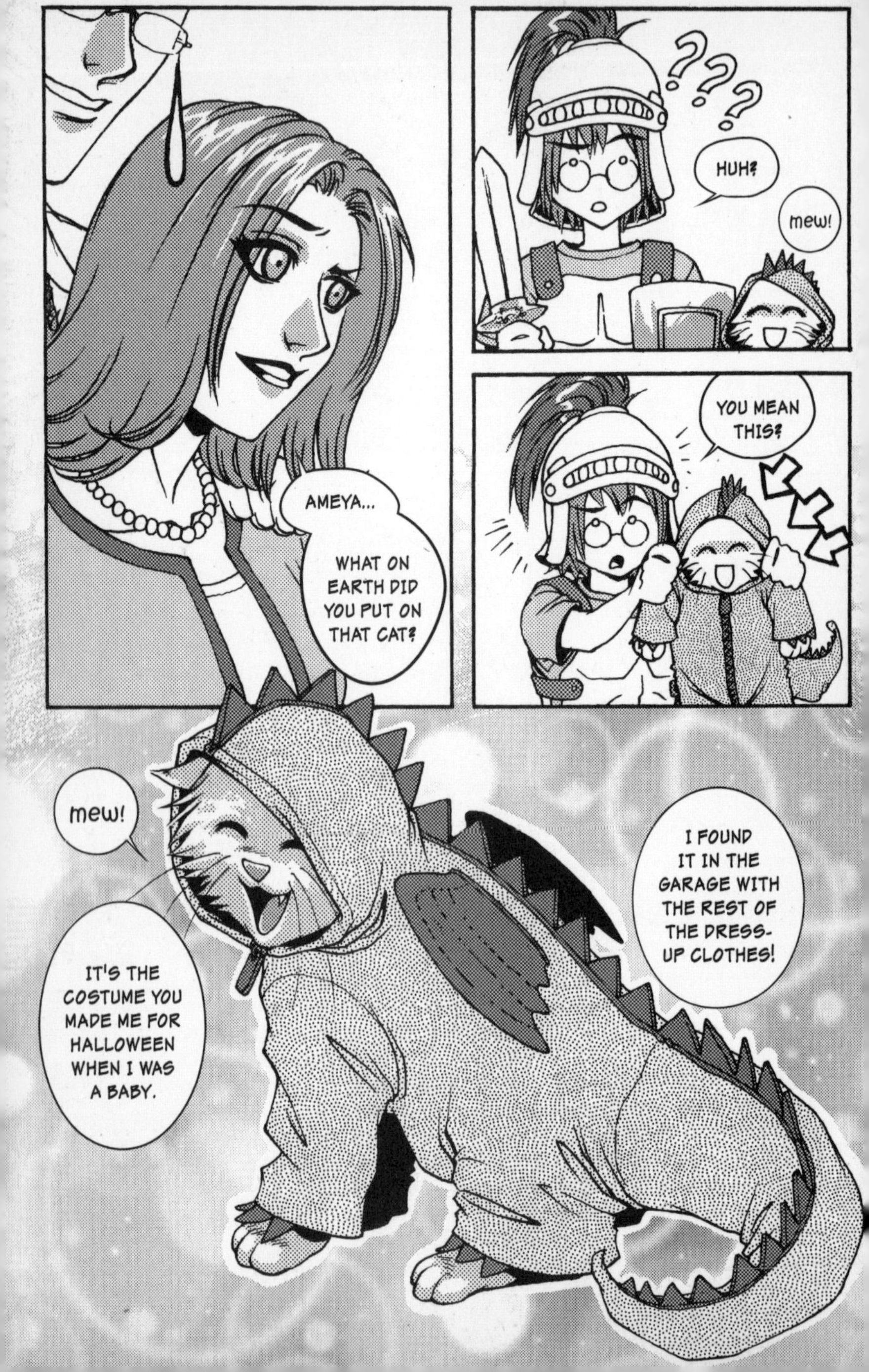
AMEYA...
WHAT ON EARTH DID YOU PUT ON THAT CAT?
HUH?
mew!
YOU MEAN THIS?
mew!
IT'S THE COSTUME YOU MADE ME FOR HALLOWEEN WHEN I WAS A BABY.
I FOUND IT IN THE GARAGE WITH THE REST OF THE DRESS-UP CLOTHES!

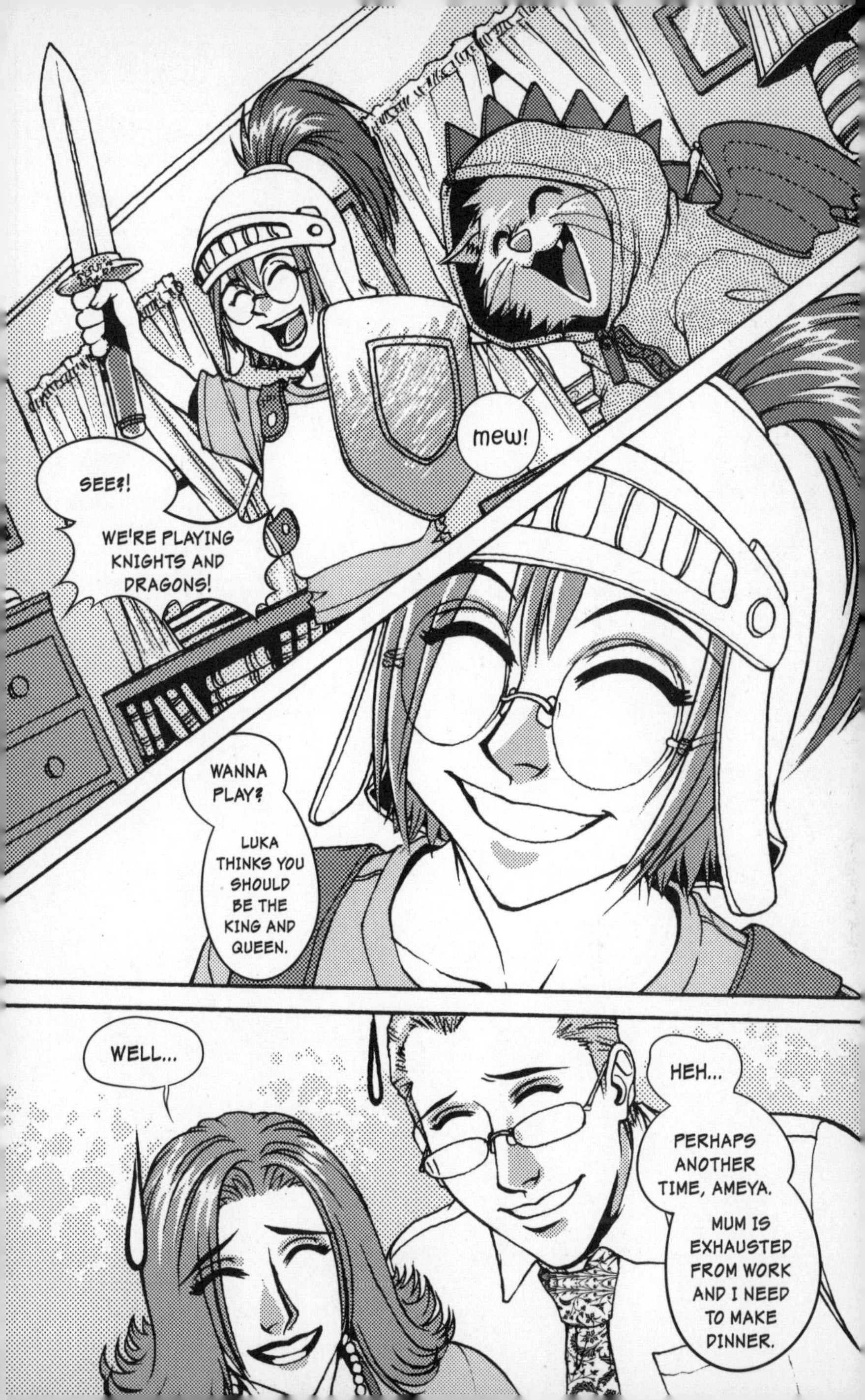
SEE?!
WE'RE PLAYING KNIGHTS AND DRAGONS!
mew!
WANNA PLAY?
LUKA THINKS YOU SHOULD BE THE KING AND QUEEN.
WELL...
HEH...
PERHAPS ANOTHER TIME, AMEYA.
MUM IS EXHAUSTED FROM WORK AND I NEED TO MAKE DINNER.

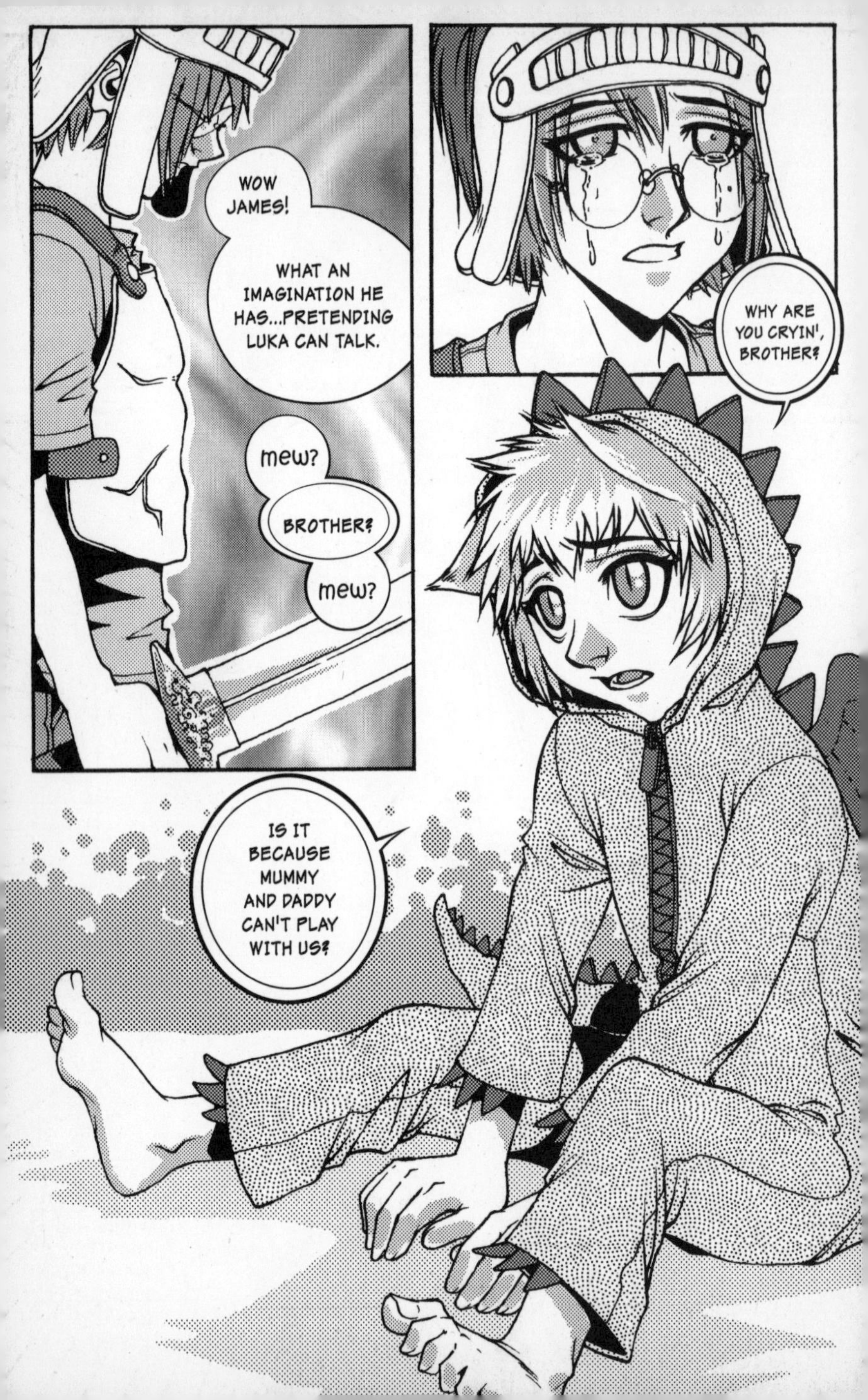
WOW JAMES!
WHAT AN IMAGINATION HE HAS...PRETENDING LUKA CAN TALK.
mew?
BROTHER?
mew?
WHY ARE YOU CRYIN', BROTHER?
IS IT BECAUSE MUMMY AND DADDY CAN'T PLAY WITH US?

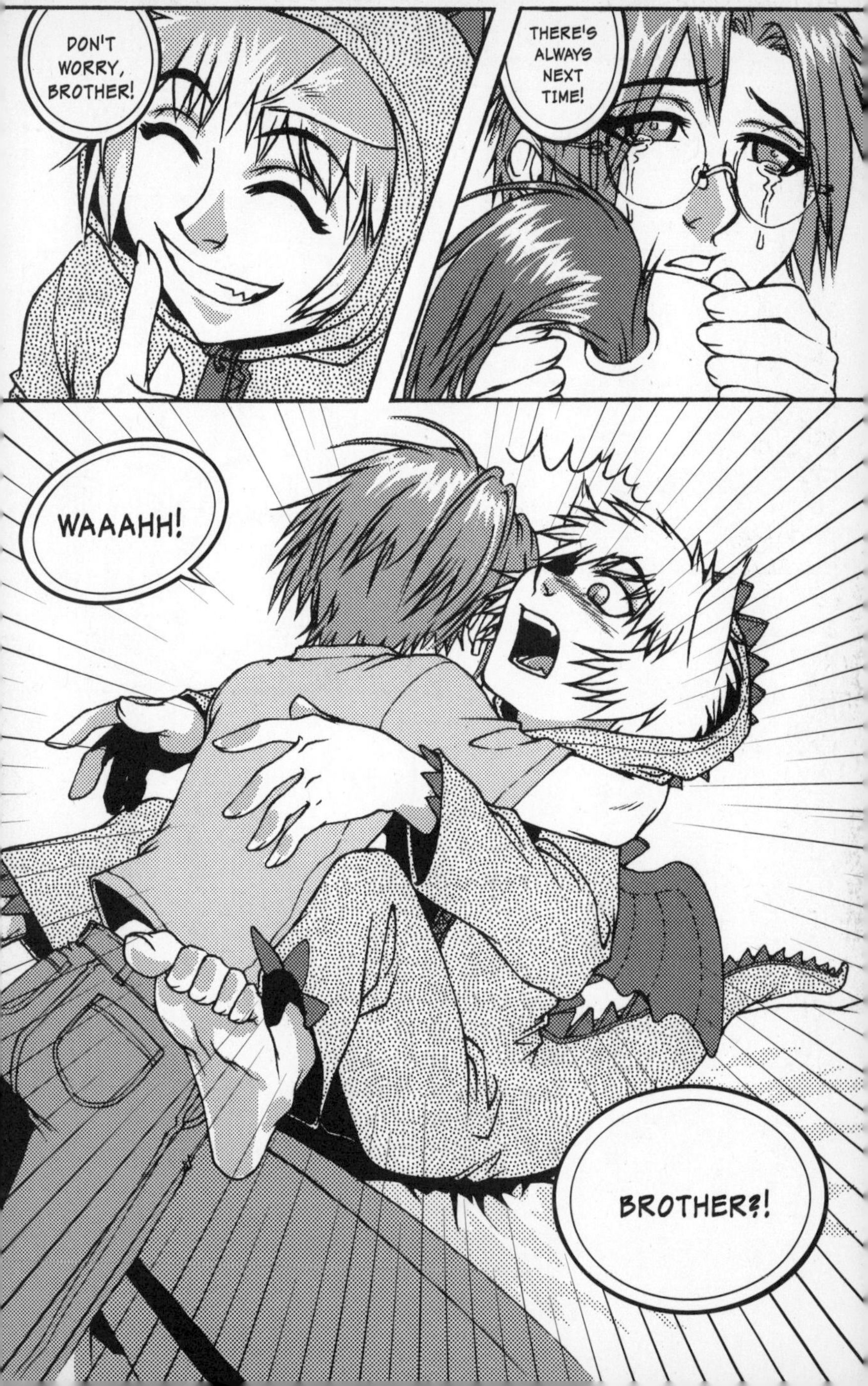
DON'T WORRY, BROTHER!
THERE'S ALWAYS NEXT TIME!
WAAAHH!
BROTHER?!

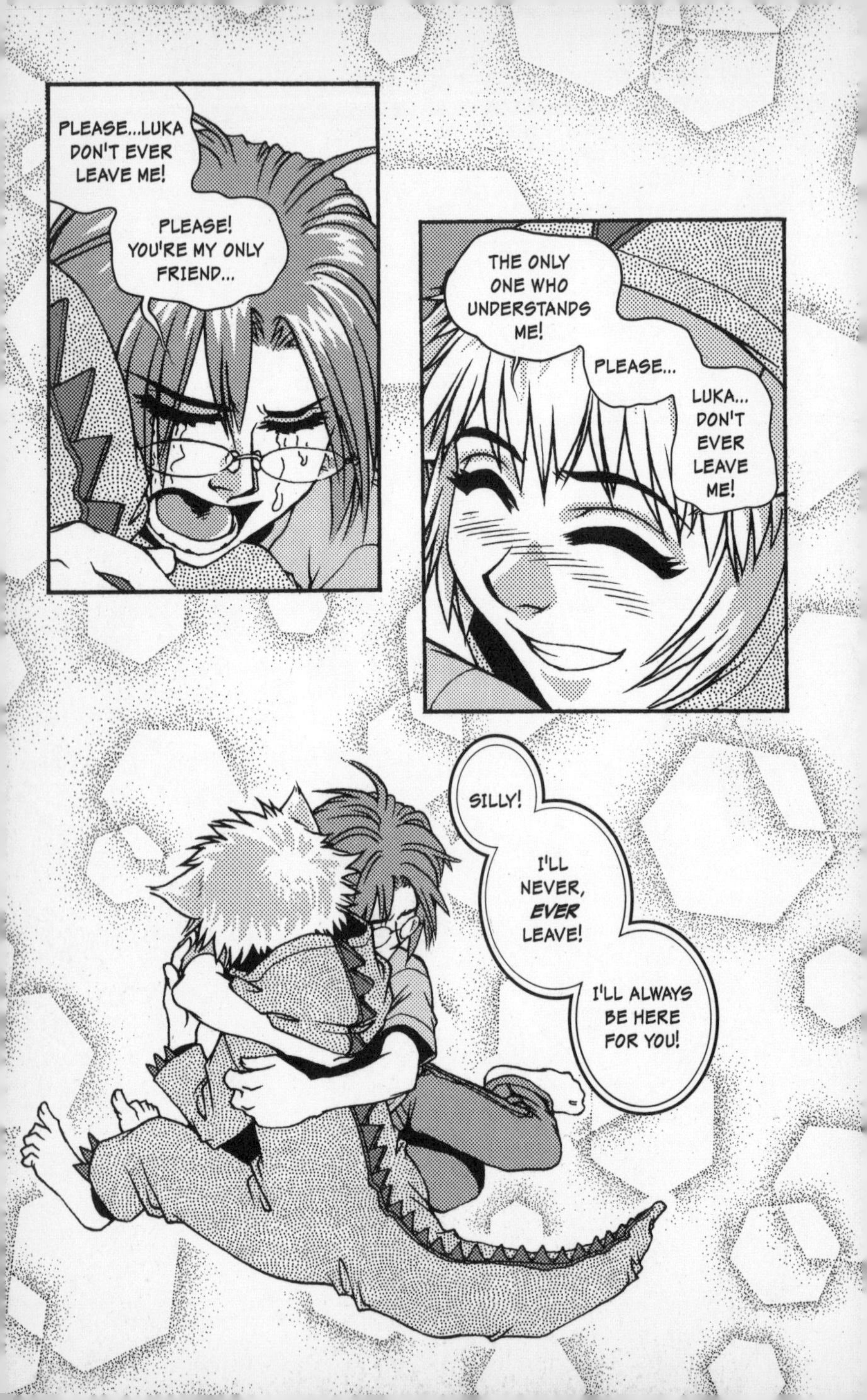
PLEASE...LUKA DON'T EVER LEAVE ME!
PLEASE! YOU'RE MY ONLY FRIEND...
THE ONLY ONE WHO UNDERSTANDS ME!
PLEASE...
LUKA... DON'T EVER LEAVE ME!
SILLY!
I'LL NEVER, *EVER* LEAVE!
I'LL ALWAYS BE HERE FOR YOU!

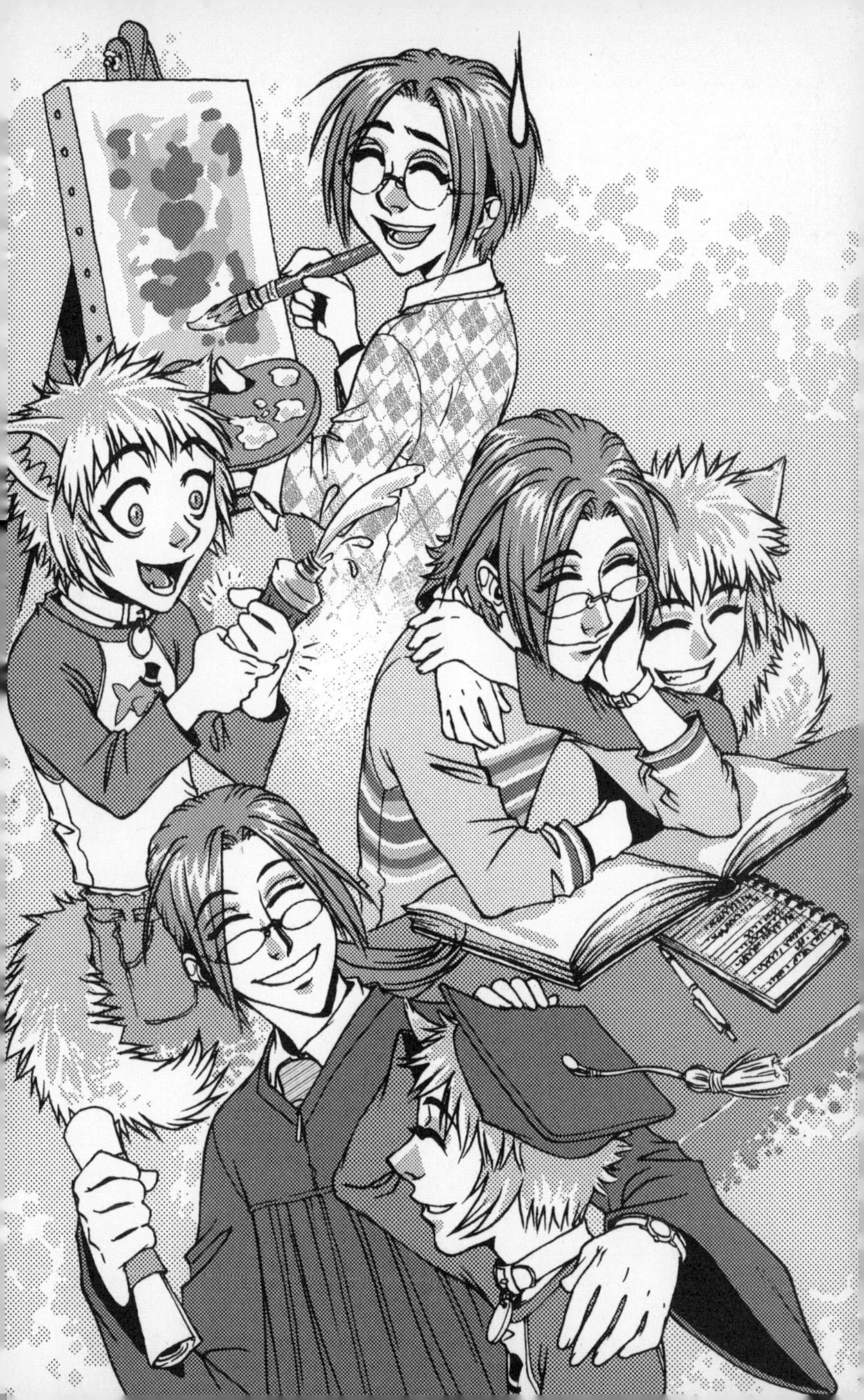

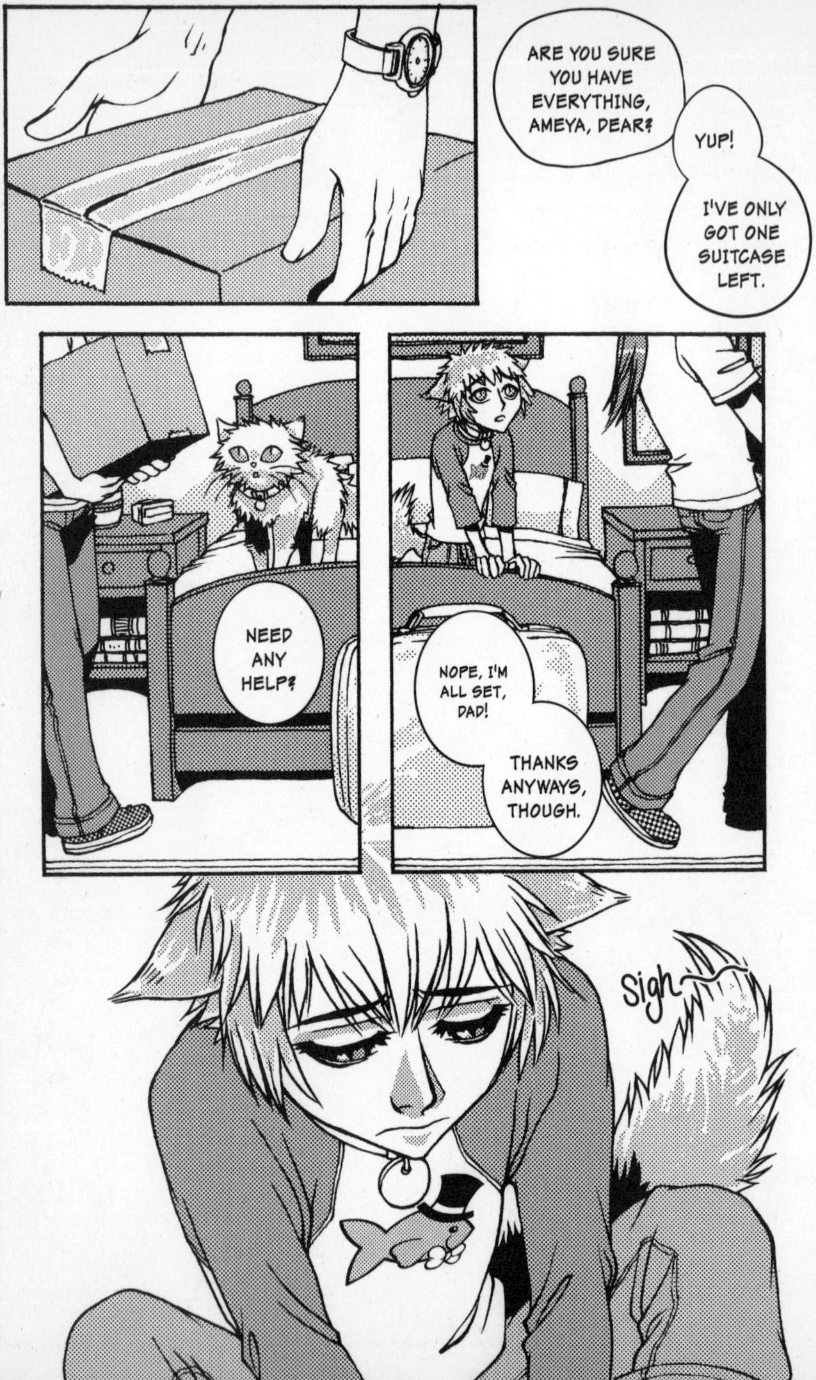

ARE YOU SURE YOU HAVE EVERYTHING, AMEYA, DEAR?
YUP!
I'VE ONLY GOT ONE SUITCASE LEFT.
NEED ANY HELP?
NOPE, I'M ALL SET, DAD!
THANKS ANYWAYS, THOUGH.
Sigh

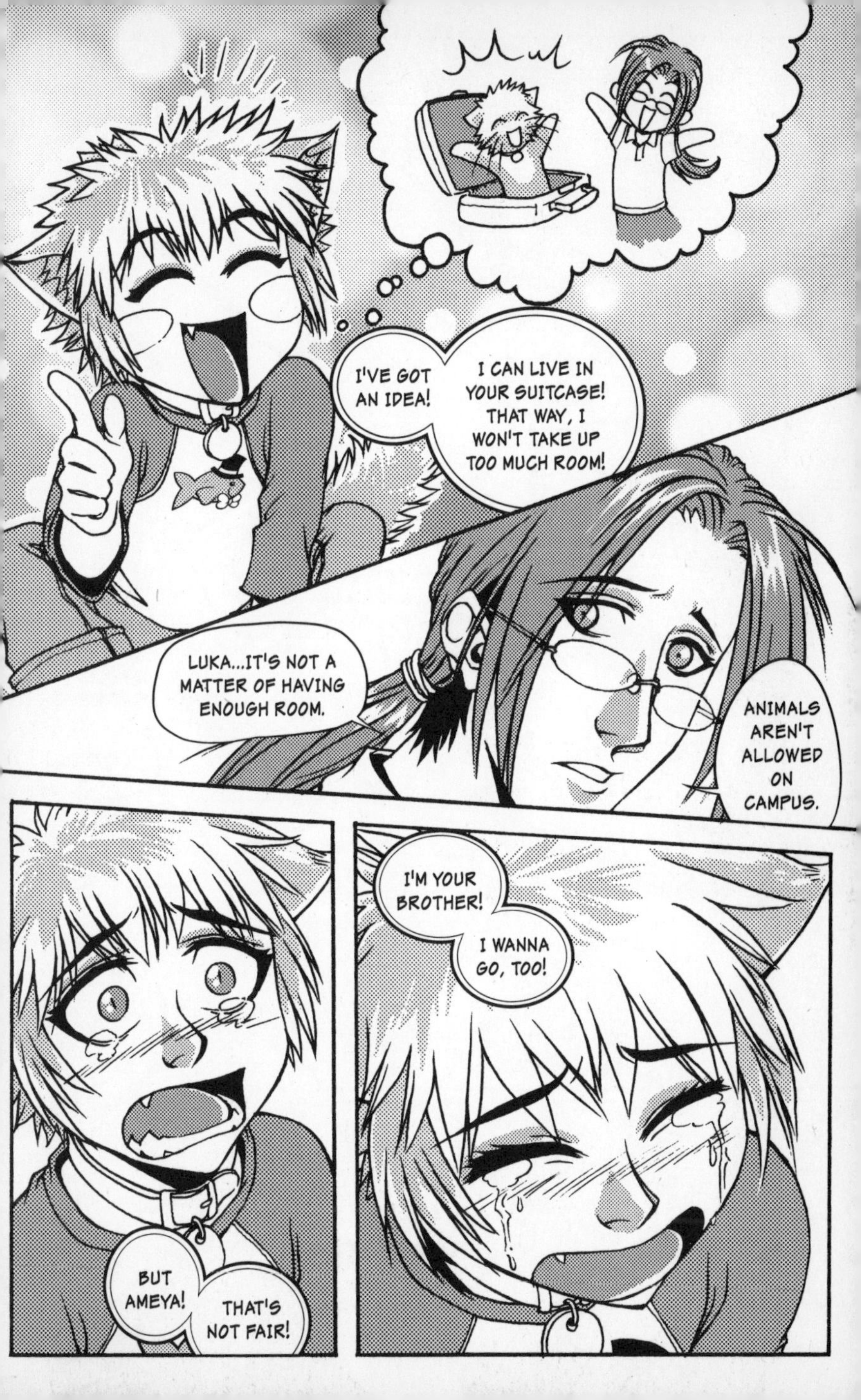
I'VE GOT AN IDEA!
I CAN LIVE IN YOUR SUITCASE! THAT WAY, I WON'T TAKE UP TOO MUCH ROOM!
LUKA...IT'S NOT A MATTER OF HAVING ENOUGH ROOM.
ANIMALS AREN'T ALLOWED ON CAMPUS.
BUT AMEYA!
THAT'S NOT FAIR!
I'M YOUR BROTHER!
I WANNA GO, TOO!

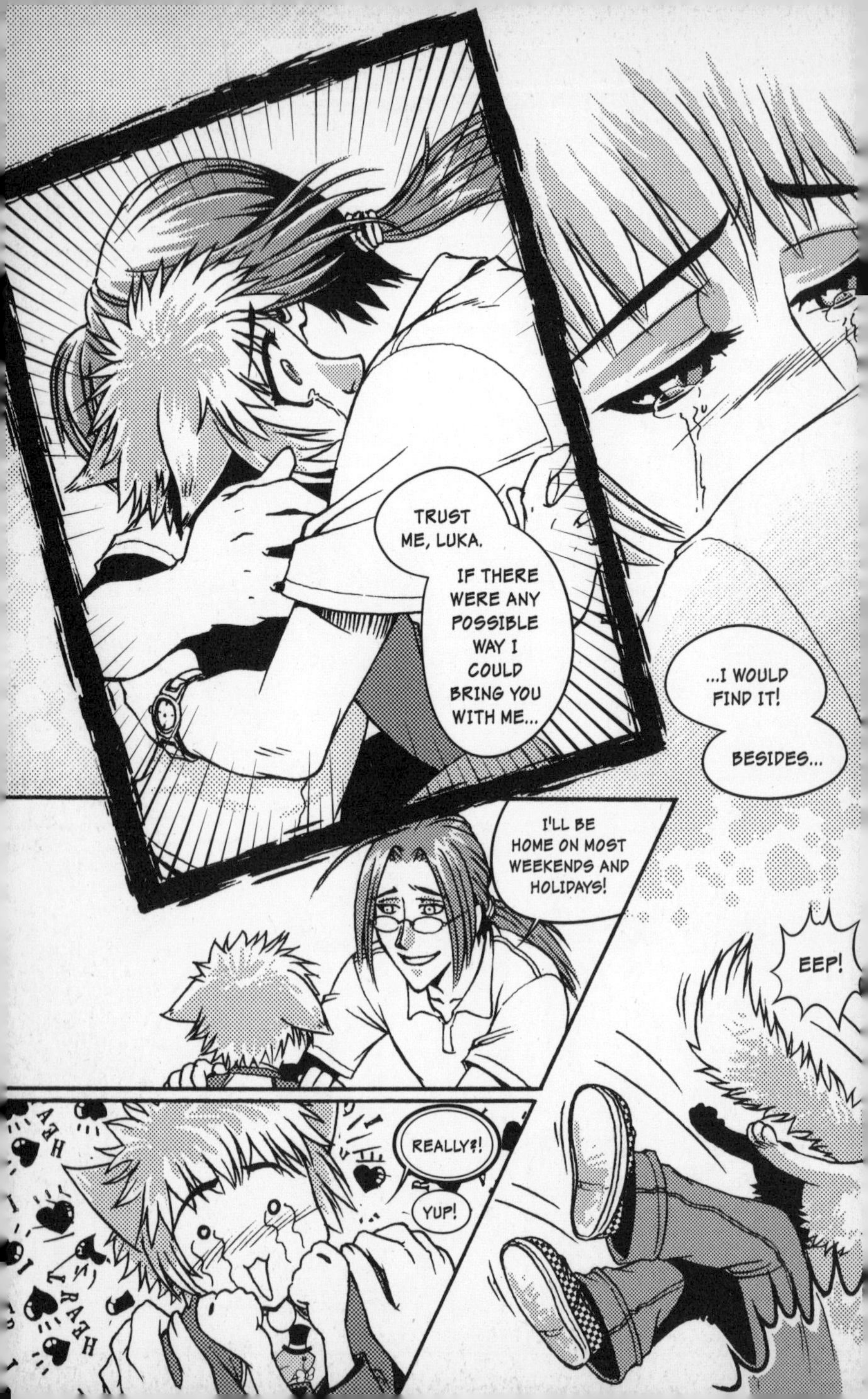
TRUST ME, LUKA.
IF THERE WERE ANY POSSIBLE WAY I COULD BRING YOU WITH ME...
...I WOULD FIND IT!
BESIDES...
I'LL BE HOME ON MOST WEEKENDS AND HOLIDAYS!
REALLY?!
YUP!
EEP!

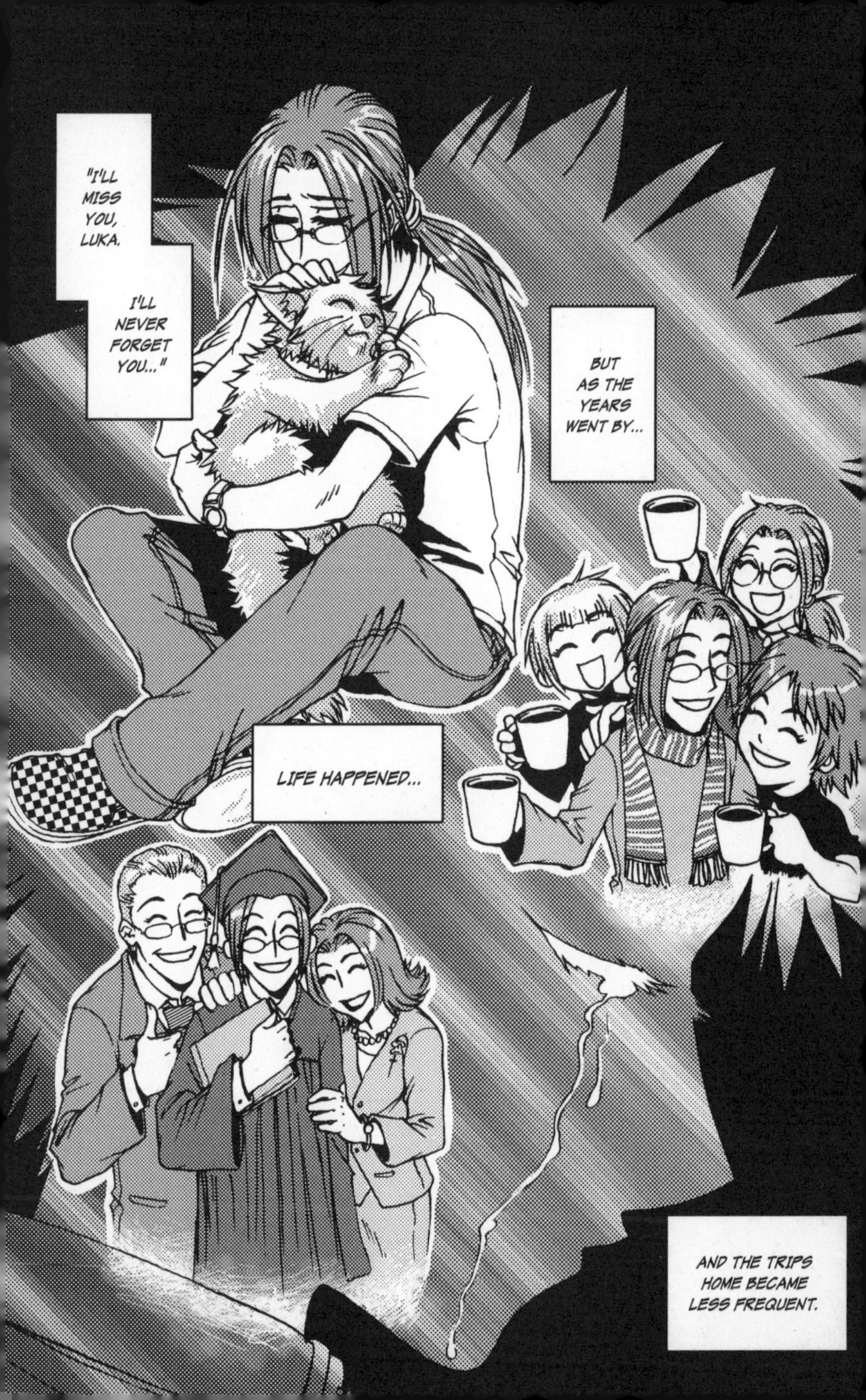
"I'LL MISS YOU, LUKA.
I'LL NEVER FORGET YOU..."
BUT AS THE YEARS WENT BY...
LIFE HAPPENED...
AND THE TRIPS HOME BECAME LESS FREQUENT.

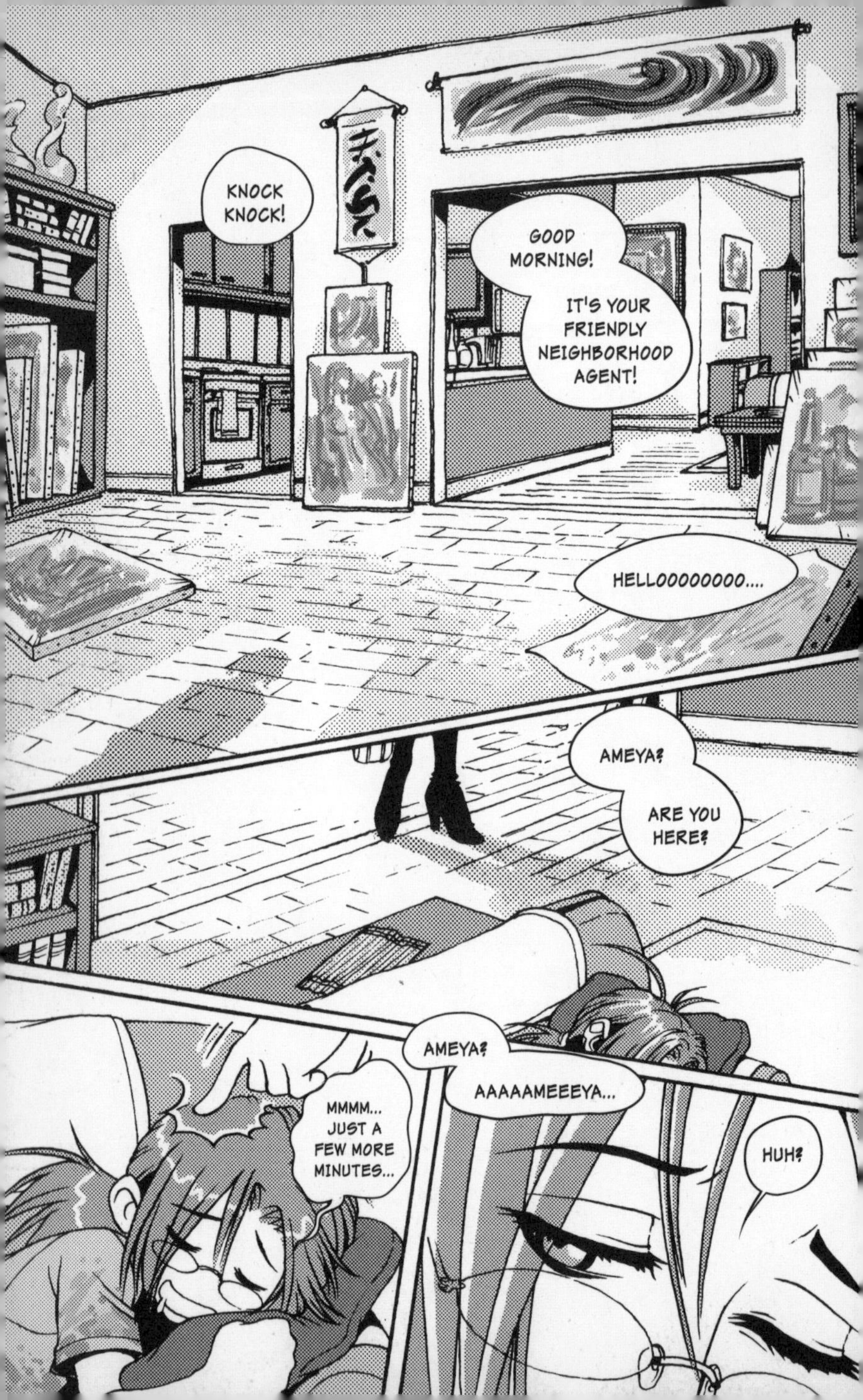
KNOCK KNOCK!
GOOD MORNING!
IT'S YOUR FRIENDLY NEIGHBORHOOD AGENT!
HELLOOOOOOOO....
AMEYA?
ARE YOU HERE?
AMEYA?
AAAAAMEEEYA...
MMMM... JUST A FEW MORE MINUTES...
HUH?

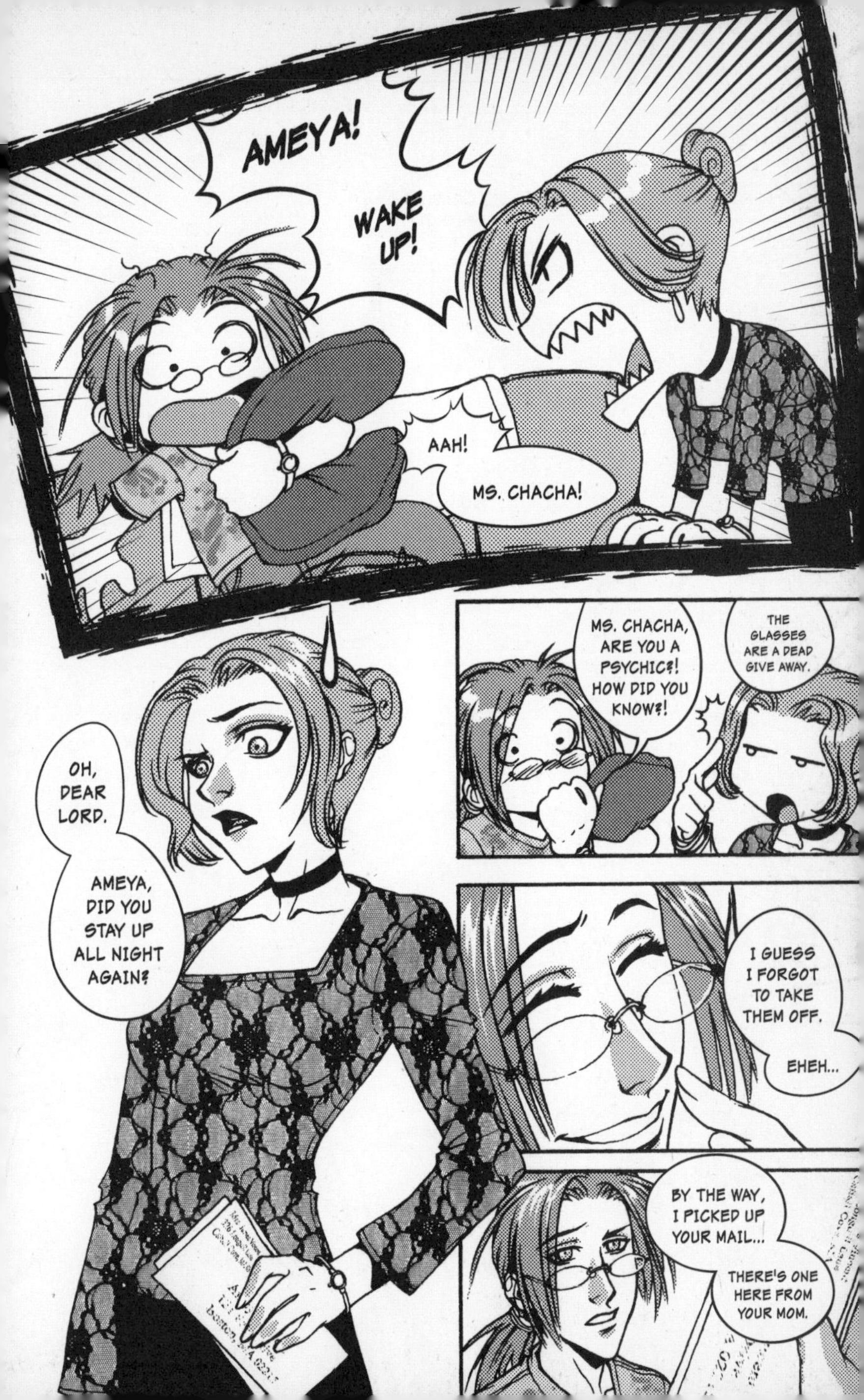
AMEYA!
WAKE UP!
AAH!
MS. CHACHA!
OH, DEAR LORD.
AMEYA, DID YOU STAY UP ALL NIGHT AGAIN?
MS. CHACHA, ARE YOU A PSYCHIC?! HOW DID YOU KNOW?!
THE GLASSES ARE A DEAD GIVE AWAY.
I GUESS I FORGOT TO TAKE THEM OFF.
EHEH...
BY THE WAY, I PICKED UP YOUR MAIL...
THERE'S ONE HERE FROM YOUR MOM.

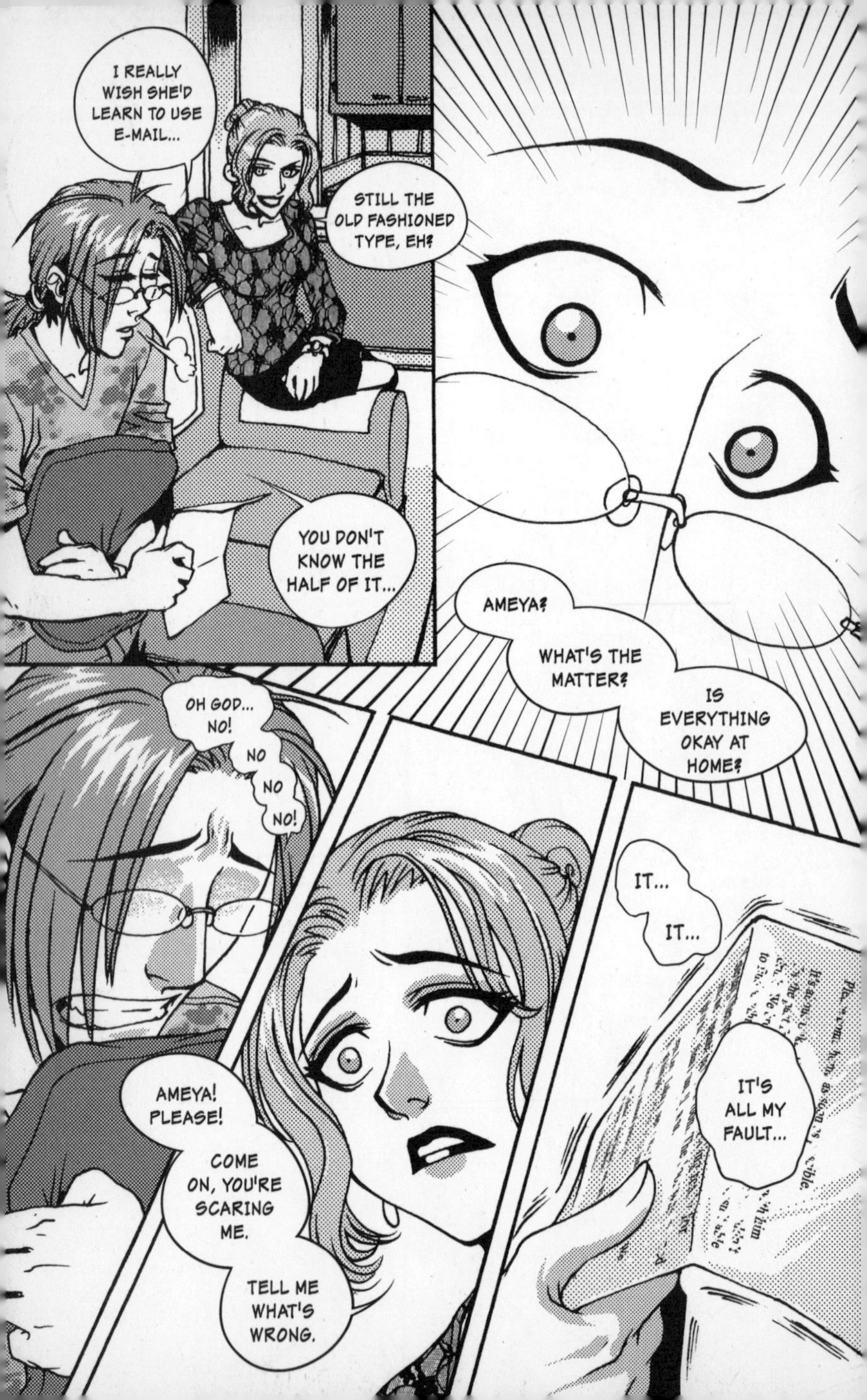
I REALLY WISH SHE'D LEARN TO USE E-MAIL...
STILL THE OLD FASHIONED TYPE, EH?
YOU DON'T KNOW THE HALF OF IT...
AMEYA?
WHAT'S THE MATTER?
IS EVERYTHING OKAY AT HOME?
OH GOD... NO!
NO
NO
NO!
AMEYA! PLEASE!
COME ON, YOU'RE SCARING ME.
TELL ME WHAT'S WRONG.
IT...
IT...
IT'S ALL MY FAULT...

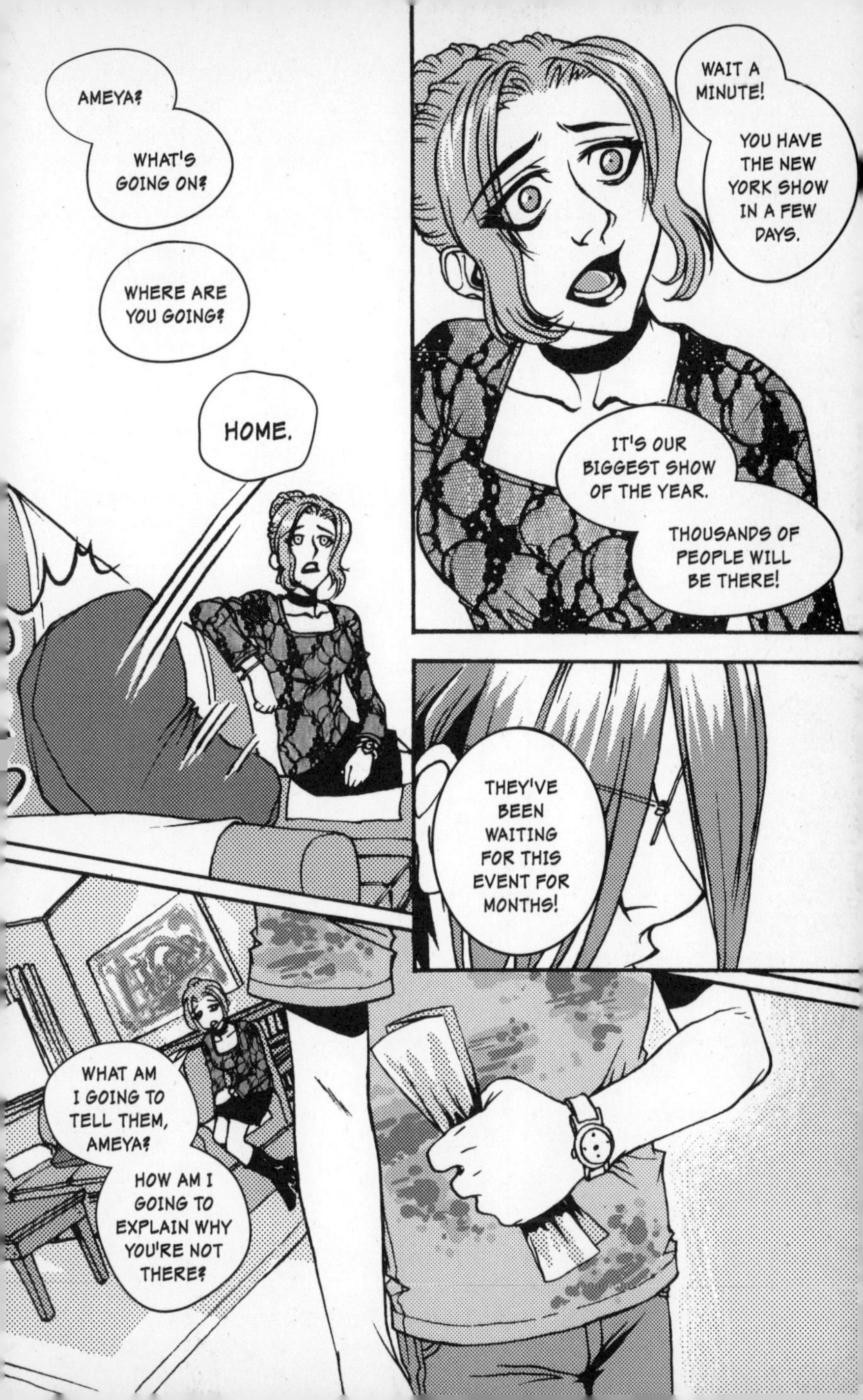
AMEYA?
WHAT'S GOING ON?
WHERE ARE YOU GOING?
HOME.
WAIT A MINUTE!
YOU HAVE THE NEW YORK SHOW IN A FEW DAYS.
IT'S OUR BIGGEST SHOW OF THE YEAR.
THOUSANDS OF PEOPLE WILL BE THERE!
THEY'VE BEEN WAITING FOR THIS EVENT FOR MONTHS!
WHAT AM I GOING TO TELL THEM, AMEYA?
HOW AM I GOING TO EXPLAIN WHY YOU'RE NOT THERE?

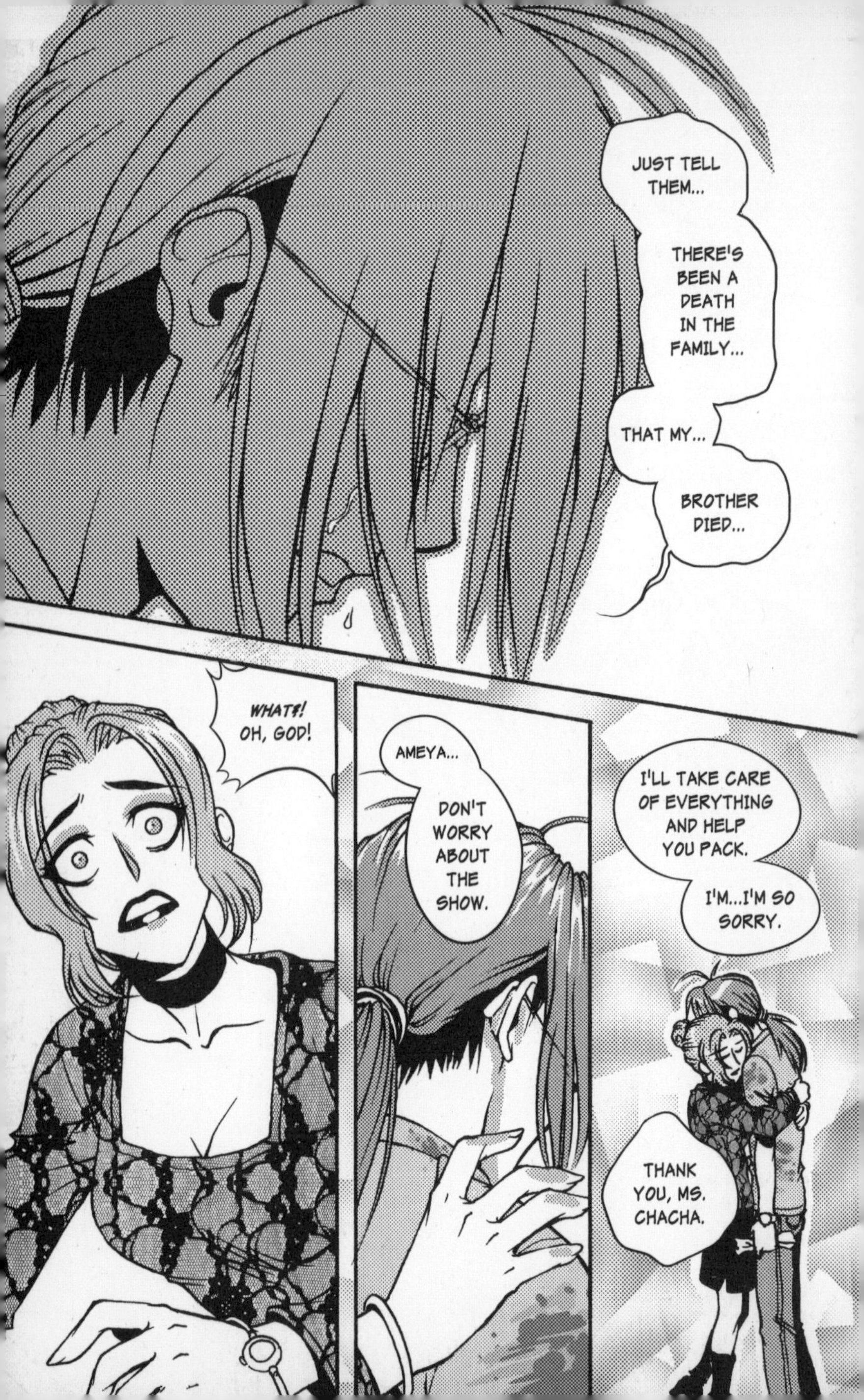

JUST TELL THEM...
THERE'S BEEN A DEATH IN THE FAMILY...
THAT MY...
BROTHER DIED...
WHAT?! OH, GOD!
AMEYA...
DON'T WORRY ABOUT THE SHOW.
I'LL TAKE CARE OF EVERYTHING AND HELP YOU PACK.
I'M...I'M SO SORRY.
THANK YOU, MS. CHACHA.

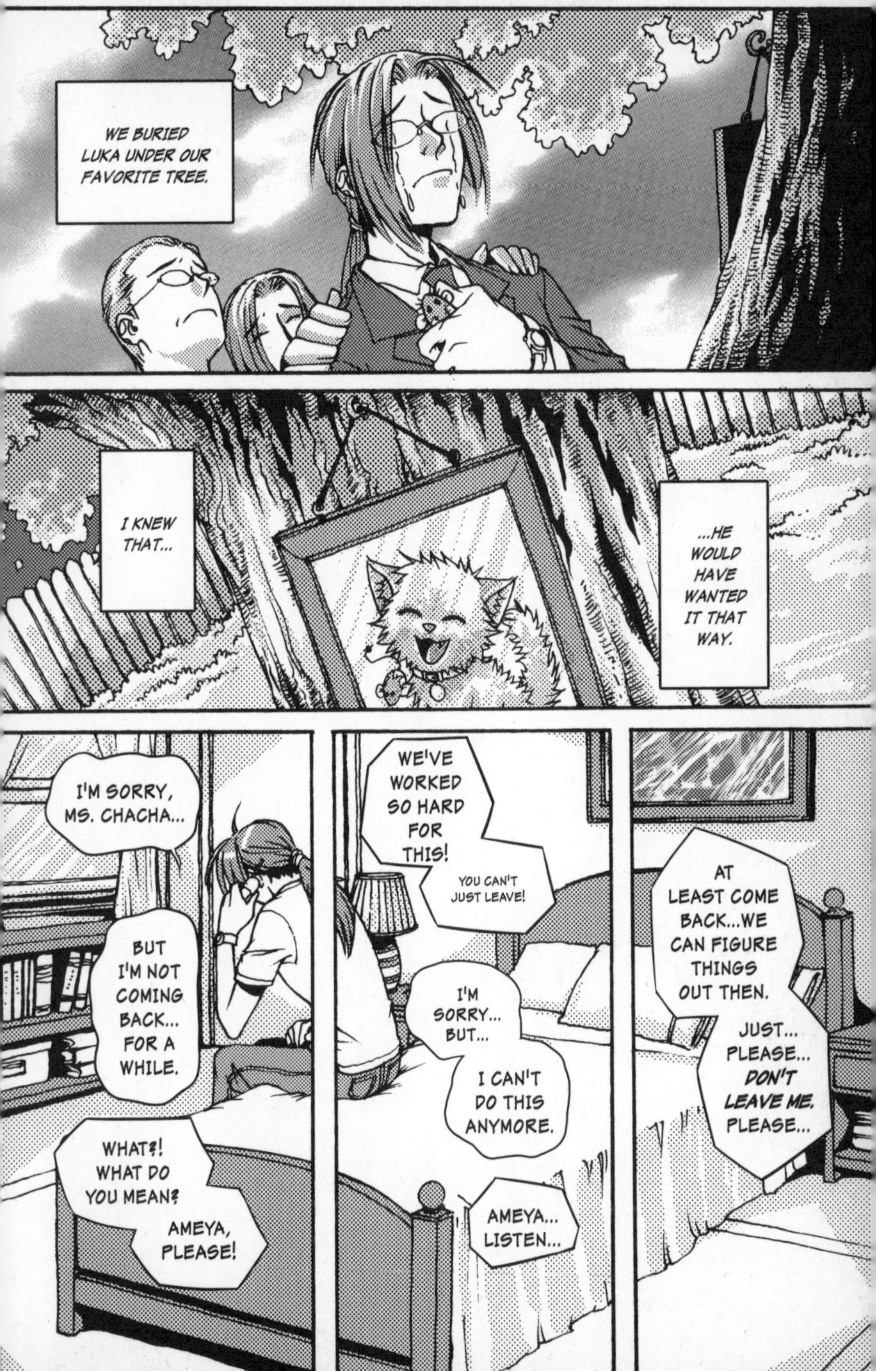
WE BURIED LUKA UNDER OUR FAVORITE TREE.
I KNEW THAT...
...HE WOULD HAVE WANTED IT THAT WAY.
I'M SORRY, MS. CHACHA...
BUT I'M NOT COMING BACK... FOR A WHILE.
WHAT?! WHAT DO YOU MEAN?
AMEYA, PLEASE!
WE'VE WORKED SO HARD FOR THIS!
YOU CAN'T JUST LEAVE!
I'M SORRY... BUT...
I CAN'T DO THIS ANYMORE.
AMEYA... LISTEN...
AT LEAST COME BACK...WE CAN FIGURE THINGS OUT THEN.
JUST... PLEASE... DON'T LEAVE ME. PLEASE...

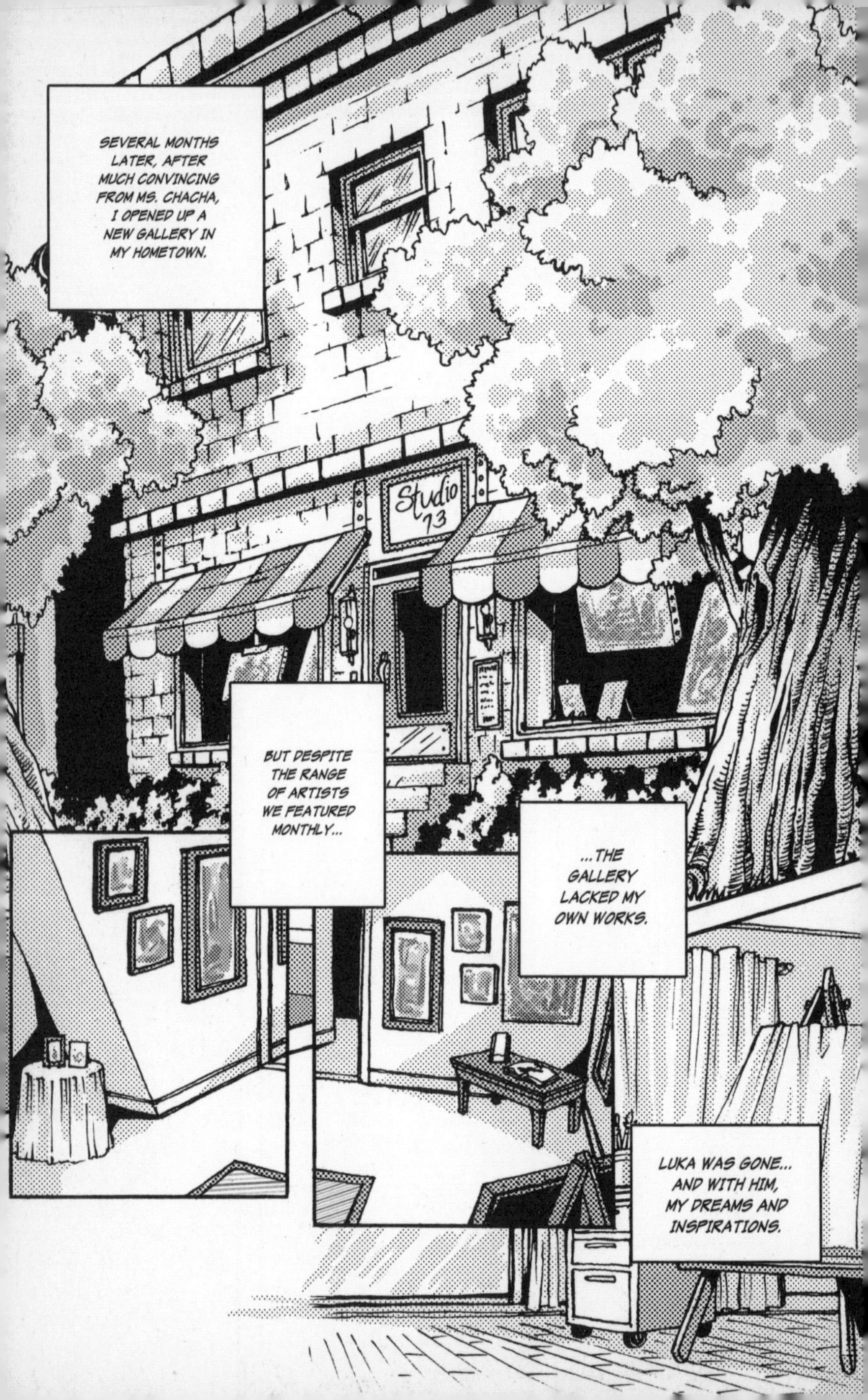
SEVERAL MONTHS LATER, AFTER MUCH CONVINCING FROM MS. CHACHA, I OPENED UP A NEW GALLERY IN MY HOMETOWN.
Studio 73
BUT DESPITE THE RANGE OF ARTISTS WE FEATURED MONTHLY...
...THE GALLERY LACKED MY OWN WORKS.
LUKA WAS GONE... AND WITH HIM, MY DREAMS AND INSPIRATIONS.

THREE YEARS LATER, MS. CHACHA SURPRISED ME WITH AN ANNOUNCEMENT...

Cattail Cove Convention Center is proud to present:

GRAND ART GALA

Featuring reknown local artist:

AMEVA

In honor of his return to the art world, the Cattail Cove Convention Center will be celebrating the event on April 3rd. Admission begins at 6pm. Show starts at 8pm.

TADA! IT'S AN ART GALA FEATURING YOU!

SHUT UP!!! YOU HAVE NO IDEA WHAT IT'S LIKE!

BUT...ME BEING THE STUBBORN ONE, WOULDN'T HEAR OF IT...

AND IT ONLY MADE MATTERS WORSE.

IN A FIT OF ANGER AND FRUSTRATION, I FOUND MYSELF OUT IN THE RAIN...

LITTLE DID I KNOW WHAT FATE HAD IN STORE FOR ME...

NOPE... I DEFINITELY HEARD IT!

I DON'T THINK I CAN FACE HER AGAIN AFTER BLOWING UP AT HER LIKE THAT...

...IN THE FORM OF A LITTLE WET CAT.

mew?

GASP

flick flick

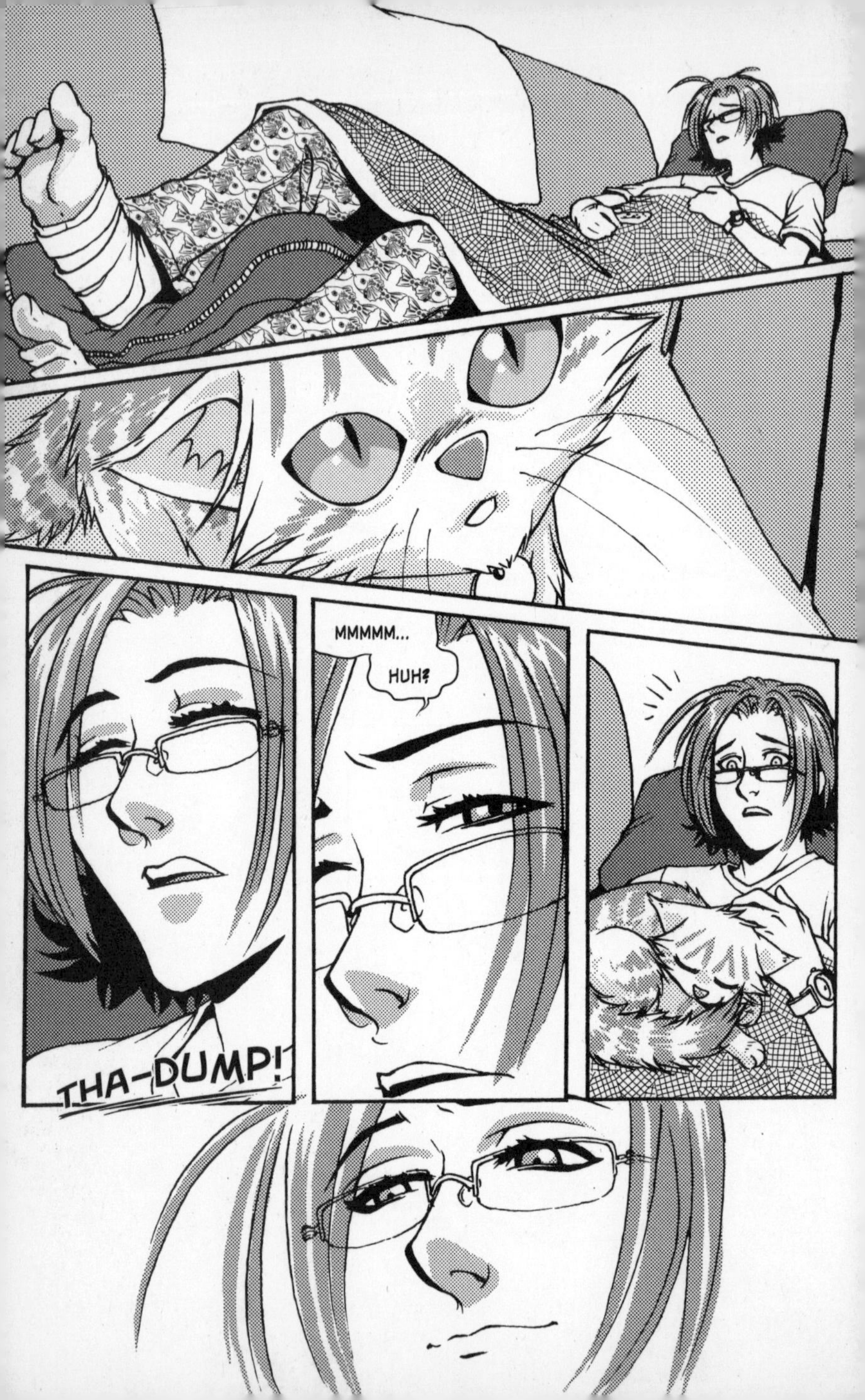
THA-DUMP!
MMMMM...
HUH?

CHAPTER 2

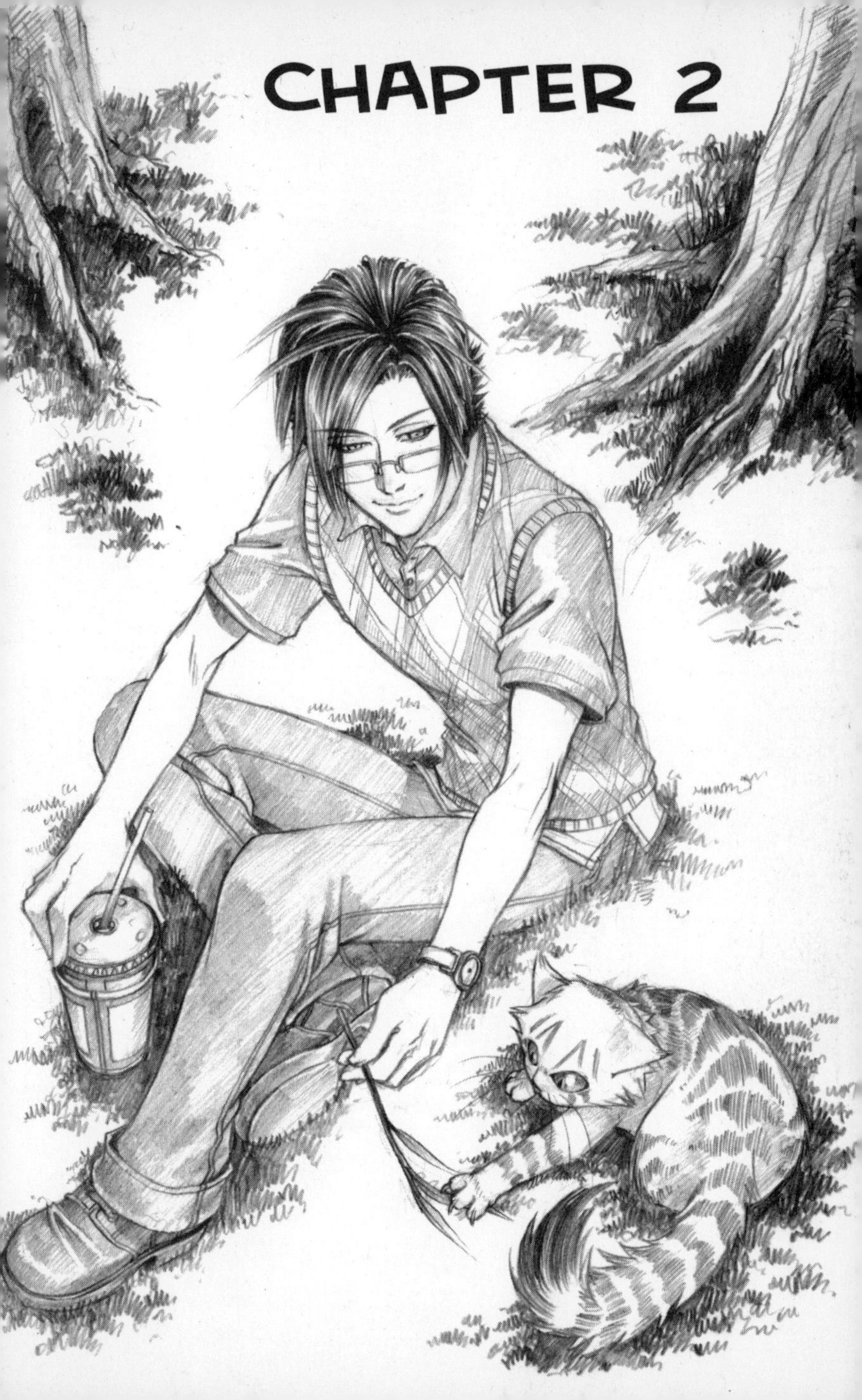

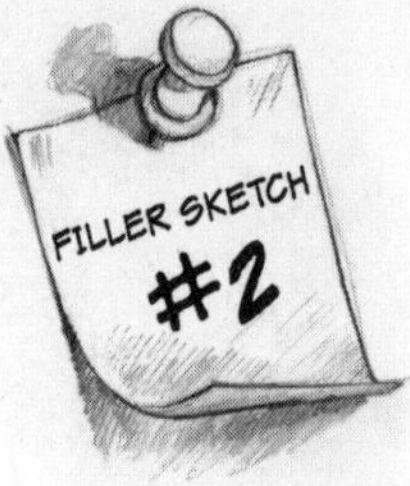
FILLER SKETCH
#2

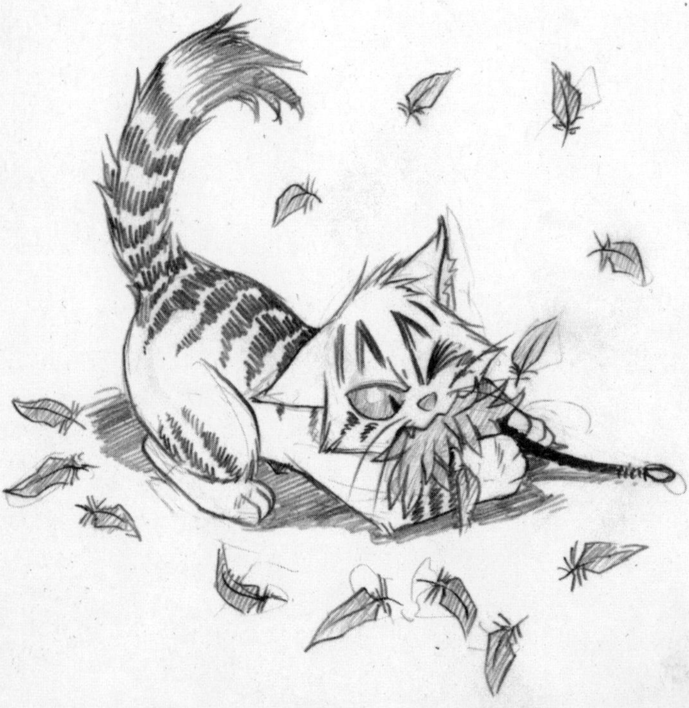

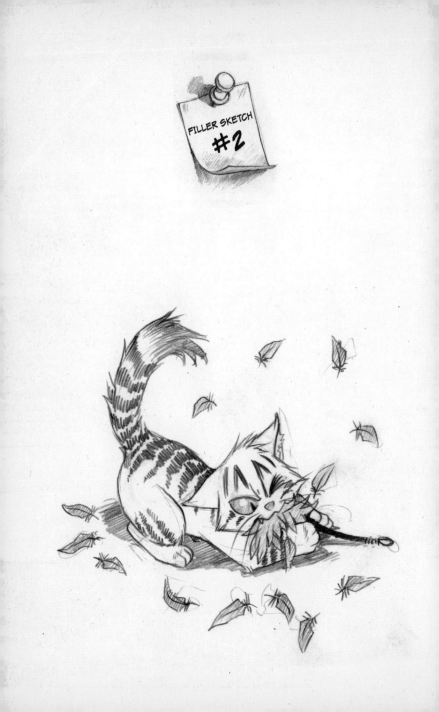

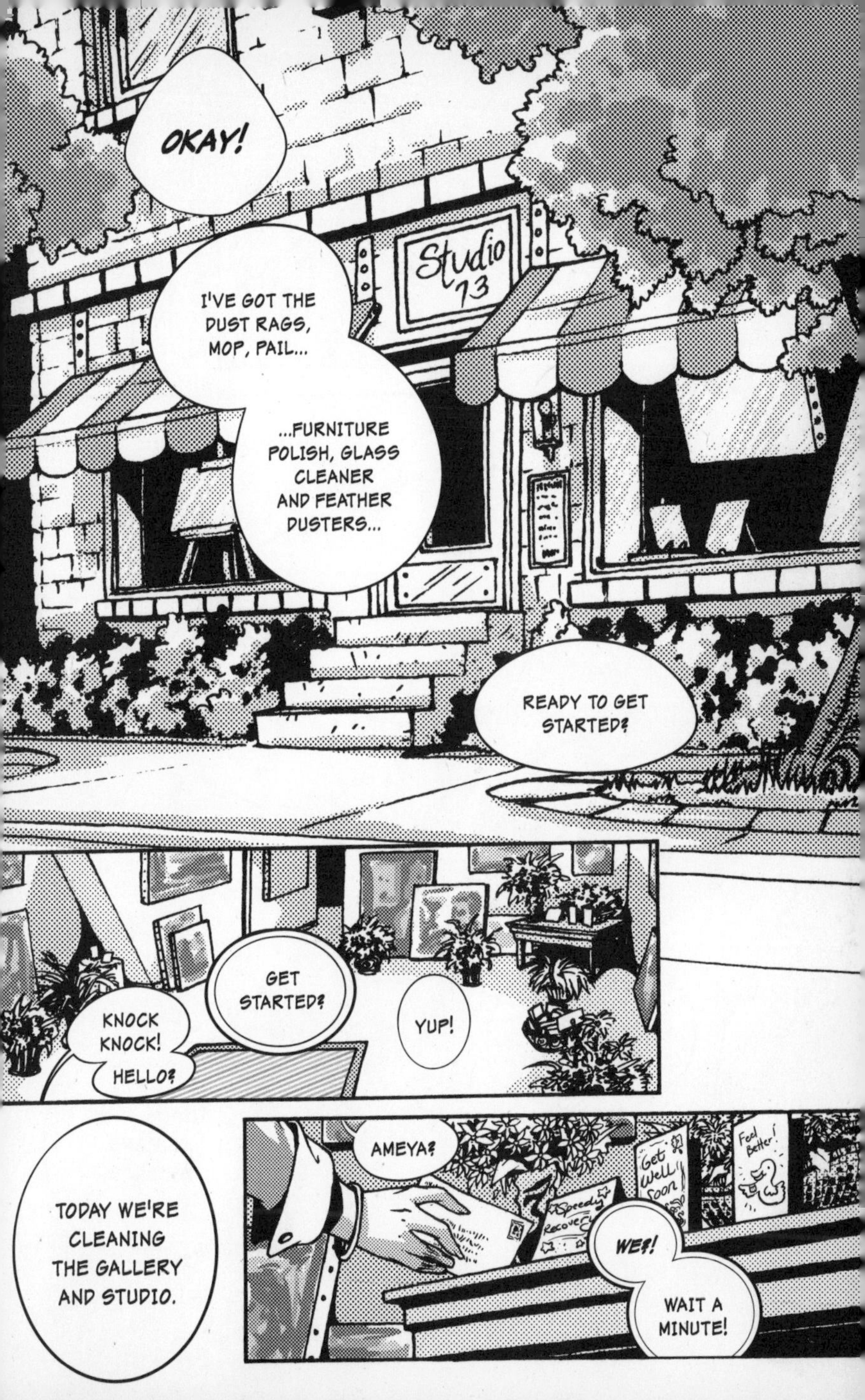
Studio 73
OKAY!
I'VE GOT THE DUST RAGS, MOP, PAIL...
...FURNITURE POLISH, GLASS CLEANER AND FEATHER DUSTERS...
READY TO GET STARTED?
GET STARTED?
YUP!
KNOCK KNOCK! HELLO?
TODAY WE'RE CLEANING THE GALLERY AND STUDIO.
AMEYA?
Get Well Soon
Feel Better!
Speedy Recovery
WE?!
WAIT A MINUTE!

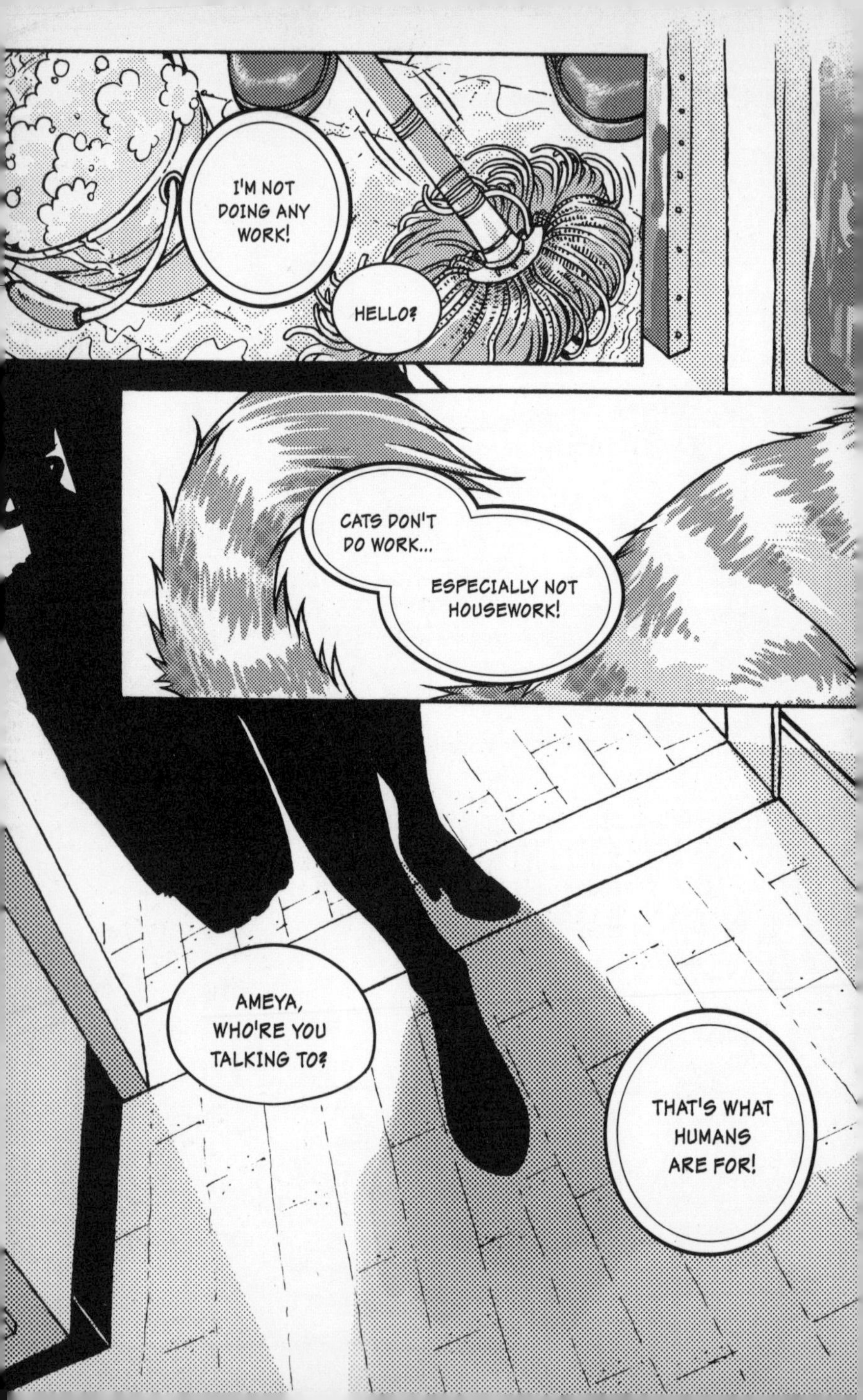
I'M NOT DOING ANY WORK!
HELLO?
CATS DON'T DO WORK...
ESPECIALLY NOT HOUSEWORK!
AMEYA, WHO'RE YOU TALKING TO?
THAT'S WHAT HUMANS ARE FOR!

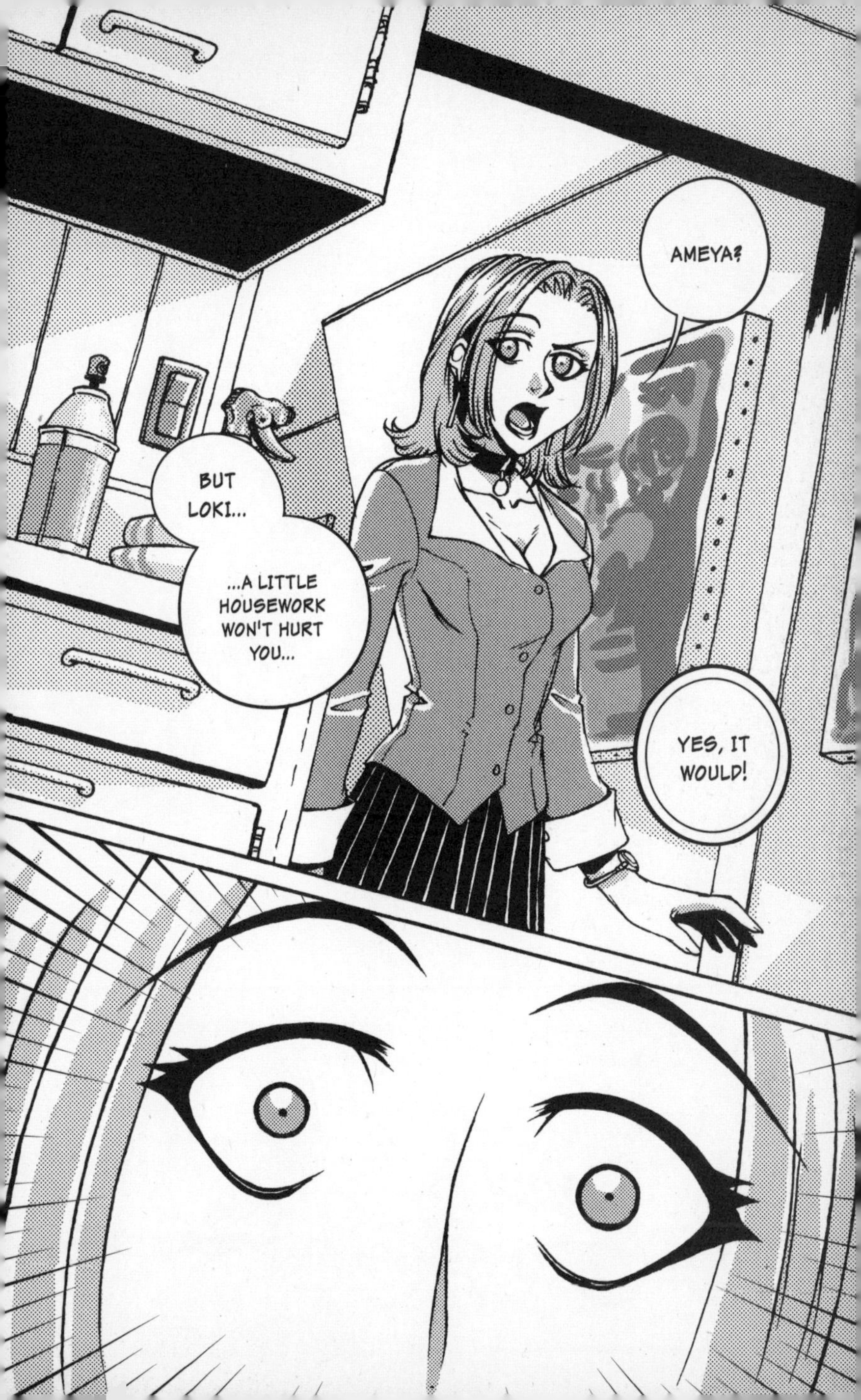
AMEYA?
BUT LOKI...
...A LITTLE HOUSEWORK WON'T HURT YOU...
YES, IT WOULD!

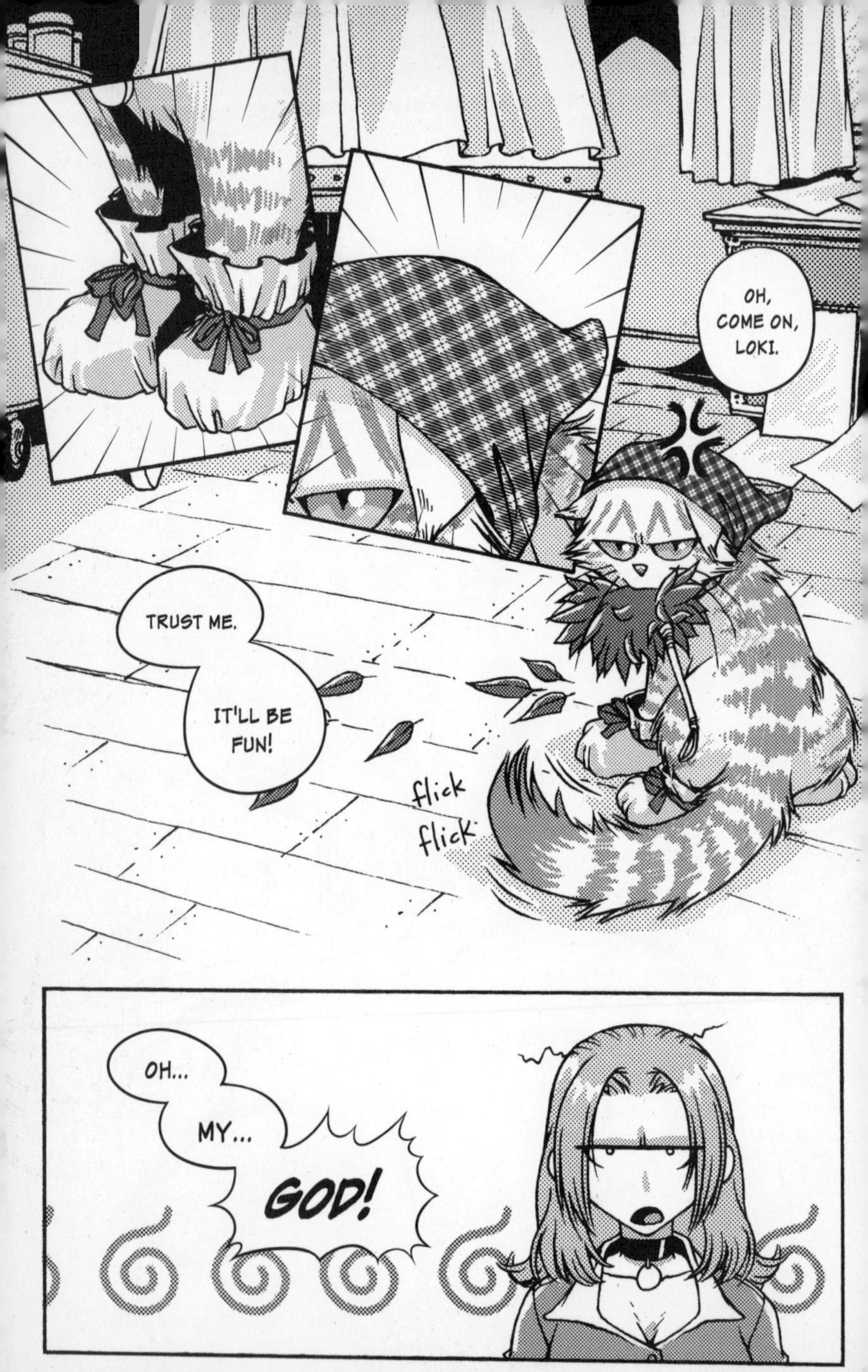
OH, COME ON, LOKI.
TRUST ME.
IT'LL BE FUN!
flick
flick
OH...
MY...
GOD!

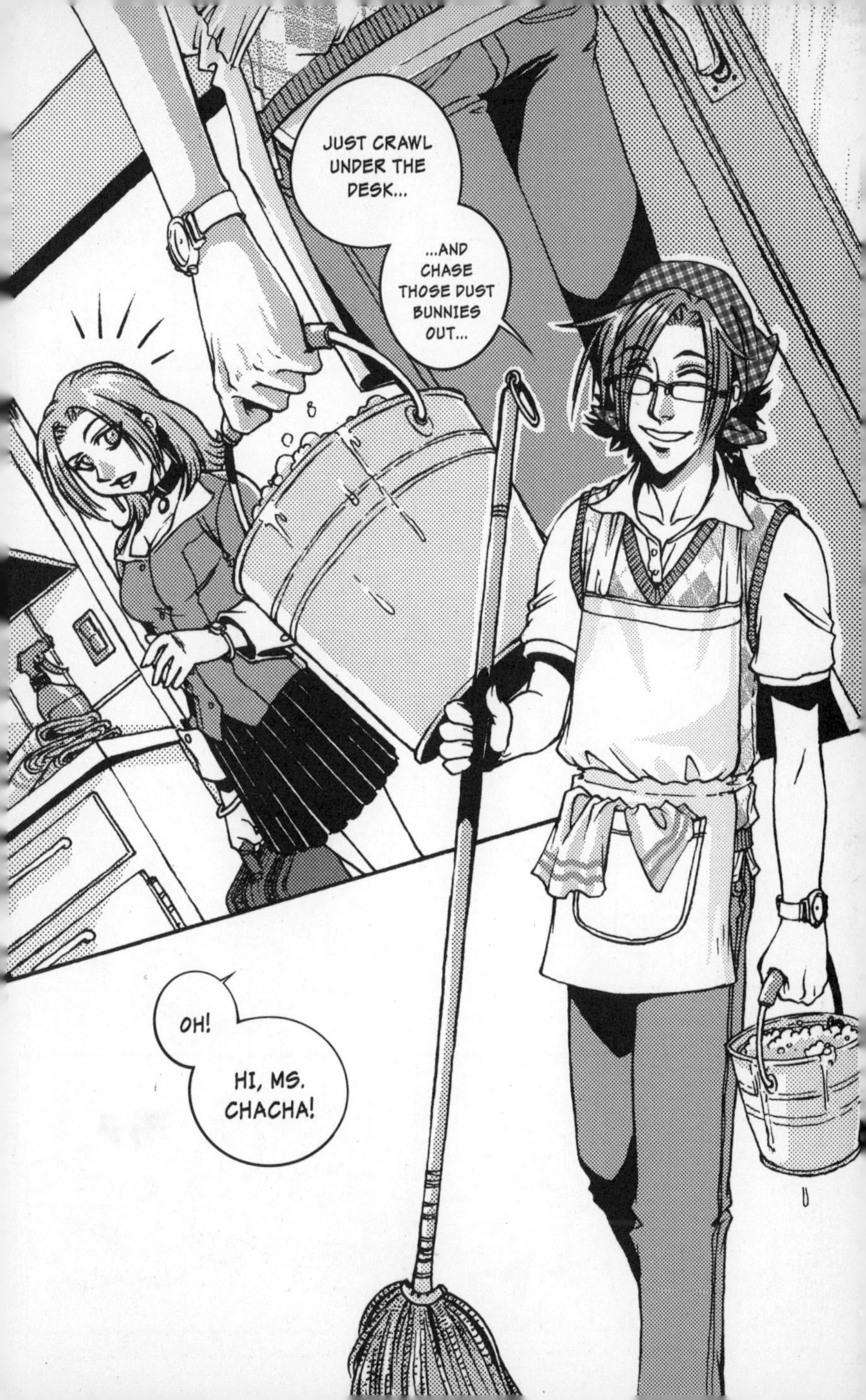
JUST CRAWL UNDER THE DESK...
...AND CHASE THOSE DUST BUNNIES OUT...
OH!
HI, MS. CHACHA!

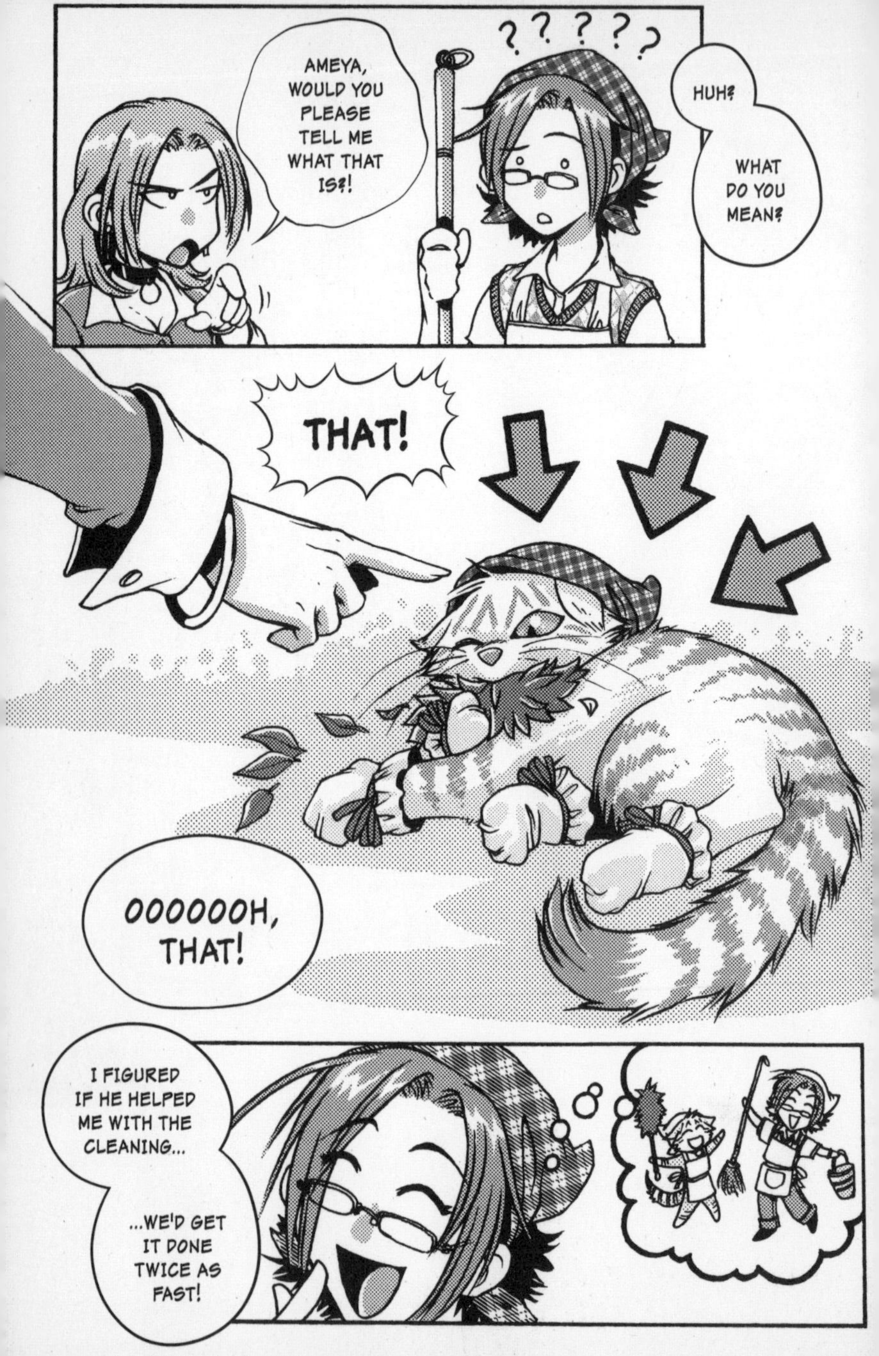
AMEYA, WOULD YOU PLEASE TELL ME WHAT THAT IS?!
HUH?
WHAT DO YOU MEAN?
THAT!
OOOOOOH, THAT!
I FIGURED IF HE HELPED ME WITH THE CLEANING...
...WE'D GET IT DONE TWICE AS FAST!

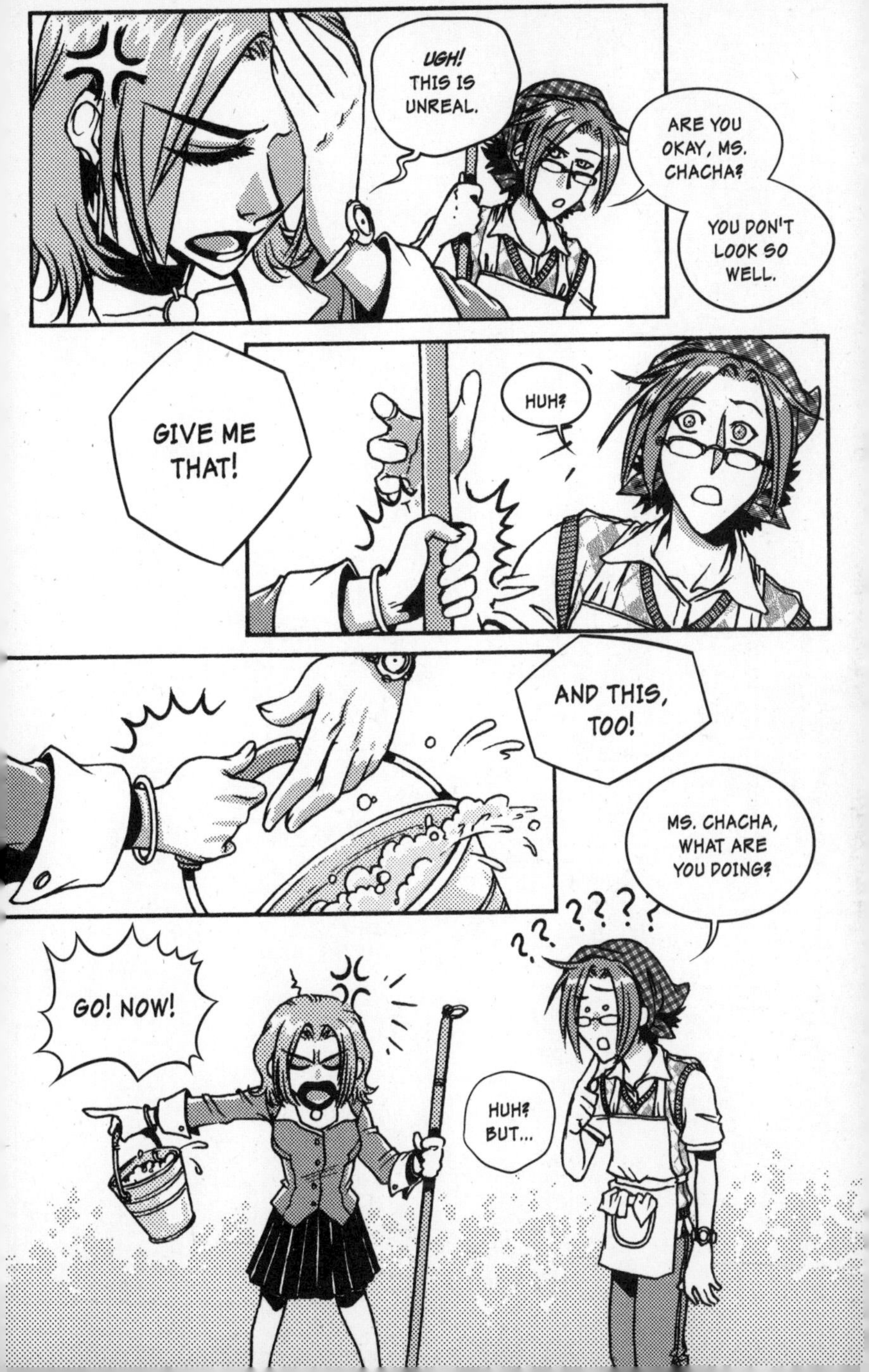
UGH! THIS IS UNREAL.
ARE YOU OKAY, MS. CHACHA?
YOU DON'T LOOK SO WELL.
GIVE ME THAT!
HUH?
AND THIS, TOO!
MS. CHACHA, WHAT ARE YOU DOING?
???? ??
GO! NOW!
HUH? BUT...

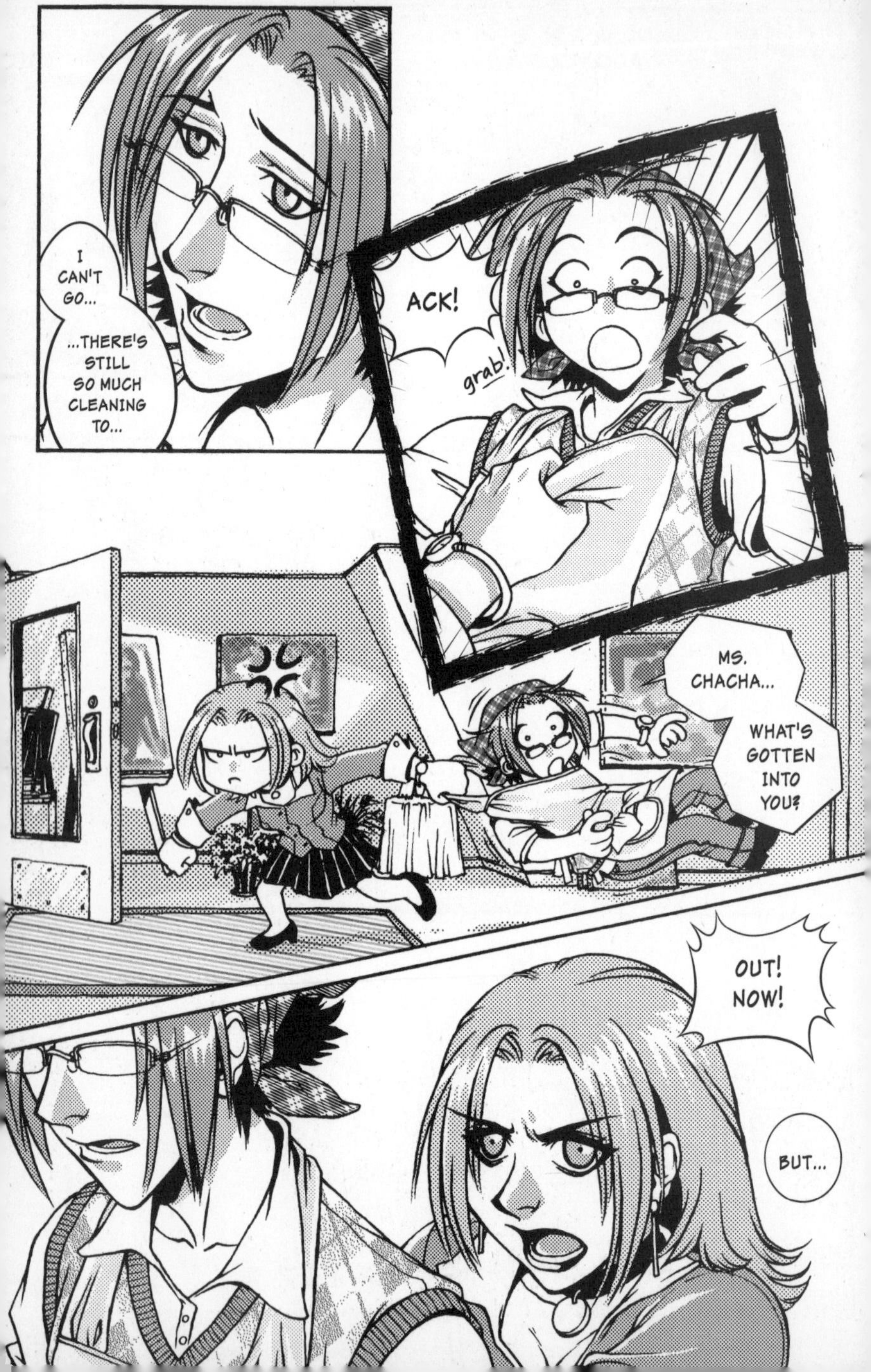
I CAN'T GO...
...THERE'S STILL SO MUCH CLEANING TO...
ACK!
grab!
MS. CHACHA...
WHAT'S GOTTEN INTO YOU?
OUT! NOW!
BUT...

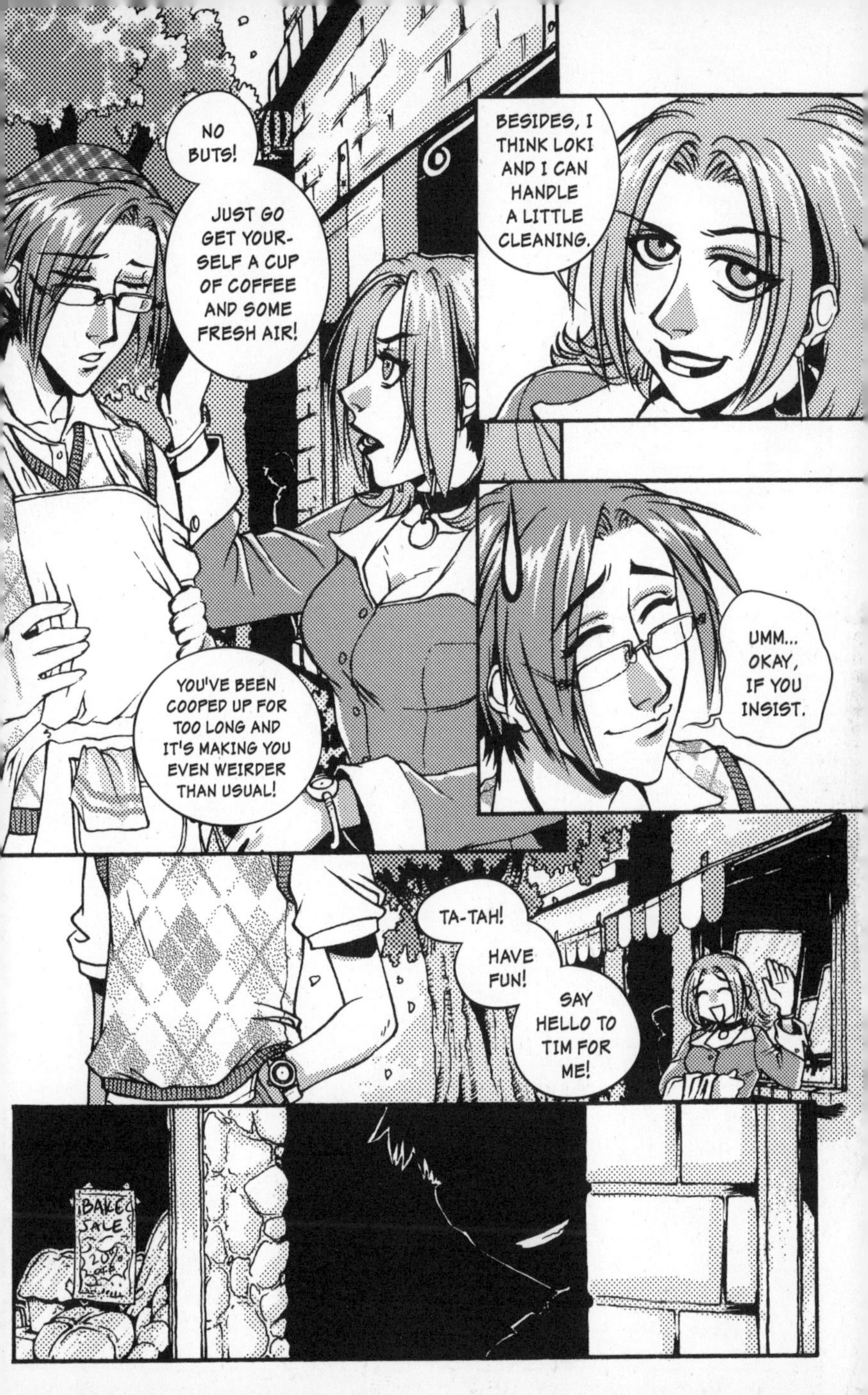
NO BUTS!
JUST GO GET YOUR-SELF A CUP OF COFFEE AND SOME FRESH AIR!
YOU'VE BEEN COOPED UP FOR TOO LONG AND IT'S MAKING YOU EVEN WEIRDER THAN USUAL!
BESIDES, I THINK LOKI AND I CAN HANDLE A LITTLE CLEANING.
UMM... OKAY, IF YOU INSIST.
TA-TAH!
HAVE FUN!
SAY HELLO TO TIM FOR ME!
BAKE SALE

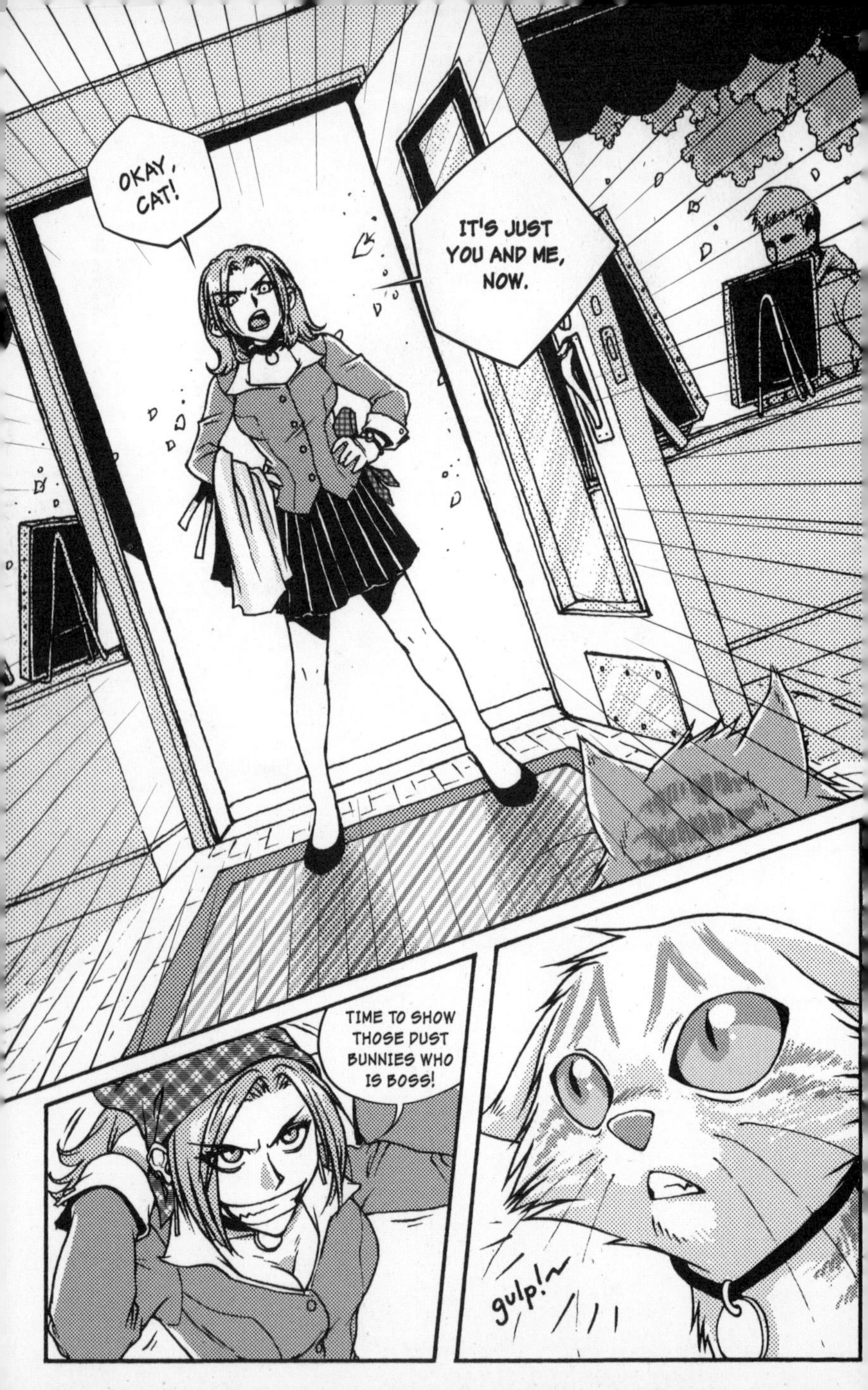
OKAY, CAT!
IT'S JUST YOU AND ME, NOW.
TIME TO SHOW THOSE DUST BUNNIES WHO IS BOSS!
gulp!

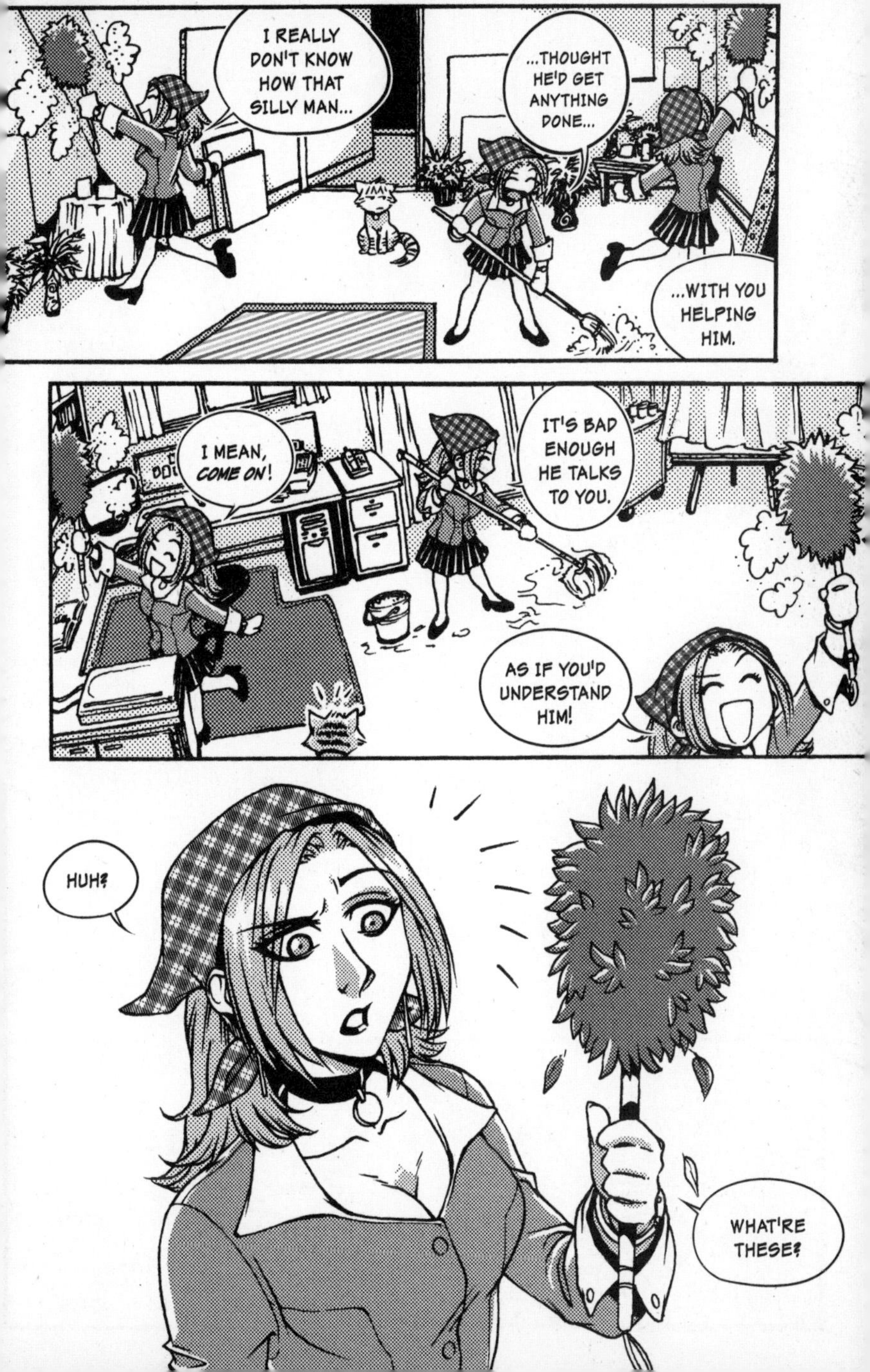
I REALLY DON'T KNOW HOW THAT SILLY MAN...
...THOUGHT HE'D GET ANYTHING DONE...
...WITH YOU HELPING HIM.
I MEAN, COME ON!
IT'S BAD ENOUGH HE TALKS TO YOU.
AS IF YOU'D UNDERSTAND HIM!
HUH?
WHAT'RE THESE?

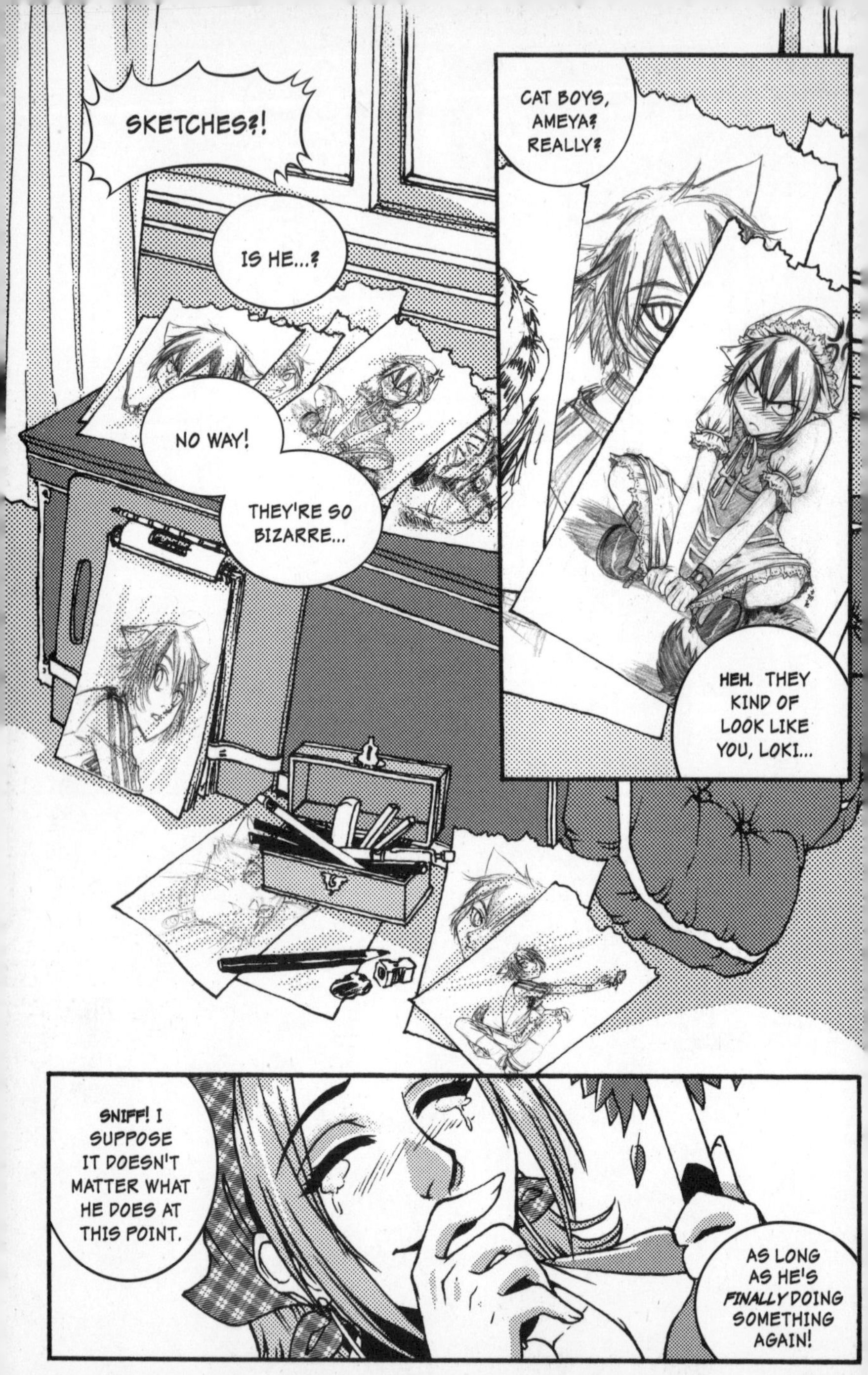
SKETCHES?!
IS HE...?
NO WAY!
THEY'RE SO BIZARRE...
CAT BOYS, AMEYA? REALLY?
HEH. THEY KIND OF LOOK LIKE YOU, LOKI...
SNIFF! I SUPPOSE IT DOESN'T MATTER WHAT HE DOES AT THIS POINT.
AS LONG AS HE'S *FINALLY* DOING SOMETHING AGAIN!

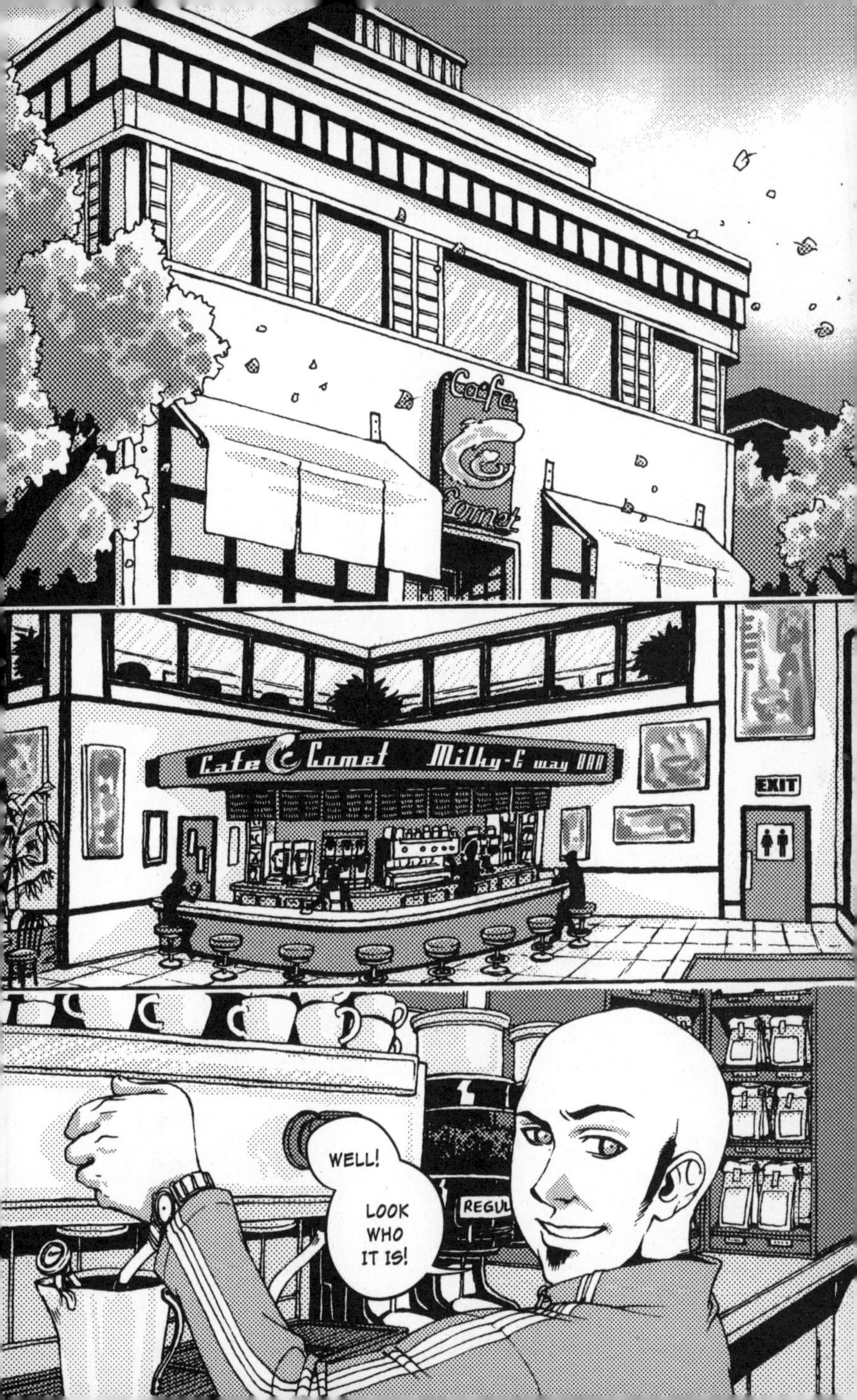
Cafe Comet
Cafe Comet Milky-C way BAR
EXIT
REGUL
WELL!
LOOK WHO IT IS!

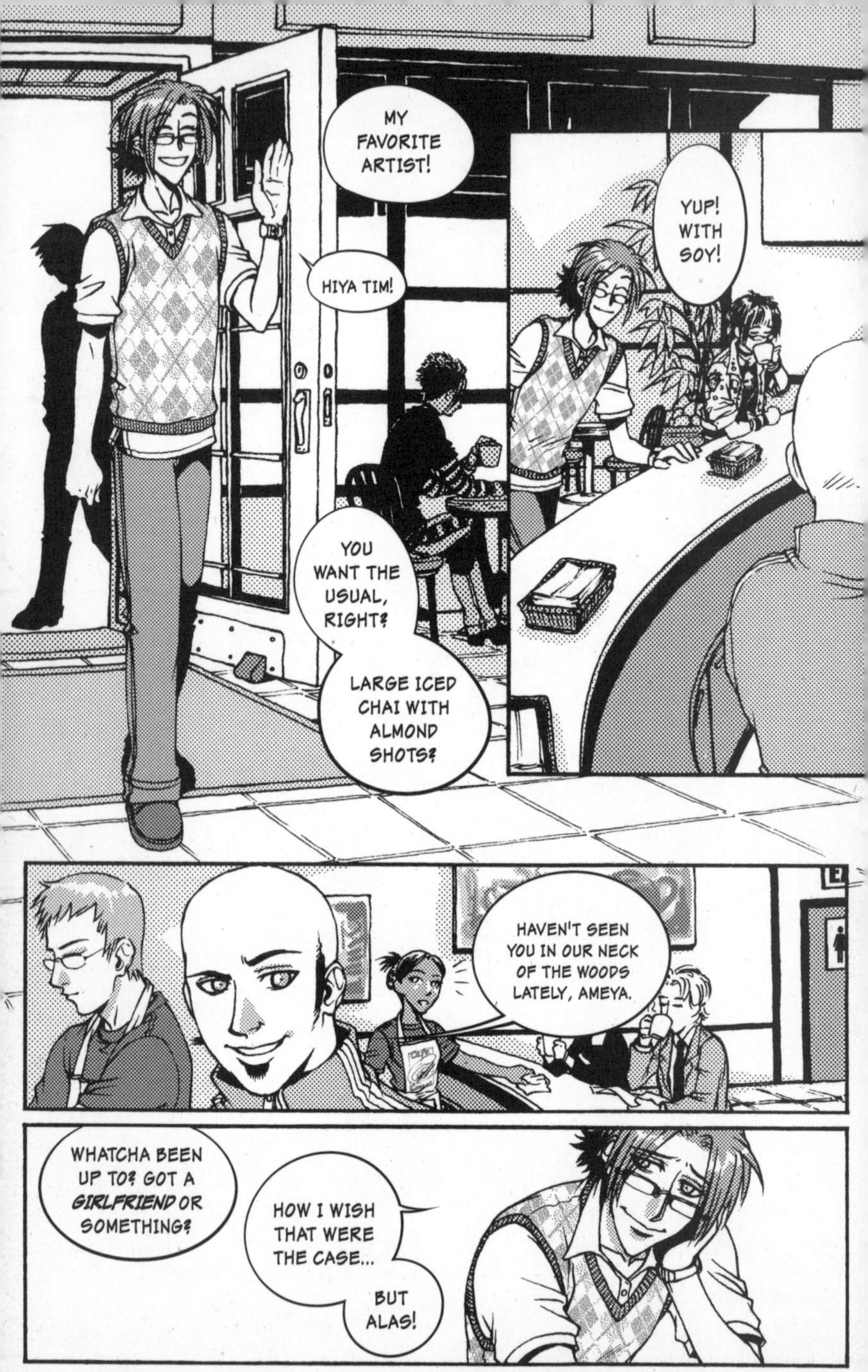
MY FAVORITE ARTIST!
HIYA TIM!
YUP! WITH SOY!
YOU WANT THE USUAL, RIGHT?
LARGE ICED CHAI WITH ALMOND SHOTS?
HAVEN'T SEEN YOU IN OUR NECK OF THE WOODS LATELY, AMEYA.
WHATCHA BEEN UP TO? GOT A *GIRLFRIEND* OR SOMETHING?
HOW I WISH THAT WERE THE CASE...
BUT ALAS!

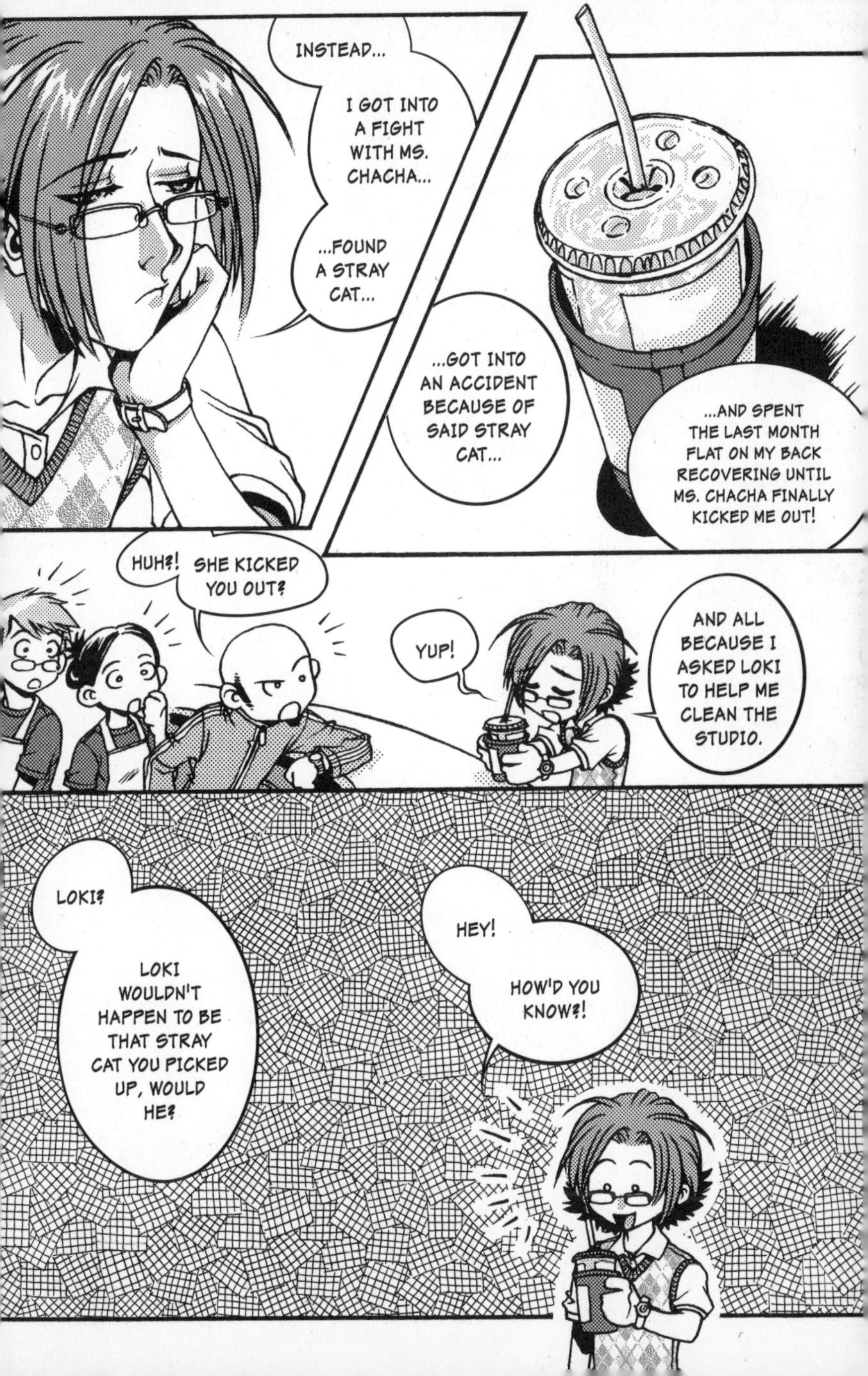
INSTEAD...
I GOT INTO A FIGHT WITH MS. CHACHA...
...FOUND A STRAY CAT...
...GOT INTO AN ACCIDENT BECAUSE OF SAID STRAY CAT...
...AND SPENT THE LAST MONTH FLAT ON MY BACK RECOVERING UNTIL MS. CHACHA FINALLY KICKED ME OUT!
HUH?!
SHE KICKED YOU OUT?
YUP!
AND ALL BECAUSE I ASKED LOKI TO HELP ME CLEAN THE STUDIO.
LOKI?
LOKI WOULDN'T HAPPEN TO BE THAT STRAY CAT YOU PICKED UP, WOULD HE?
HEY!
HOW'D YOU KNOW?!

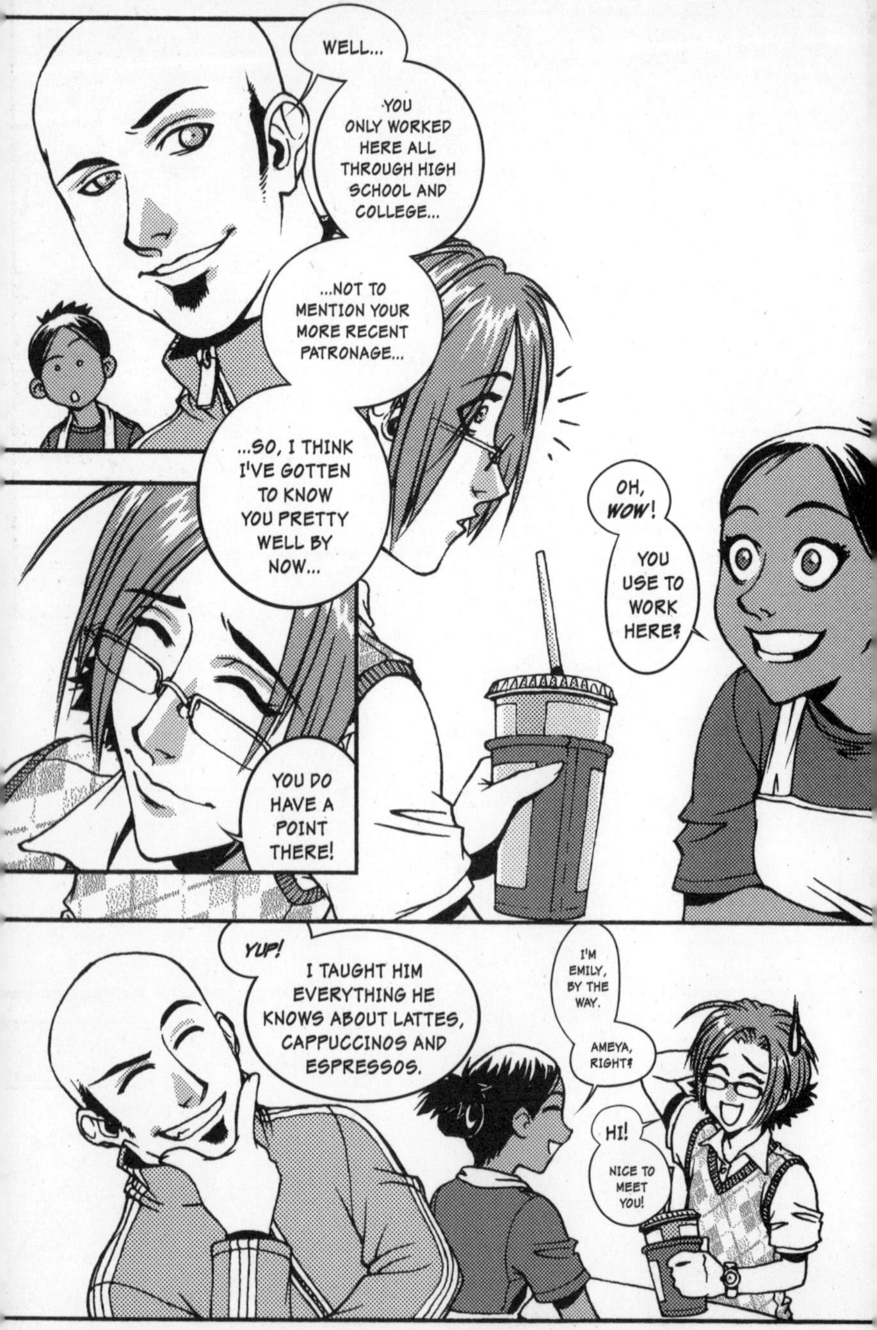
WELL...
YOU ONLY WORKED HERE ALL THROUGH HIGH SCHOOL AND COLLEGE...
...NOT TO MENTION YOUR MORE RECENT PATRONAGE...
...SO, I THINK I'VE GOTTEN TO KNOW YOU PRETTY WELL BY NOW...
YOU DO HAVE A POINT THERE!
OH, WOW!
YOU USE TO WORK HERE?
YUP!
I TAUGHT HIM EVERYTHING HE KNOWS ABOUT LATTES, CAPPUCCINOS AND ESPRESSOS.
I'M EMILY, BY THE WAY.
AMEYA, RIGHT?
HI!
NICE TO MEET YOU!

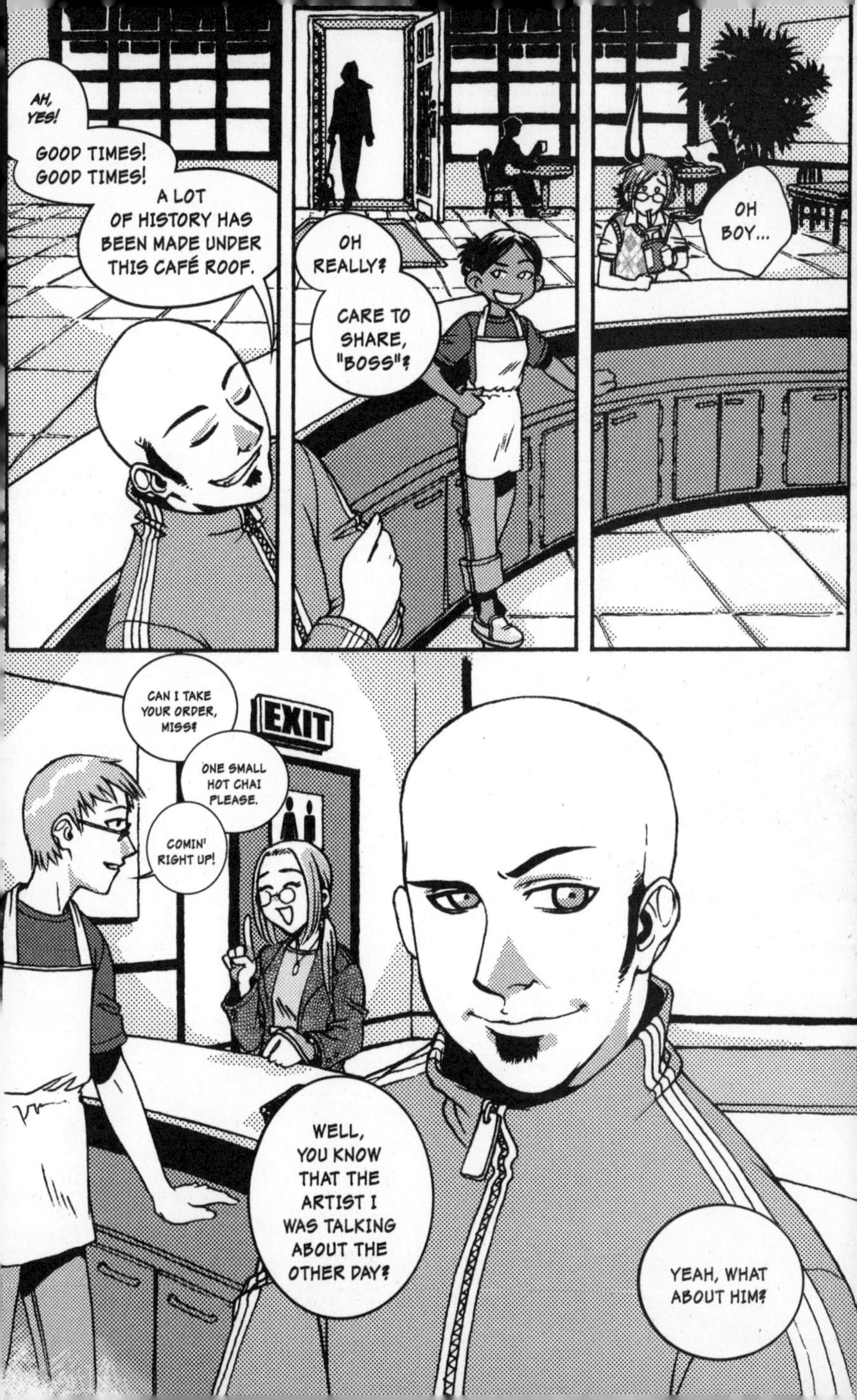

AH, YES!
GOOD TIMES! GOOD TIMES!
A LOT OF HISTORY HAS BEEN MADE UNDER THIS CAFÉ ROOF.
OH REALLY?
CARE TO SHARE, "BOSS"?
OH BOY...
CAN I TAKE YOUR ORDER, MISS?
EXIT
ONE SMALL HOT CHAI PLEASE.
COMIN' RIGHT UP!
WELL, YOU KNOW THAT THE ARTIST I WAS TALKING ABOUT THE OTHER DAY?
YEAH, WHAT ABOUT HIM?

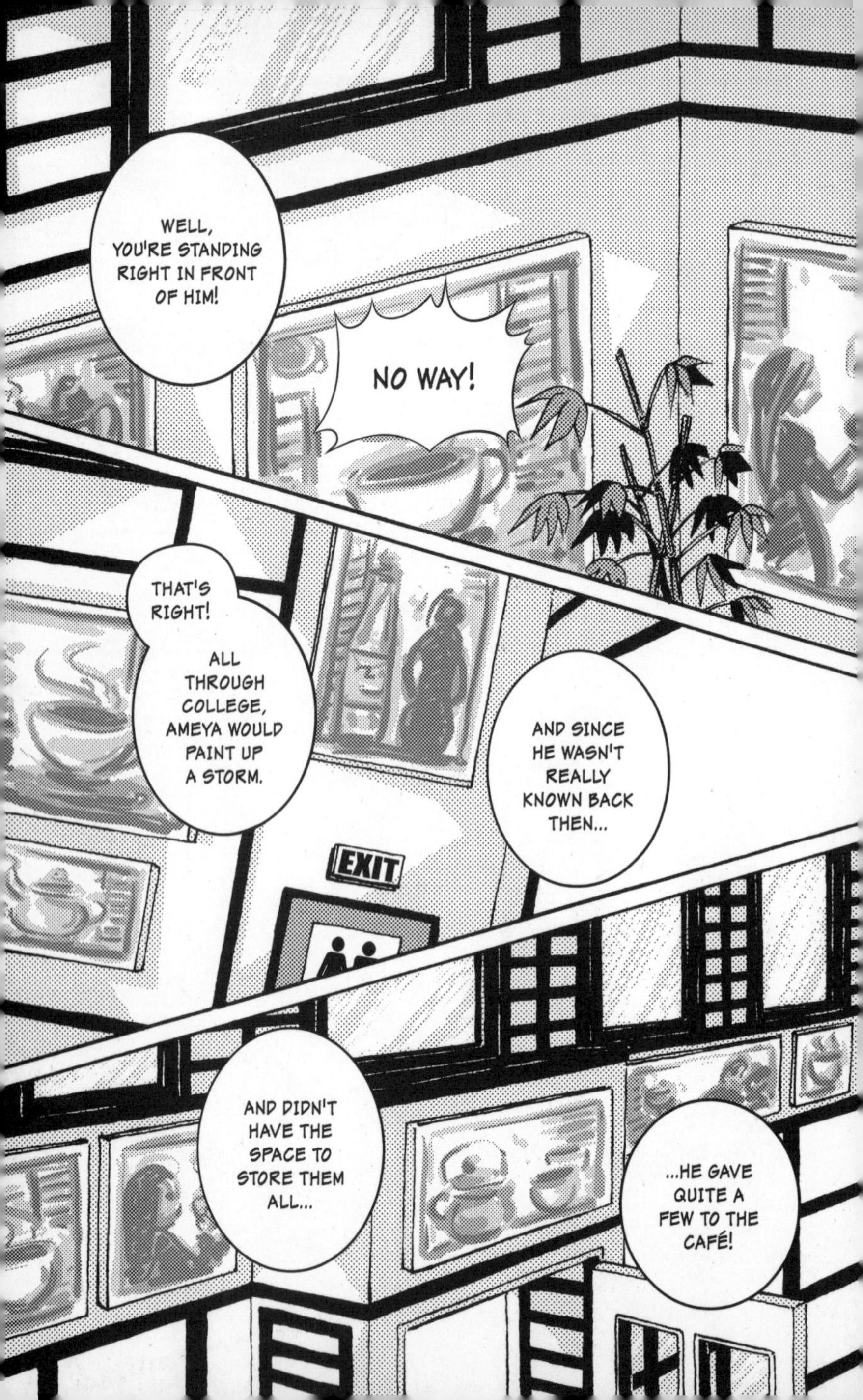

WELL, YOU'RE STANDING RIGHT IN FRONT OF HIM!
NO WAY!
THAT'S RIGHT!
ALL THROUGH COLLEGE, AMEYA WOULD PAINT UP A STORM.
AND SINCE HE WASN'T REALLY KNOWN BACK THEN...
EXIT
AND DIDN'T HAVE THE SPACE TO STORE THEM ALL...
...HE GAVE QUITE A FEW TO THE CAFÉ!

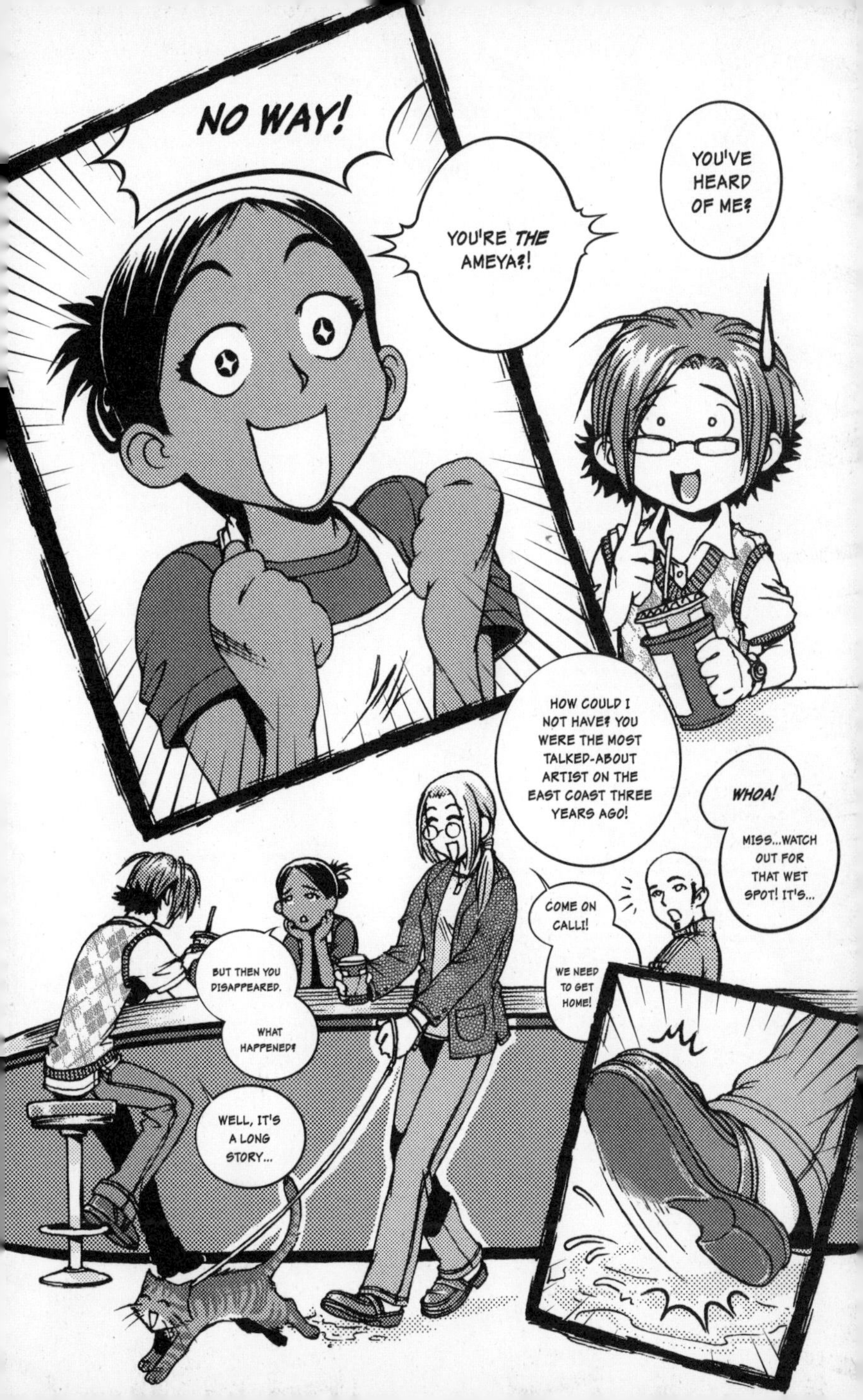
NO WAY!
YOU'RE *THE* AMEYA?!
YOU'VE HEARD OF ME?
HOW COULD I NOT HAVE? YOU WERE THE MOST TALKED-ABOUT ARTIST ON THE EAST COAST THREE YEARS AGO!
BUT THEN YOU DISAPPEARED.
WHAT HAPPENED?
WELL, IT'S A LONG STORY...
COME ON CALLI!
WE NEED TO GET HOME!
WHOA!
MISS...WATCH OUT FOR THAT WET SPOT! IT'S...

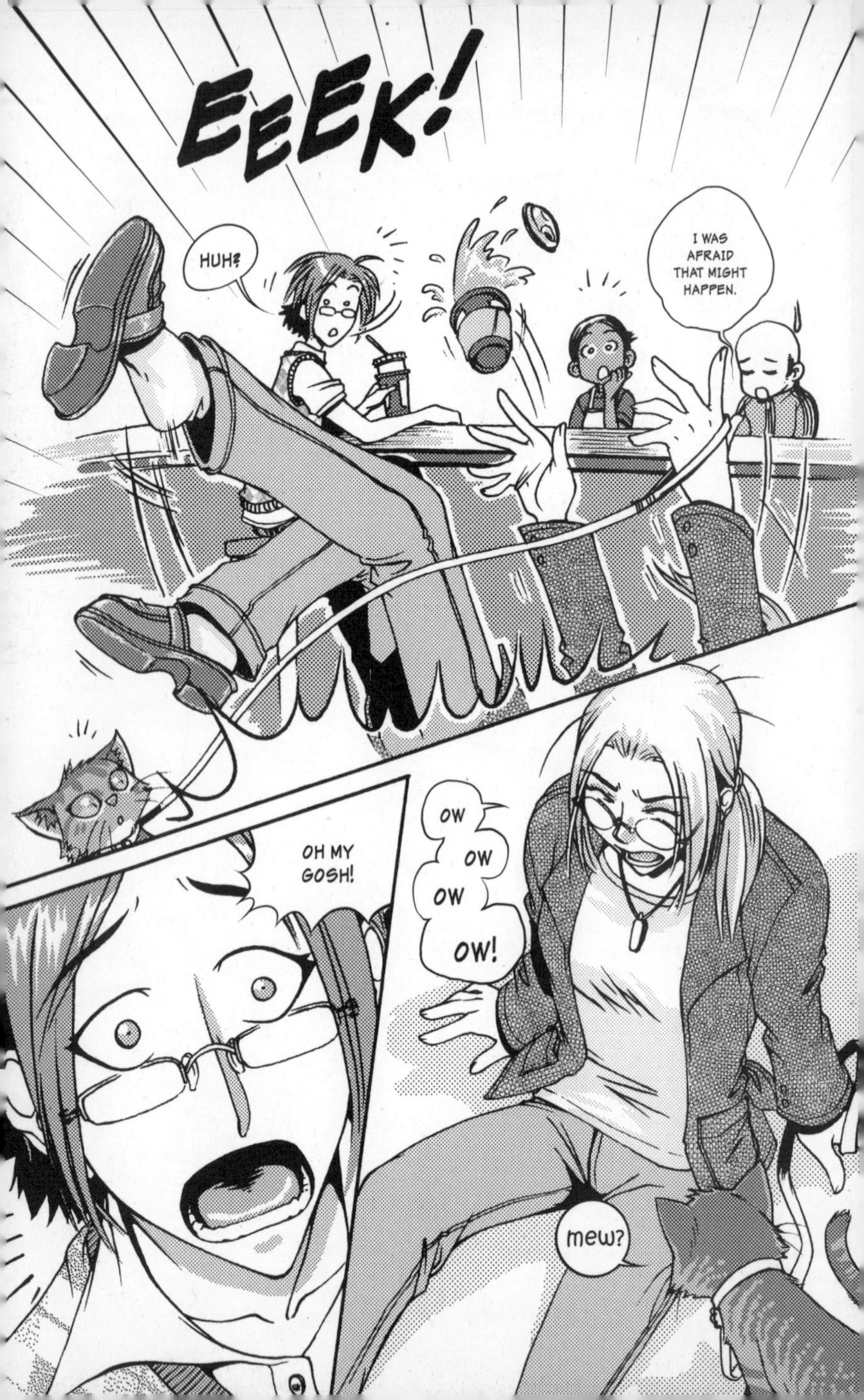
EEEK!
HUH?
I WAS AFRAID THAT MIGHT HAPPEN.
OH MY GOSH!
OW
OW
OW
OW!
mew?

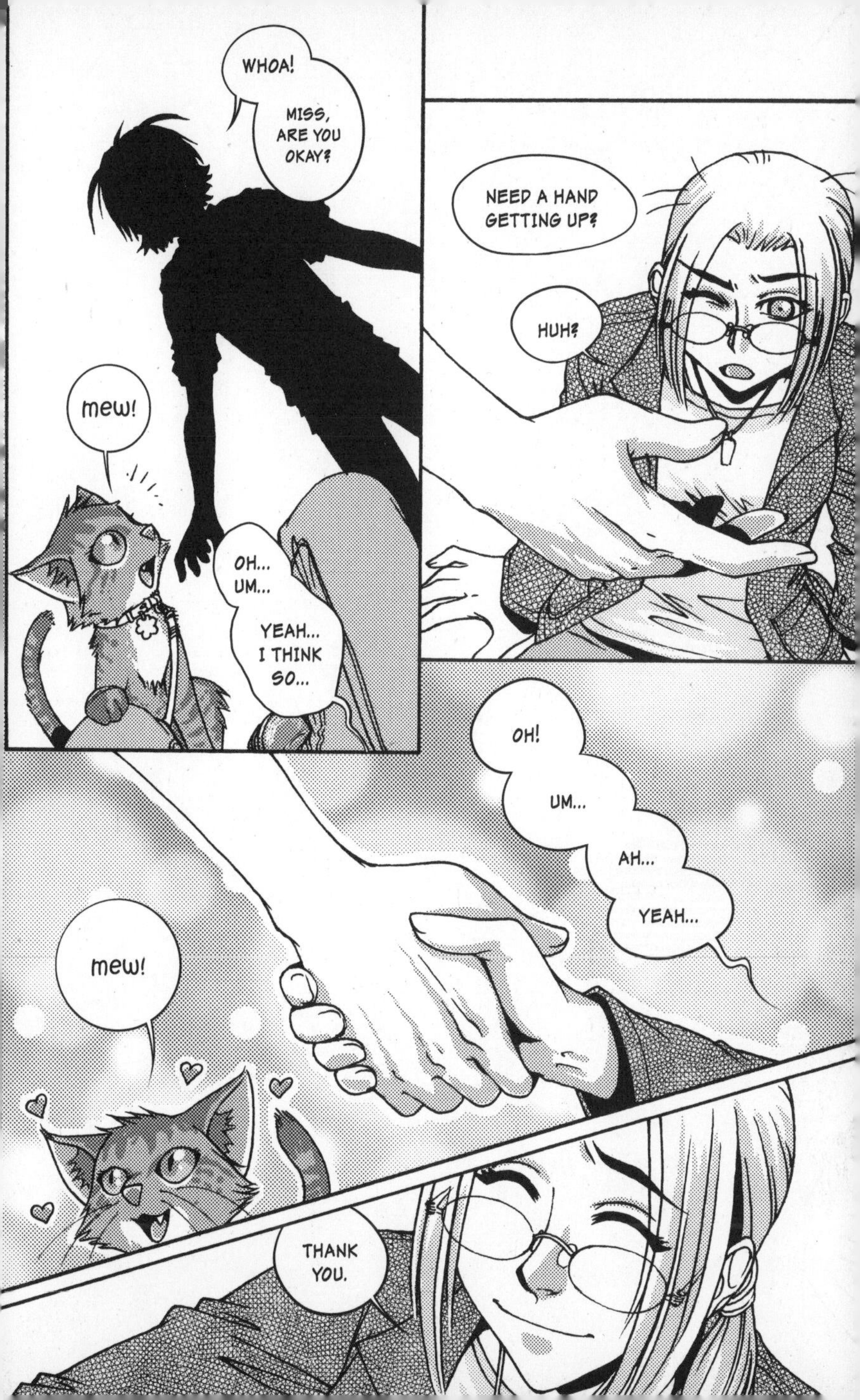
WHOA!
MISS, ARE YOU OKAY?
mew!
OH... UM...
YEAH... I THINK SO...
NEED A HAND GETTING UP?
HUH?
OH!
UM...
AH...
YEAH...
mew!
THANK YOU.

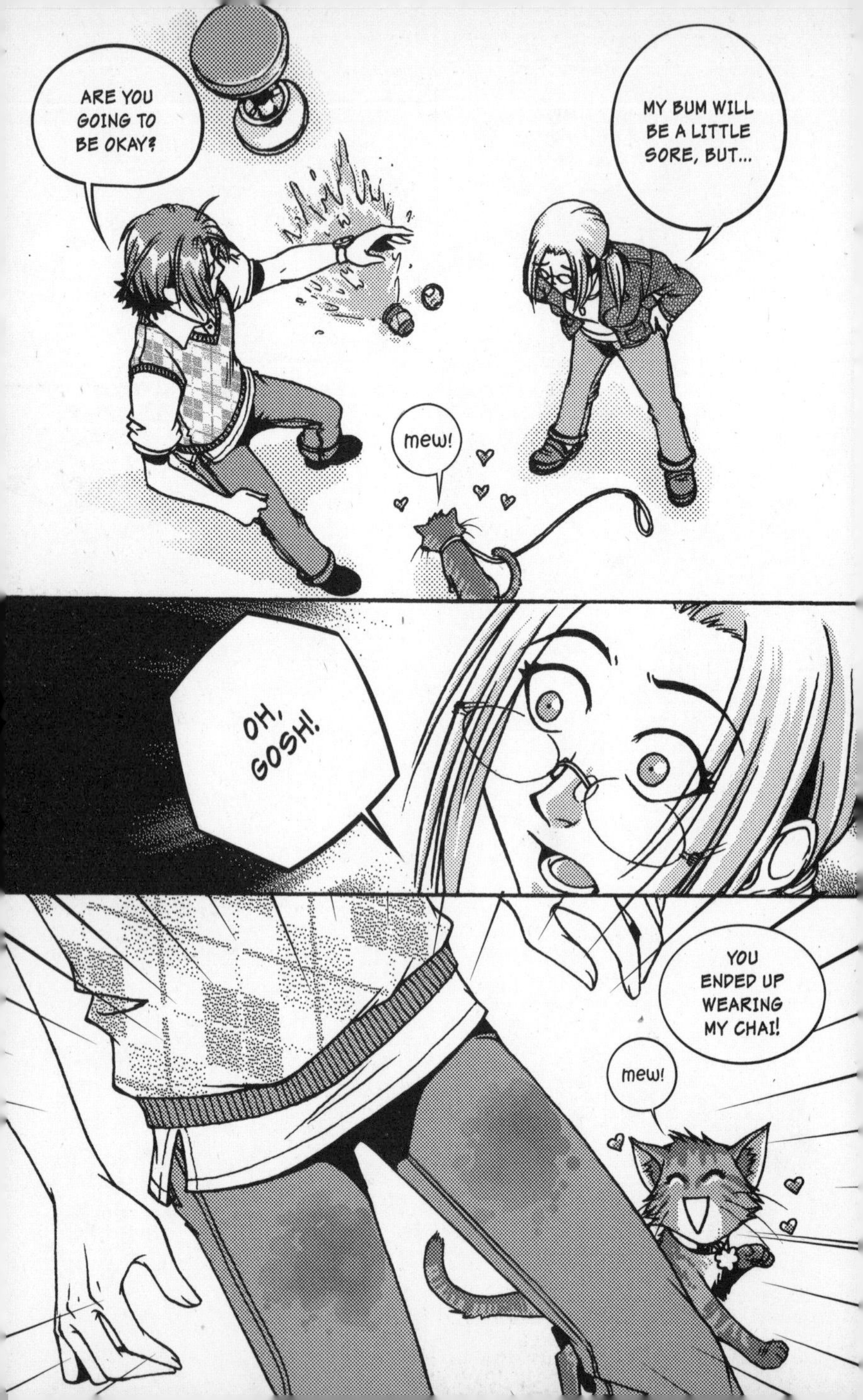
ARE YOU GOING TO BE OKAY?
MY BUM WILL BE A LITTLE SORE, BUT...
mew!
OH, GOSH!
YOU ENDED UP WEARING MY CHAI!
mew!

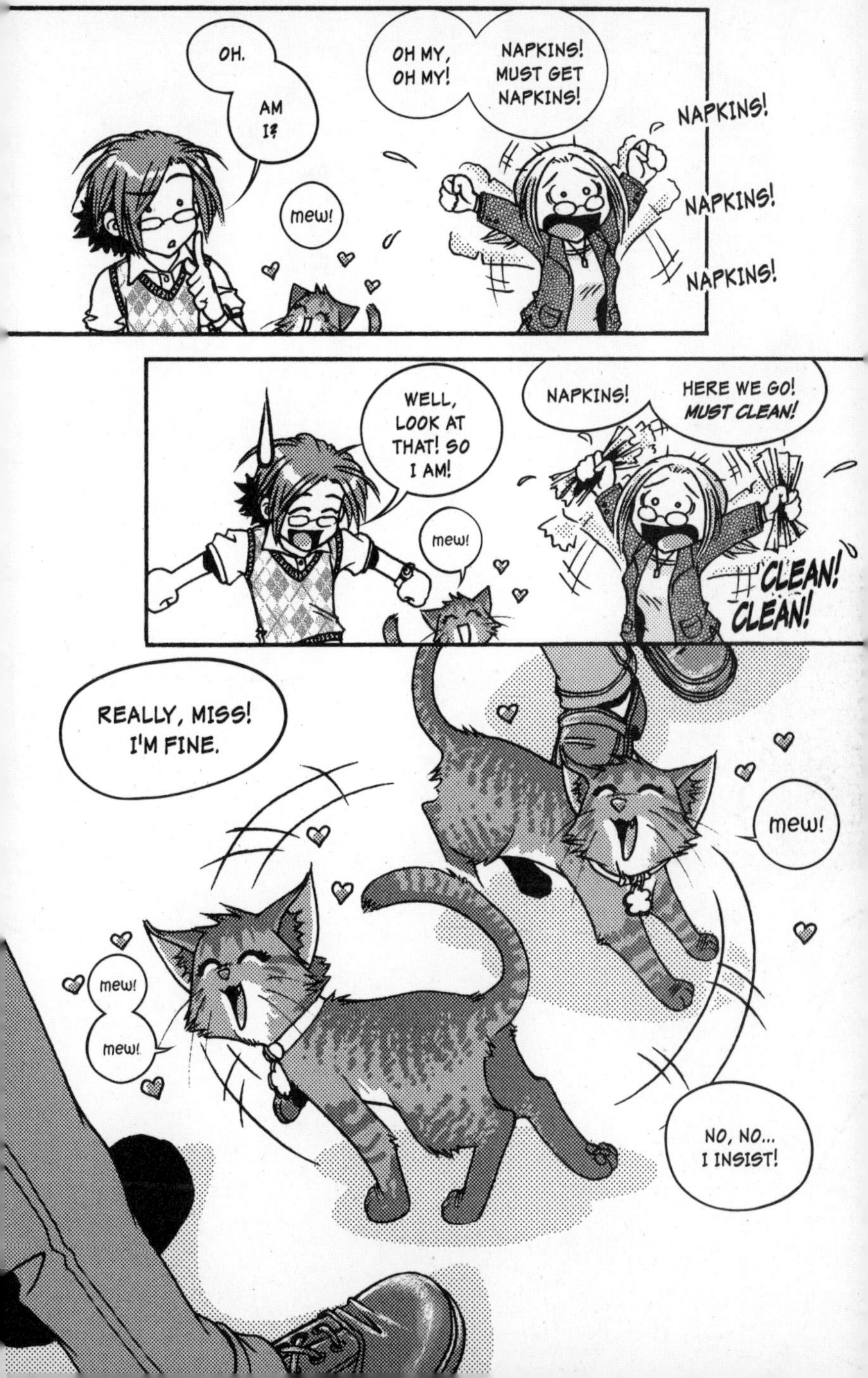
OH.
AM I?
mew!
OH MY, OH MY!
NAPKINS! MUST GET NAPKINS!
NAPKINS!
NAPKINS!
NAPKINS!
WELL, LOOK AT THAT! SO I AM!
mew!
NAPKINS!
HERE WE GO! *MUST CLEAN!*
CLEAN! CLEAN!
REALLY, MISS! I'M FINE.
mew!
mew!
mew!
NO, NO... I INSIST!

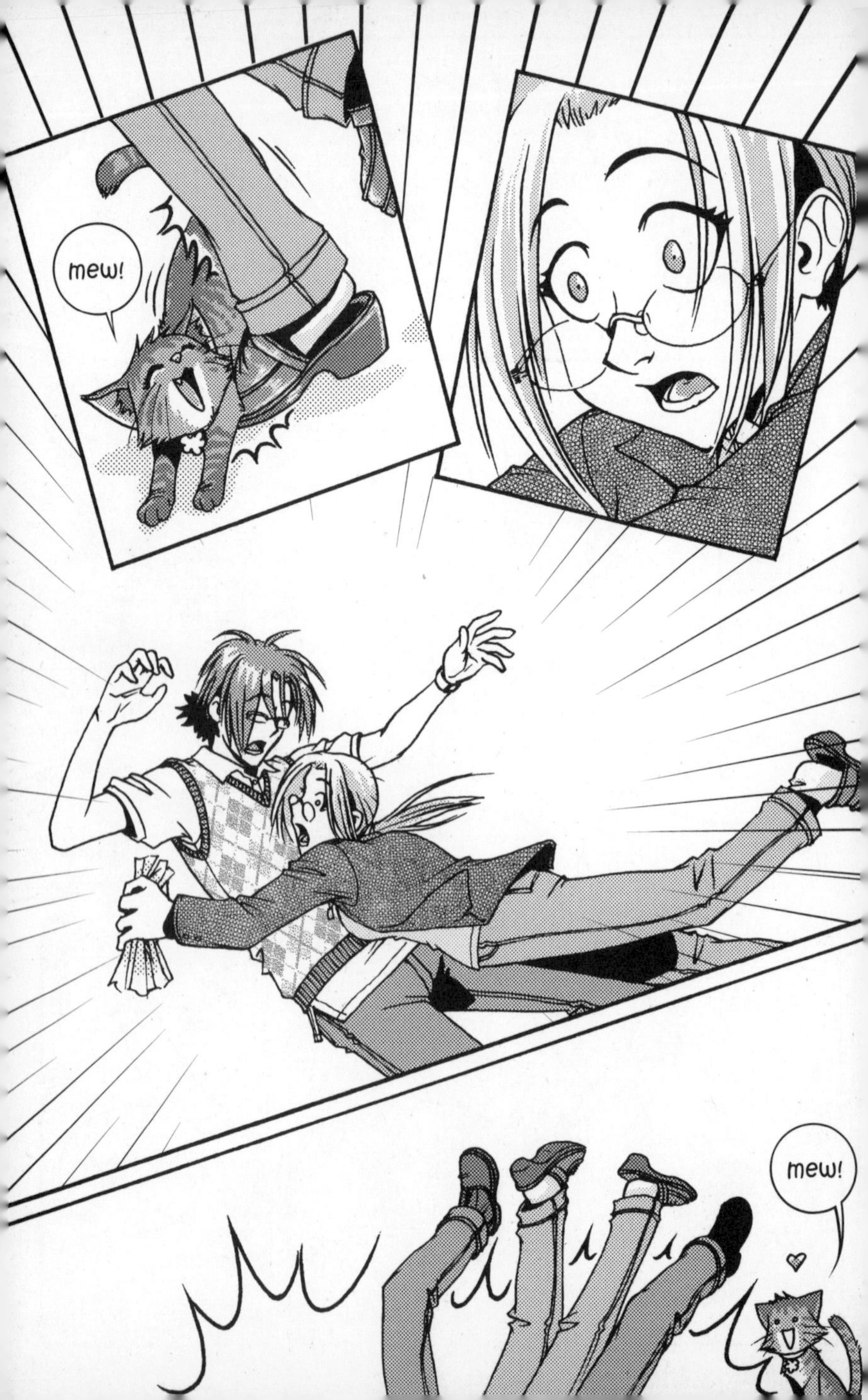
mew!
mew!

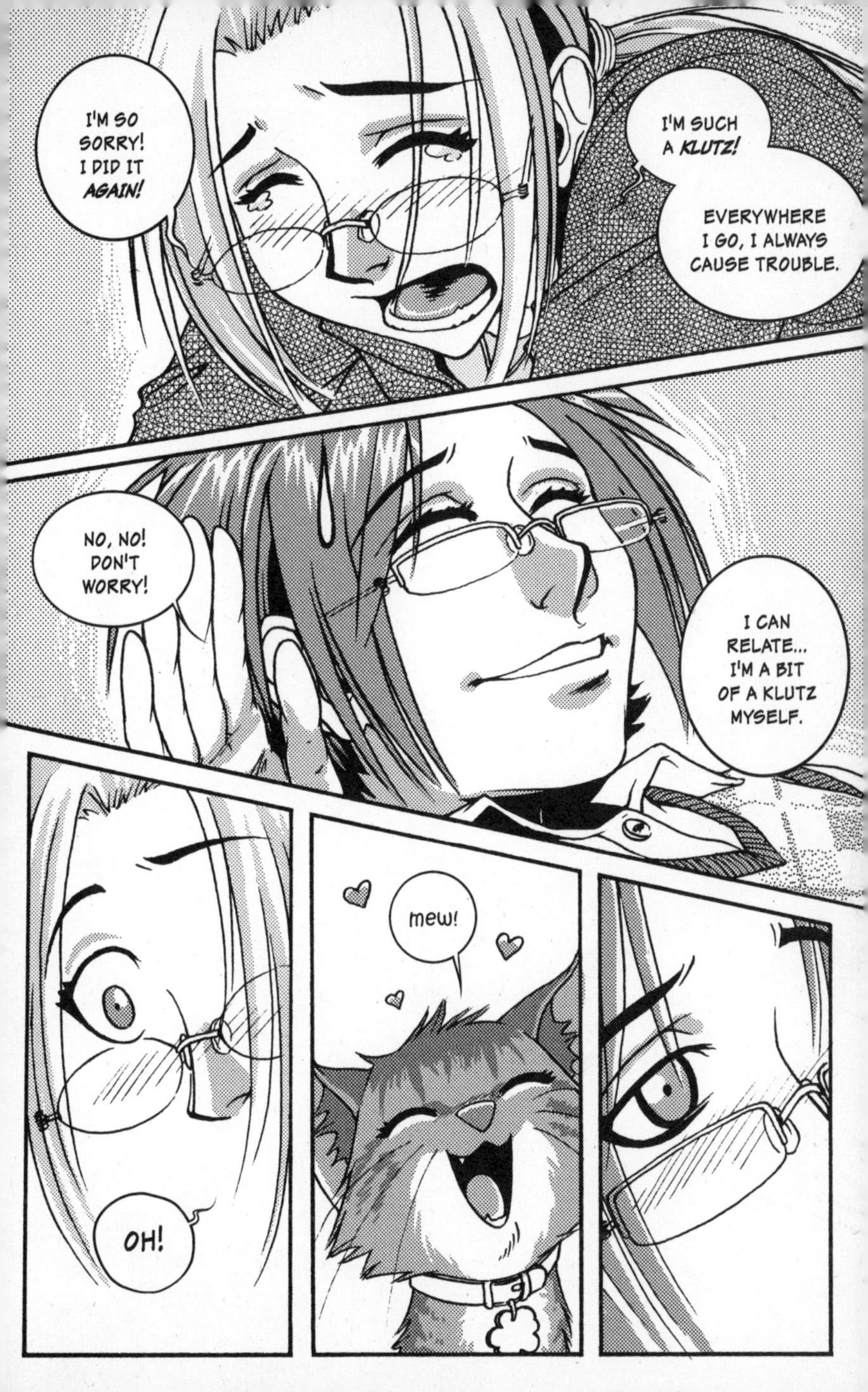

I'M SO SORRY! I DID IT *AGAIN!*
I'M SUCH A *KLUTZ!*
EVERYWHERE I GO, I ALWAYS CAUSE TROUBLE.
NO, NO! DON'T WORRY!
I CAN RELATE... I'M A BIT OF A KLUTZ MYSELF.
OH!
mew!

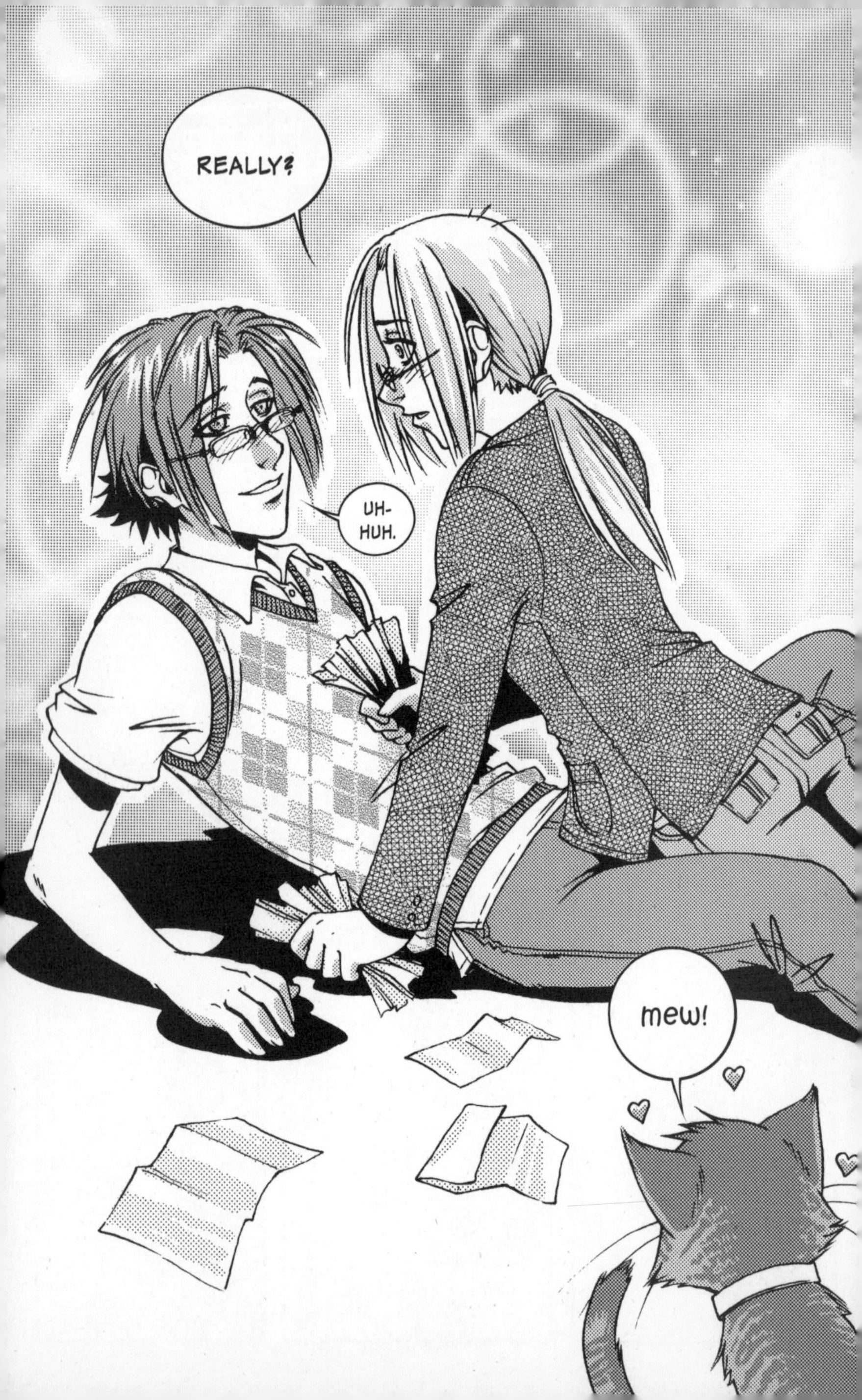
REALLY?
UH-HUH.
mew!

CHAPTER 3

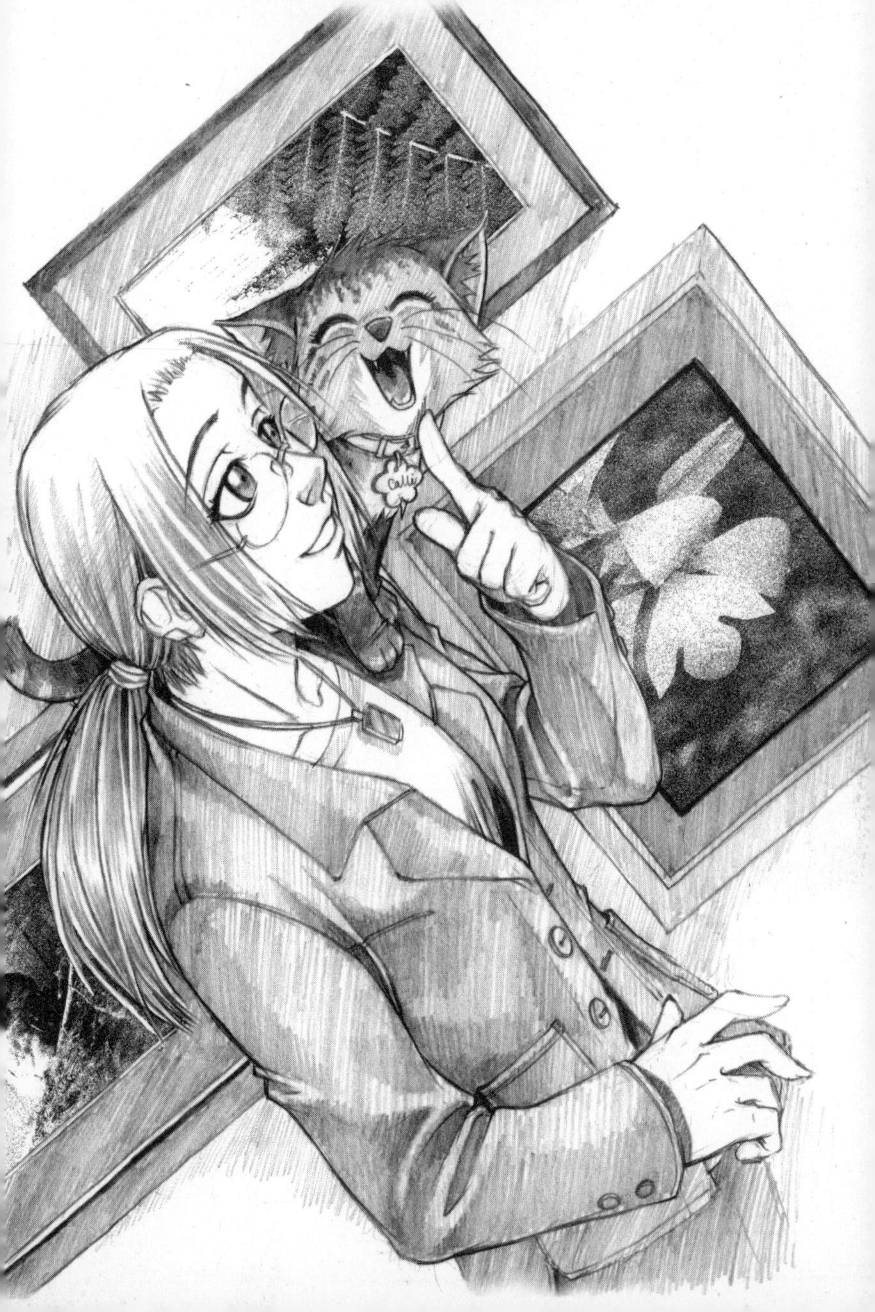

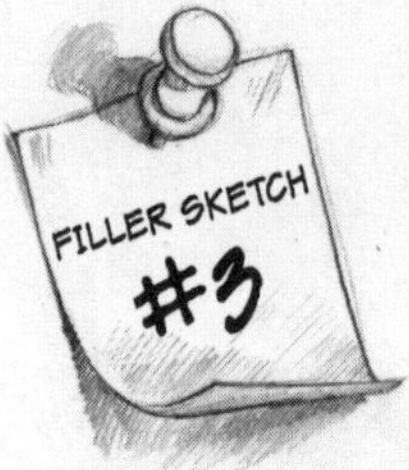
FILLER SKETCH
#3

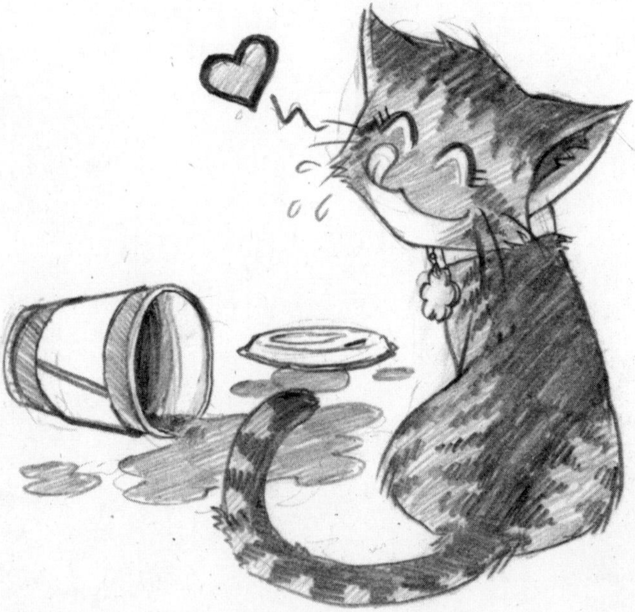

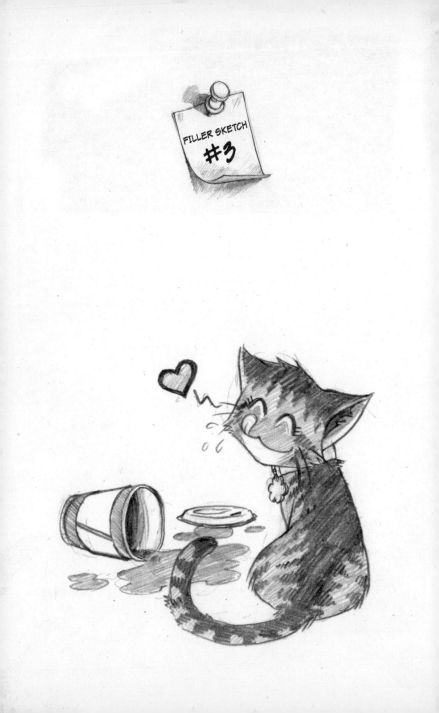

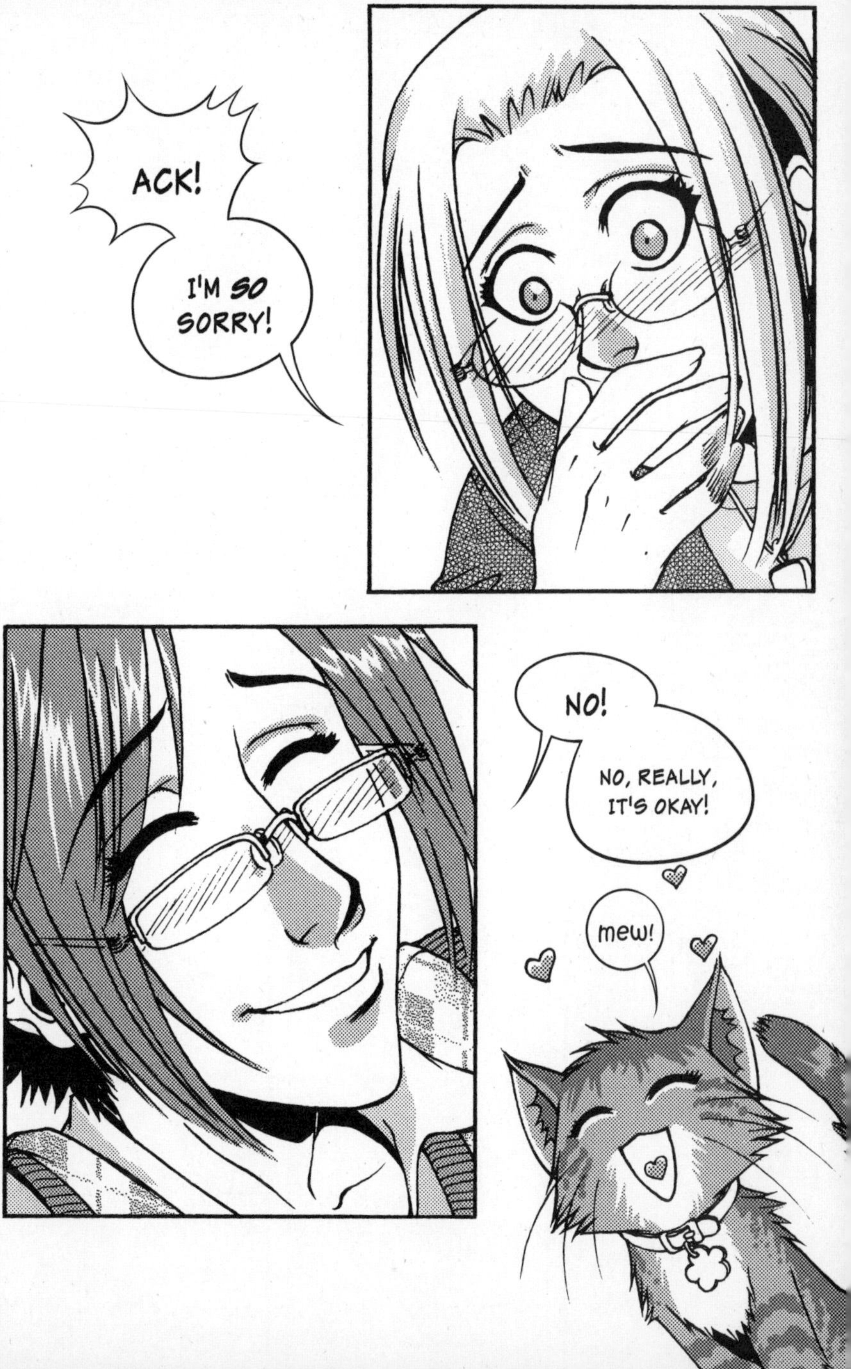
ACK!
I'M SO SORRY!
NO!
NO, REALLY, IT'S OKAY!
mew!

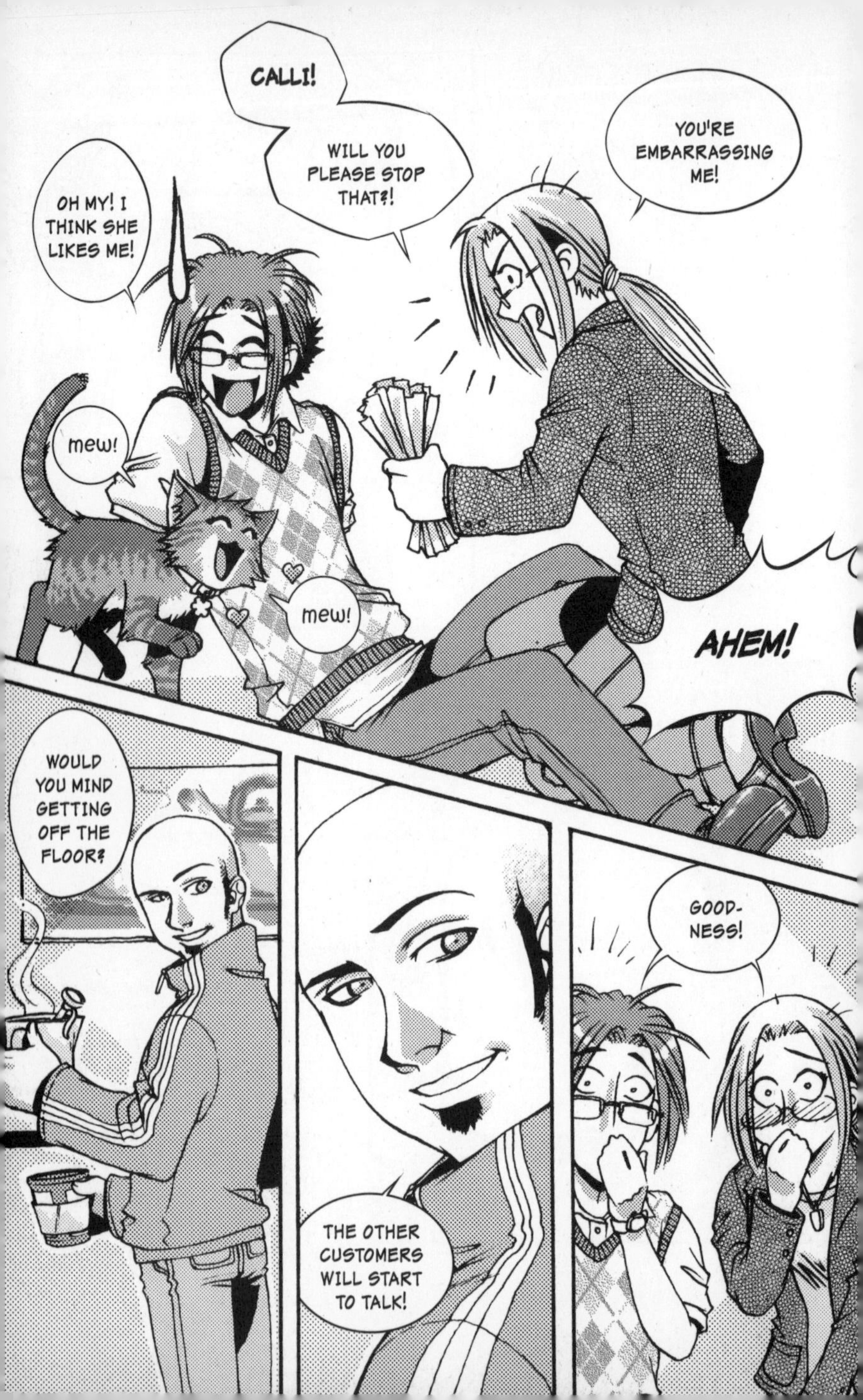
OH MY! I THINK SHE LIKES ME!
CALLI!
WILL YOU PLEASE STOP THAT?!
YOU'RE EMBARRASSING ME!
mew!
mew!
AHEM!
WOULD YOU MIND GETTING OFF THE FLOOR?
THE OTHER CUSTOMERS WILL START TO TALK!
GOOD-NESS!

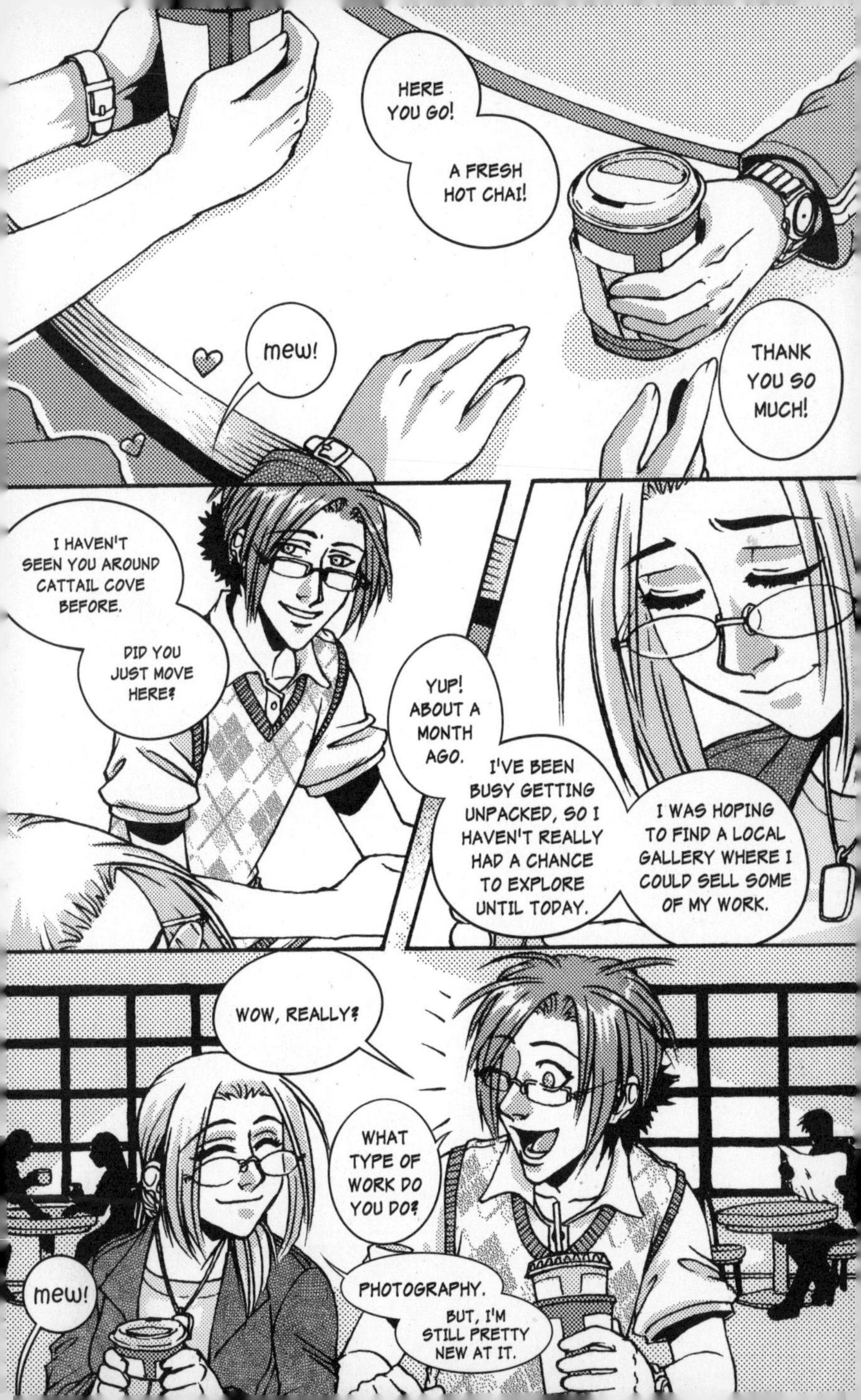
HERE YOU GO!
A FRESH HOT CHAI!
mew!
THANK YOU SO MUCH!
I HAVEN'T SEEN YOU AROUND CATTAIL COVE BEFORE.
DID YOU JUST MOVE HERE?
YUP! ABOUT A MONTH AGO.
I'VE BEEN BUSY GETTING UNPACKED, SO I HAVEN'T REALLY HAD A CHANCE TO EXPLORE UNTIL TODAY.
I WAS HOPING TO FIND A LOCAL GALLERY WHERE I COULD SELL SOME OF MY WORK.
WOW, REALLY?
WHAT TYPE OF WORK DO YOU DO?
mew!
PHOTOGRAPHY.
BUT, I'M STILL PRETTY NEW AT IT.

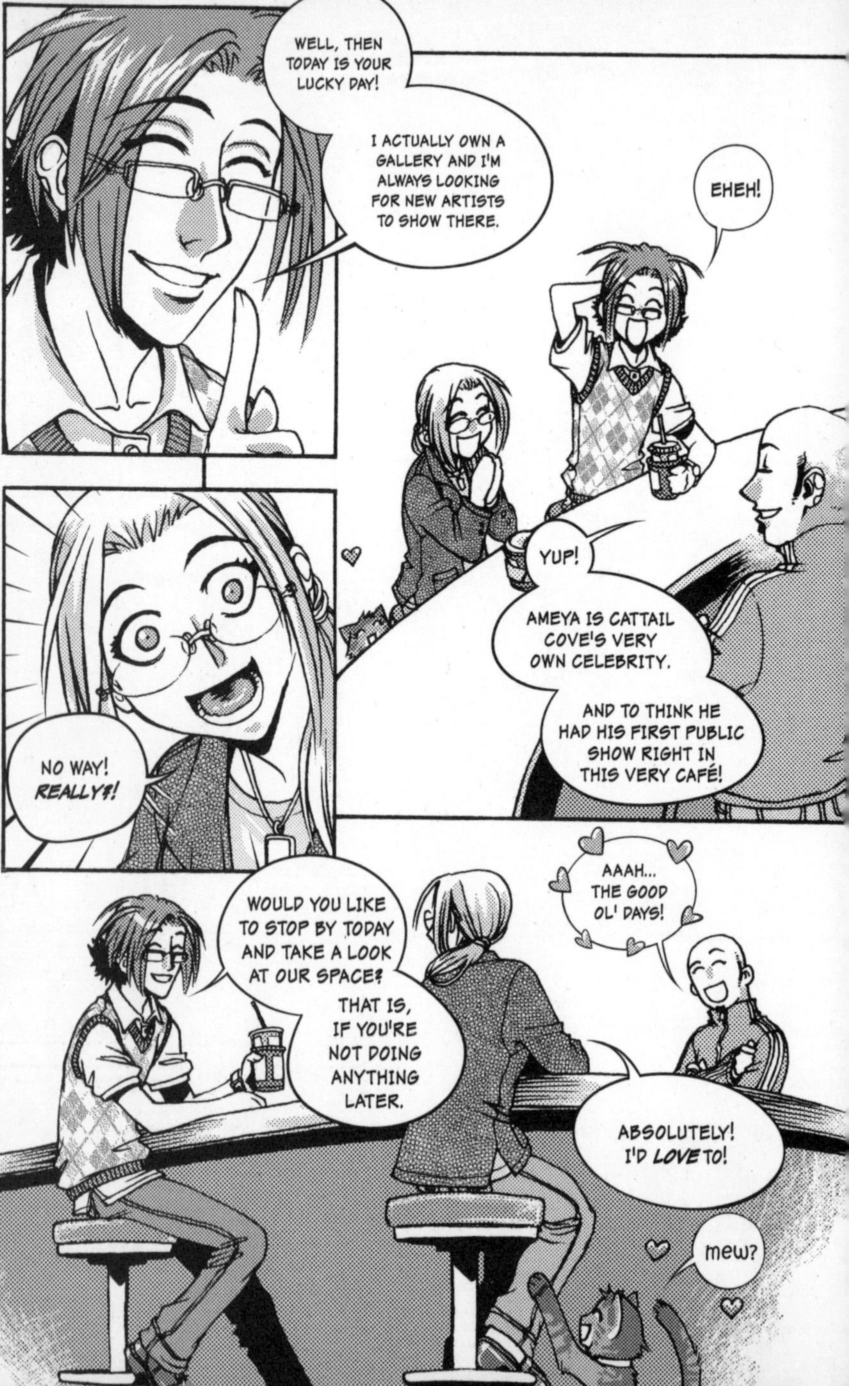
WELL, THEN TODAY IS YOUR LUCKY DAY!
I ACTUALLY OWN A GALLERY AND I'M ALWAYS LOOKING FOR NEW ARTISTS TO SHOW THERE.
NO WAY! *REALLY?!*
EHEH!
YUP!
AMEYA IS CATTAIL COVE'S VERY OWN CELEBRITY.
AND TO THINK HE HAD HIS FIRST PUBLIC SHOW RIGHT IN THIS VERY CAFÉ!
WOULD YOU LIKE TO STOP BY TODAY AND TAKE A LOOK AT OUR SPACE?
THAT IS, IF YOU'RE NOT DOING ANYTHING LATER.
AAAH... THE GOOD OL' DAYS!
ABSOLUTELY! I'D *LOVE* TO!
mew?

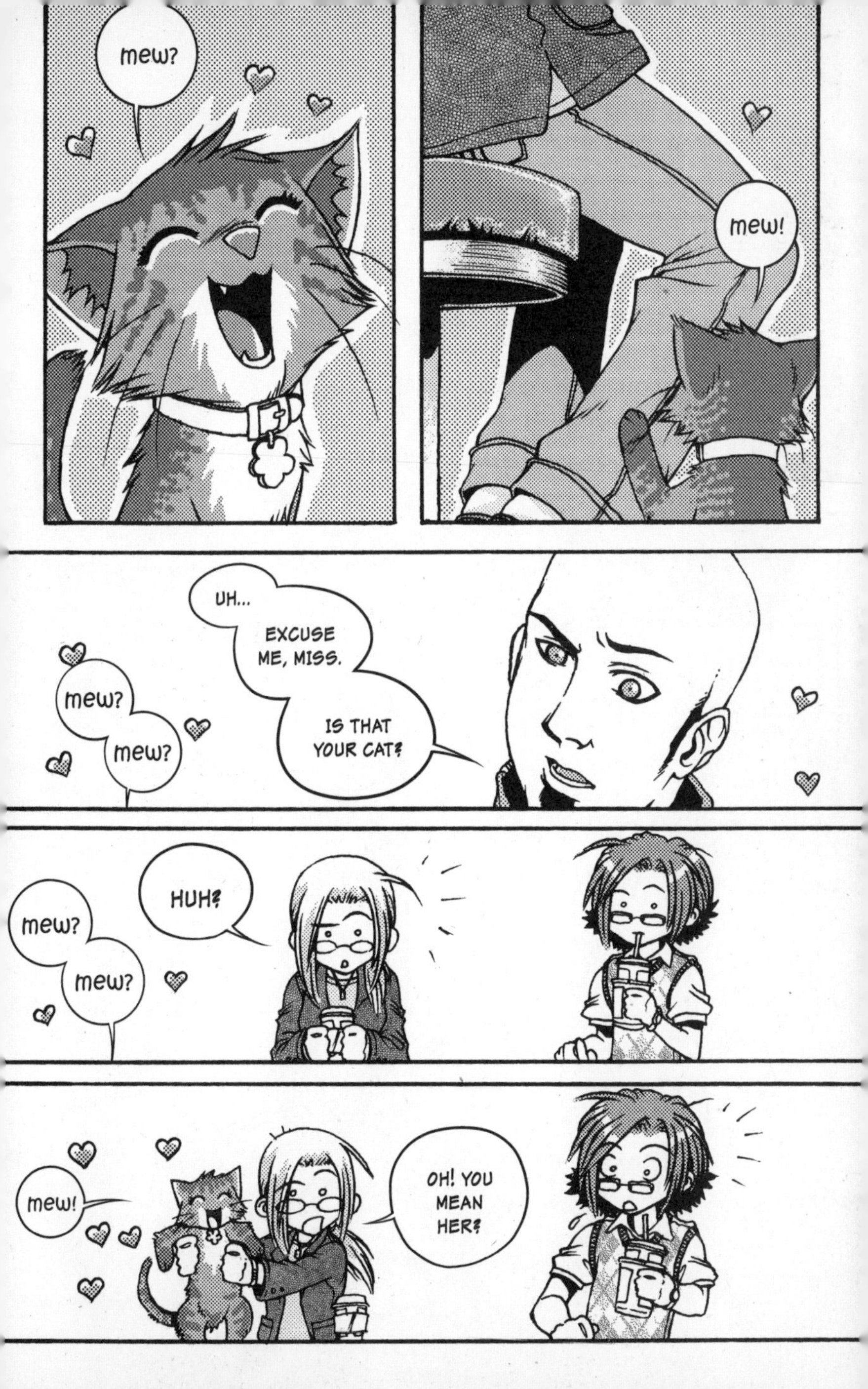
mew?
mew!
UH...
EXCUSE ME, MISS.
IS THAT YOUR CAT?
mew?
mew?
mew?
mew?
HUH?
mew!
OH! YOU MEAN HER?

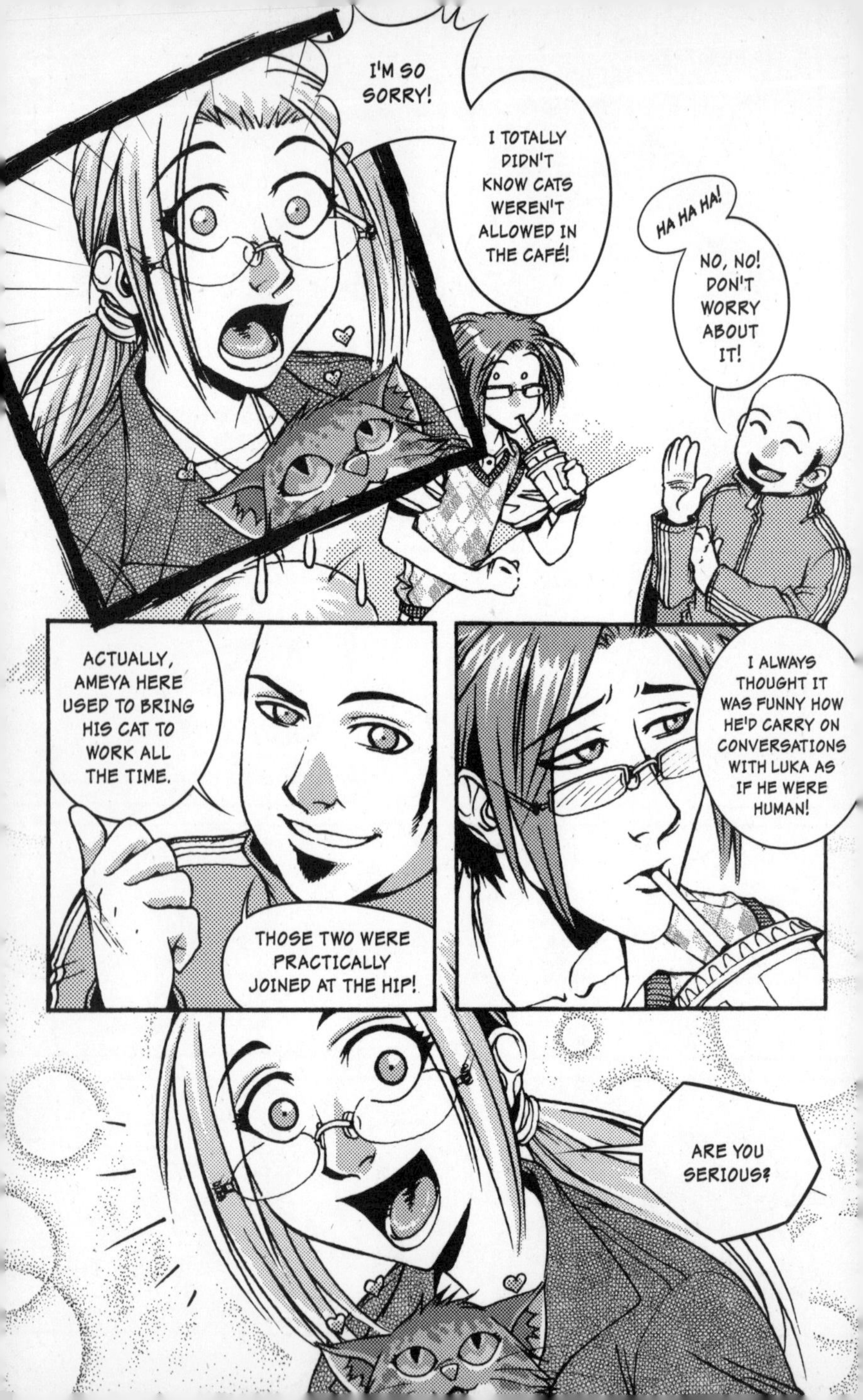
I'M SO SORRY!
I TOTALLY DIDN'T KNOW CATS WEREN'T ALLOWED IN THE CAFÉ!
HA HA HA!
NO, NO! DON'T WORRY ABOUT IT!
ACTUALLY, AMEYA HERE USED TO BRING HIS CAT TO WORK ALL THE TIME.
THOSE TWO WERE PRACTICALLY JOINED AT THE HIP!
I ALWAYS THOUGHT IT WAS FUNNY HOW HE'D CARRY ON CONVERSATIONS WITH LUKA AS IF HE WERE HUMAN!
ARE YOU SERIOUS?

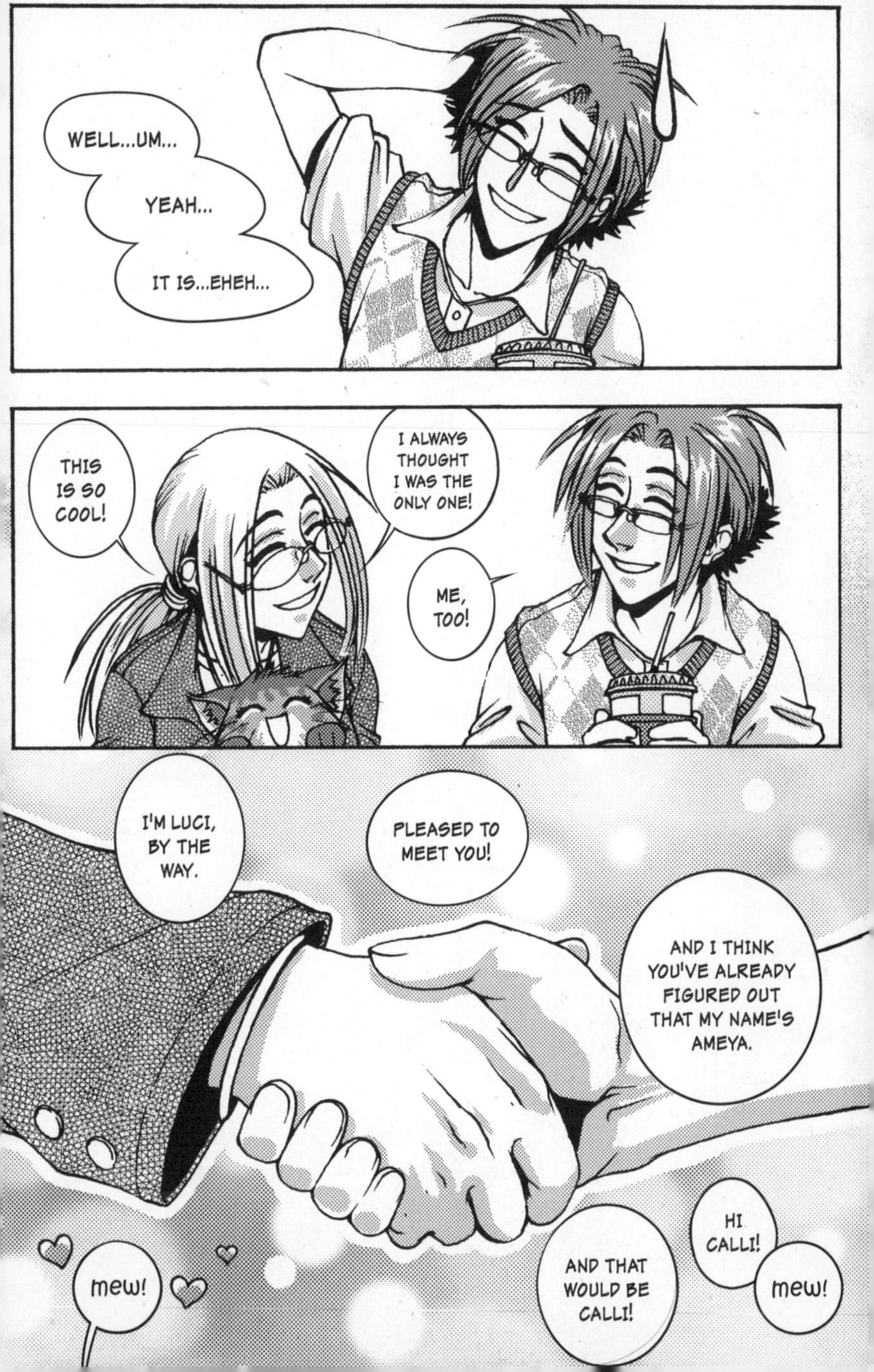
WELL...UM...
YEAH...
IT IS...EHEH...
THIS IS SO COOL!
I ALWAYS THOUGHT I WAS THE ONLY ONE!
ME, TOO!
I'M LUCI, BY THE WAY.
PLEASED TO MEET YOU!
AND I THINK YOU'VE ALREADY FIGURED OUT THAT MY NAME'S AMEYA.
mew!
AND THAT WOULD BE CALLI!
HI CALLI!
mew!

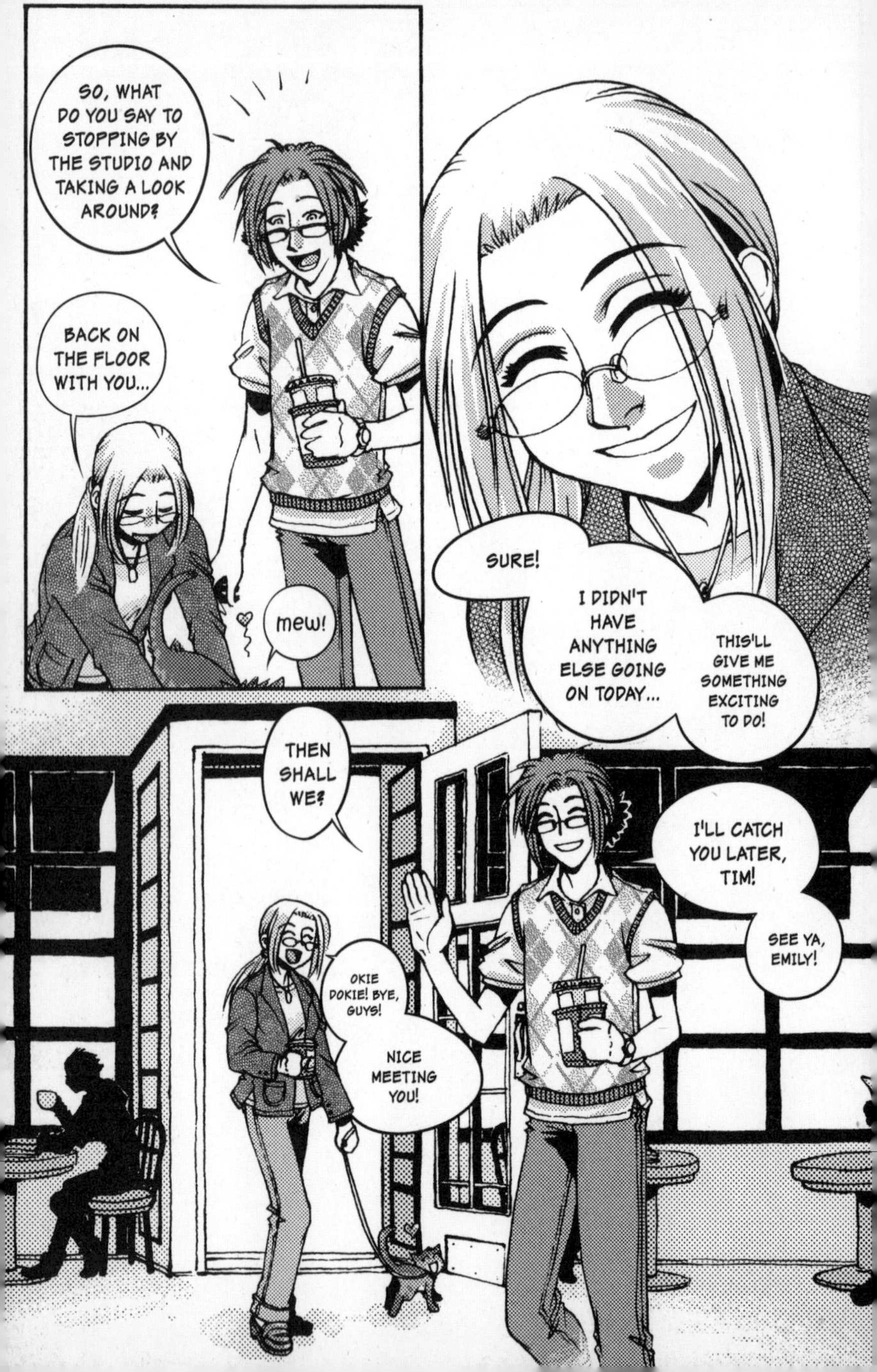
SO, WHAT DO YOU SAY TO STOPPING BY THE STUDIO AND TAKING A LOOK AROUND?
BACK ON THE FLOOR WITH YOU...
mew!
SURE!
I DIDN'T HAVE ANYTHING ELSE GOING ON TODAY...
THIS'LL GIVE ME SOMETHING EXCITING TO DO!
THEN SHALL WE?
I'LL CATCH YOU LATER, TIM!
SEE YA, EMILY!
OKIE DOKIE! BYE, GUYS!
NICE MEETING YOU!

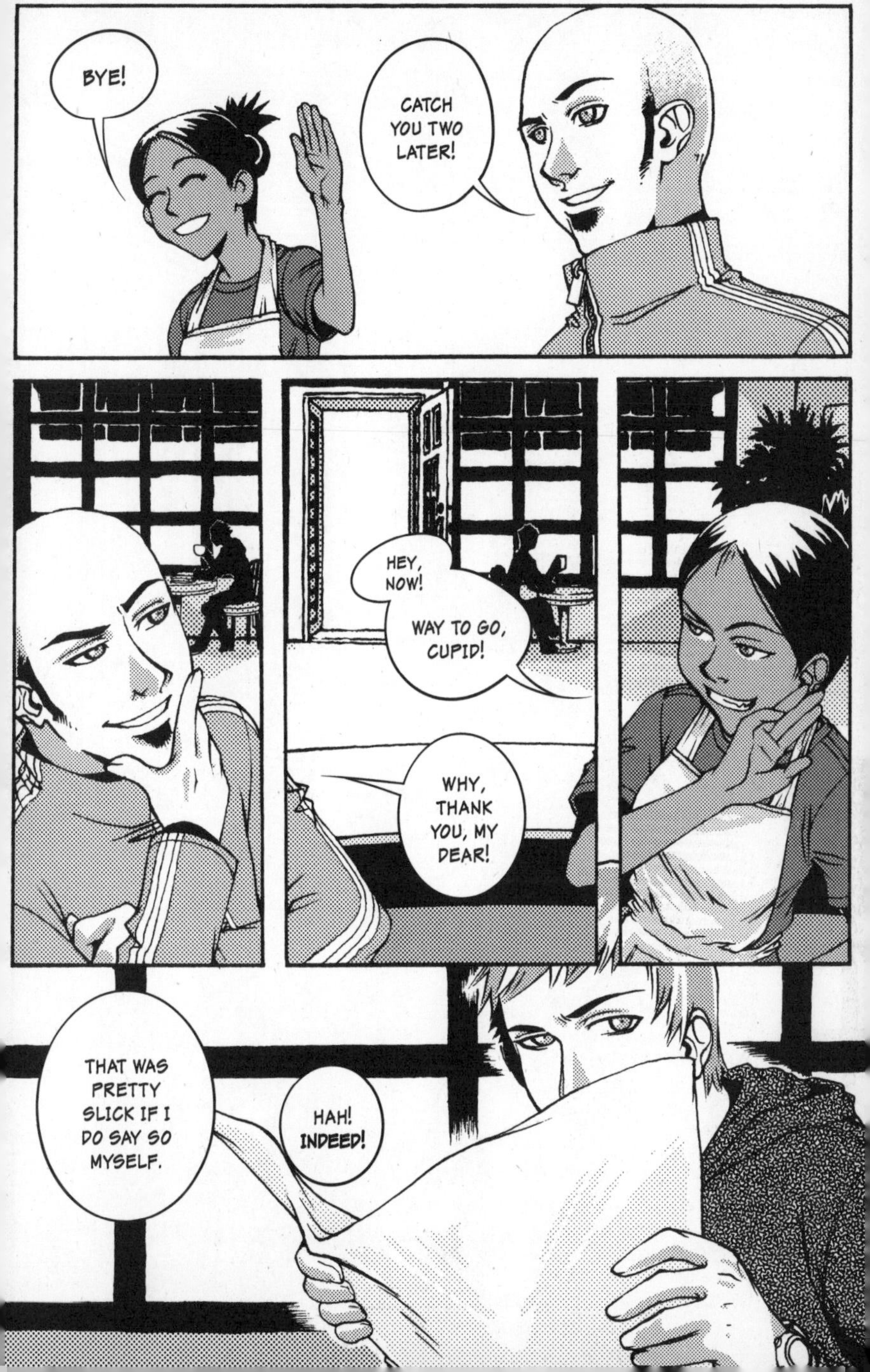
BYE!
CATCH YOU TWO LATER!
HEY, NOW!
WAY TO GO, CUPID!
WHY, THANK YOU, MY DEAR!
THAT WAS PRETTY SLICK IF I DO SAY SO MYSELF.
HAH! INDEED!

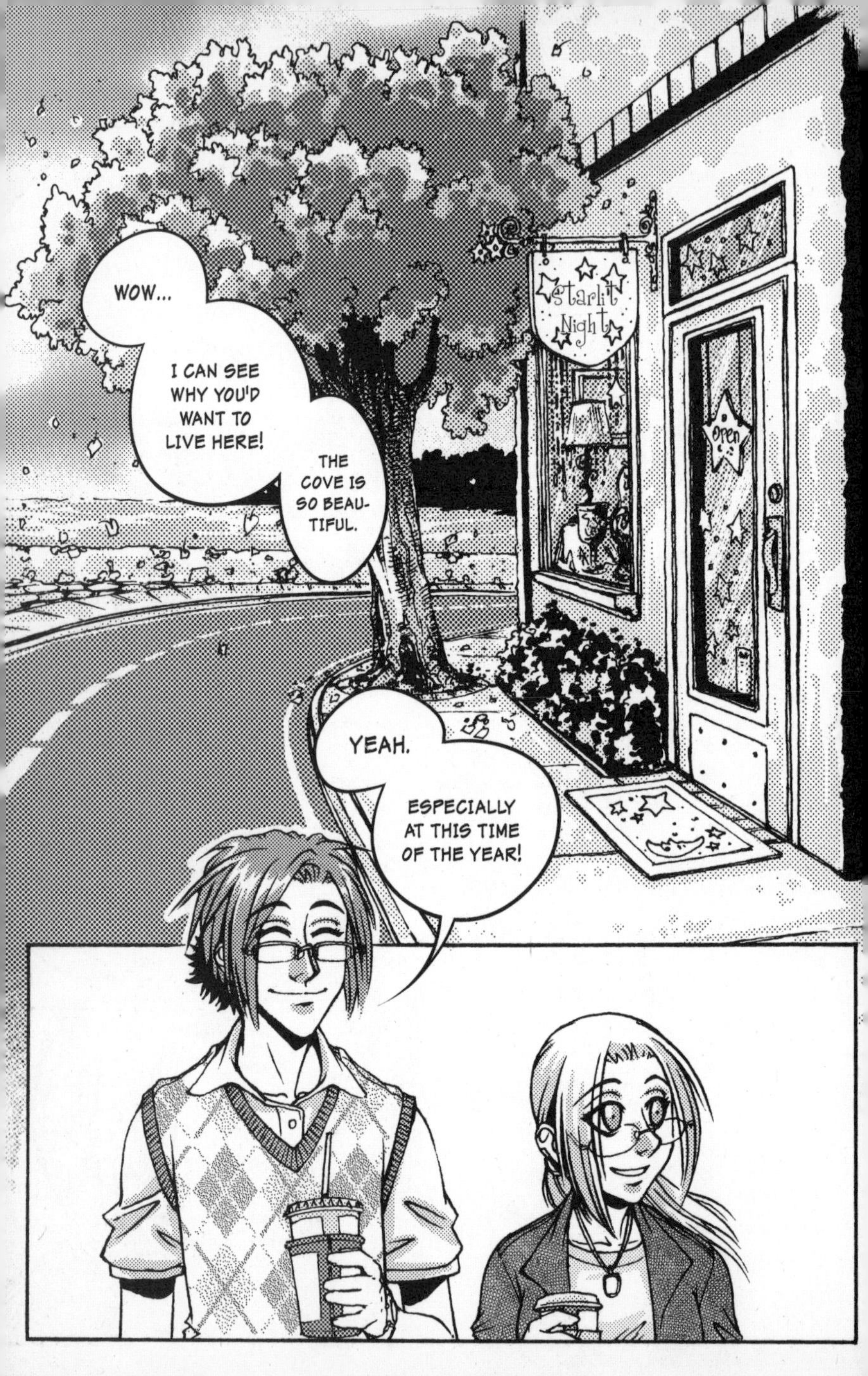
starlit Night
open
WOW...
I CAN SEE WHY YOU'D WANT TO LIVE HERE!
THE COVE IS SO BEAU-TIFUL.
YEAH.
ESPECIALLY AT THIS TIME OF THE YEAR!

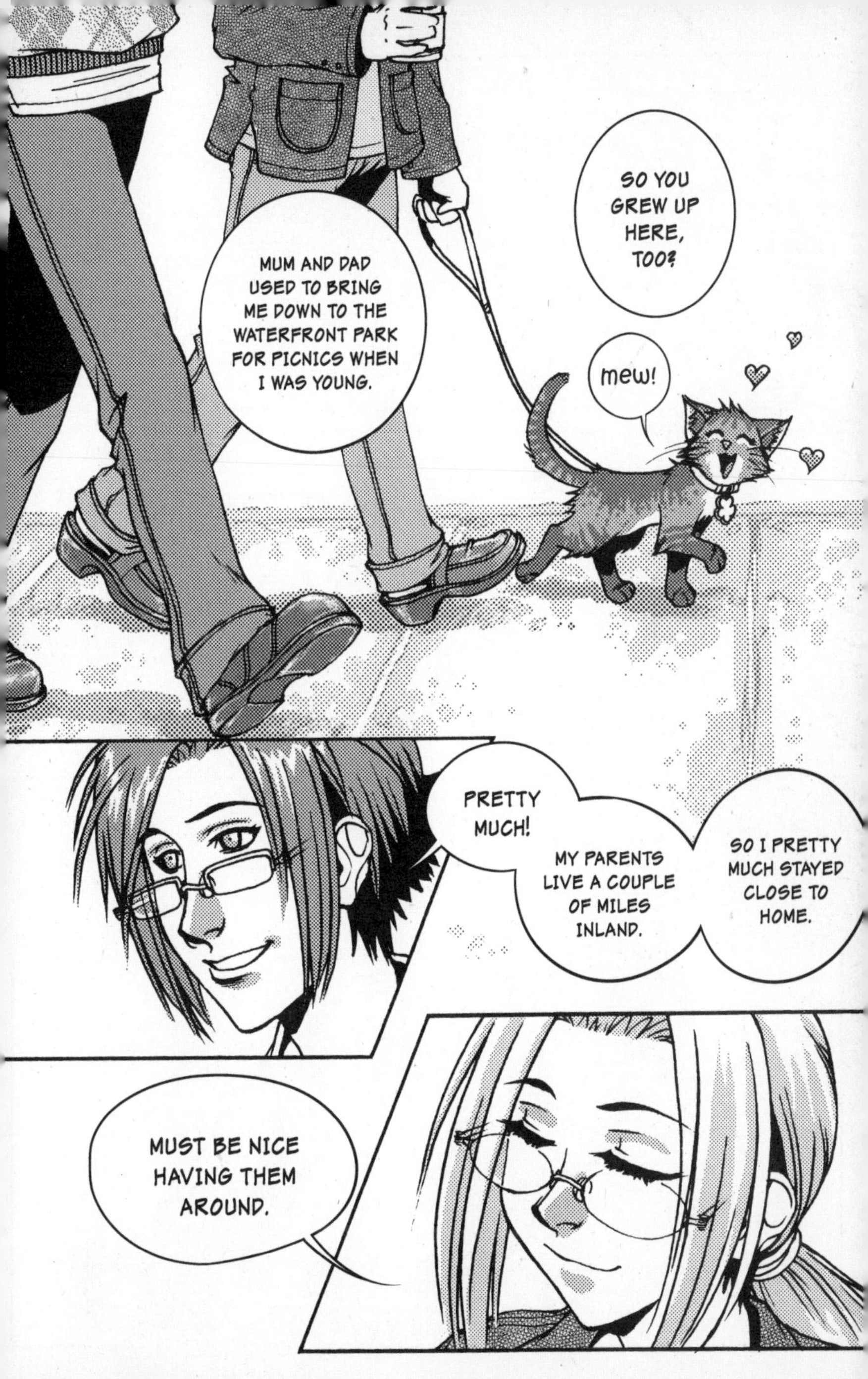
MUM AND DAD USED TO BRING ME DOWN TO THE WATERFRONT PARK FOR PICNICS WHEN I WAS YOUNG.
SO YOU GREW UP HERE, TOO?
mew!
PRETTY MUCH!
MY PARENTS LIVE A COUPLE OF MILES INLAND.
SO I PRETTY MUCH STAYED CLOSE TO HOME.
MUST BE NICE HAVING THEM AROUND.

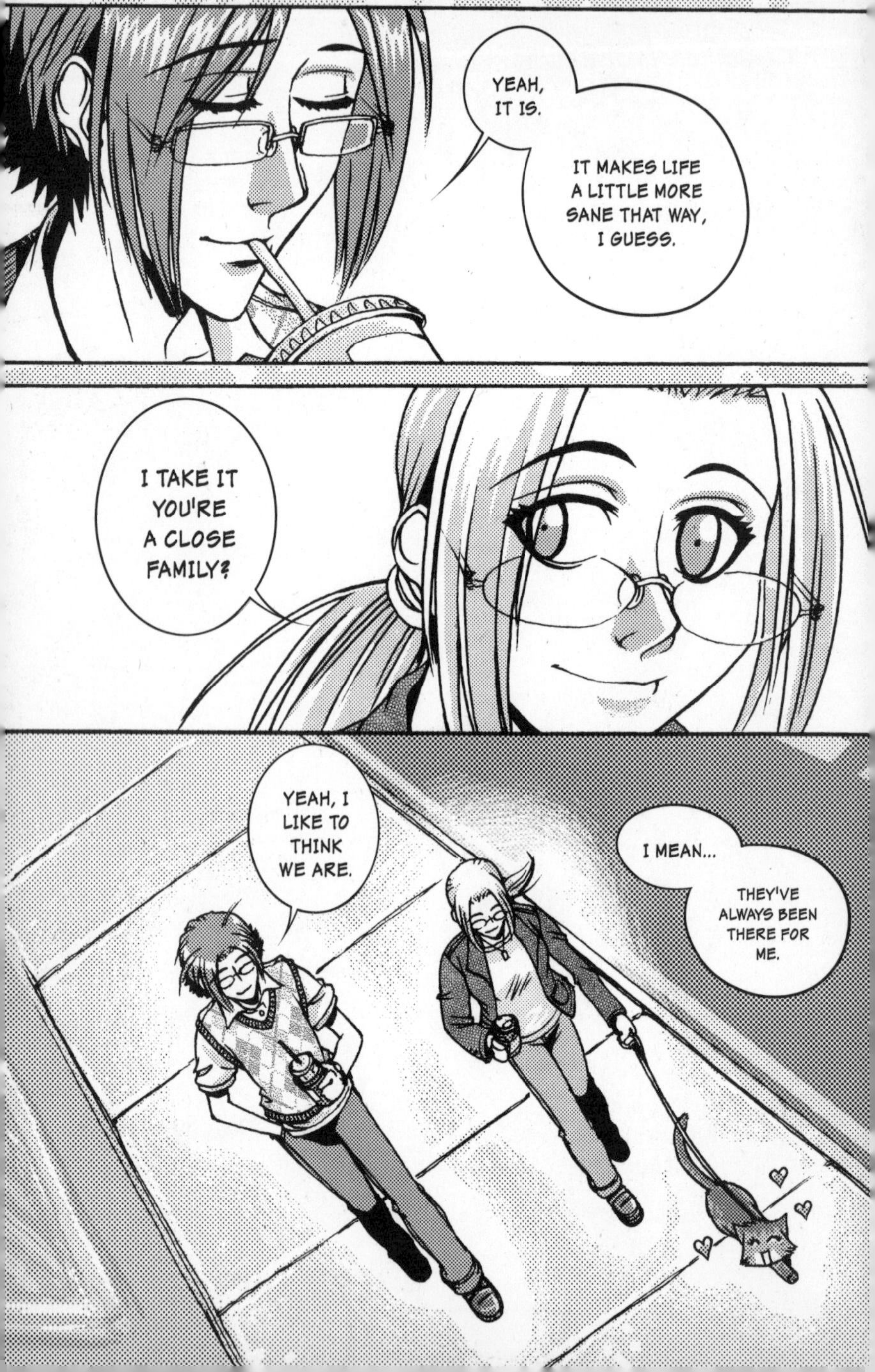
YEAH, IT IS.
IT MAKES LIFE A LITTLE MORE SANE THAT WAY, I GUESS.
I TAKE IT YOU'RE A CLOSE FAMILY?
YEAH, I LIKE TO THINK WE ARE.
I MEAN...
THEY'VE ALWAYS BEEN THERE FOR ME.

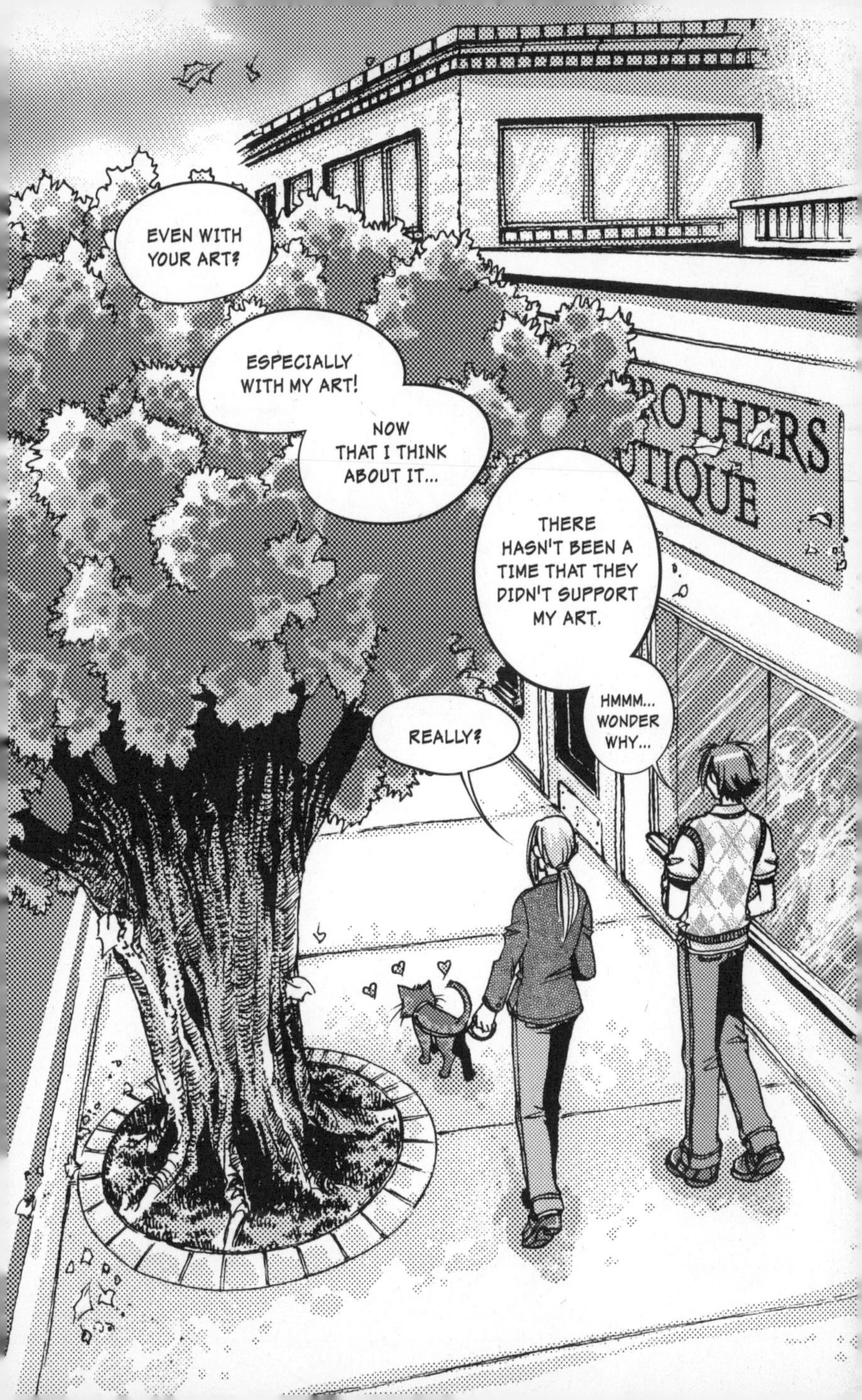
EVEN WITH YOUR ART?
ESPECIALLY WITH MY ART!
NOW THAT I THINK ABOUT IT...
THERE HASN'T BEEN A TIME THAT THEY DIDN'T SUPPORT MY ART.
REALLY?
HMMM... WONDER WHY...

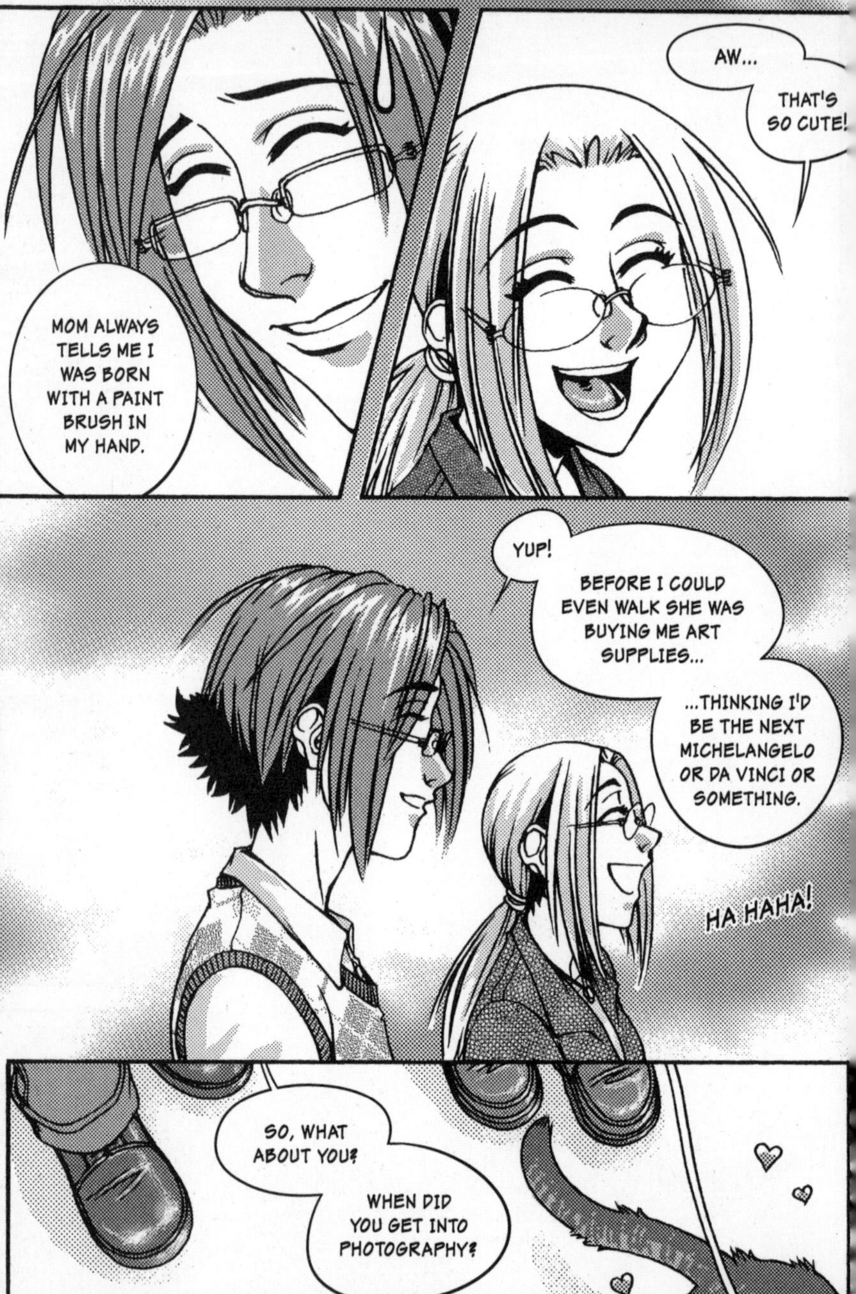
MOM ALWAYS TELLS ME I WAS BORN WITH A PAINT BRUSH IN MY HAND.
AW...
THAT'S SO CUTE!
YUP!
BEFORE I COULD EVEN WALK SHE WAS BUYING ME ART SUPPLIES...
...THINKING I'D BE THE NEXT MICHELANGELO OR DA VINCI OR SOMETHING.
HA HAHA!
SO, WHAT ABOUT YOU?
WHEN DID YOU GET INTO PHOTOGRAPHY?

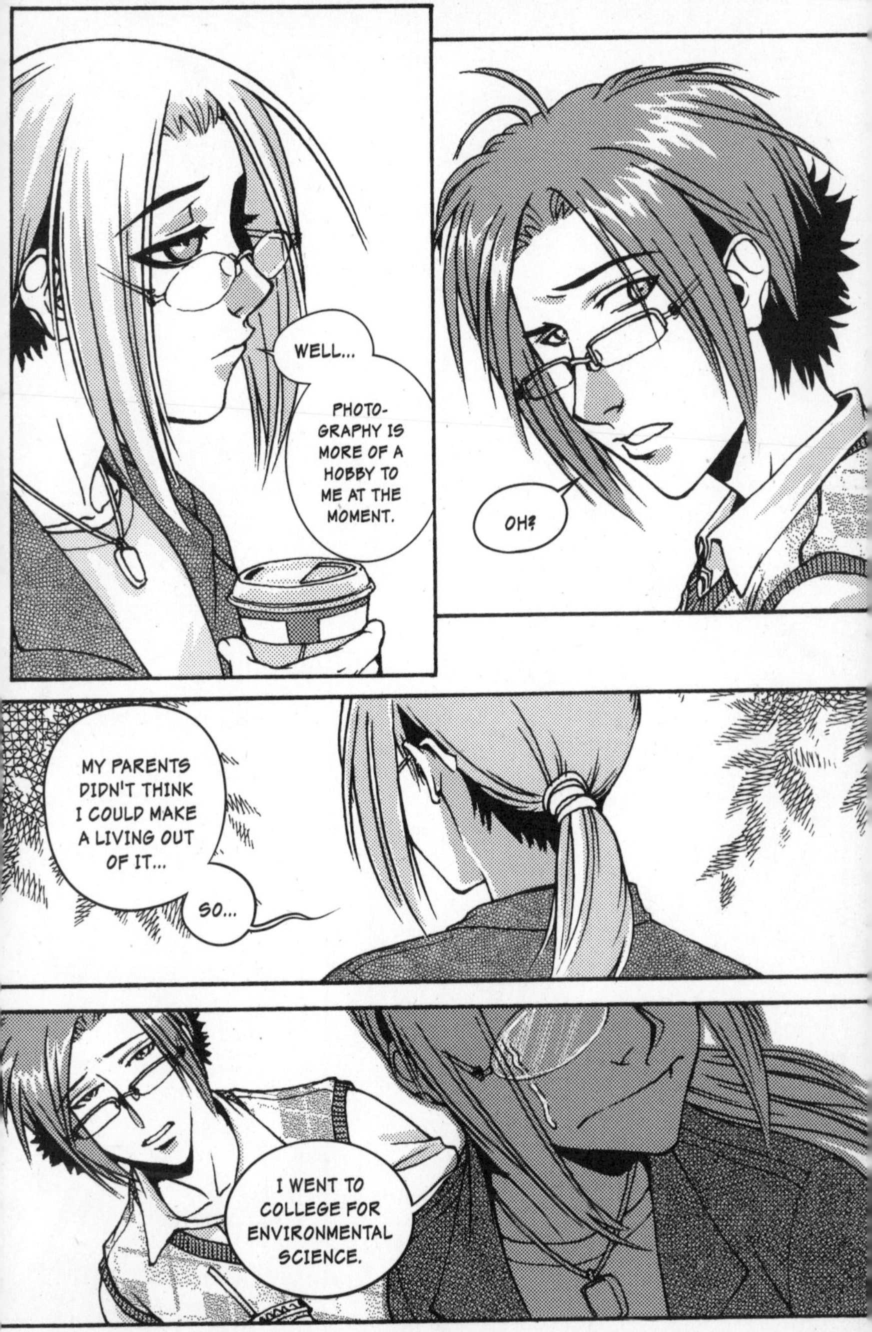
WELL...
PHOTOGRAPHY IS MORE OF A HOBBY TO ME AT THE MOMENT.
OH?
MY PARENTS DIDN'T THINK I COULD MAKE A LIVING OUT OF IT...
SO...
I WENT TO COLLEGE FOR ENVIRONMENTAL SCIENCE.

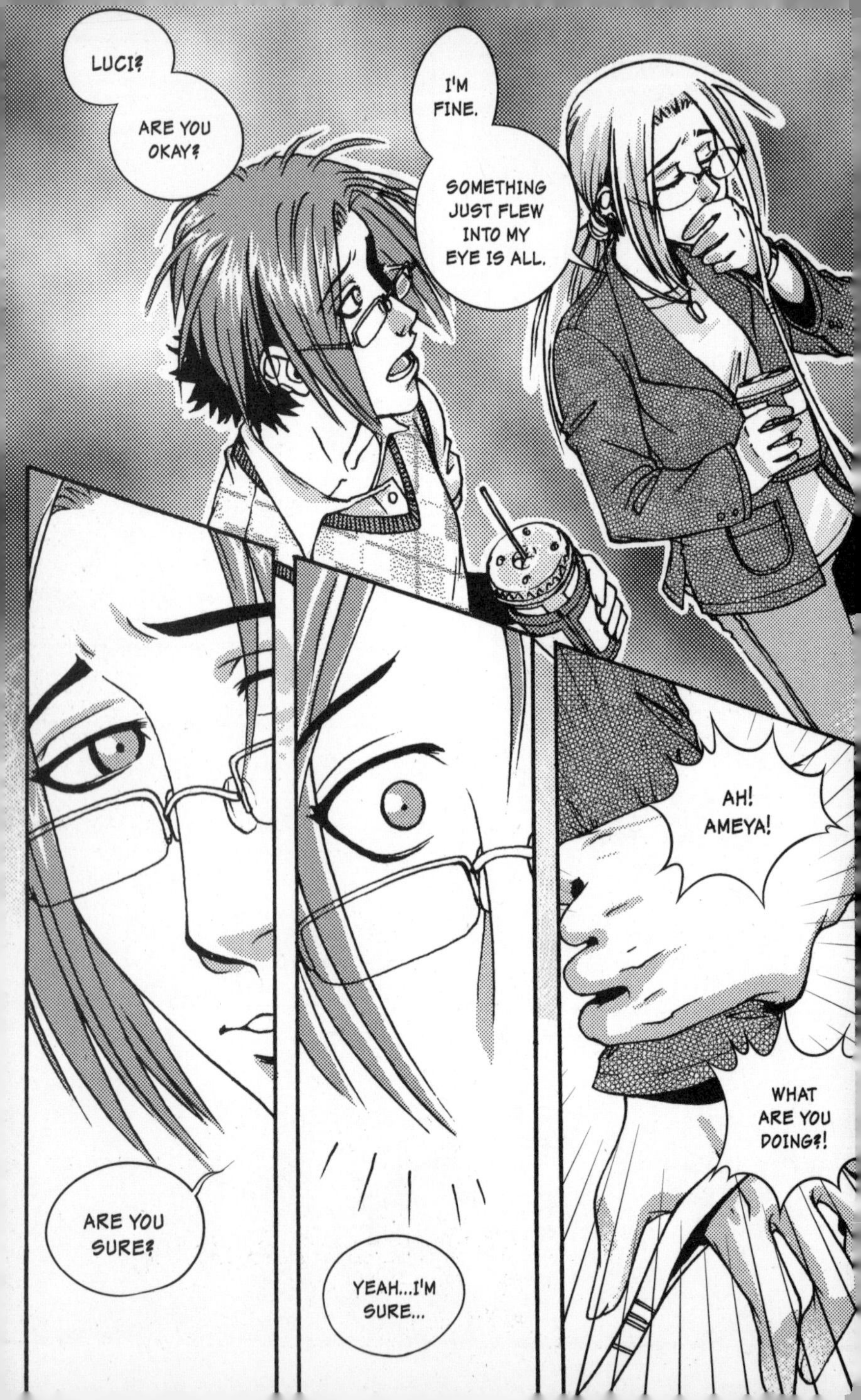

LUCI?
ARE YOU OKAY?
I'M FINE.
SOMETHING JUST FLEW INTO MY EYE IS ALL.
ARE YOU SURE?
YEAH...I'M SURE...
AH! AMEYA!
WHAT ARE YOU DOING?!

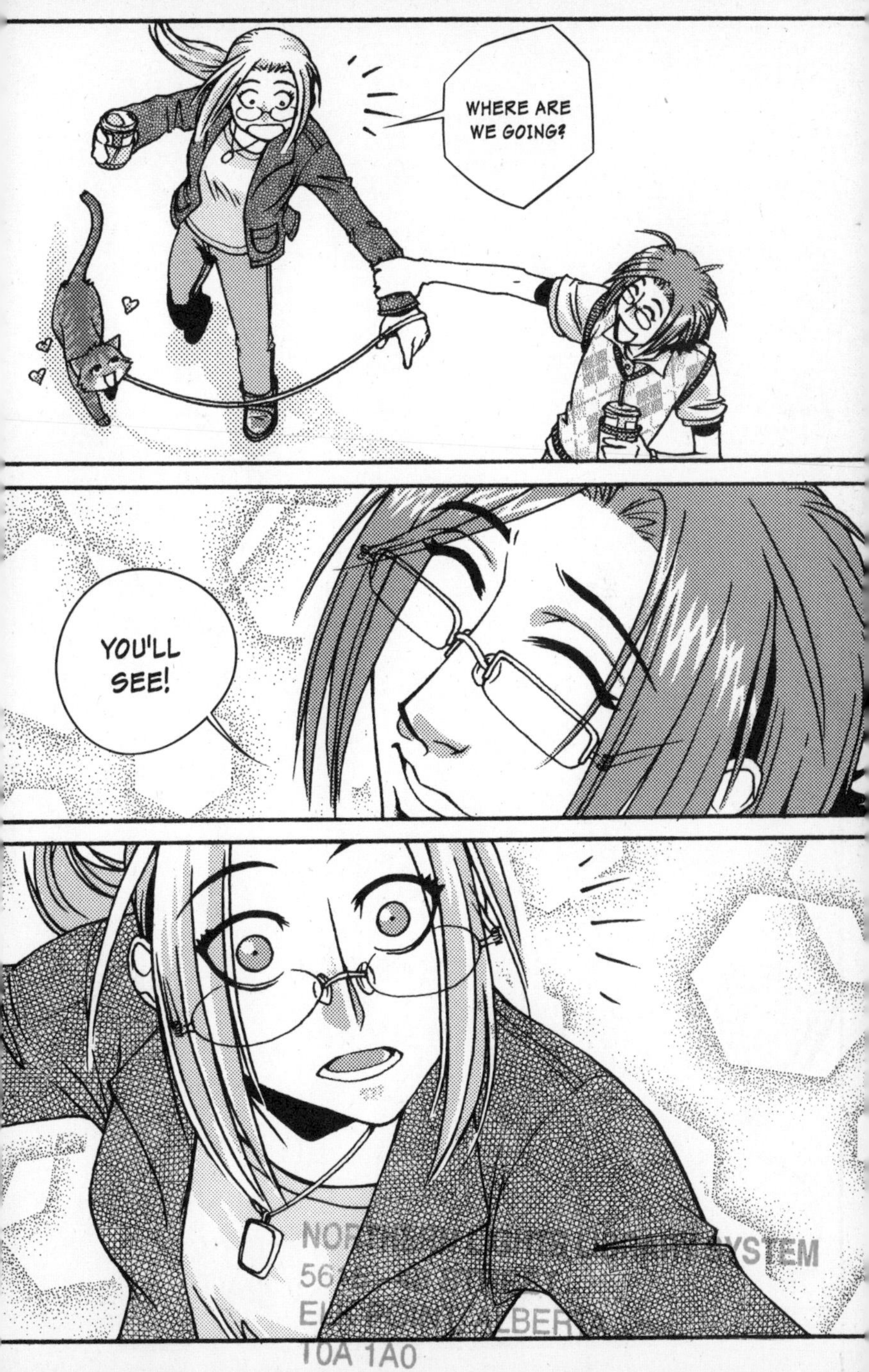
WHERE ARE WE GOING?
YOU'LL SEE!

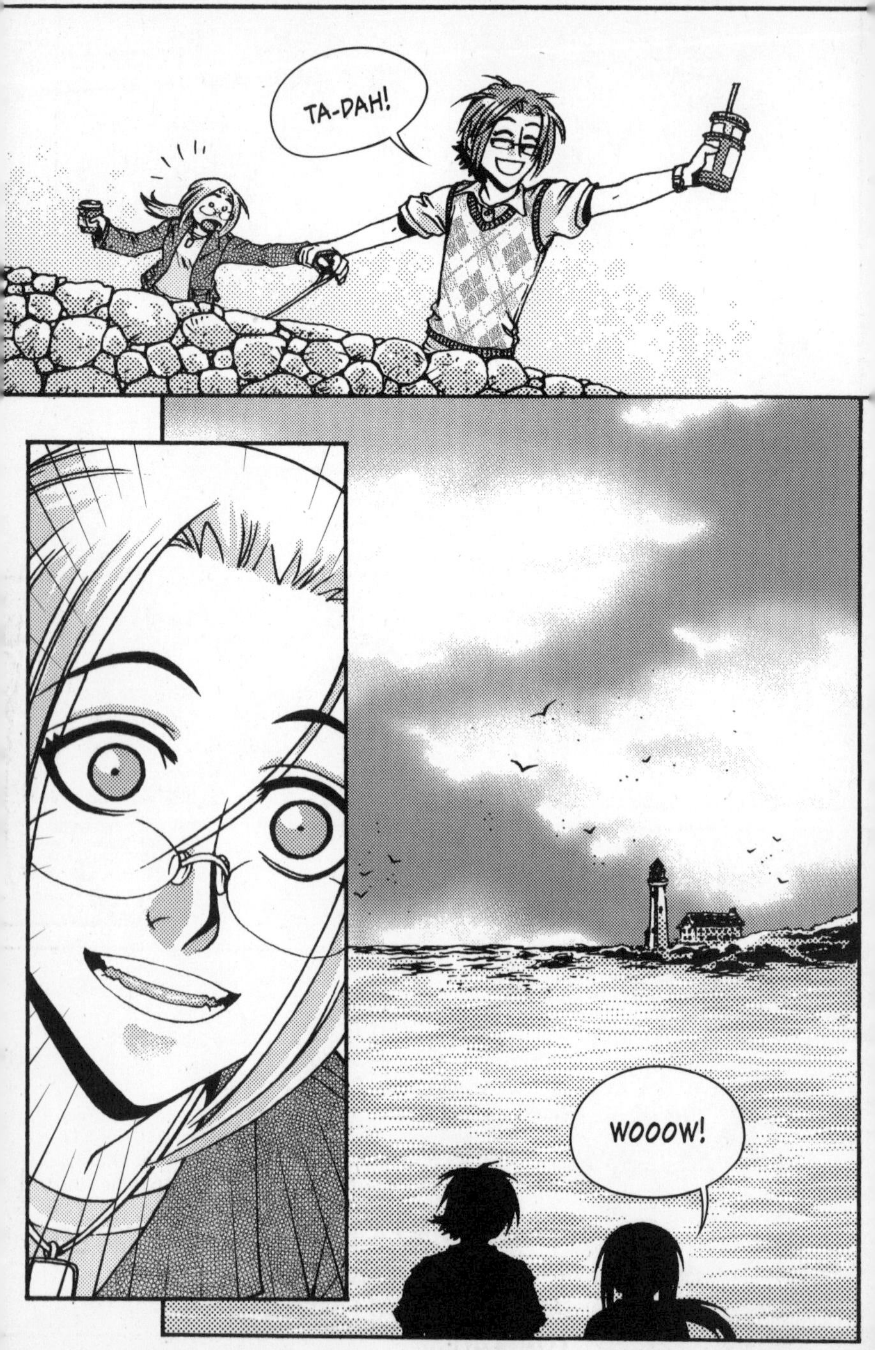
TA-DAH!
WOOOW!

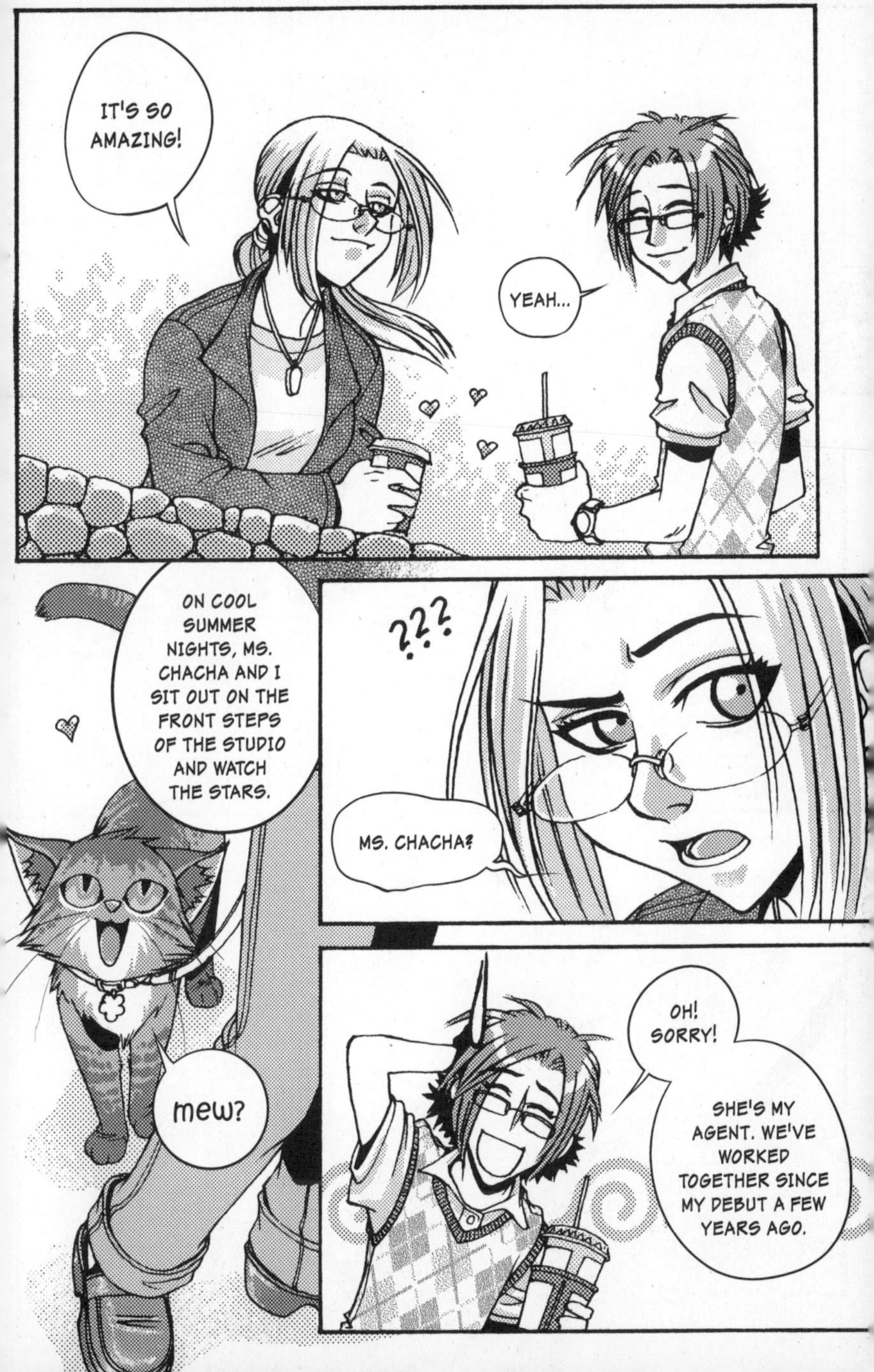
IT'S SO AMAZING!
YEAH...
ON COOL SUMMER NIGHTS, MS. CHACHA AND I SIT OUT ON THE FRONT STEPS OF THE STUDIO AND WATCH THE STARS.
mew?
???
MS. CHACHA?
OH! SORRY!
SHE'S MY AGENT. WE'VE WORKED TOGETHER SINCE MY DEBUT A FEW YEARS AGO.

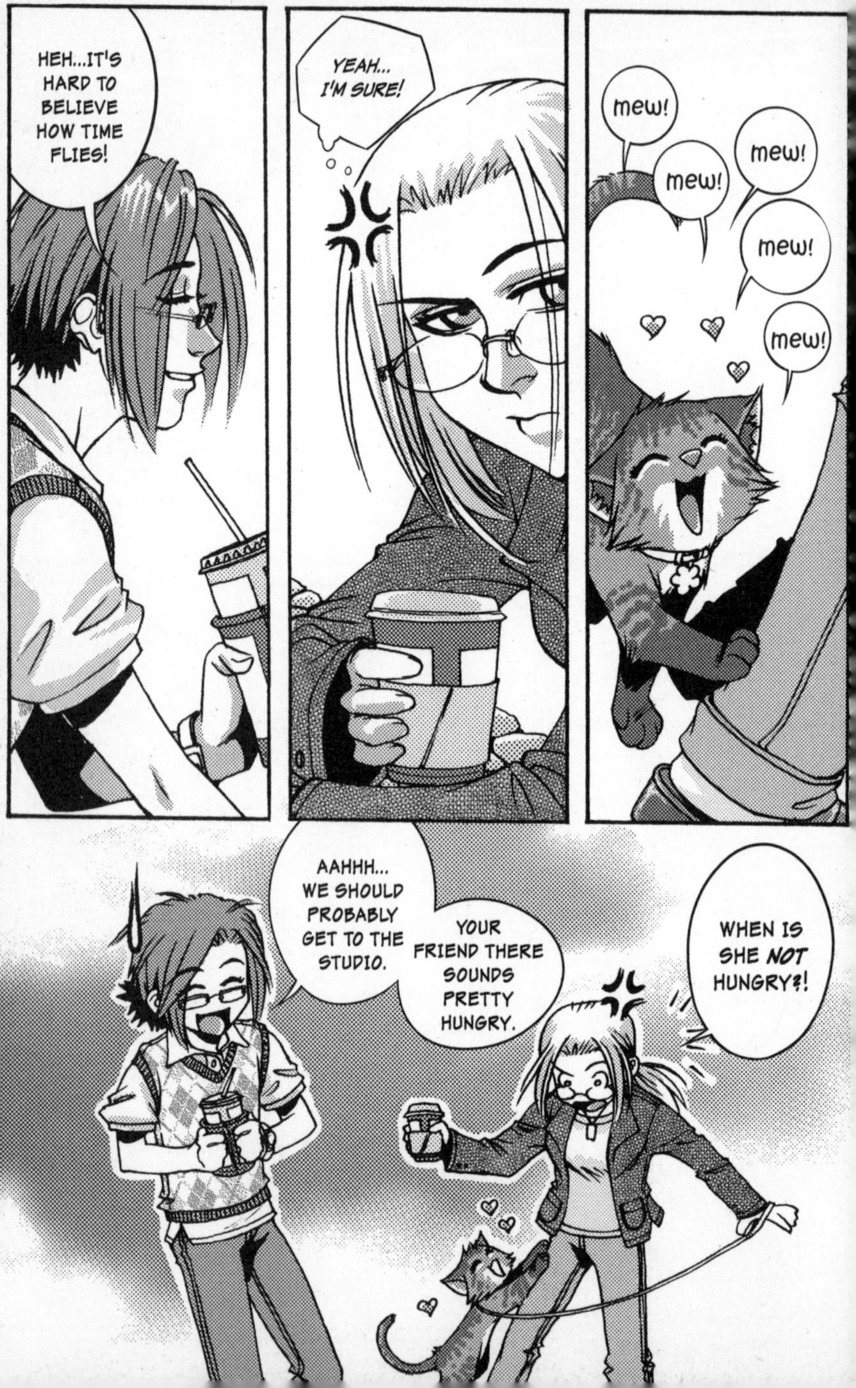
HEH...IT'S HARD TO BELIEVE HOW TIME FLIES!
YEAH... I'M SURE!
mew!
mew!
mew!
mew!
mew!
AAHHH... WE SHOULD PROBABLY GET TO THE STUDIO.
YOUR FRIEND THERE SOUNDS PRETTY HUNGRY.
WHEN IS SHE *NOT* HUNGRY?!

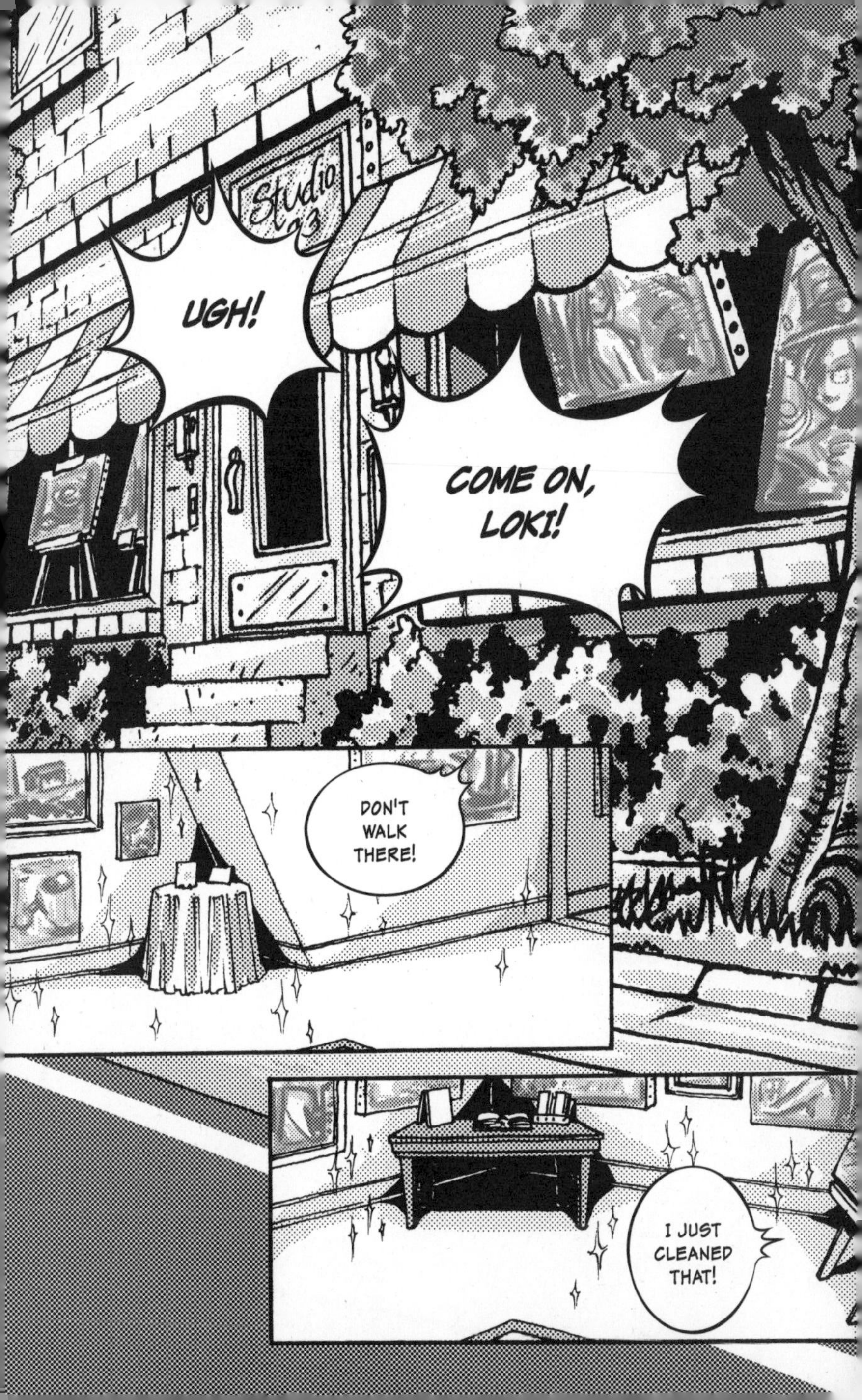
Studio 3
UGH!
COME ON, LOKI!
DON'T WALK THERE!
I JUST CLEANED THAT!

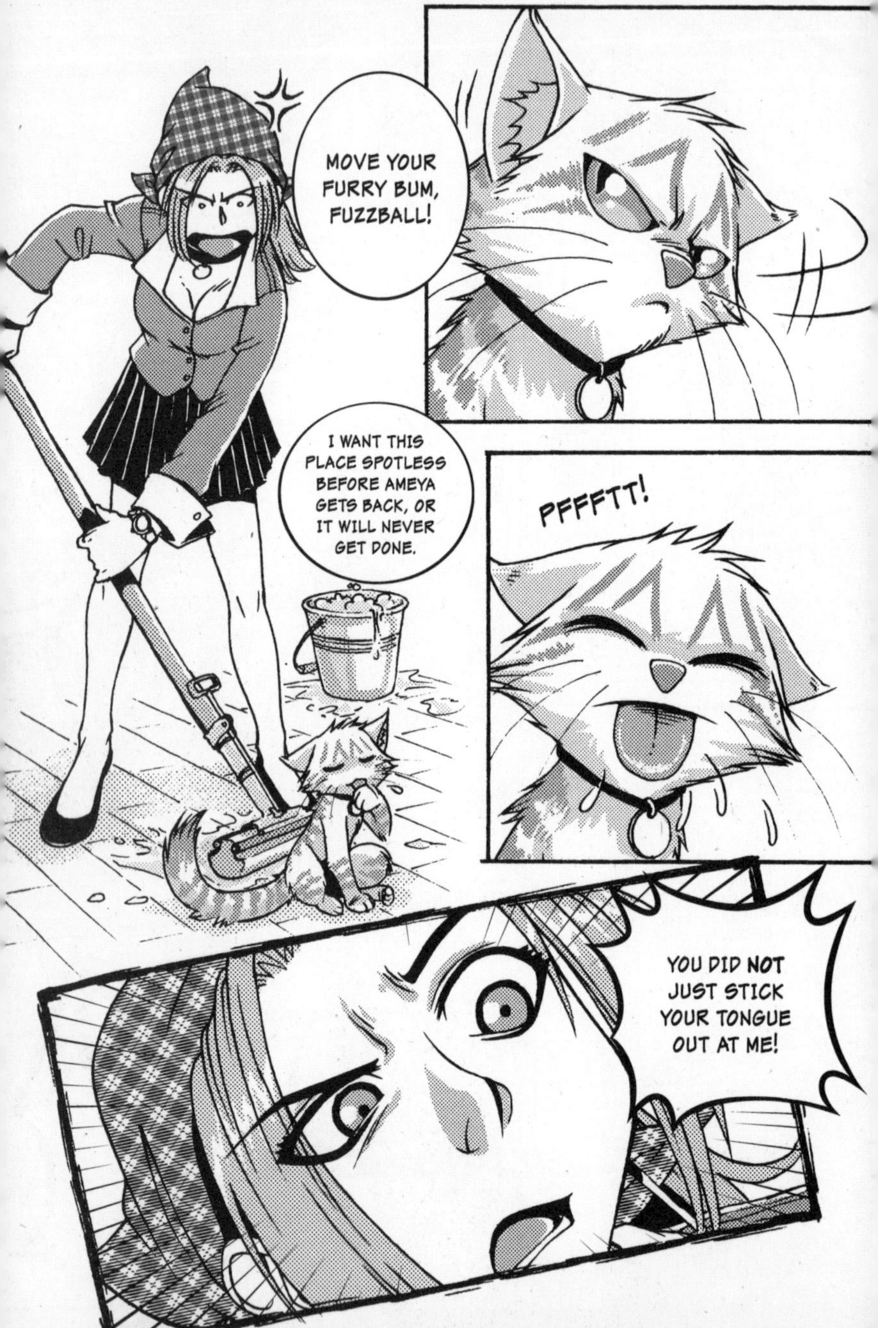
MOVE YOUR FURRY BUM, FUZZBALL!
I WANT THIS PLACE SPOTLESS BEFORE AMEYA GETS BACK, OR IT WILL NEVER GET DONE.
PFFFTT!
YOU DID NOT JUST STICK YOUR TONGUE OUT AT ME!

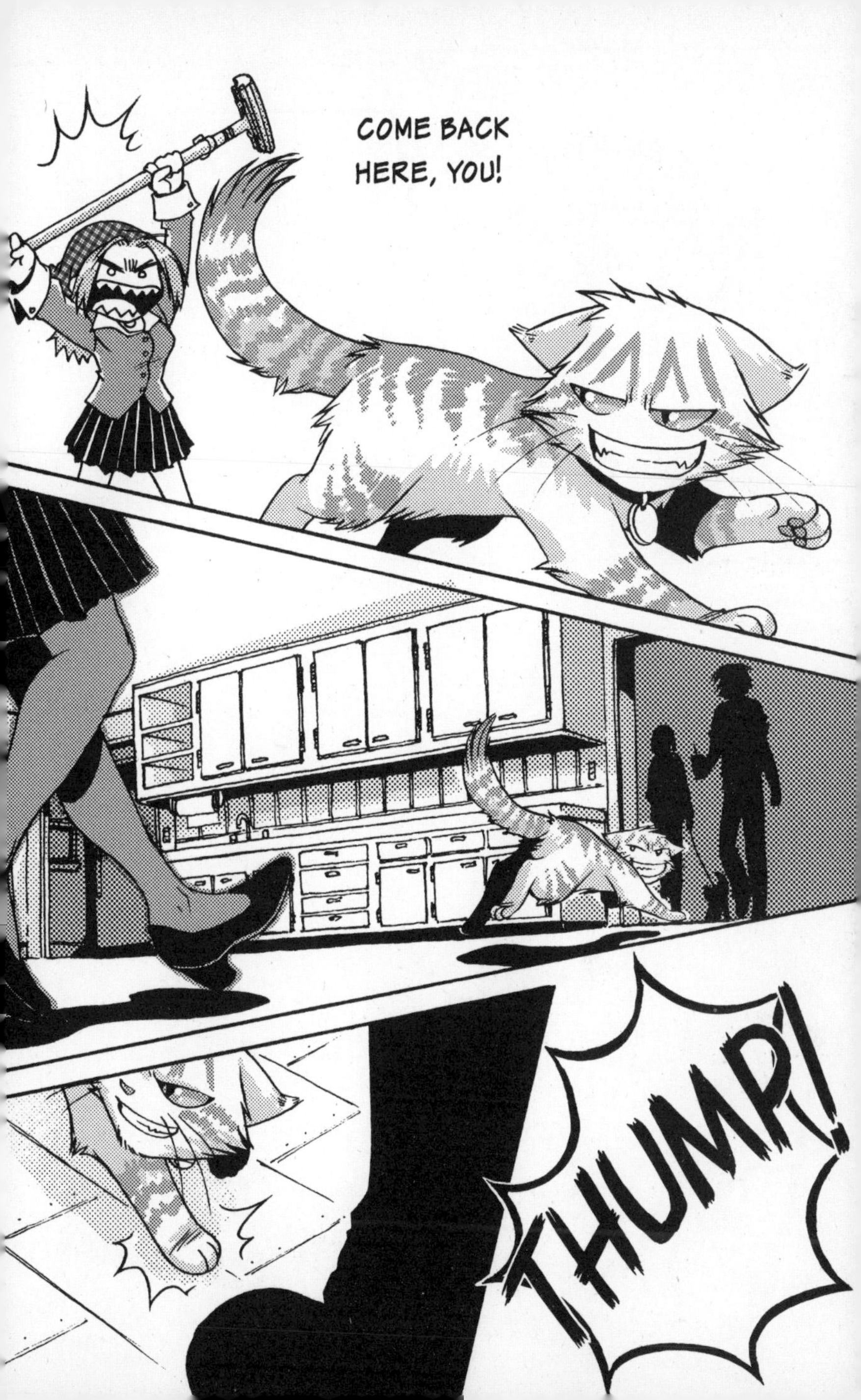
COME BACK HERE, YOU!
THUMP!

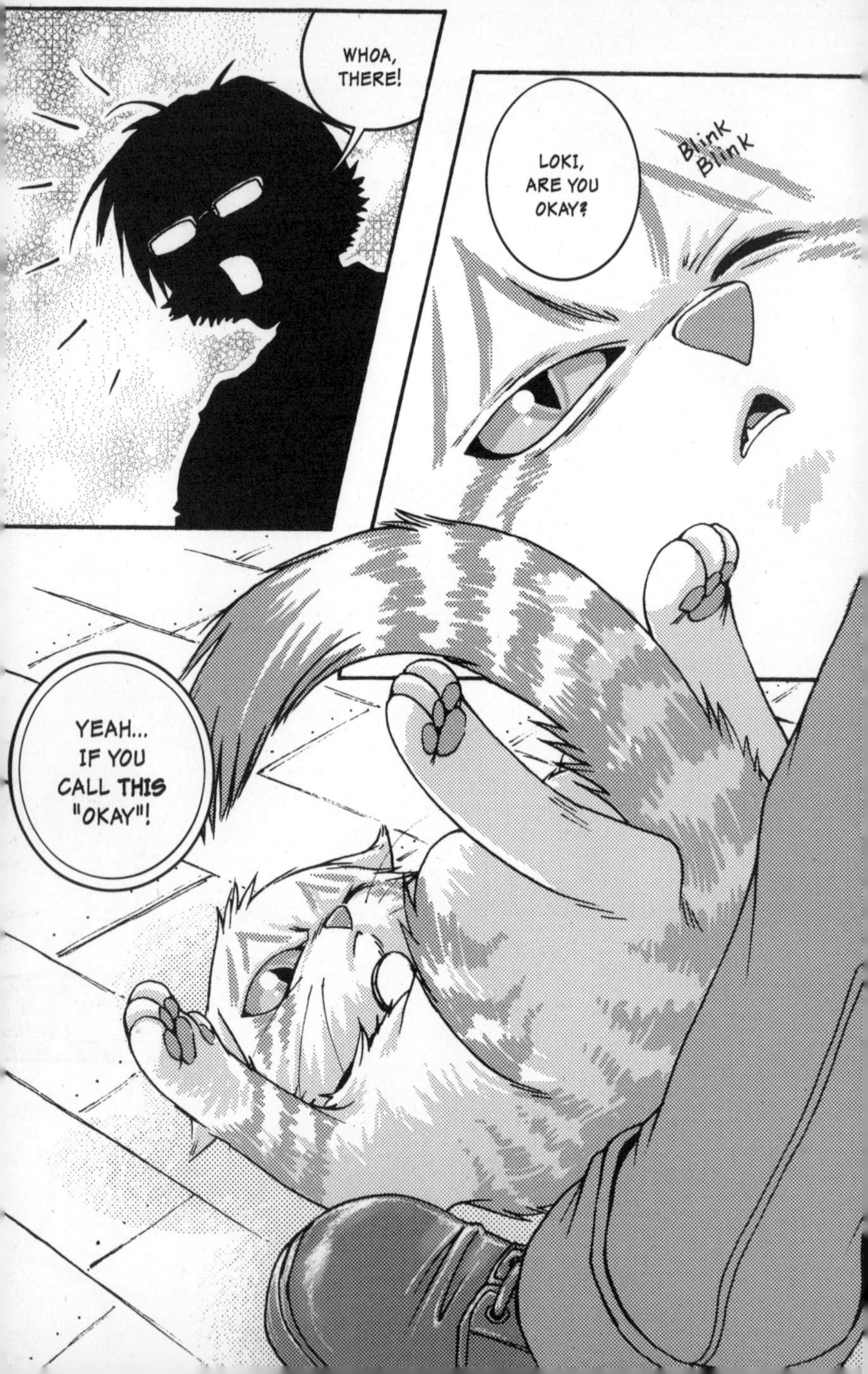
WHOA, THERE!
LOKI, ARE YOU OKAY?
Blink Blink
YEAH... IF YOU CALL THIS "OKAY"!

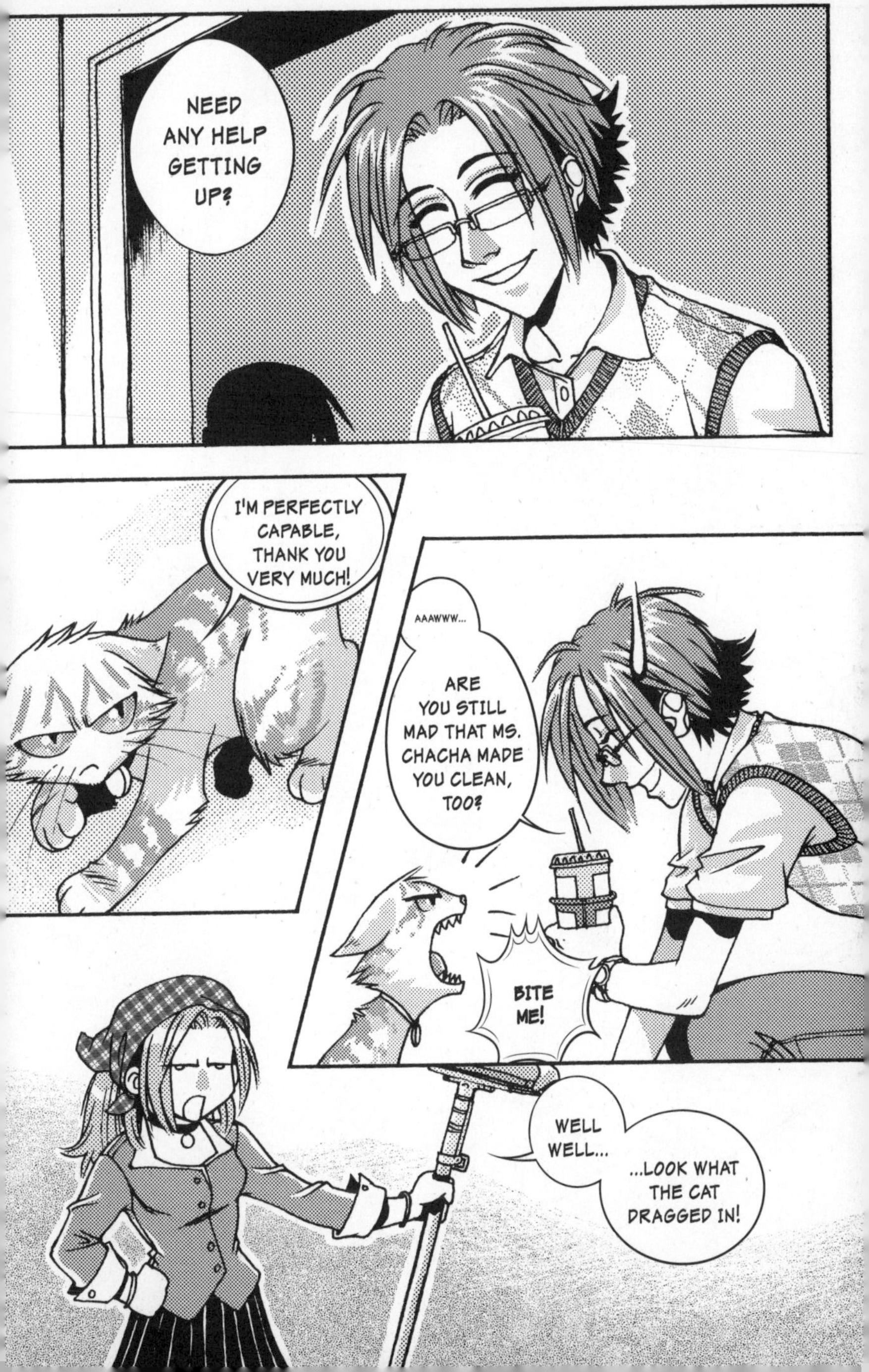
NEED ANY HELP GETTING UP?
I'M PERFECTLY CAPABLE, THANK YOU VERY MUCH!
AAAWWW...
ARE YOU STILL MAD THAT MS. CHACHA MADE YOU CLEAN, TOO?
BITE ME!
WELL WELL...
...LOOK WHAT THE CAT DRAGGED IN!

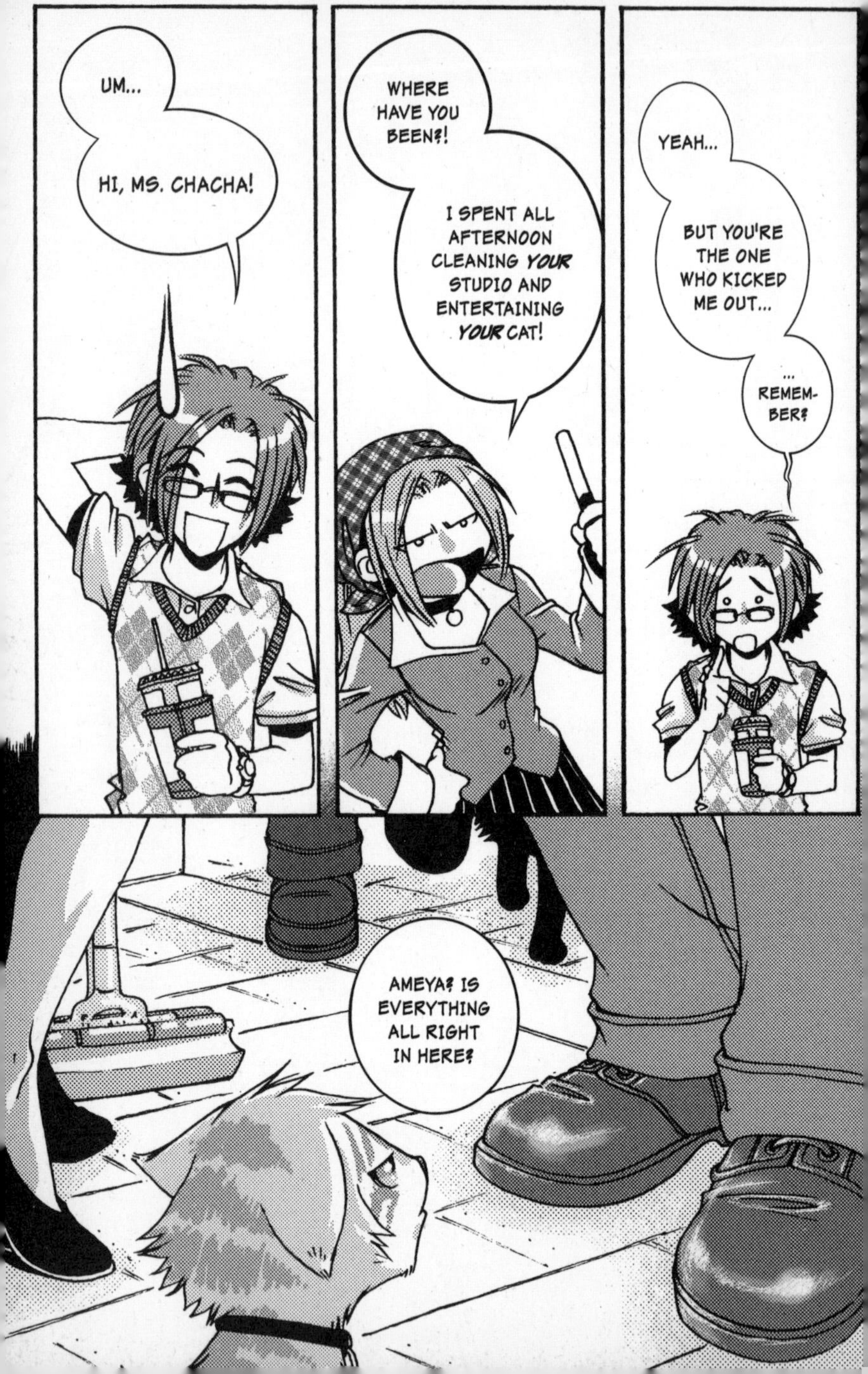
UM...
HI, MS. CHACHA!
WHERE HAVE YOU BEEN?!
I SPENT ALL AFTERNOON CLEANING YOUR STUDIO AND ENTERTAINING YOUR CAT!
YEAH...
BUT YOU'RE THE ONE WHO KICKED ME OUT...
... REMEMBER?
AMEYA? IS EVERYTHING ALL RIGHT IN HERE?

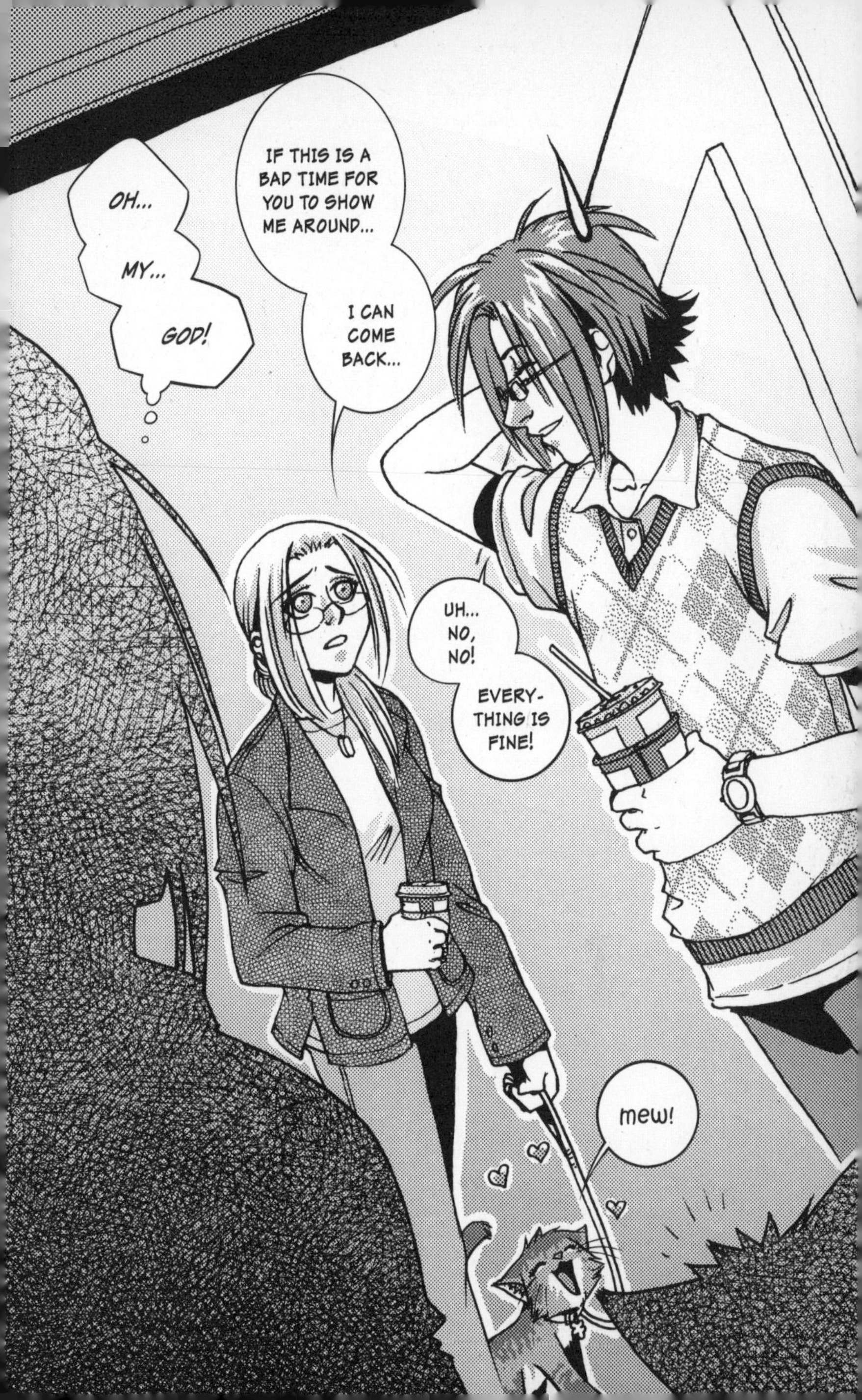
OH...
MY...
GOD!
IF THIS IS A BAD TIME FOR YOU TO SHOW ME AROUND...
I CAN COME BACK...
UH... NO, NO!
EVERY-THING IS FINE!
mew!

DON'T WORRY
ABOUT IT.

EVERYTHING IS JUST...

...FINE.

CHAPTER 4

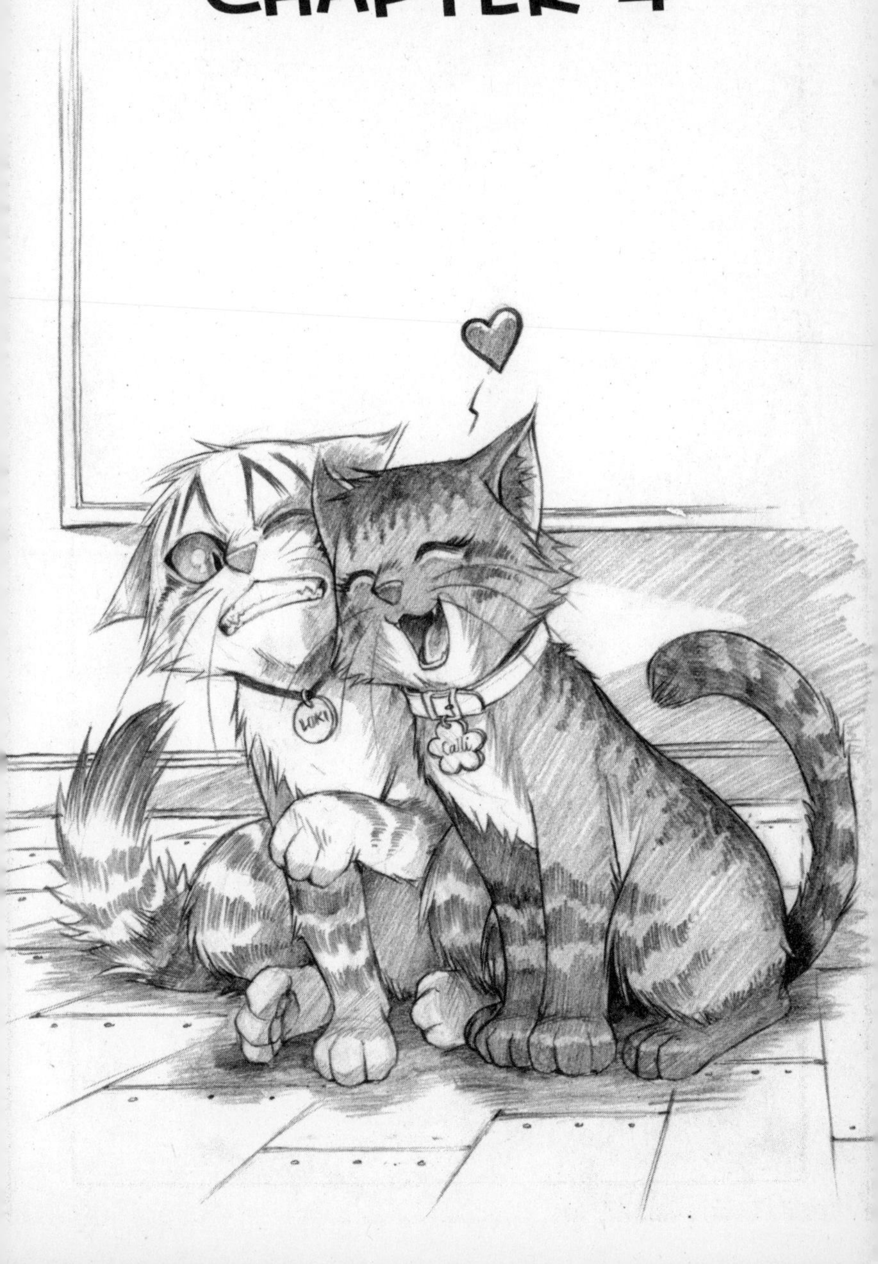
LOKI
Calli

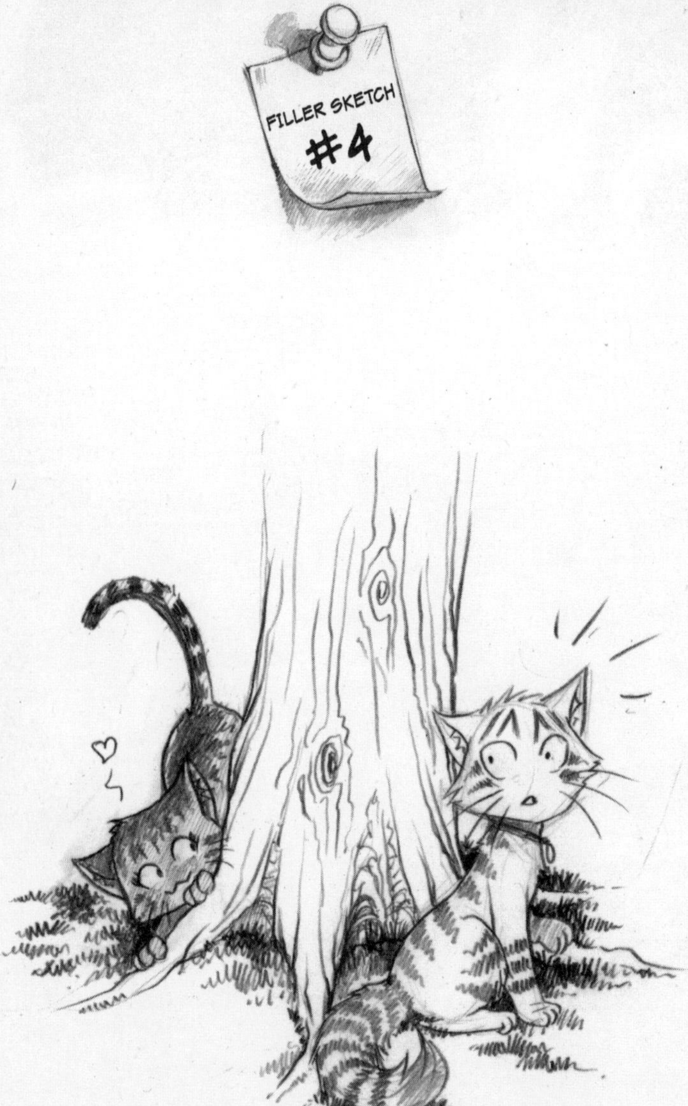
FILLER SKETCH
#4

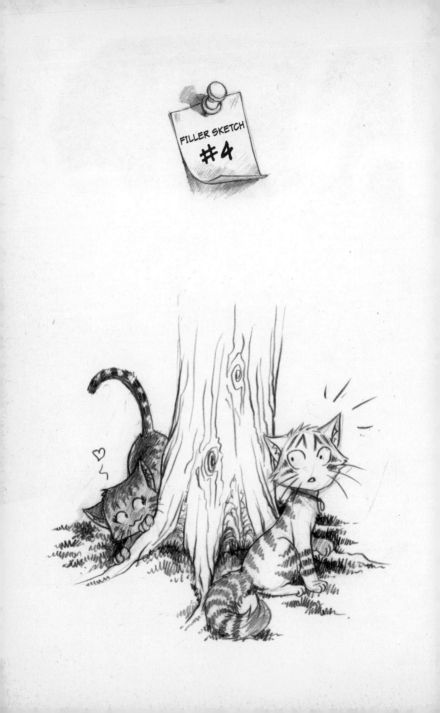

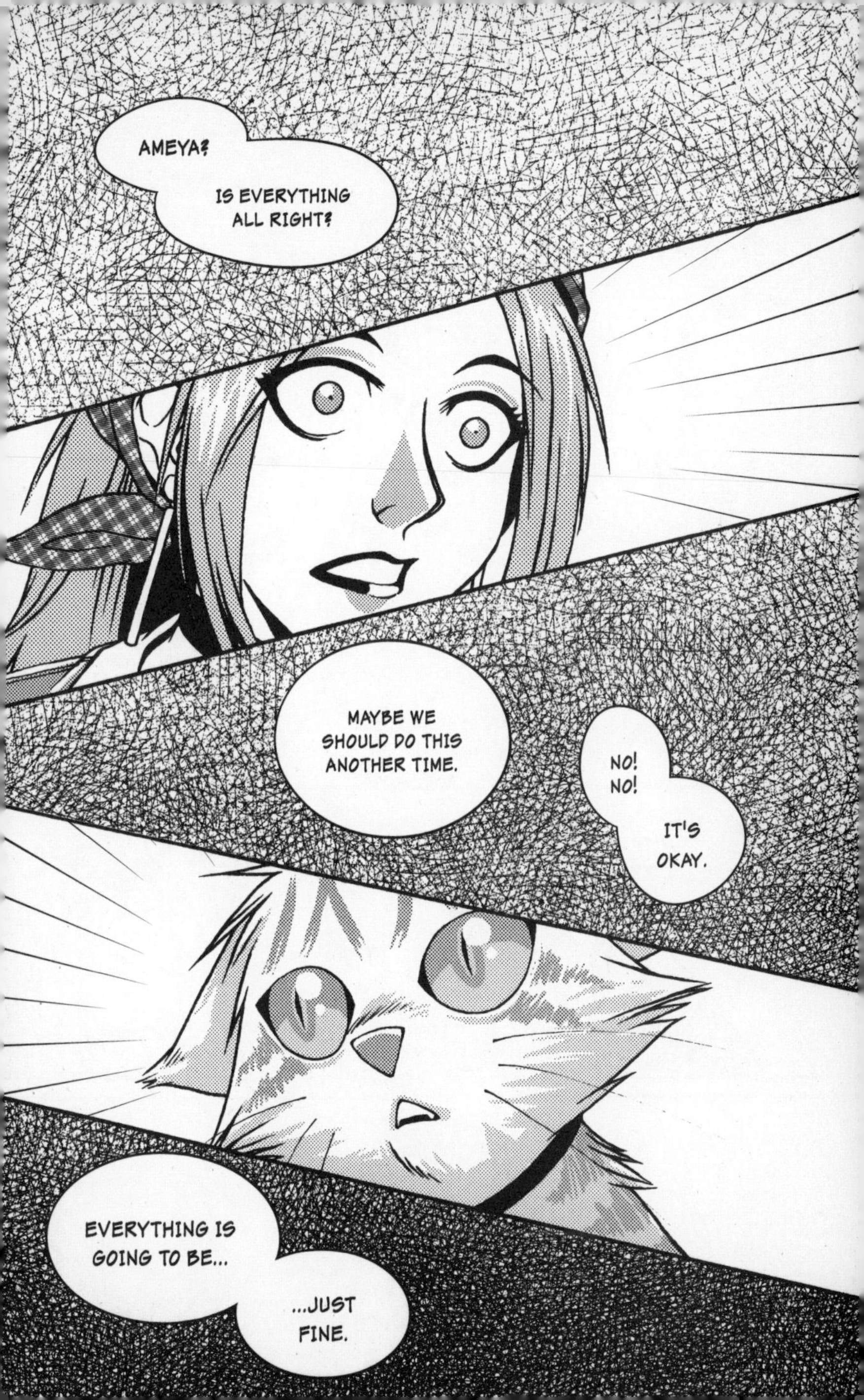
AMEYA?
IS EVERYTHING ALL RIGHT?
MAYBE WE SHOULD DO THIS ANOTHER TIME.
NO! NO!
IT'S OKAY.
EVERYTHING IS GOING TO BE...
...JUST FINE.

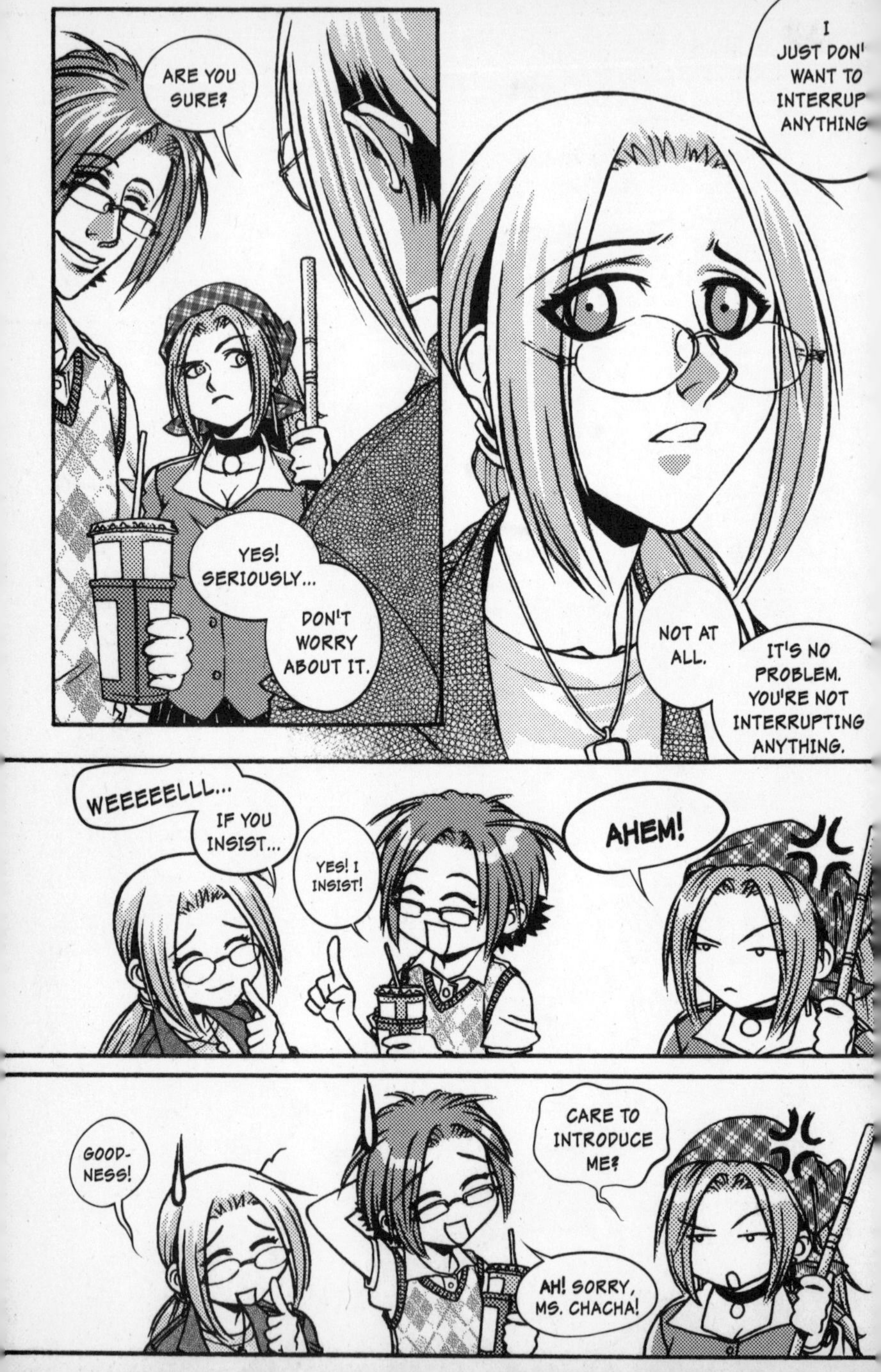
ARE YOU SURE?
YES! SERIOUSLY...
DON'T WORRY ABOUT IT.
I JUST DON' WANT TO INTERRUP ANYTHING
NOT AT ALL.
IT'S NO PROBLEM. YOU'RE NOT INTERRUPTING ANYTHING.
WEEEEELLL... IF YOU INSIST...
YES! I INSIST!
AHEM!
GOOD-NESS!
CARE TO INTRODUCE ME?
AH! SORRY, MS. CHACHA!

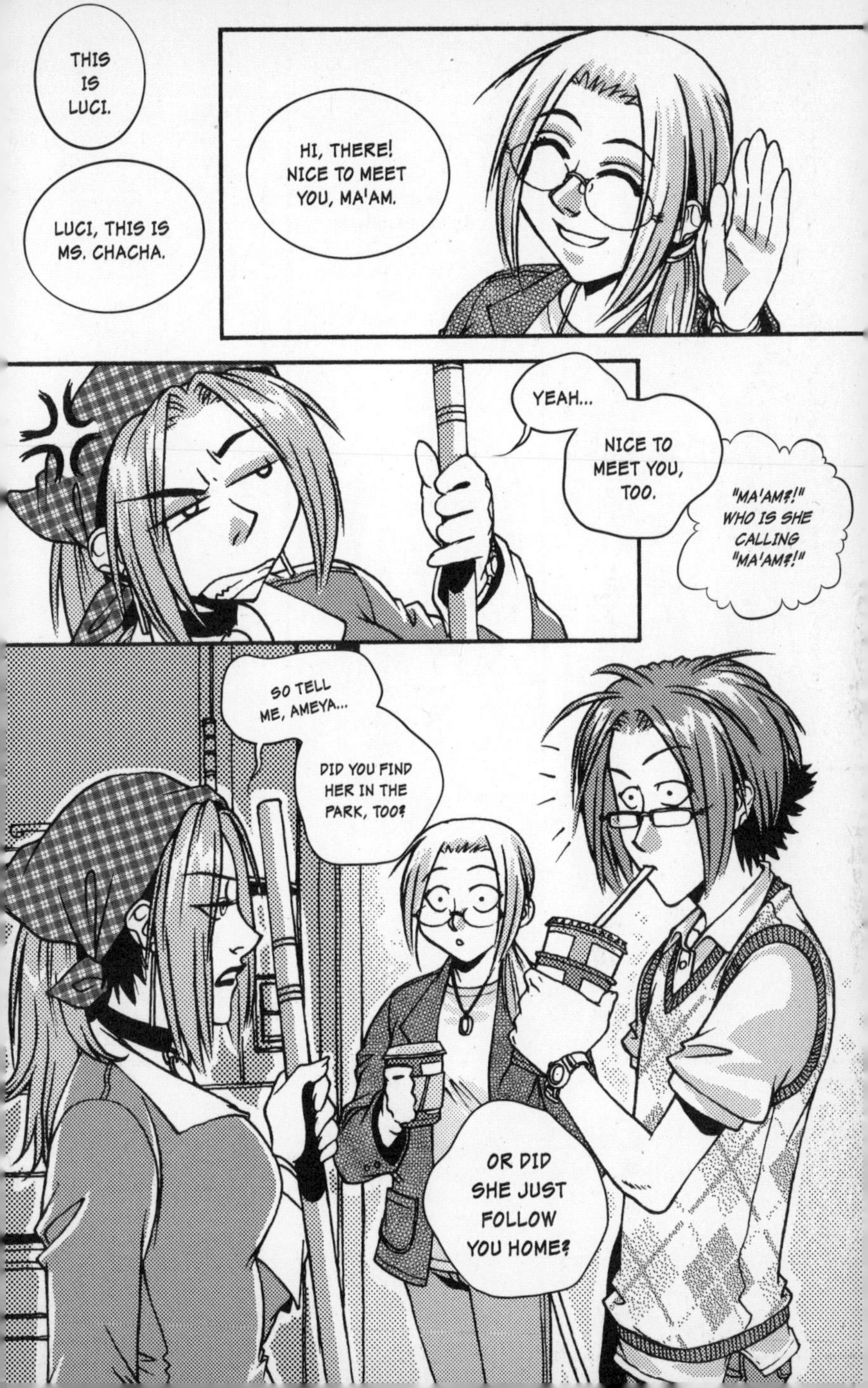

THIS IS LUCI.
LUCI, THIS IS MS. CHACHA.
HI, THERE! NICE TO MEET YOU, MA'AM.
YEAH...
NICE TO MEET YOU, TOO.
"MA'AM?!" WHO IS SHE CALLING "MA'AM?!"
SO TELL ME, AMEYA...
DID YOU FIND HER IN THE PARK, TOO?
OR DID SHE JUST FOLLOW YOU HOME?

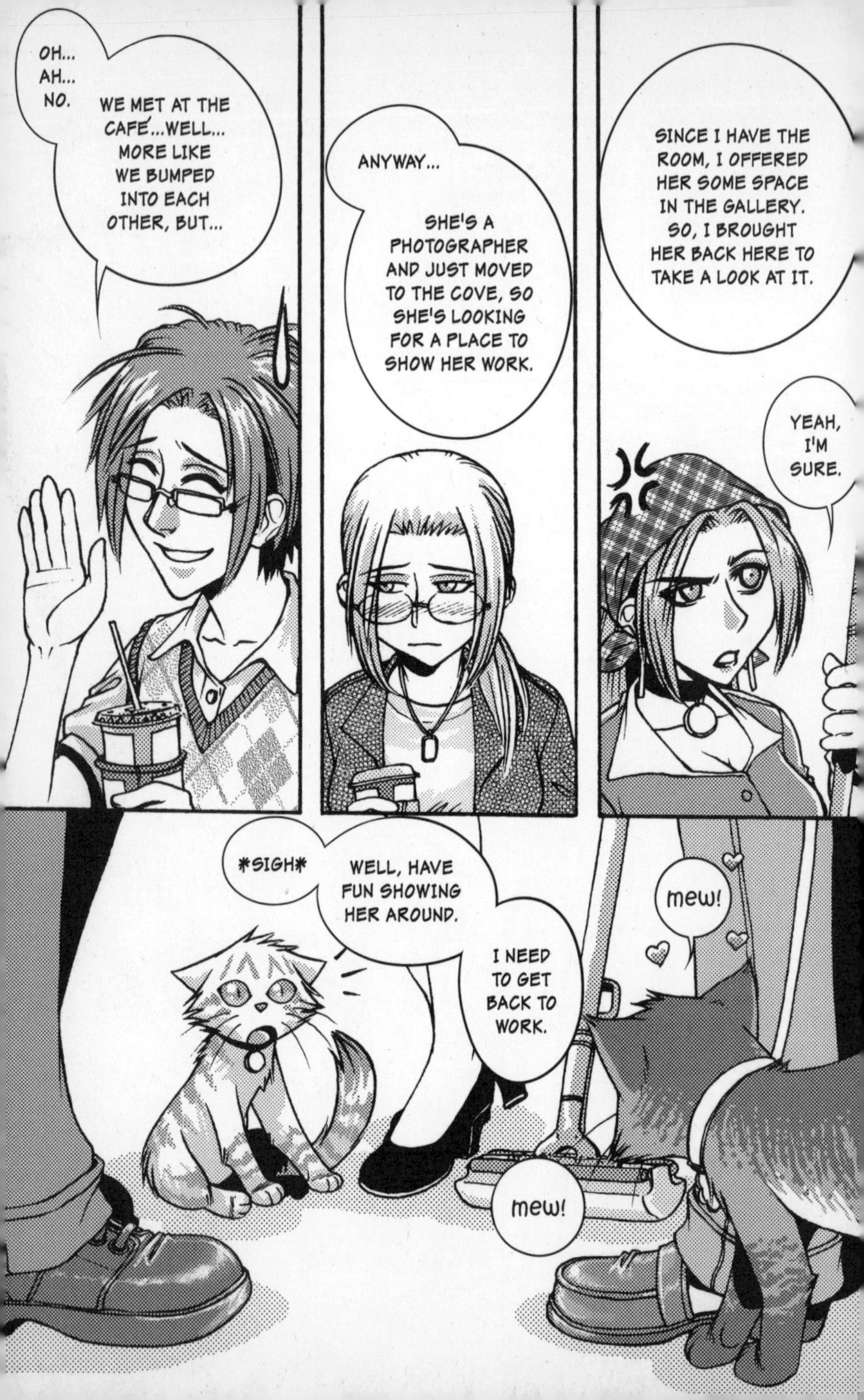
OH... AH... NO.
WE MET AT THE CAFÉ...WELL... MORE LIKE WE BUMPED INTO EACH OTHER, BUT...
ANYWAY...
SHE'S A PHOTOGRAPHER AND JUST MOVED TO THE COVE, SO SHE'S LOOKING FOR A PLACE TO SHOW HER WORK.
SINCE I HAVE THE ROOM, I OFFERED HER SOME SPACE IN THE GALLERY. SO, I BROUGHT HER BACK HERE TO TAKE A LOOK AT IT.
YEAH, I'M SURE.
SIGH
WELL, HAVE FUN SHOWING HER AROUND.
I NEED TO GET BACK TO WORK.
mew!
mew!

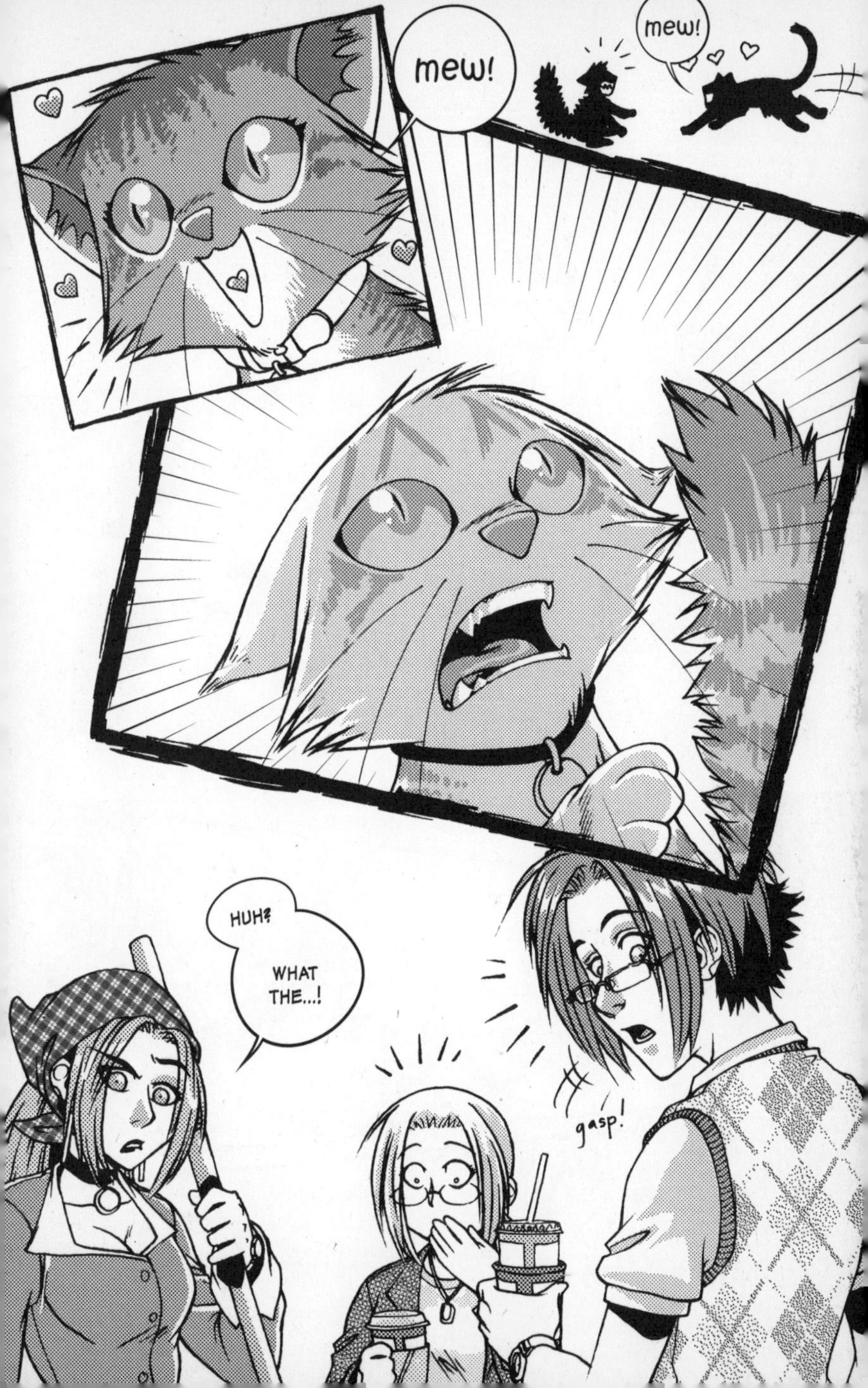
mew!
mew!
HUH?
WHAT THE...!
gasp!

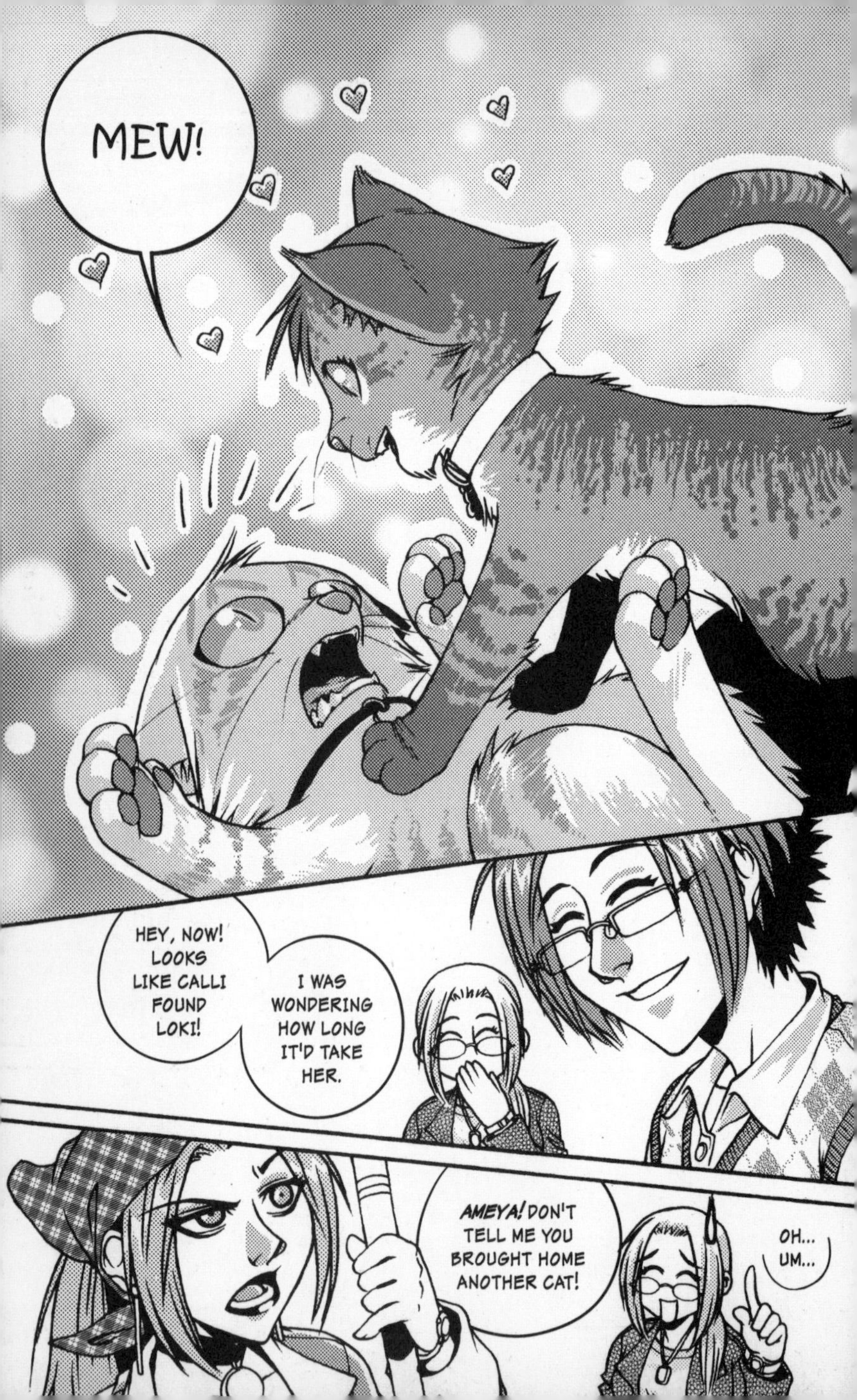

MEW!
HEY, NOW! LOOKS LIKE CALLI FOUND LOKI!
I WAS WONDERING HOW LONG IT'D TAKE HER.
AMEYA! DON'T TELL ME YOU BROUGHT HOME ANOTHER CAT!
OH... UM...

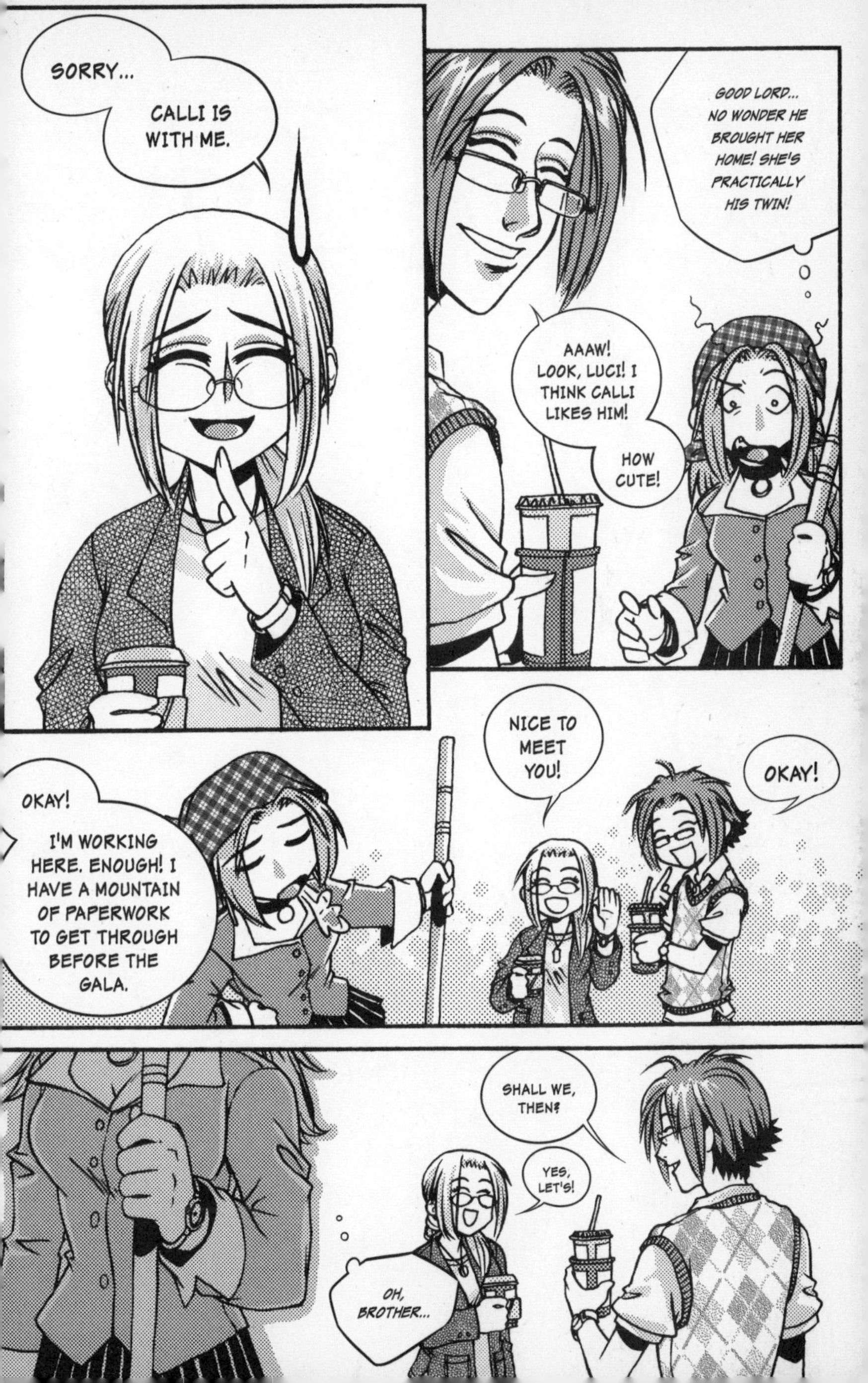
SORRY...
CALLI IS WITH ME.
GOOD LORD... NO WONDER HE BROUGHT HER HOME! SHE'S PRACTICALLY HIS TWIN!
AAAW! LOOK, LUCI! I THINK CALLI LIKES HIM!
HOW CUTE!
OKAY!
I'M WORKING HERE. ENOUGH! I HAVE A MOUNTAIN OF PAPERWORK TO GET THROUGH BEFORE THE GALA.
NICE TO MEET YOU!
OKAY!
SHALL WE, THEN?
YES, LET'S!
OH, BROTHER...

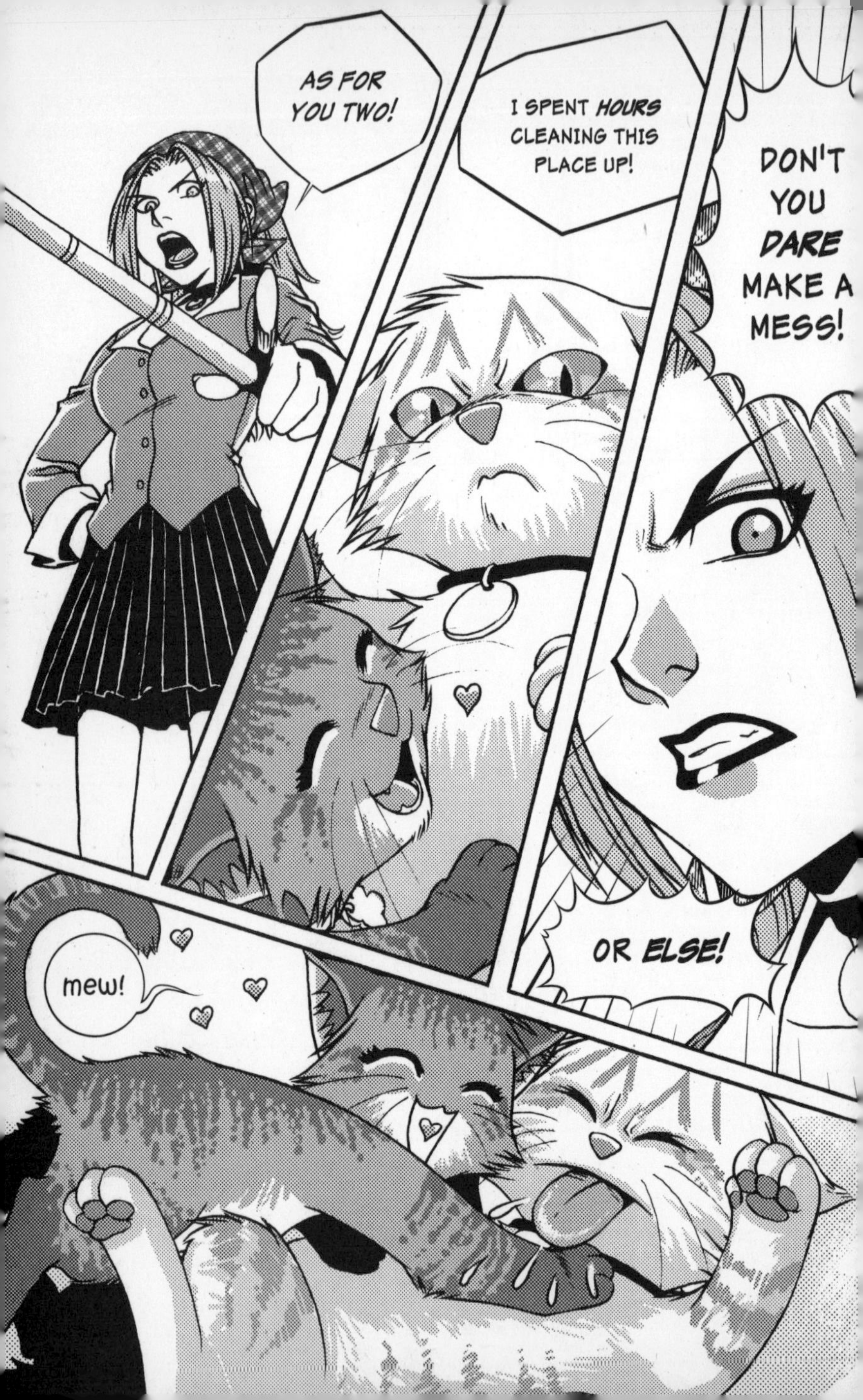
AS FOR YOU TWO!
I SPENT *HOURS* CLEANING THIS PLACE UP!
DON'T YOU *DARE* MAKE A MESS!
OR *ELSE*!
mew!

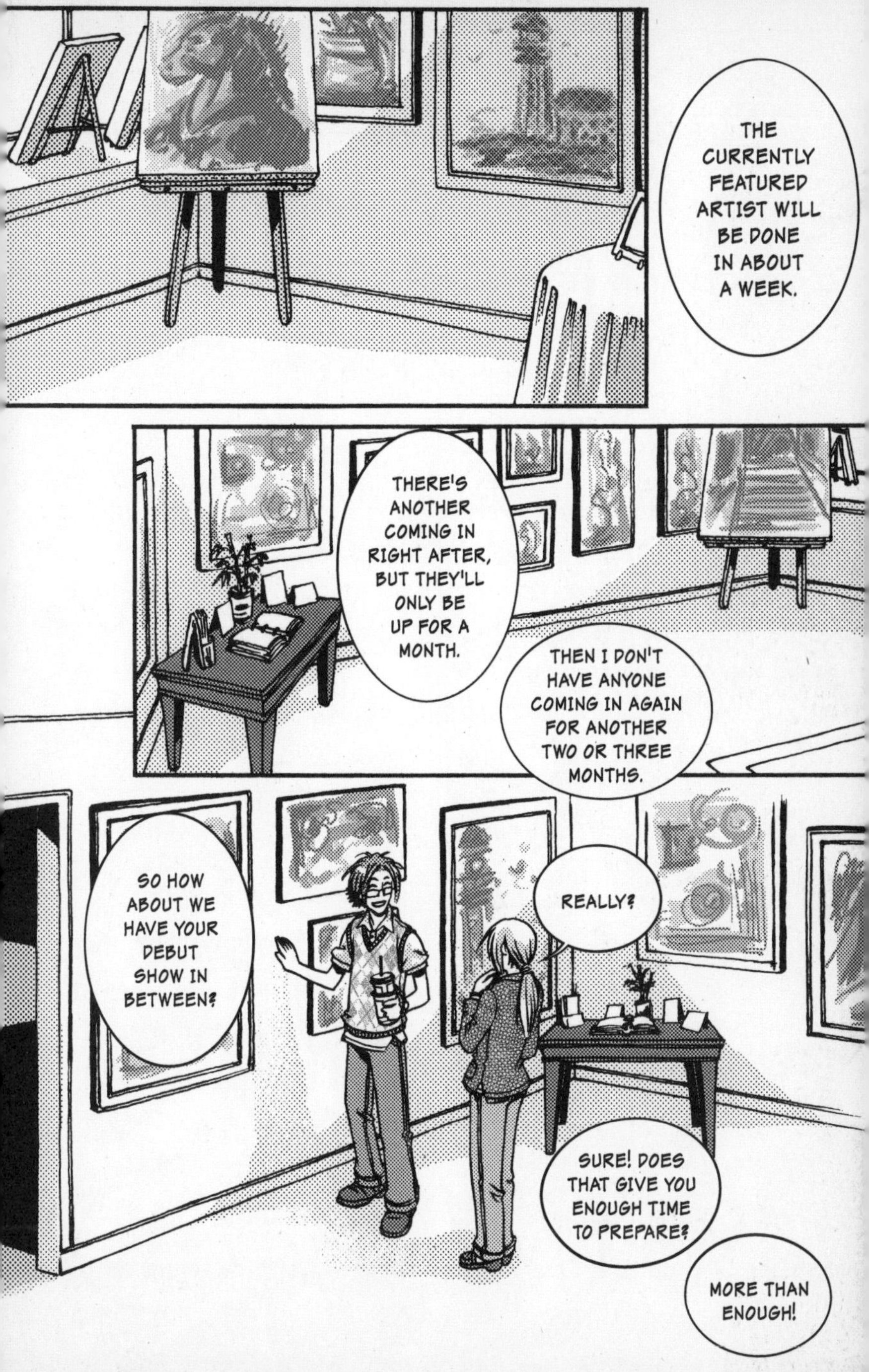
THE CURRENTLY FEATURED ARTIST WILL BE DONE IN ABOUT A WEEK.
THERE'S ANOTHER COMING IN RIGHT AFTER, BUT THEY'LL ONLY BE UP FOR A MONTH.
THEN I DON'T HAVE ANYONE COMING IN AGAIN FOR ANOTHER TWO OR THREE MONTHS.
SO HOW ABOUT WE HAVE YOUR DEBUT SHOW IN BETWEEN?
REALLY?
SURE! DOES THAT GIVE YOU ENOUGH TIME TO PREPARE?
MORE THAN ENOUGH!

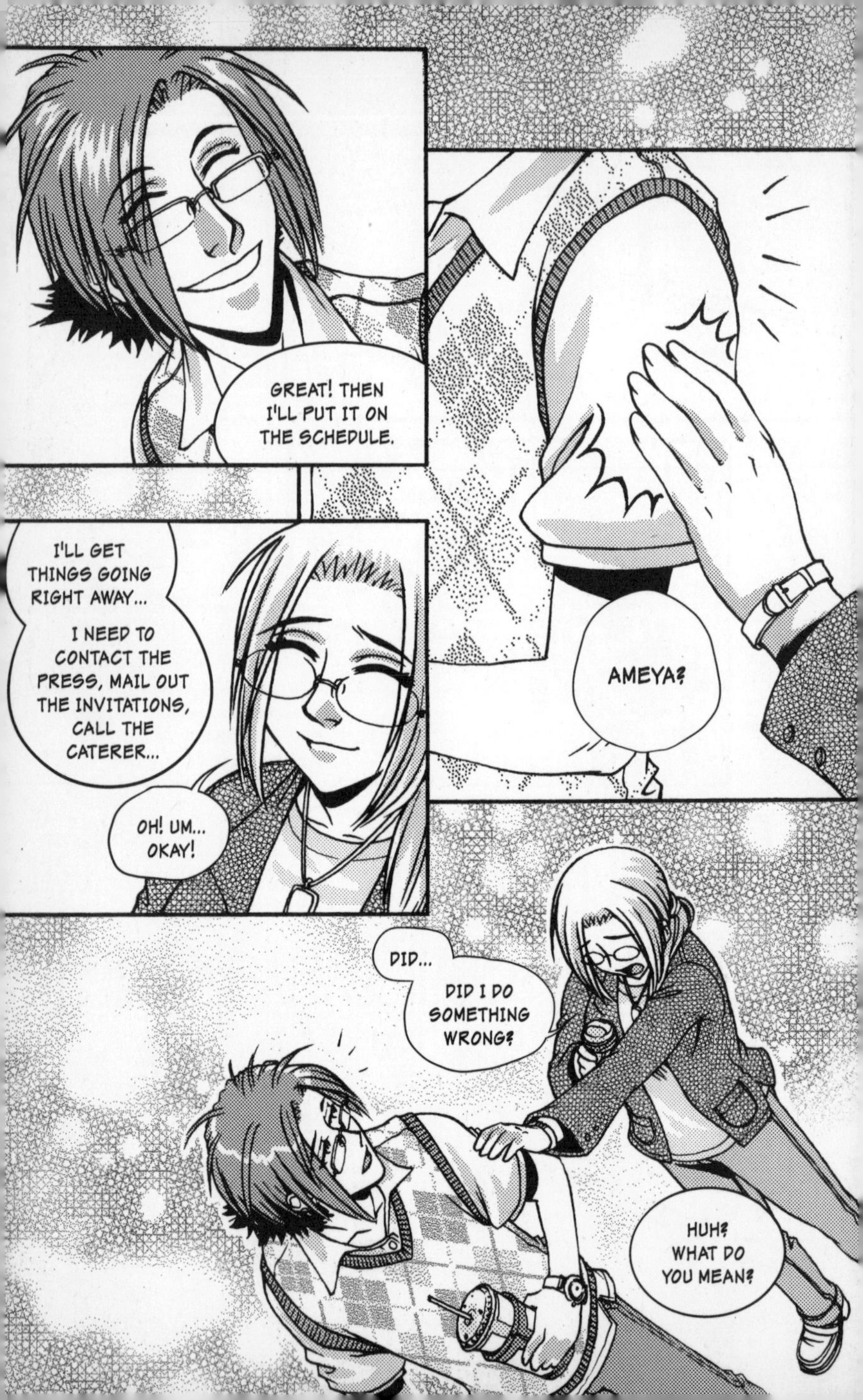
GREAT! THEN I'LL PUT IT ON THE SCHEDULE.
I'LL GET THINGS GOING RIGHT AWAY...
I NEED TO CONTACT THE PRESS, MAIL OUT THE INVITATIONS, CALL THE CATERER...
OH! UM... OKAY!
AMEYA?
DID...
DID I DO SOMETHING WRONG?
HUH? WHAT DO YOU MEAN?

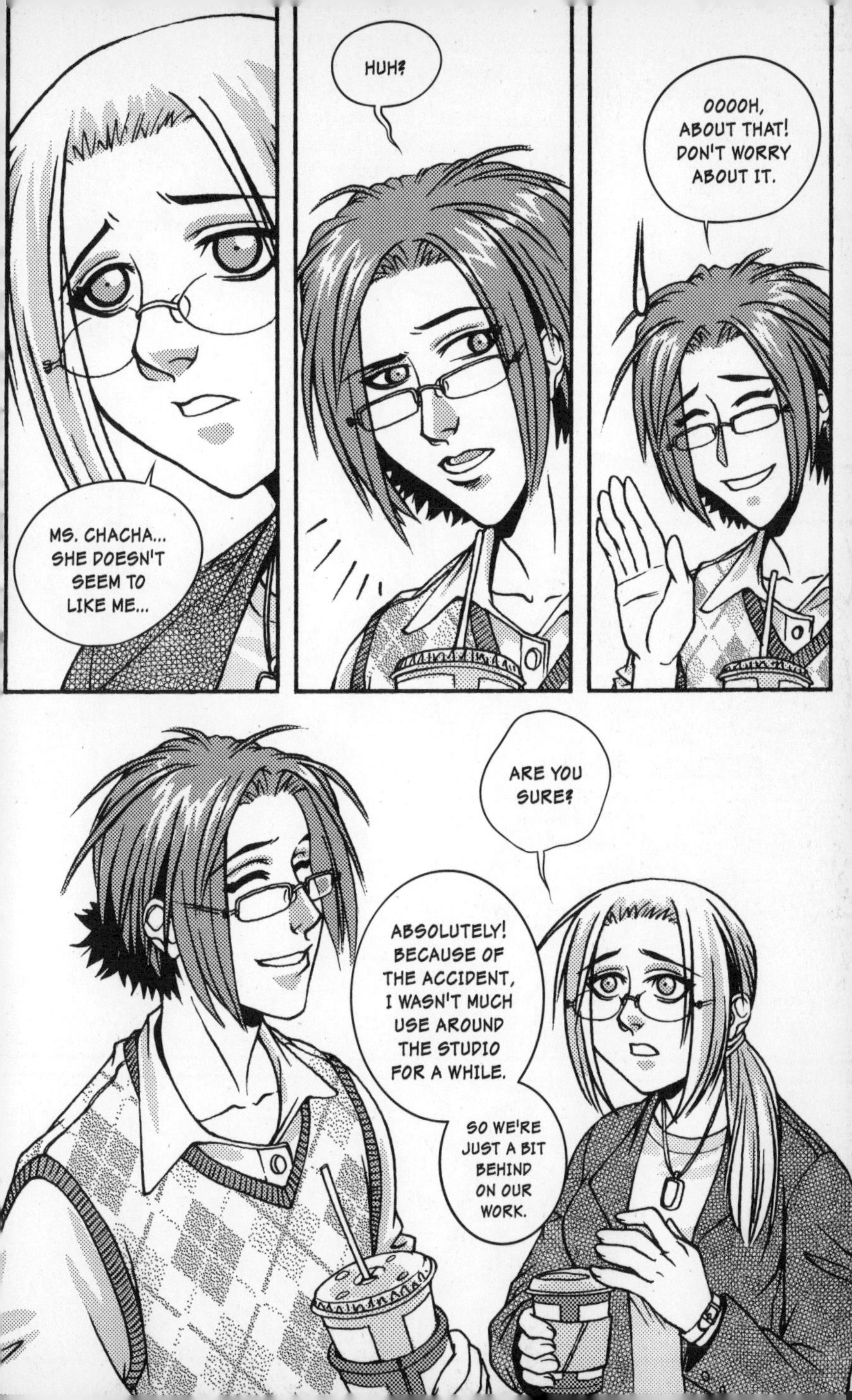
MS. CHACHA... SHE DOESN'T SEEM TO LIKE ME...
HUH?
OOOOH, ABOUT THAT! DON'T WORRY ABOUT IT.
ARE YOU SURE?
ABSOLUTELY! BECAUSE OF THE ACCIDENT, I WASN'T MUCH USE AROUND THE STUDIO FOR A WHILE.
SO WE'RE JUST A BIT BEHIND ON OUR WORK.

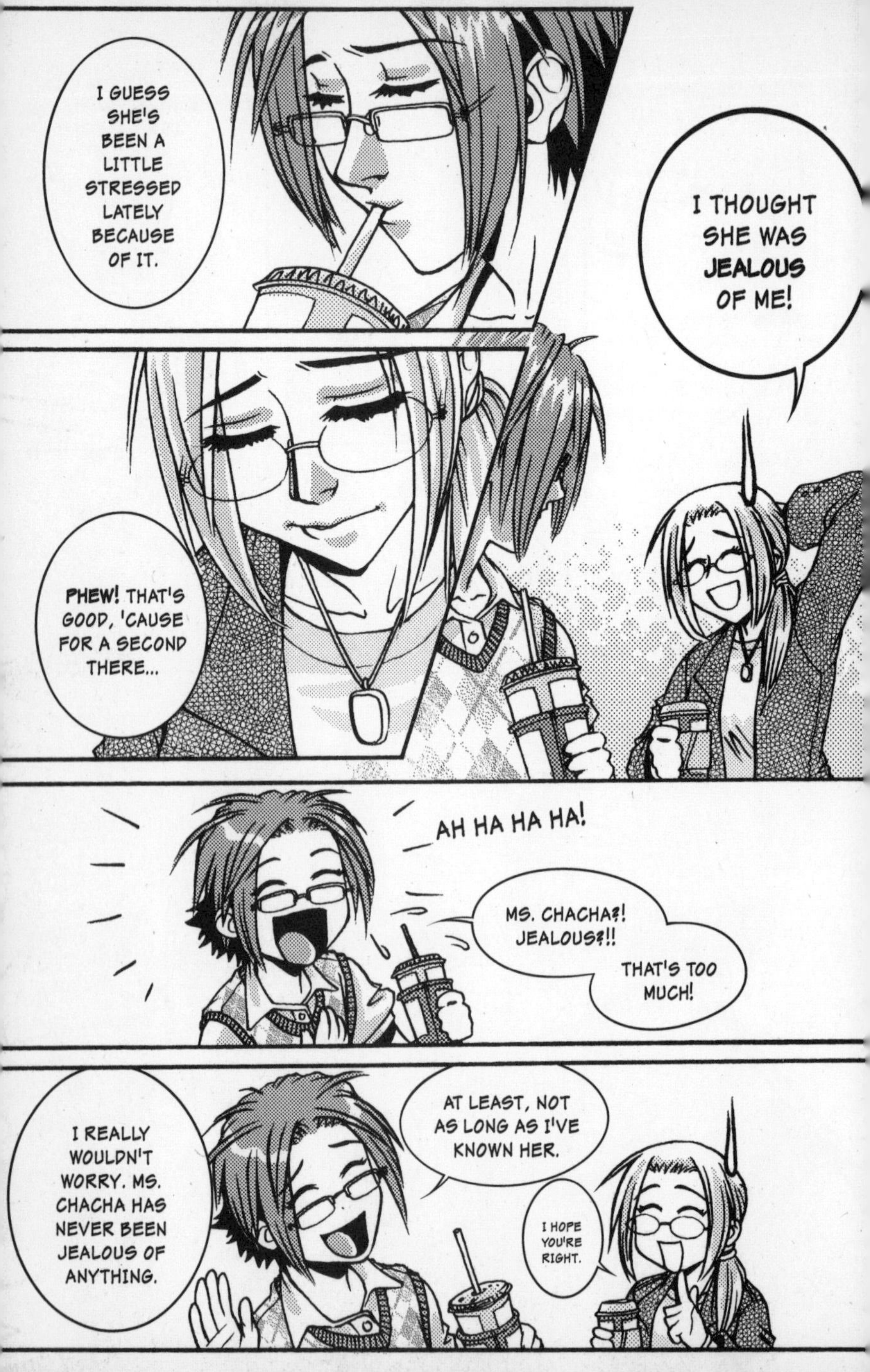
I GUESS SHE'S BEEN A LITTLE STRESSED LATELY BECAUSE OF IT.
PHEW! THAT'S GOOD, 'CAUSE FOR A SECOND THERE...
I THOUGHT SHE WAS JEALOUS OF ME!
AH HA HA HA!
MS. CHACHA?! JEALOUS?!!
THAT'S TOO MUCH!
I REALLY WOULDN'T WORRY. MS. CHACHA HAS NEVER BEEN JEALOUS OF ANYTHING.
AT LEAST, NOT AS LONG AS I'VE KNOWN HER.
I HOPE YOU'RE RIGHT.

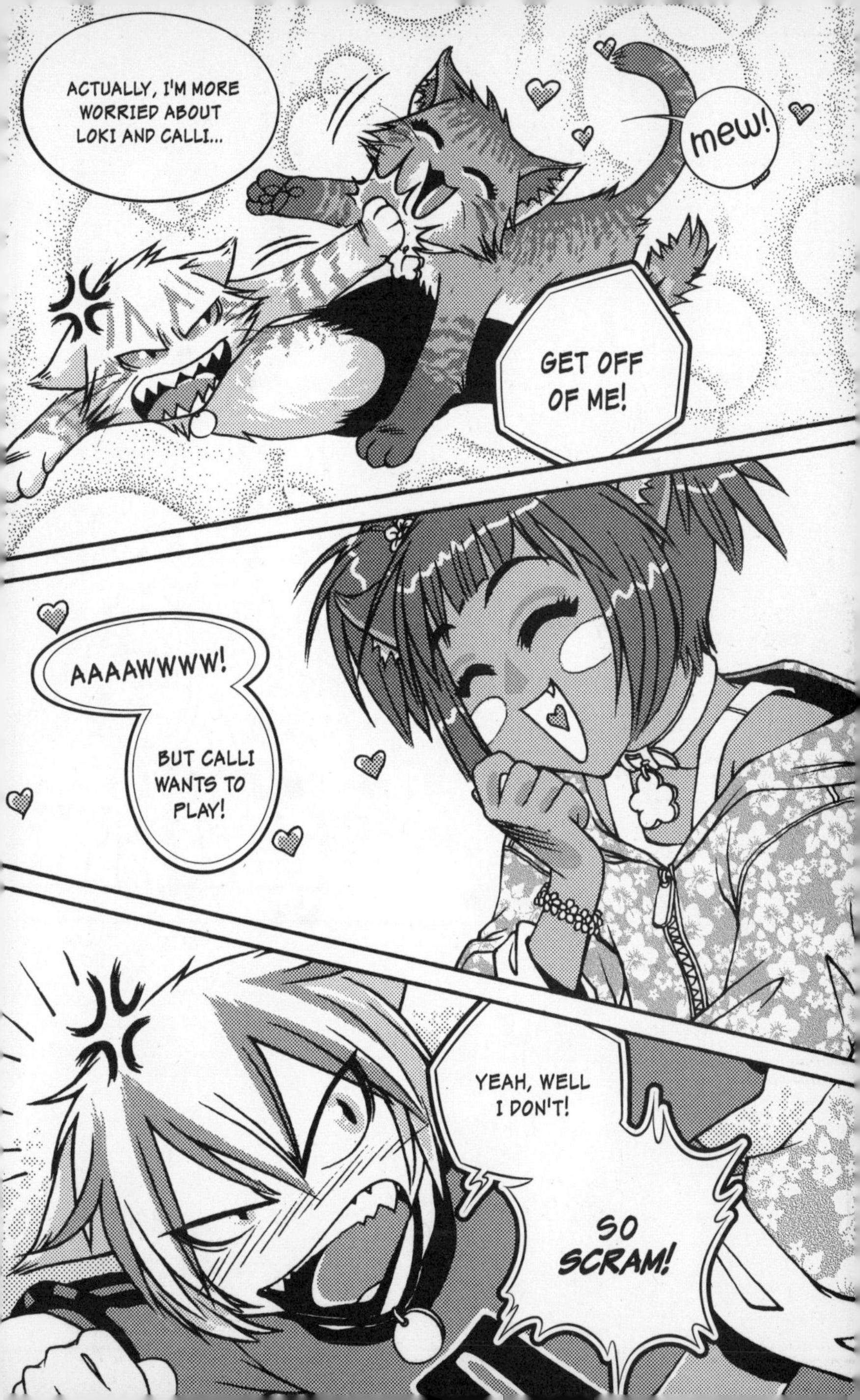
ACTUALLY, I'M MORE WORRIED ABOUT LOKI AND CALLI...
mew!
GET OFF OF ME!
AAAAWWWW!
BUT CALLI WANTS TO PLAY!
YEAH, WELL I DON'T!
SO SCRAM!

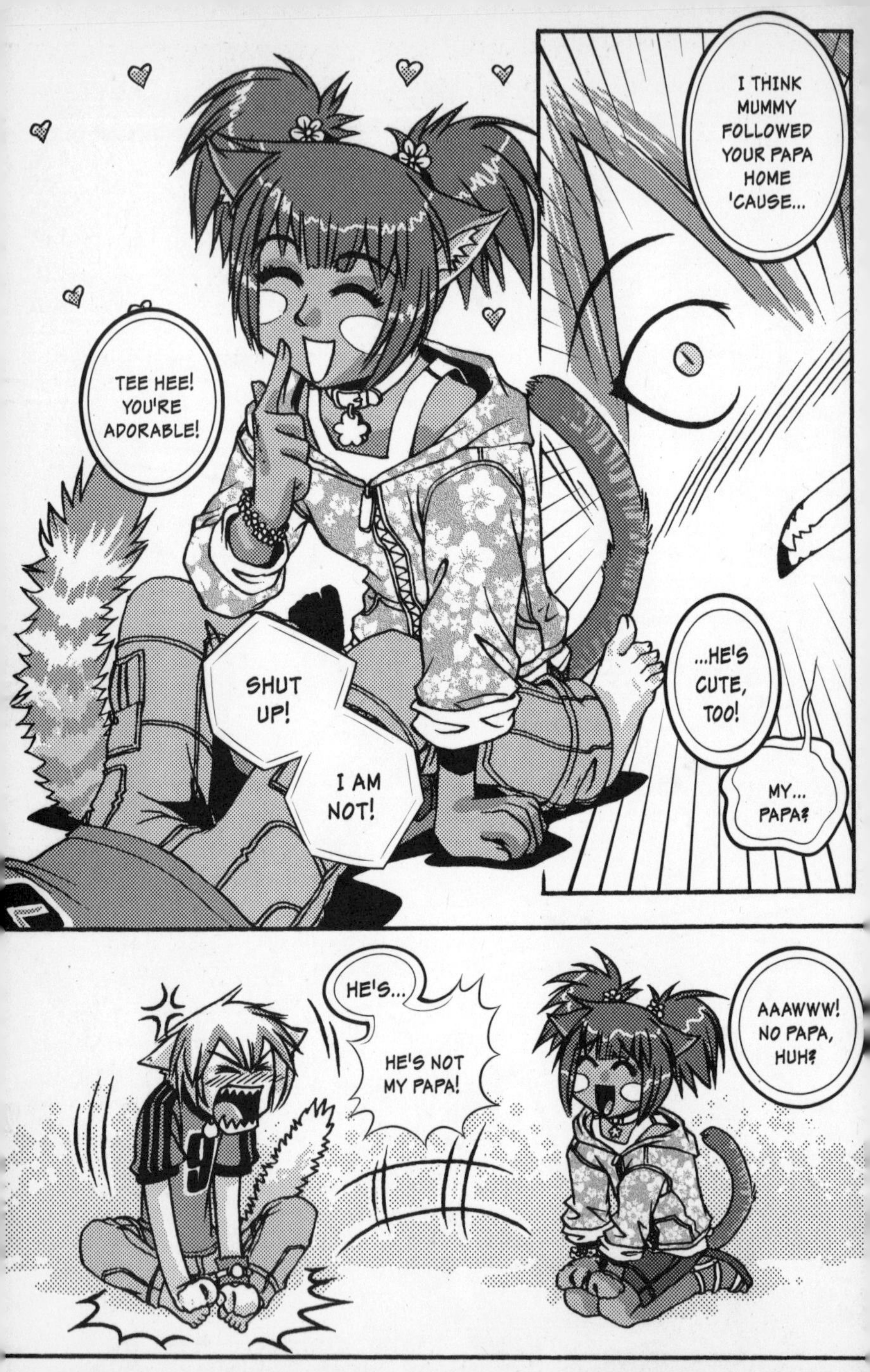
TEE HEE! YOU'RE ADORABLE!
SHUT UP!
I AM NOT!
I THINK MUMMY FOLLOWED YOUR PAPA HOME 'CAUSE...
...HE'S CUTE, TOO!
MY... PAPA?
HE'S...
HE'S NOT MY PAPA!
AAAWWW! NO PAPA, HUH?

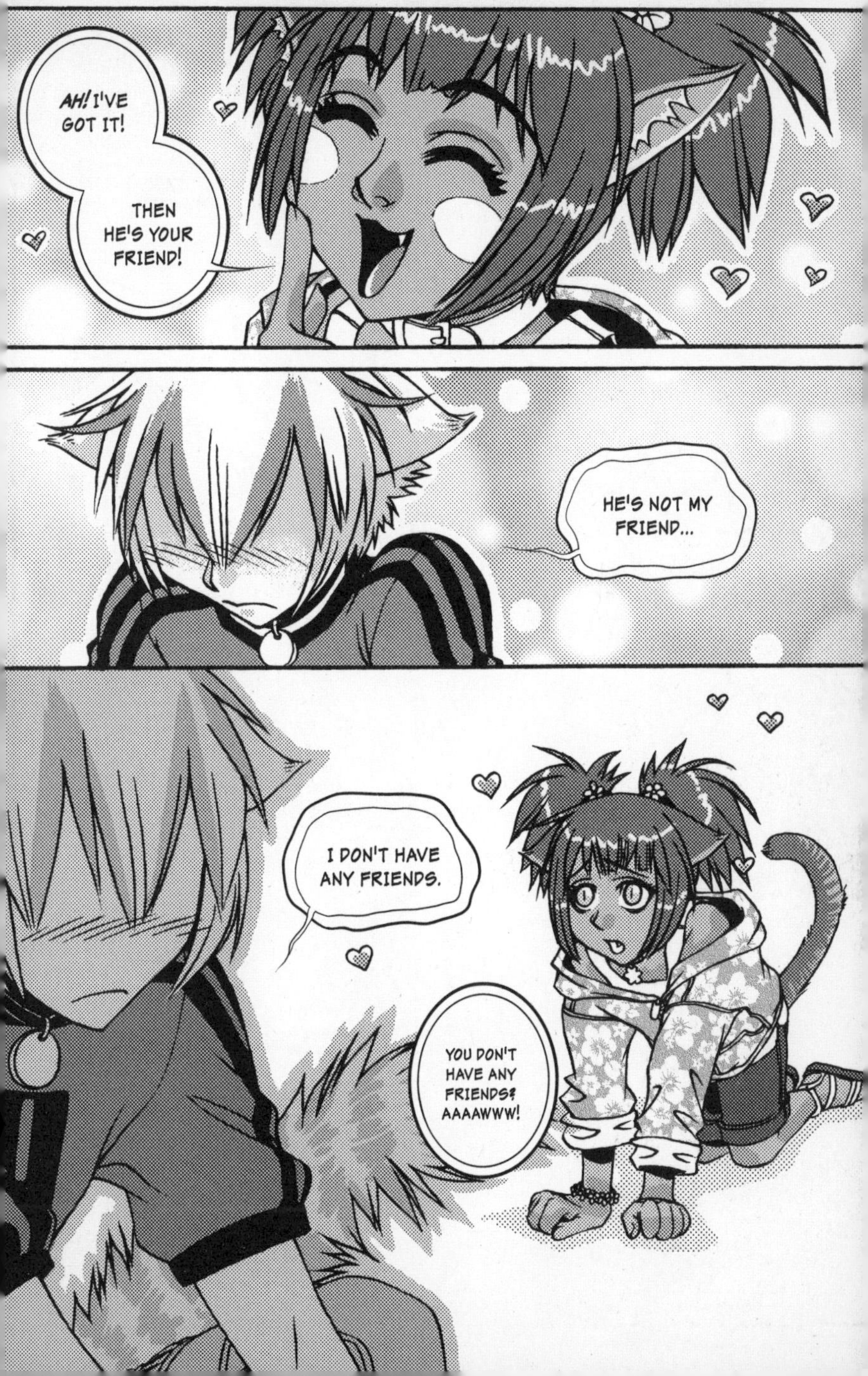
AH! I'VE GOT IT!
THEN HE'S YOUR FRIEND!
HE'S NOT MY FRIEND...
I DON'T HAVE ANY FRIENDS.
YOU DON'T HAVE ANY FRIENDS? AAAAWWW!

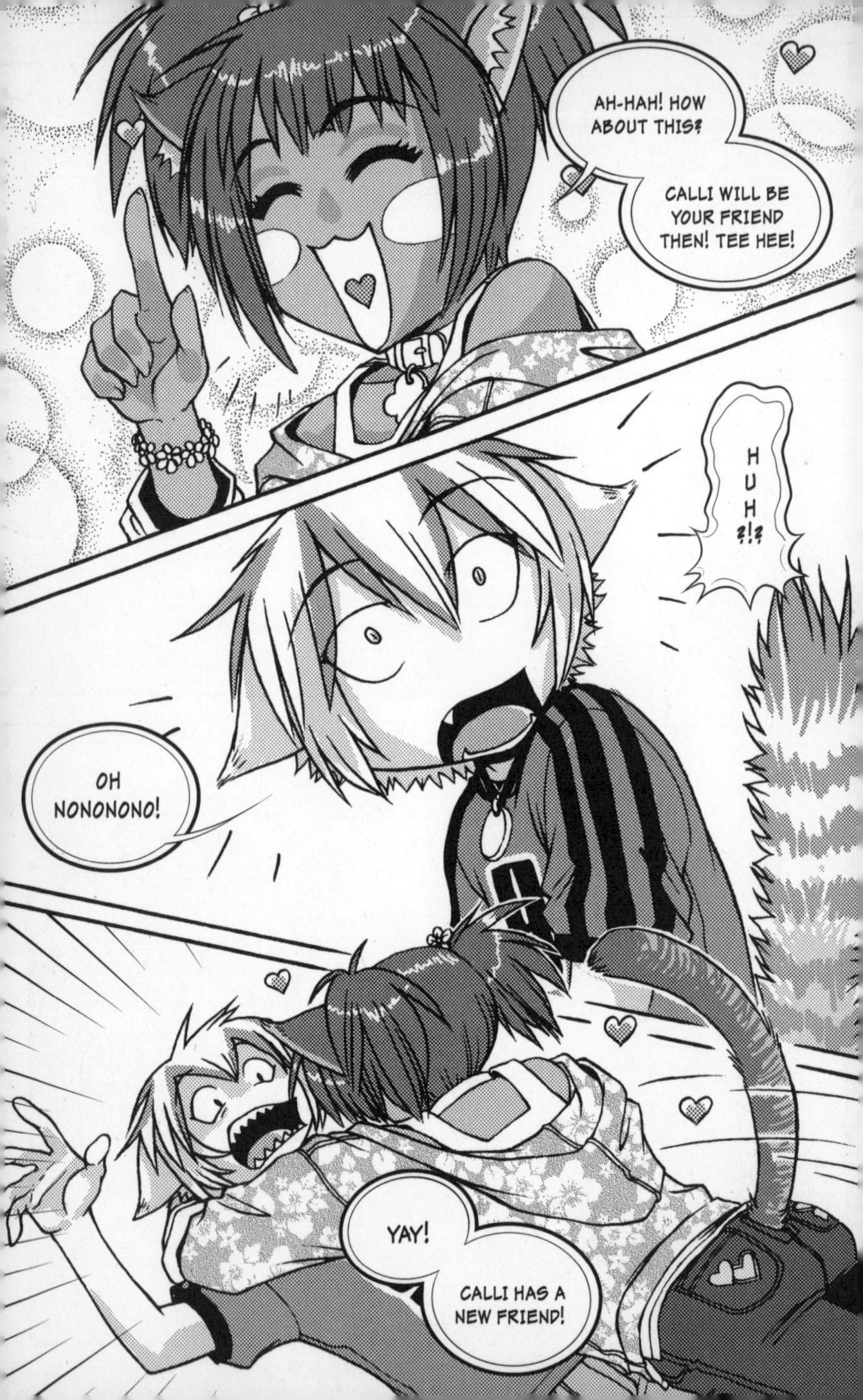
AH-HAH! HOW ABOUT THIS?
CALLI WILL BE YOUR FRIEND THEN! TEE HEE!
OH NONONONO!
HUH ?!?
YAY!
CALLI HAS A NEW FRIEND!

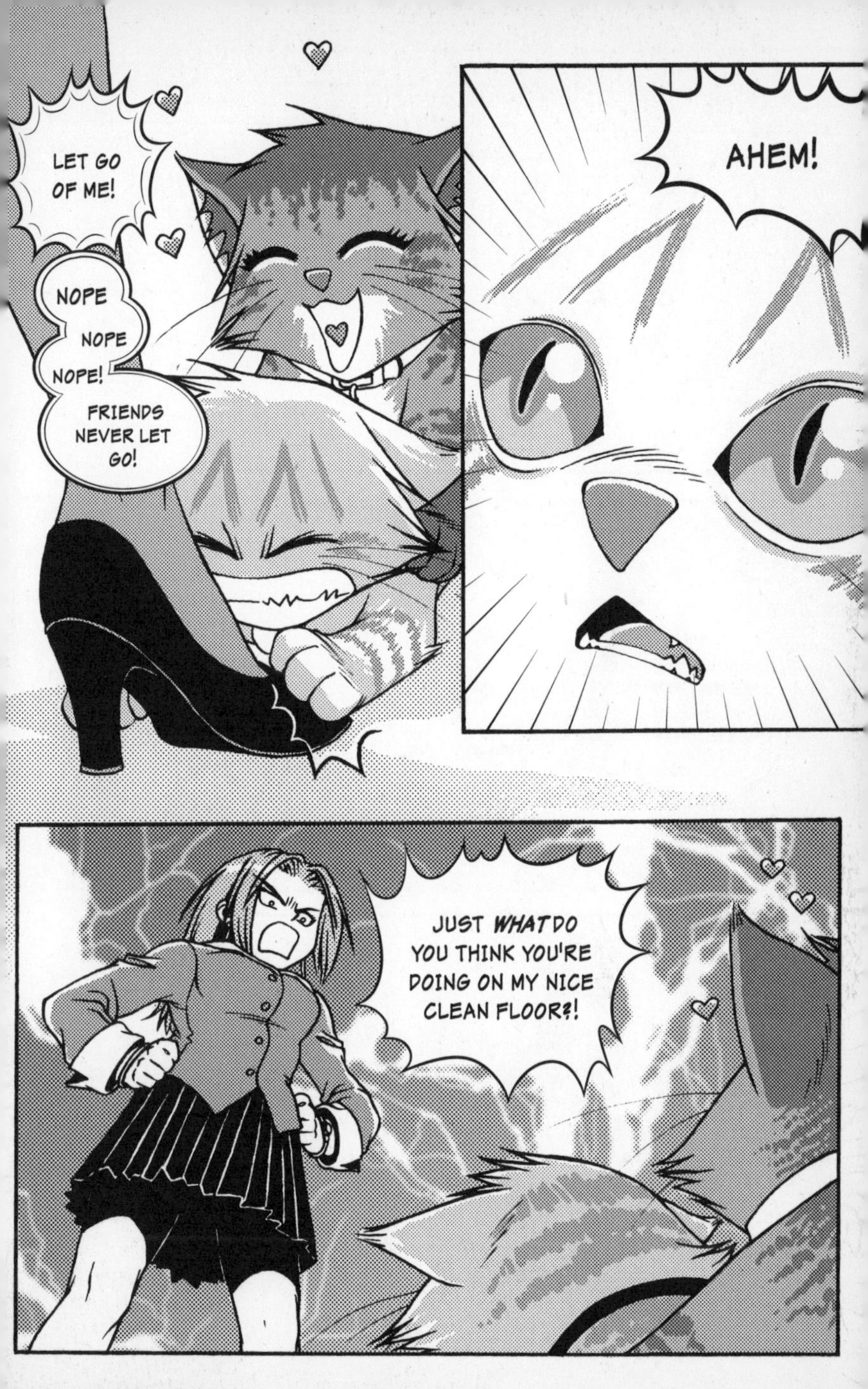
LET GO OF ME!
NOPE NOPE NOPE!
FRIENDS NEVER LET GO!
AHEM!
JUST *WHAT* DO YOU THINK YOU'RE DOING ON MY NICE CLEAN FLOOR?!

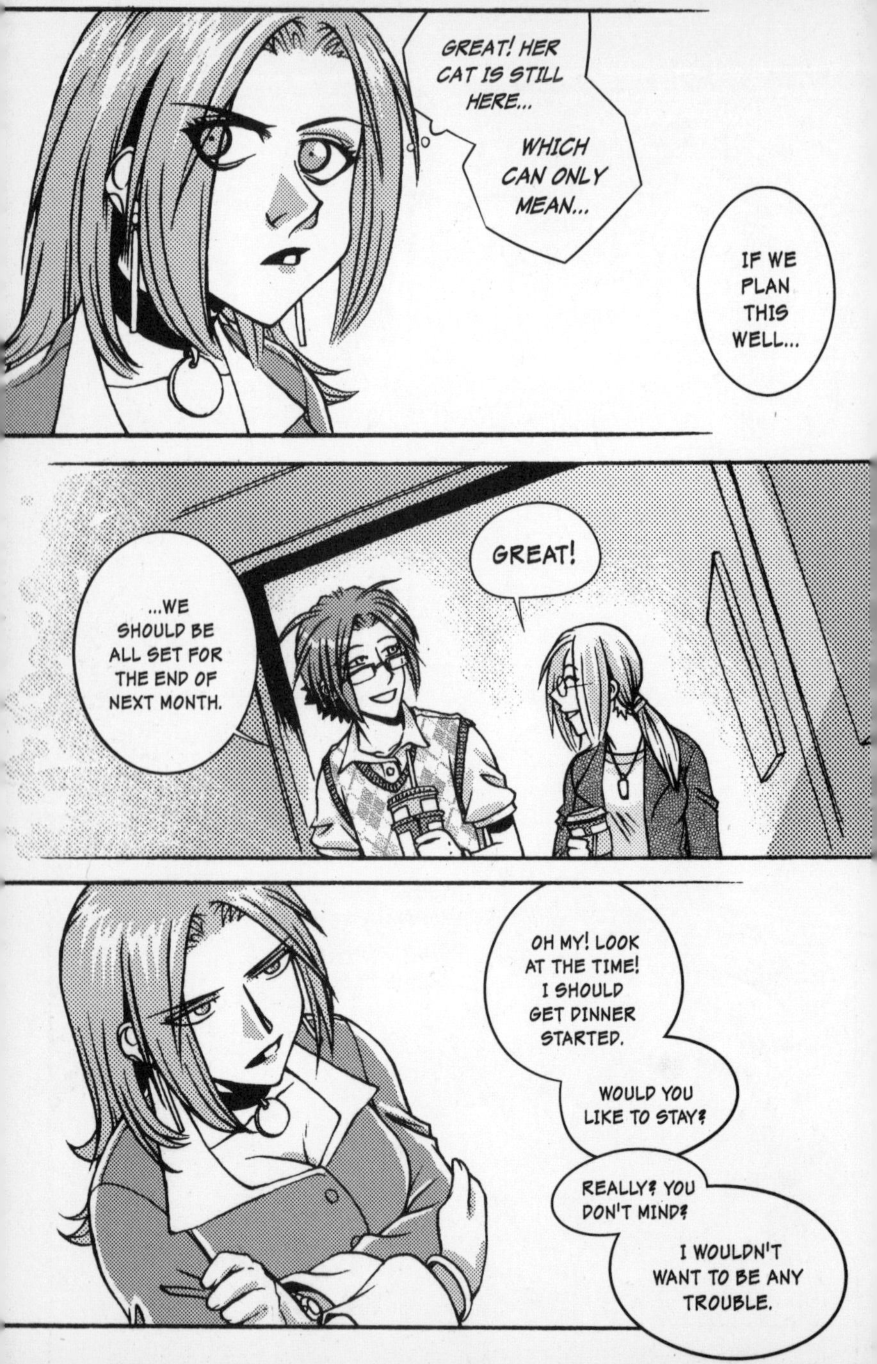
GREAT! HER CAT IS STILL HERE...
WHICH CAN ONLY MEAN...
IF WE PLAN THIS WELL...
...WE SHOULD BE ALL SET FOR THE END OF NEXT MONTH.
GREAT!
OH MY! LOOK AT THE TIME! I SHOULD GET DINNER STARTED.
WOULD YOU LIKE TO STAY?
REALLY? YOU DON'T MIND?
I WOULDN'T WANT TO BE ANY TROUBLE.

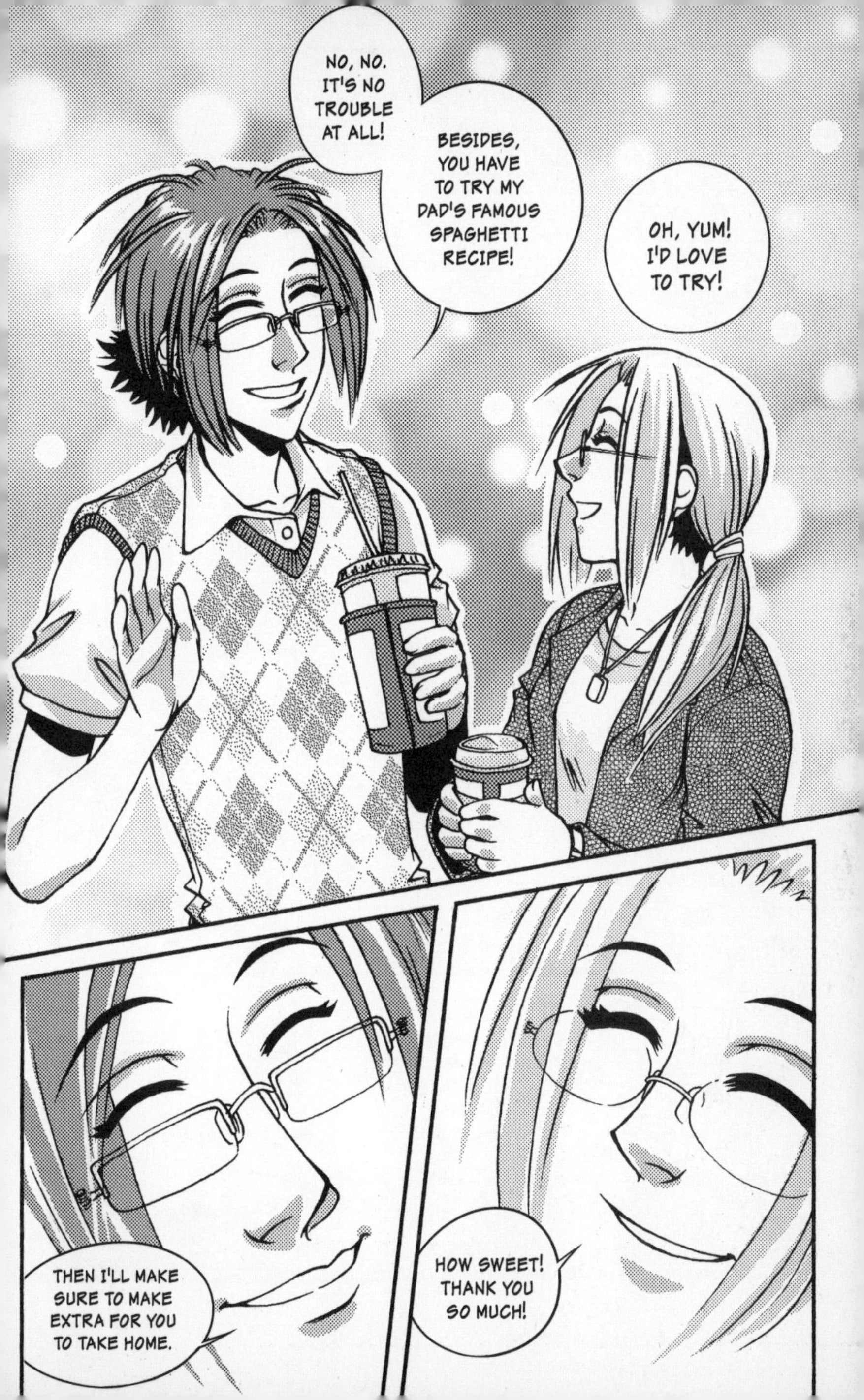
NO, NO. IT'S NO TROUBLE AT ALL!
BESIDES, YOU HAVE TO TRY MY DAD'S FAMOUS SPAGHETTI RECIPE!
OH, YUM! I'D LOVE TO TRY!
THEN I'LL MAKE SURE TO MAKE EXTRA FOR YOU TO TAKE HOME.
HOW SWEET! THANK YOU SO MUCH!

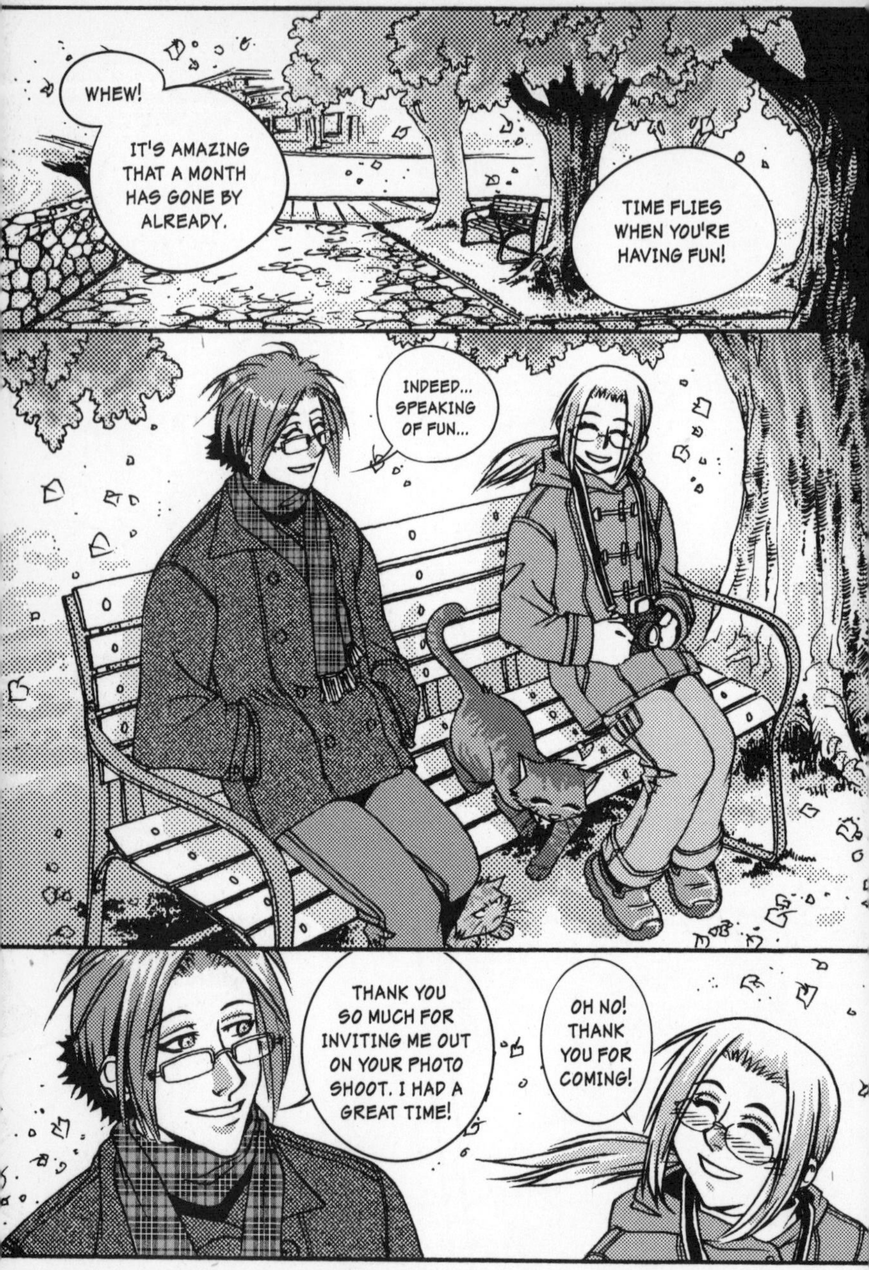
WHEW!
IT'S AMAZING THAT A MONTH HAS GONE BY ALREADY.
TIME FLIES WHEN YOU'RE HAVING FUN!
INDEED... SPEAKING OF FUN...
THANK YOU SO MUCH FOR INVITING ME OUT ON YOUR PHOTO SHOOT. I HAD A GREAT TIME!
OH NO! THANK YOU FOR COMING!

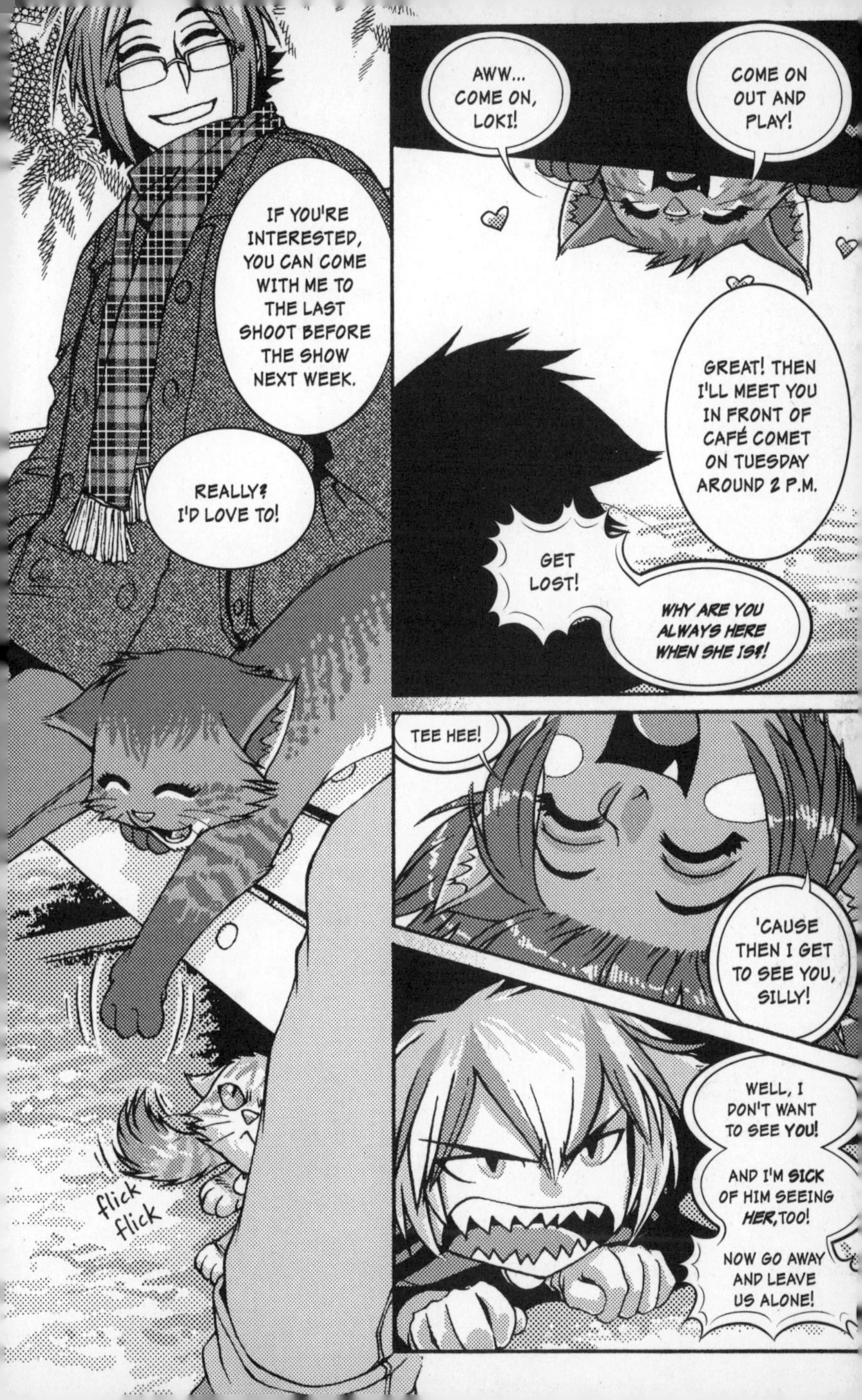
IF YOU'RE INTERESTED, YOU CAN COME WITH ME TO THE LAST SHOOT BEFORE THE SHOW NEXT WEEK.
REALLY? I'D LOVE TO!
flick flick
AWW... COME ON, LOKI!
COME ON OUT AND PLAY!
GREAT! THEN I'LL MEET YOU IN FRONT OF CAFÉ COMET ON TUESDAY AROUND 2 P.M.
GET LOST!
WHY ARE YOU ALWAYS HERE WHEN SHE IS?!
TEE HEE!
'CAUSE THEN I GET TO SEE YOU, SILLY!
WELL, I DON'T WANT TO SEE YOU!
AND I'M SICK OF HIM SEEING HER, TOO!
NOW GO AWAY AND LEAVE US ALONE!

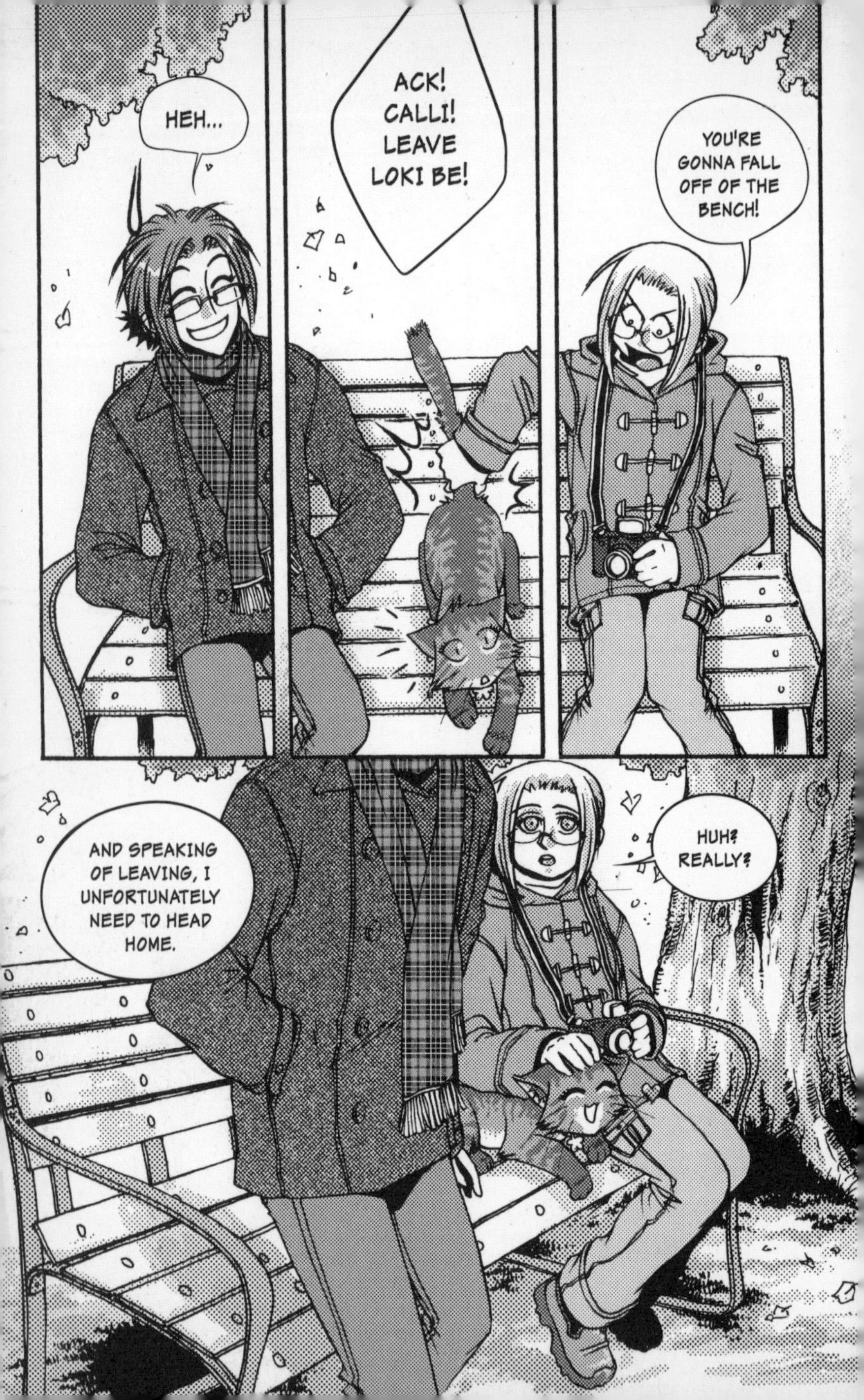
HEH...
ACK! CALLI! LEAVE LOKI BE!
YOU'RE GONNA FALL OFF OF THE BENCH!
AND SPEAKING OF LEAVING, I UNFORTUNATELY NEED TO HEAD HOME.
HUH? REALLY?

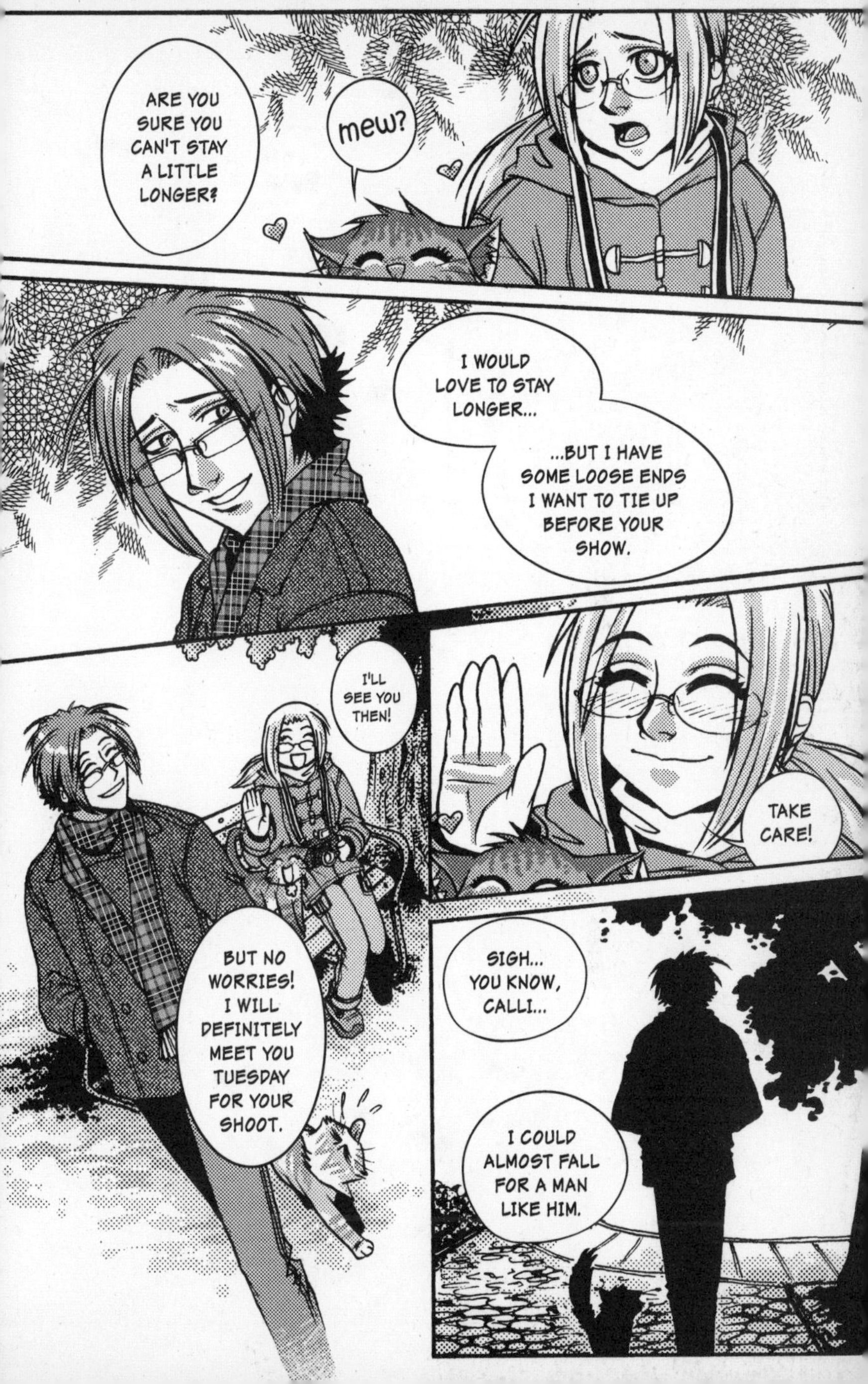
ARE YOU SURE YOU CAN'T STAY A LITTLE LONGER?
mew?
I WOULD LOVE TO STAY LONGER...
...BUT I HAVE SOME LOOSE ENDS I WANT TO TIE UP BEFORE YOUR SHOW.
BUT NO WORRIES! I WILL DEFINITELY MEET YOU TUESDAY FOR YOUR SHOOT.
I'LL SEE YOU THEN!
TAKE CARE!
SIGH... YOU KNOW, CALLI...
I COULD ALMOST FALL FOR A MAN LIKE HIM.

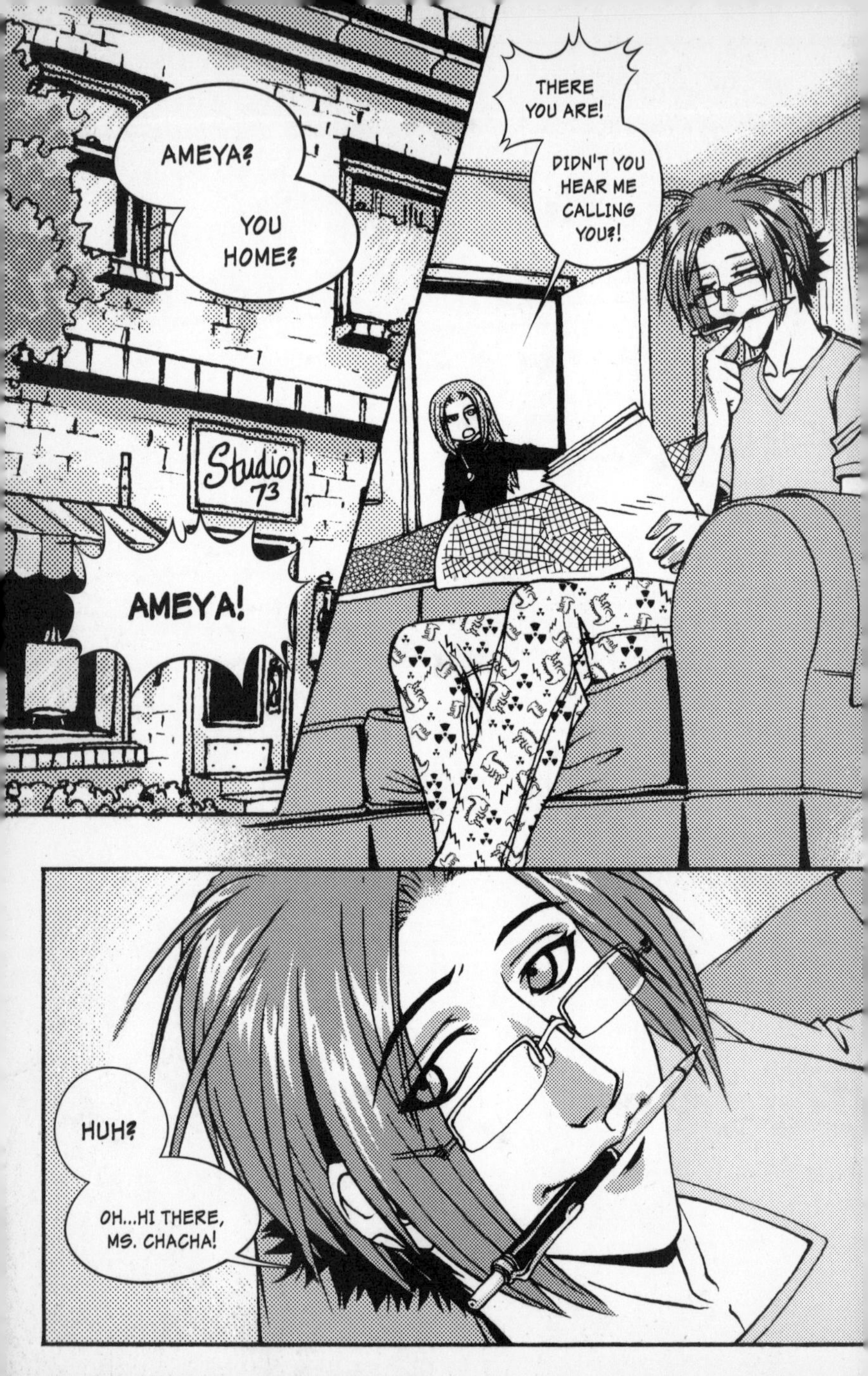
AMEYA?
YOU HOME?
Studio 73
AMEYA!
THERE YOU ARE!
DIDN'T YOU HEAR ME CALLING YOU?!
HUH?
OH...HI THERE, MS. CHACHA!

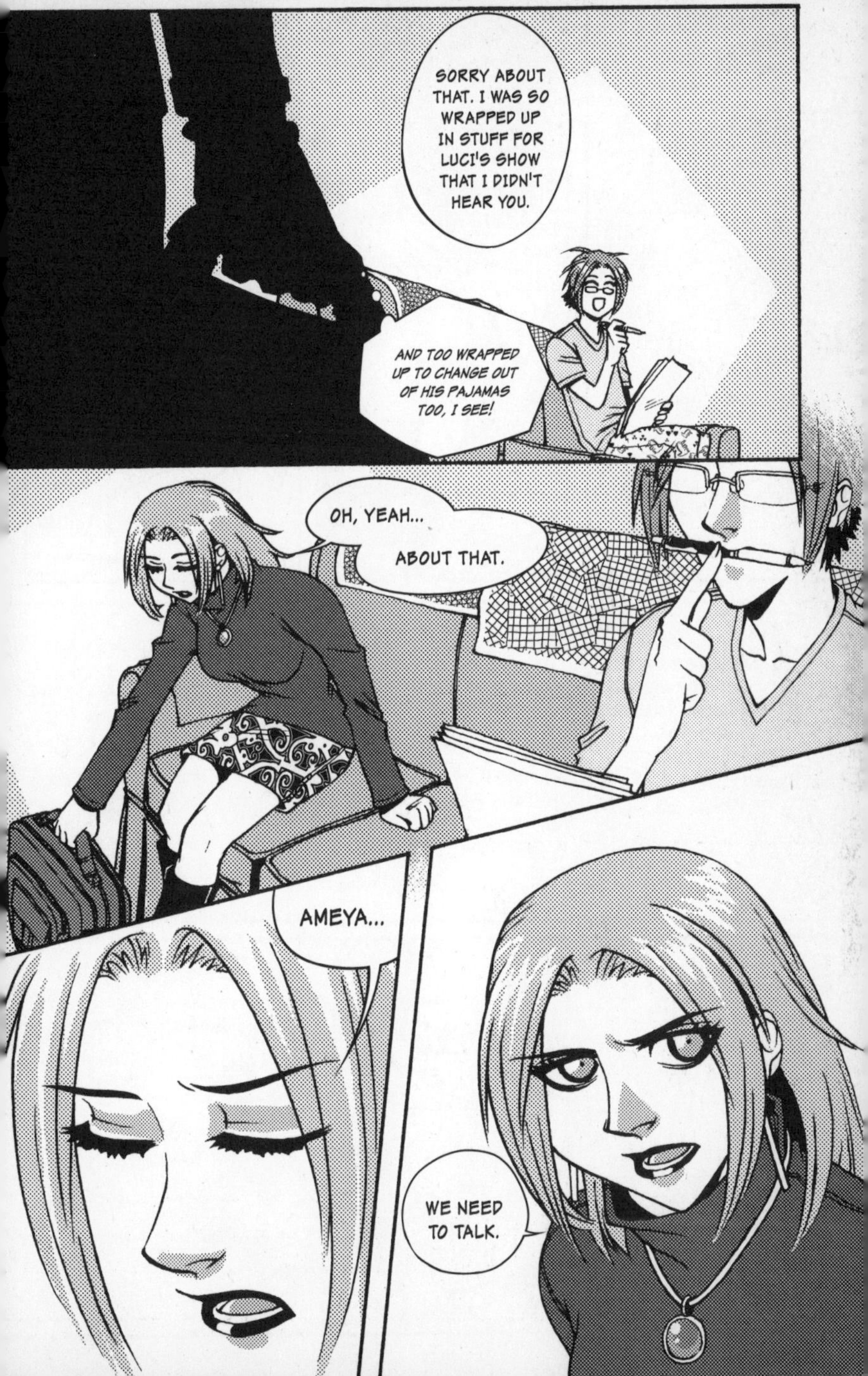
SORRY ABOUT THAT. I WAS SO WRAPPED UP IN STUFF FOR LUCI'S SHOW THAT I DIDN'T HEAR YOU.
AND TOO WRAPPED UP TO CHANGE OUT OF HIS PAJAMAS TOO, I SEE!
OH, YEAH...
ABOUT THAT.
AMEYA...
WE NEED TO TALK.

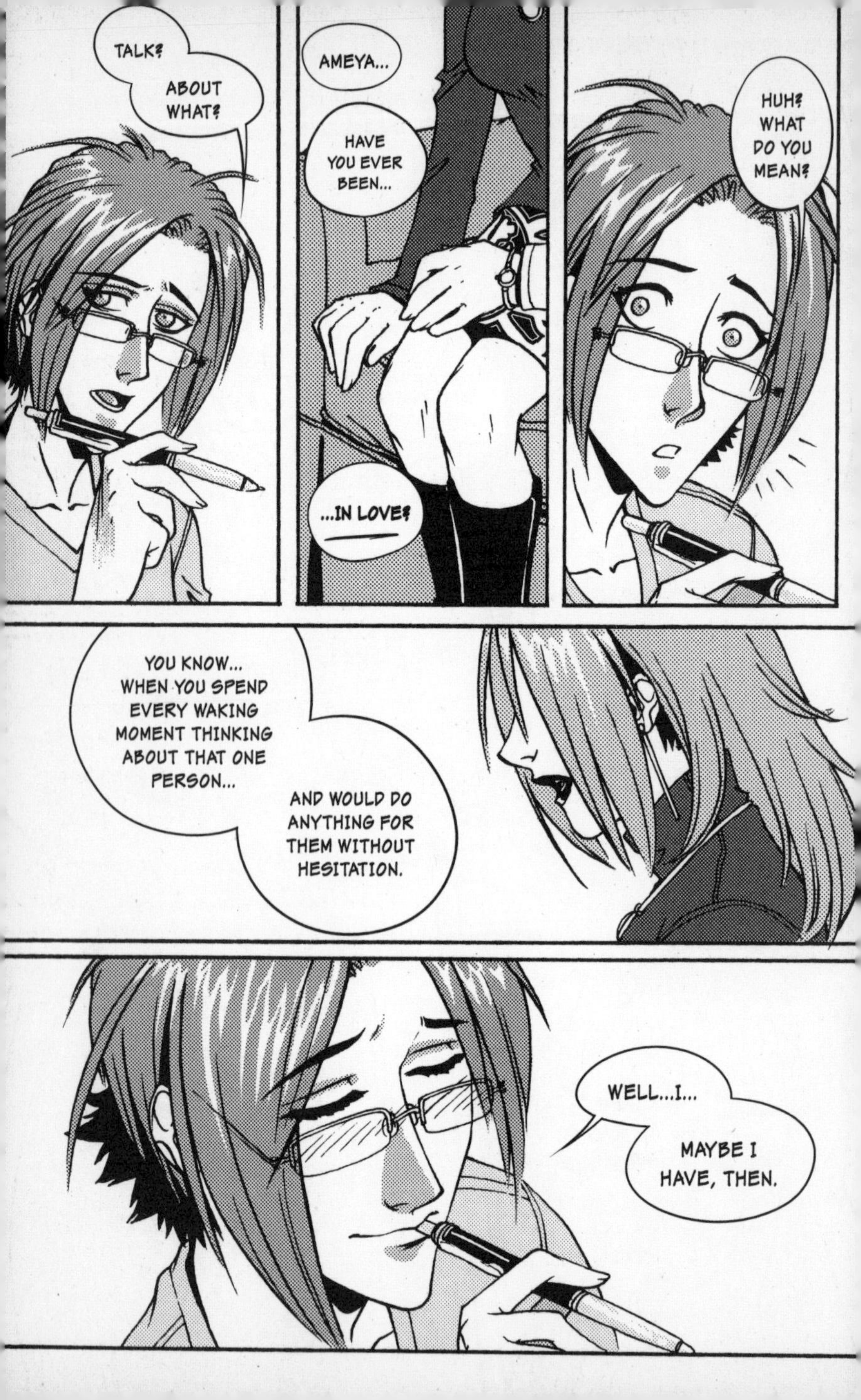
TALK? ABOUT WHAT?
AMEYA...
HAVE YOU EVER BEEN...
...IN LOVE?
HUH? WHAT DO YOU MEAN?
YOU KNOW... WHEN YOU SPEND EVERY WAKING MOMENT THINKING ABOUT THAT ONE PERSON...
AND WOULD DO ANYTHING FOR THEM WITHOUT HESITATION.
WELL...I...
MAYBE I HAVE, THEN.

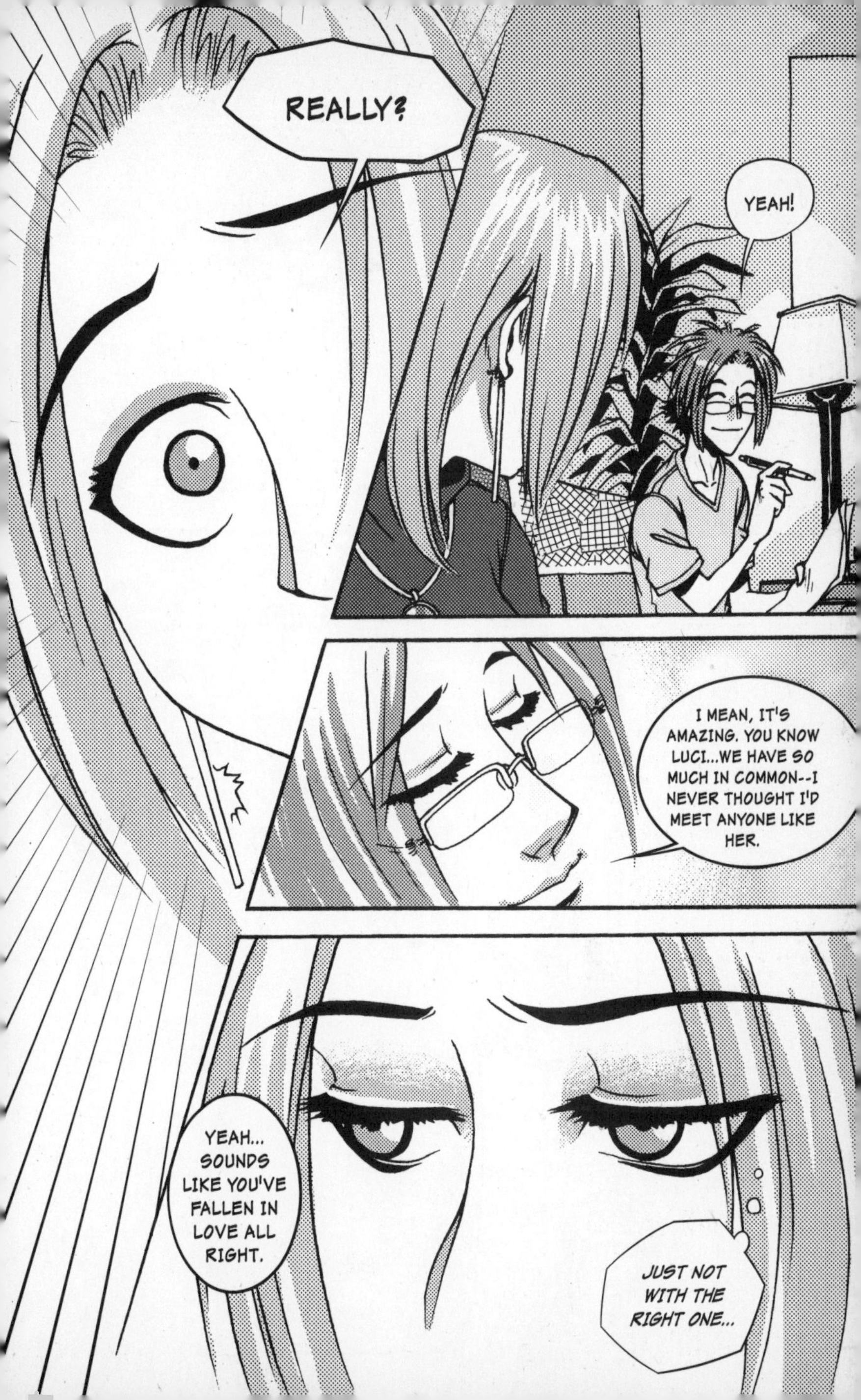
REALLY?
YEAH!
I MEAN, IT'S AMAZING. YOU KNOW LUCI...WE HAVE SO MUCH IN COMMON--I NEVER THOUGHT I'D MEET ANYONE LIKE HER.
YEAH... SOUNDS LIKE YOU'VE FALLEN IN LOVE ALL RIGHT.
JUST NOT WITH THE RIGHT ONE...

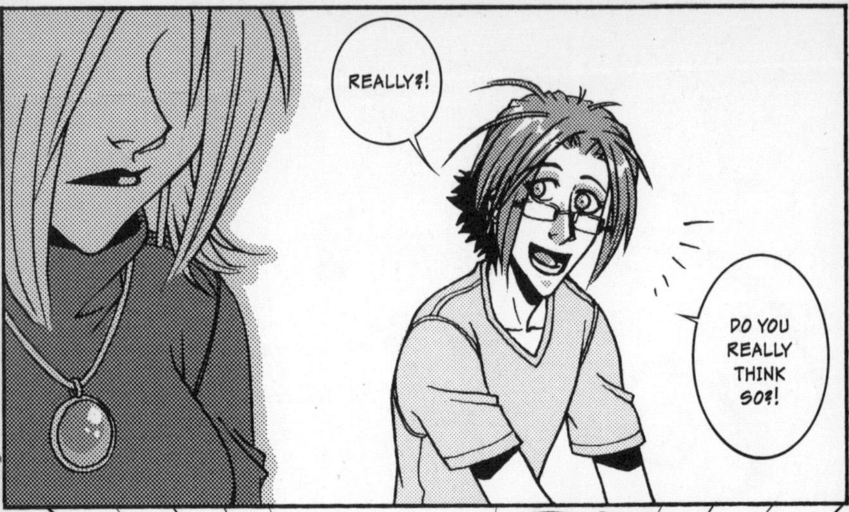
REALLY?!
DO YOU REALLY THINK SO?!

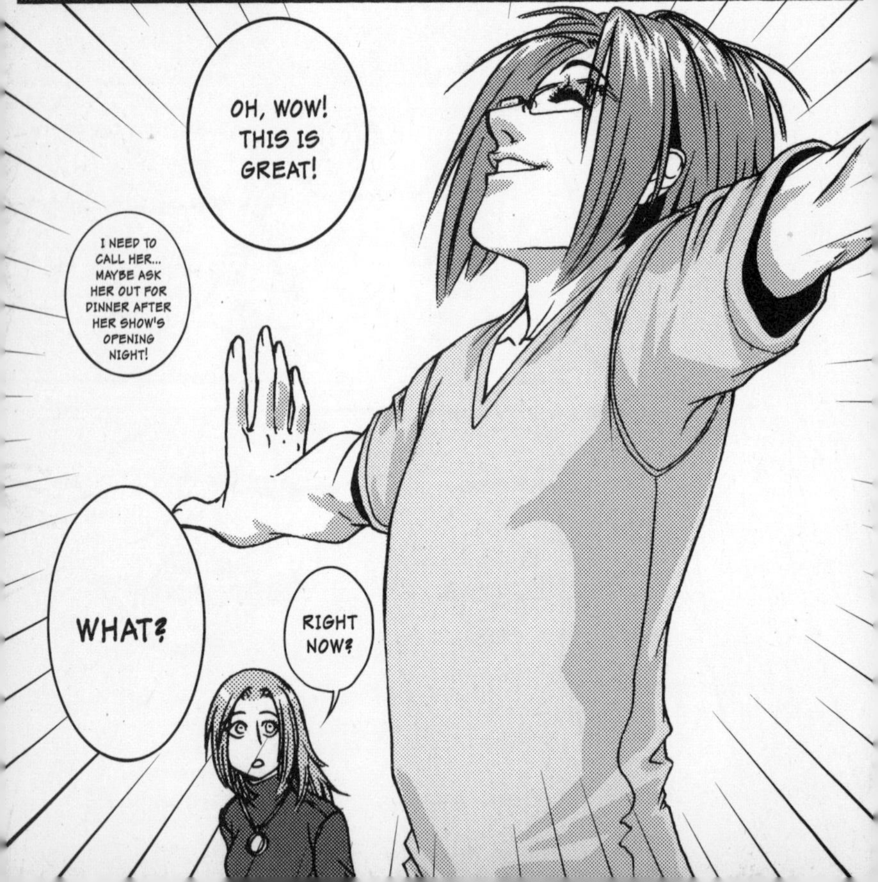
OH, WOW! THIS IS GREAT!
I NEED TO CALL HER... MAYBE ASK HER OUT FOR DINNER AFTER HER SHOW'S OPENING NIGHT!
WHAT?
RIGHT NOW?

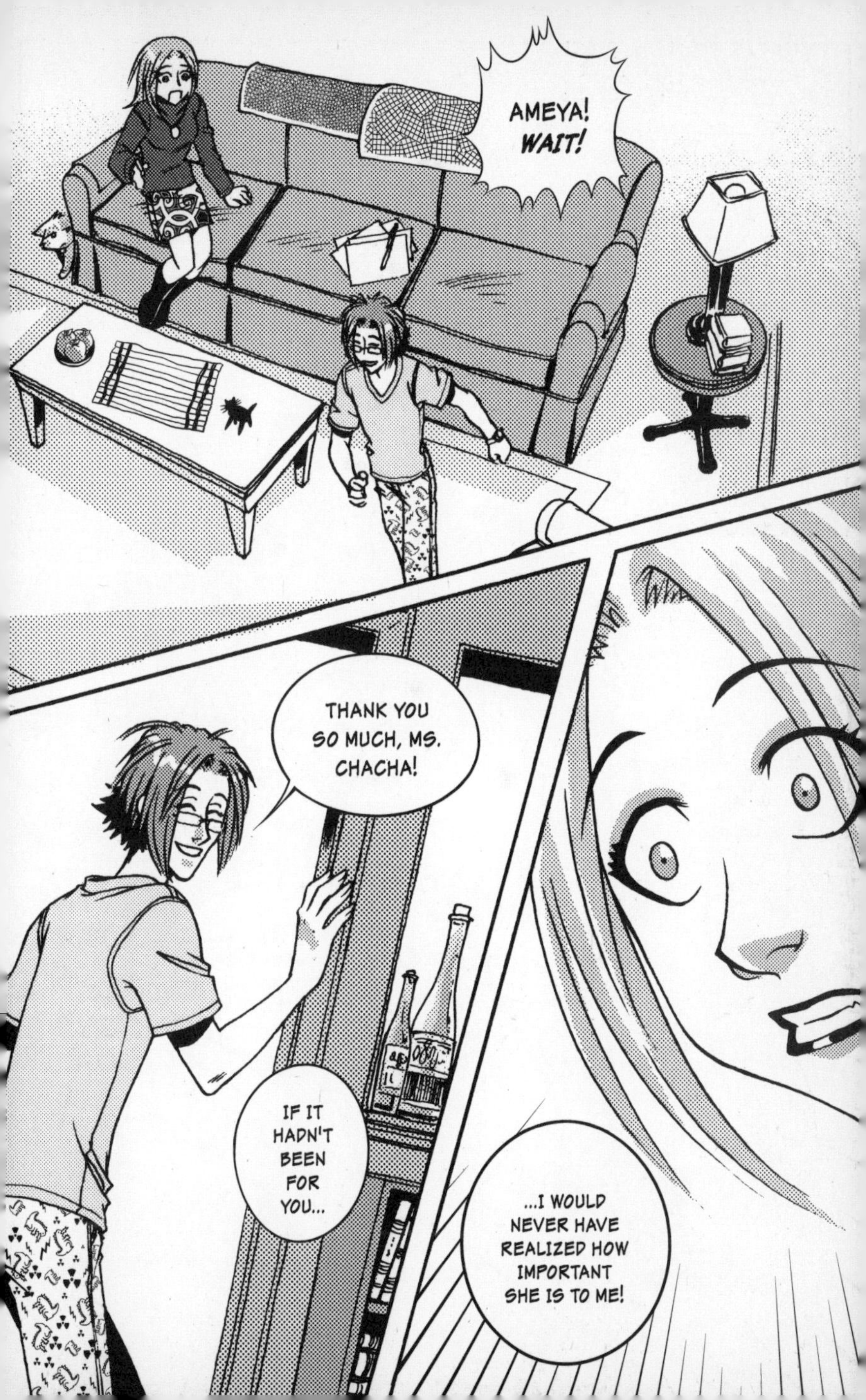
AMEYA! WAIT!
THANK YOU SO MUCH, MS. CHACHA!
IF IT HADN'T BEEN FOR YOU...
...I WOULD NEVER HAVE REALIZED HOW IMPORTANT SHE IS TO ME!

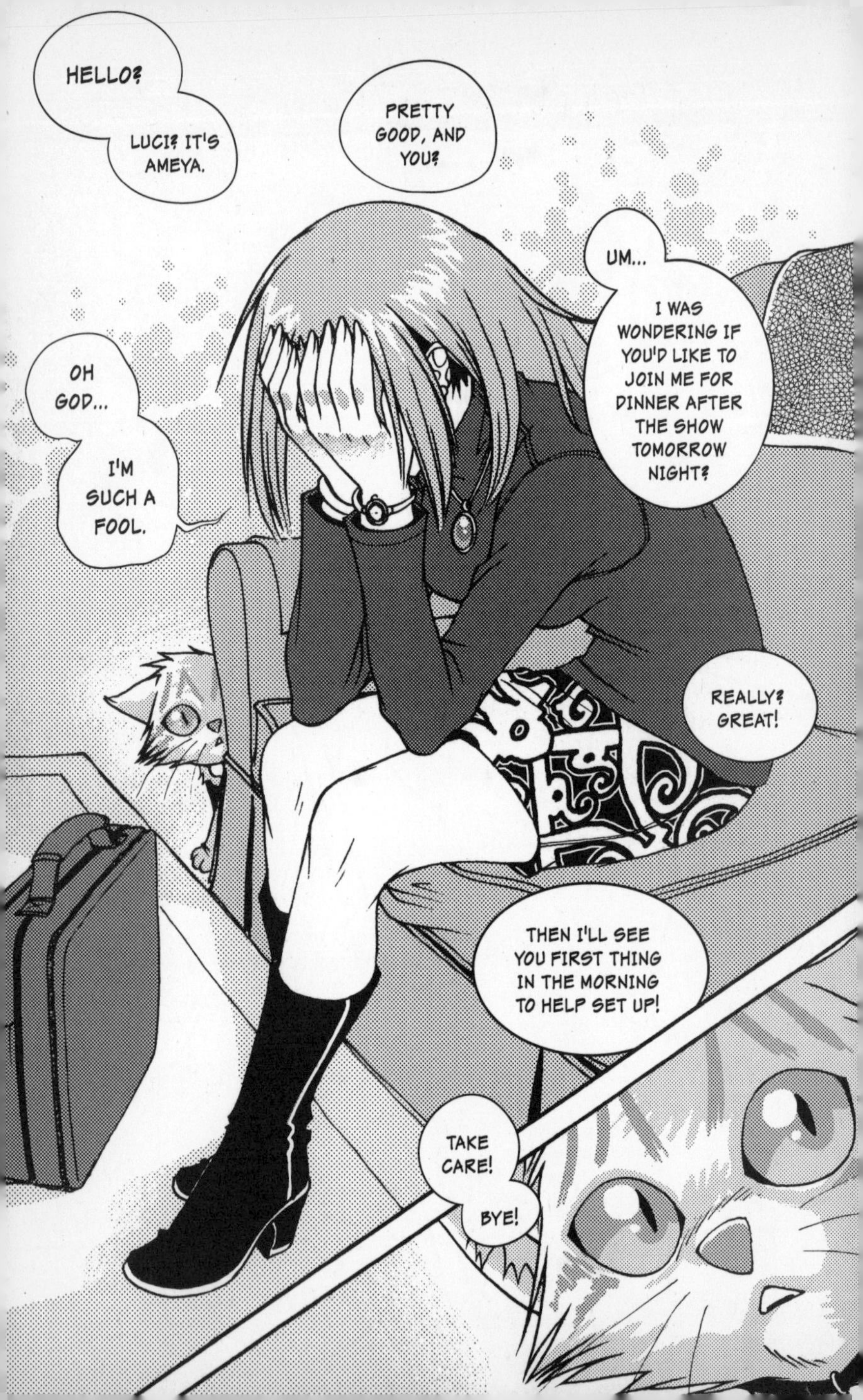
HELLO?
LUCI? IT'S AMEYA.
PRETTY GOOD, AND YOU?
UM...
I WAS WONDERING IF YOU'D LIKE TO JOIN ME FOR DINNER AFTER THE SHOW TOMORROW NIGHT?
OH GOD...
I'M SUCH A FOOL.
REALLY? GREAT!
THEN I'LL SEE YOU FIRST THING IN THE MORNING TO HELP SET UP!
TAKE CARE!
BYE!

CHAPTER 5

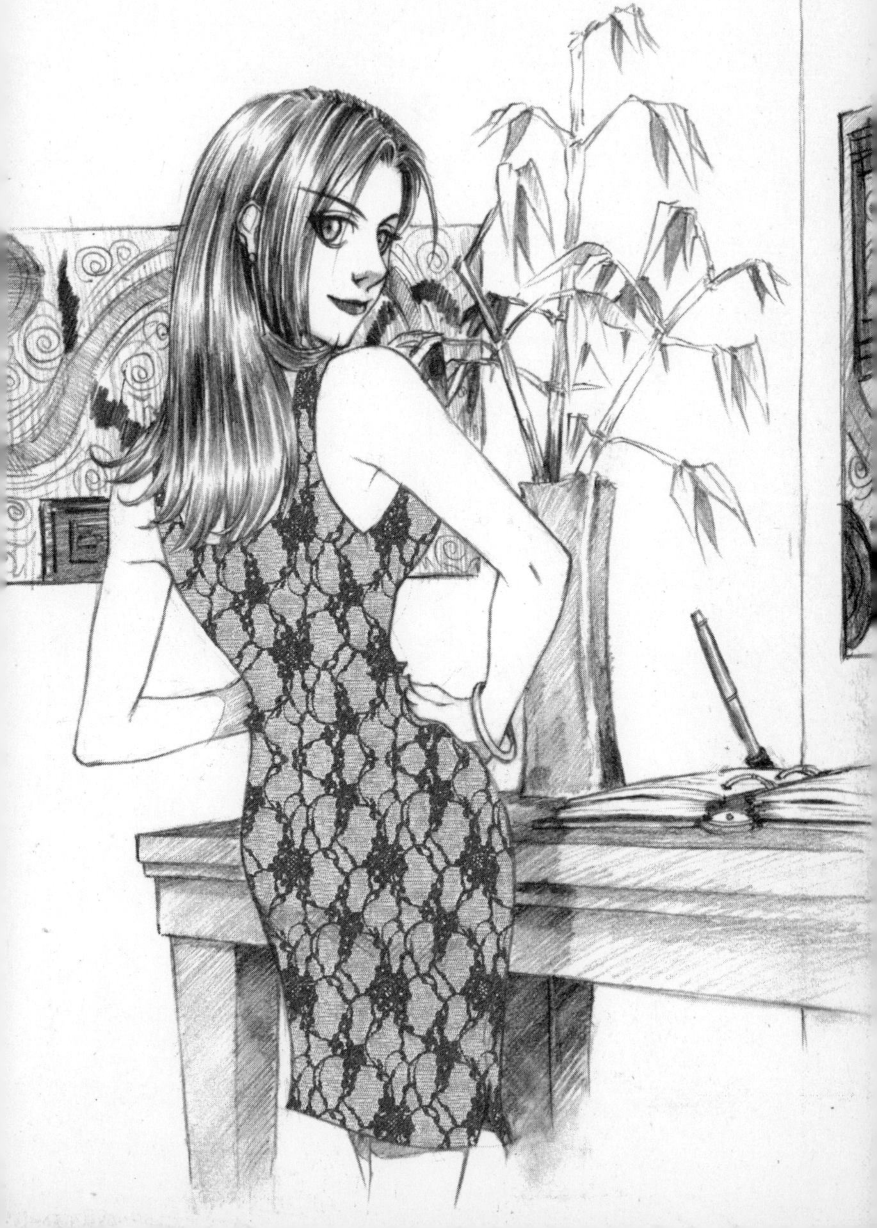

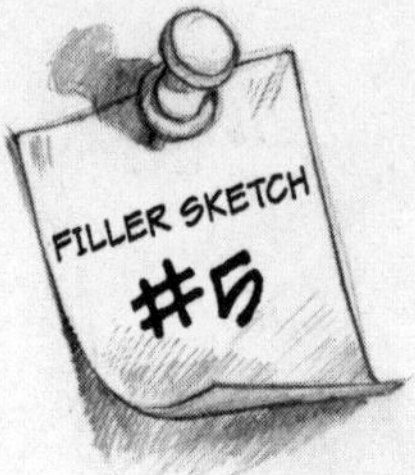
FILLER SKETCH
#5

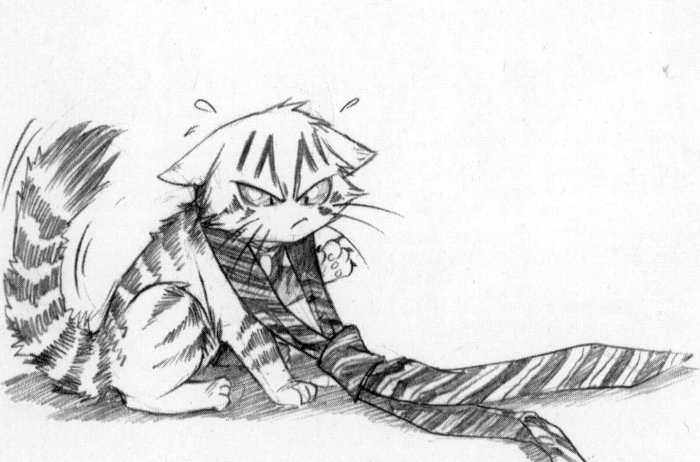

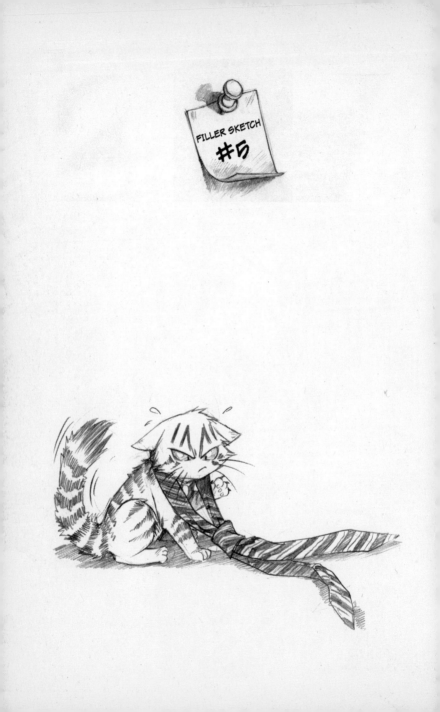

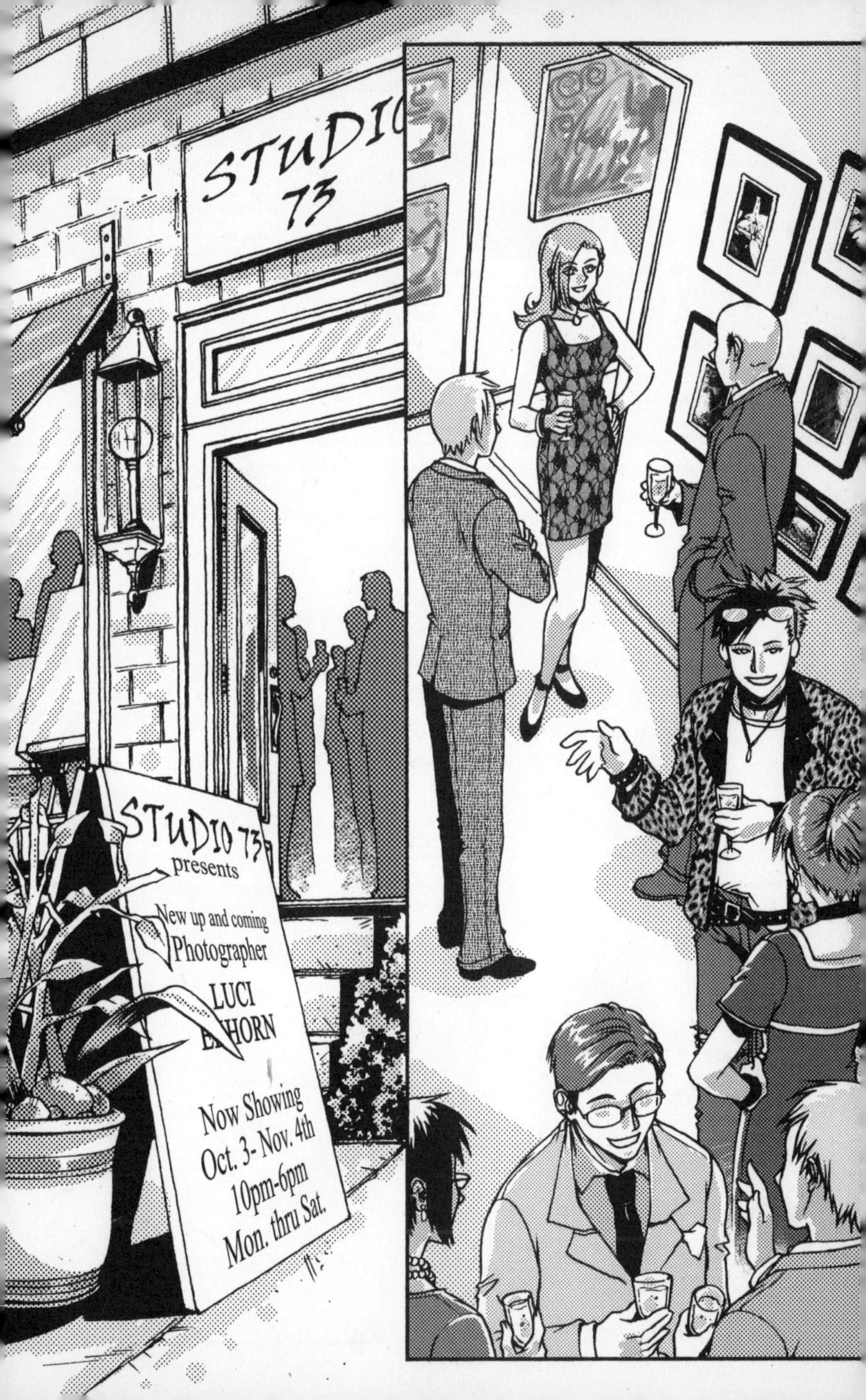
STUDIO 73
STUDIO 73
presents
New up and coming
Photographer
LUCI
Now Showing
Oct. 3- Nov. 4th
10pm-6pm
Mon. thru Sat.

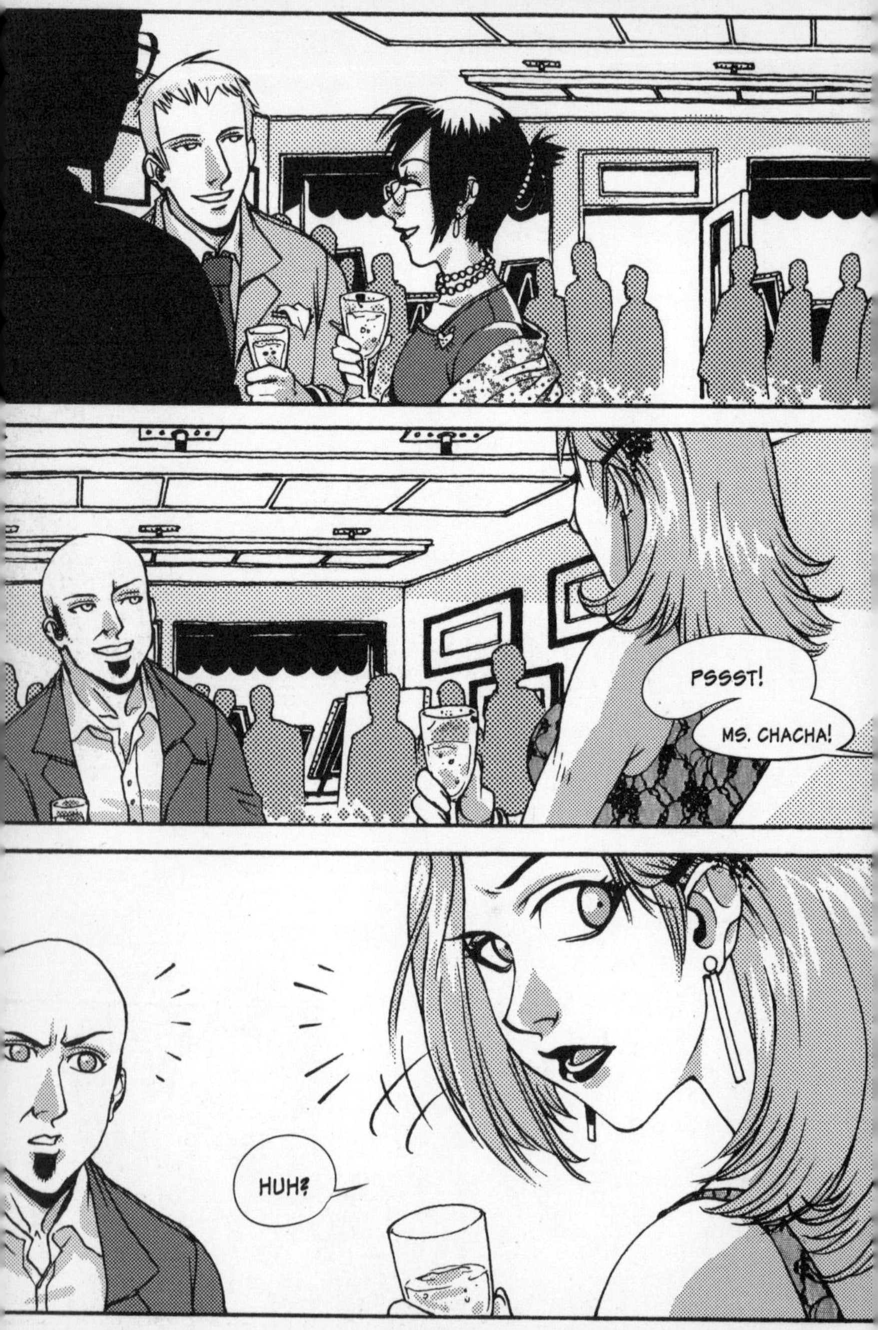
PSSST!
MS. CHACHA!
HUH?

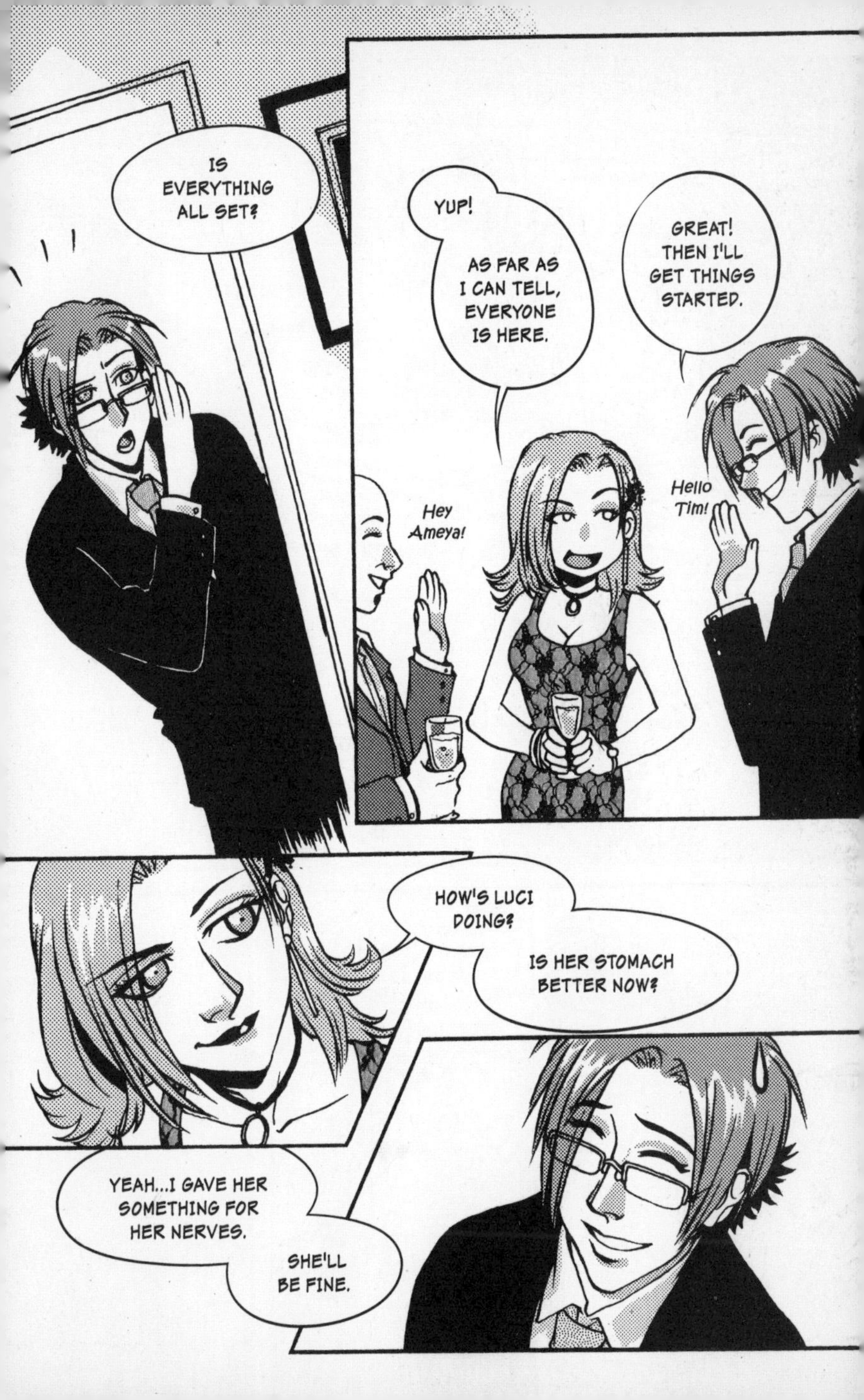
IS EVERYTHING ALL SET?
YUP!
AS FAR AS I CAN TELL, EVERYONE IS HERE.
GREAT! THEN I'LL GET THINGS STARTED.
Hey Ameya!
Hello Tim!
HOW'S LUCI DOING?
IS HER STOMACH BETTER NOW?
YEAH...I GAVE HER SOMETHING FOR HER NERVES.
SHE'LL BE FINE.

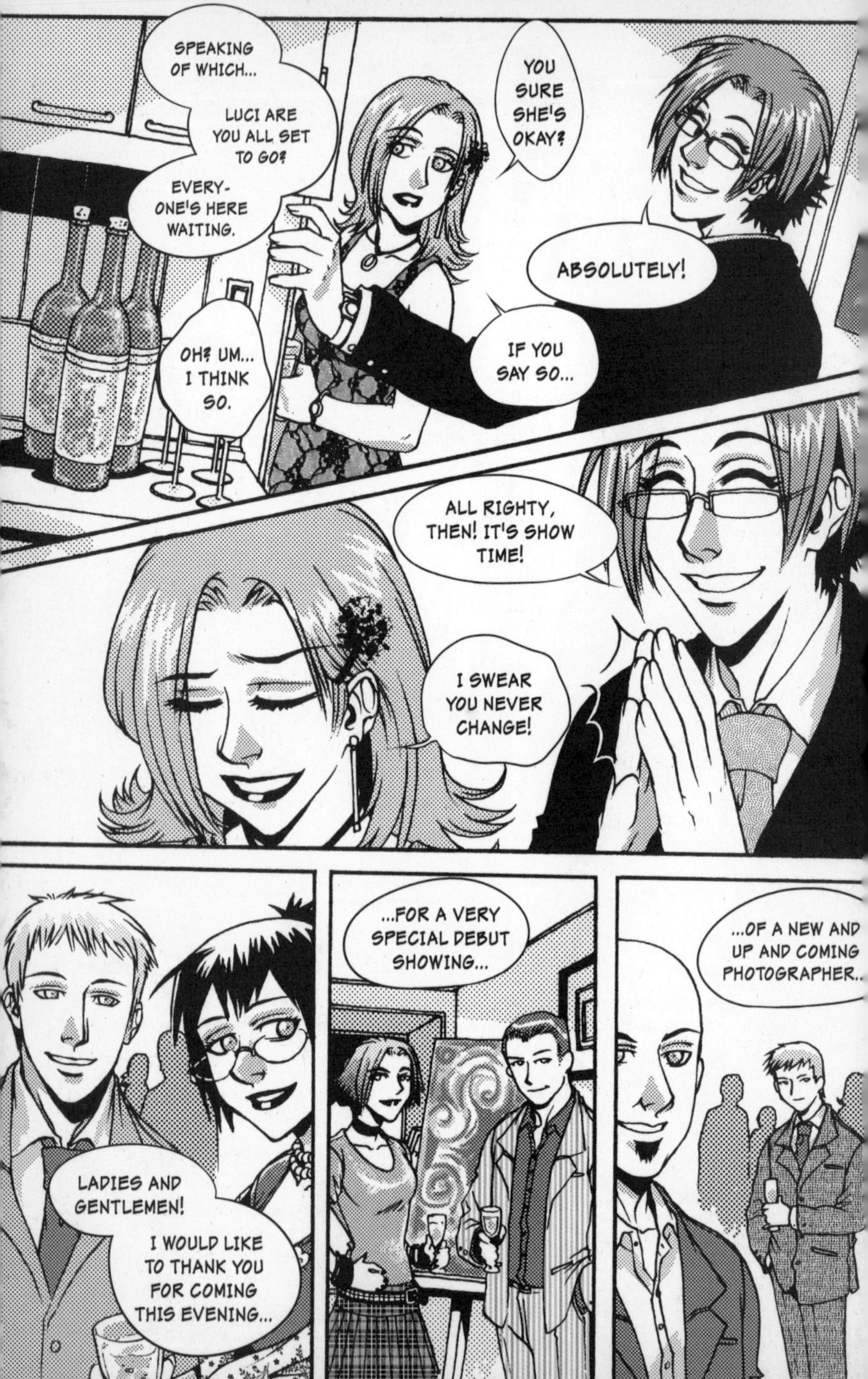
SPEAKING OF WHICH...
LUCI ARE YOU ALL SET TO GO?
EVERY-ONE'S HERE WAITING.
OH? UM... I THINK SO.
YOU SURE SHE'S OKAY?
ABSOLUTELY!
IF YOU SAY SO...
ALL RIGHTY, THEN! IT'S SHOW TIME!
I SWEAR YOU NEVER CHANGE!
LADIES AND GENTLEMEN!
I WOULD LIKE TO THANK YOU FOR COMING THIS EVENING...
...FOR A VERY SPECIAL DEBUT SHOWING...
...OF A NEW AND UP AND COMING PHOTOGRAPHER...

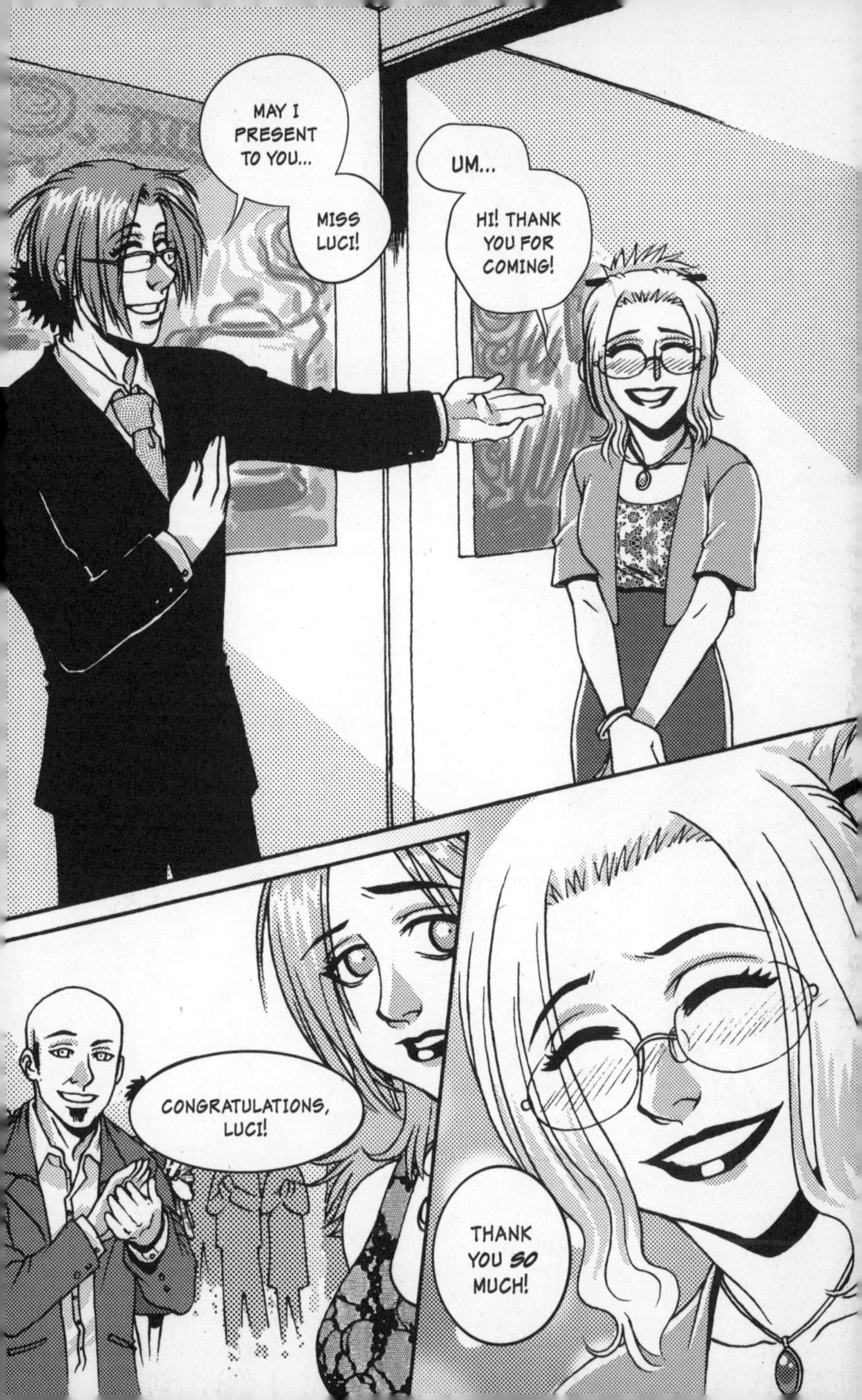
MAY I PRESENT TO YOU...
MISS LUCI!
UM...
HI! THANK YOU FOR COMING!
CONGRATULATIONS, LUCI!
THANK YOU *SO* MUCH!

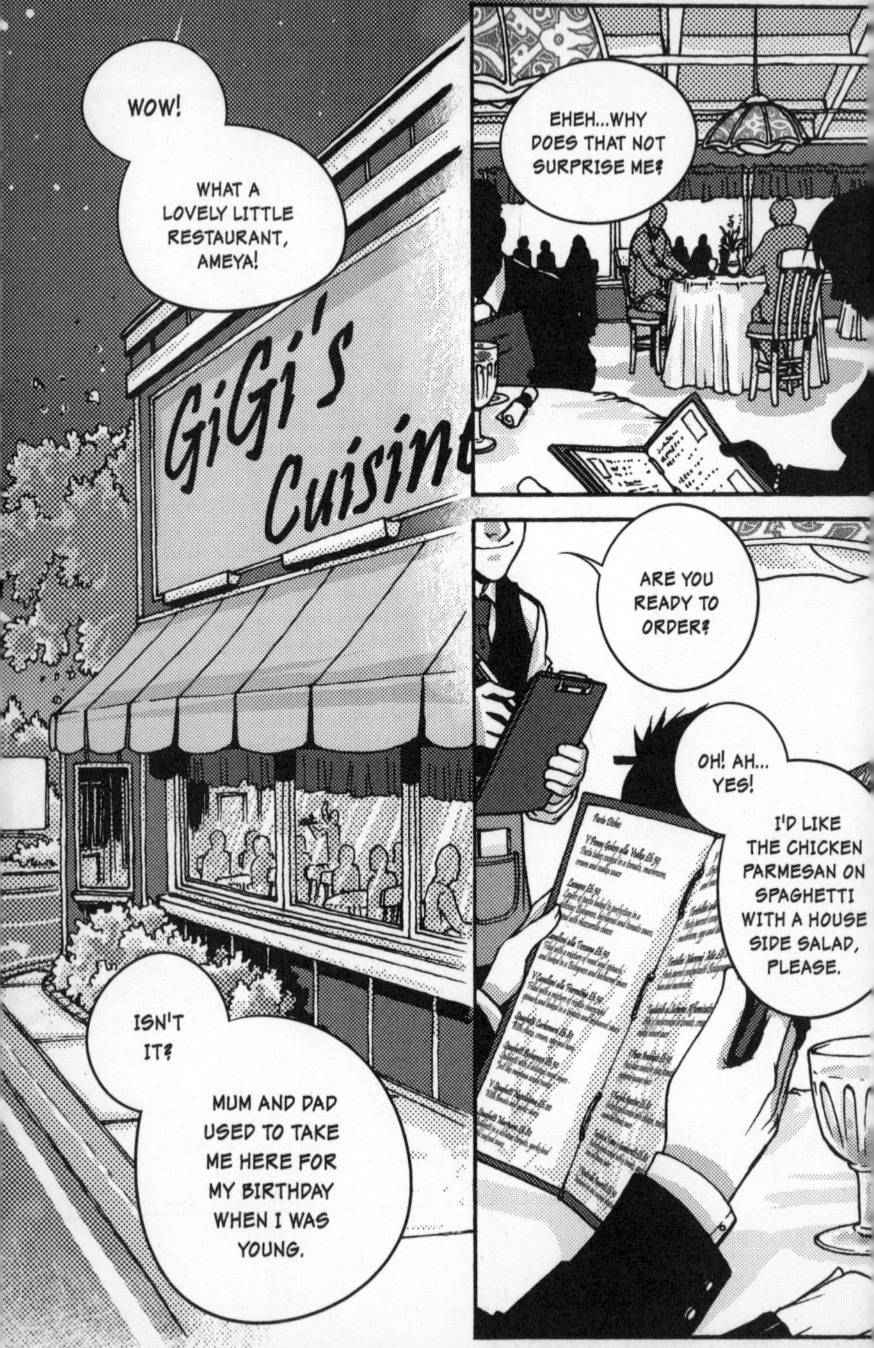
WOW!
WHAT A LOVELY LITTLE RESTAURANT, AMEYA!
GiGi's Cuisin
ISN'T IT?
MUM AND DAD USED TO TAKE ME HERE FOR MY BIRTHDAY WHEN I WAS YOUNG.
EHEH...WHY DOES THAT NOT SURPRISE ME?
ARE YOU READY TO ORDER?
OH! AH... YES!
I'D LIKE THE CHICKEN PARMESAN ON SPAGHETTI WITH A HOUSE SIDE SALAD, PLEASE.

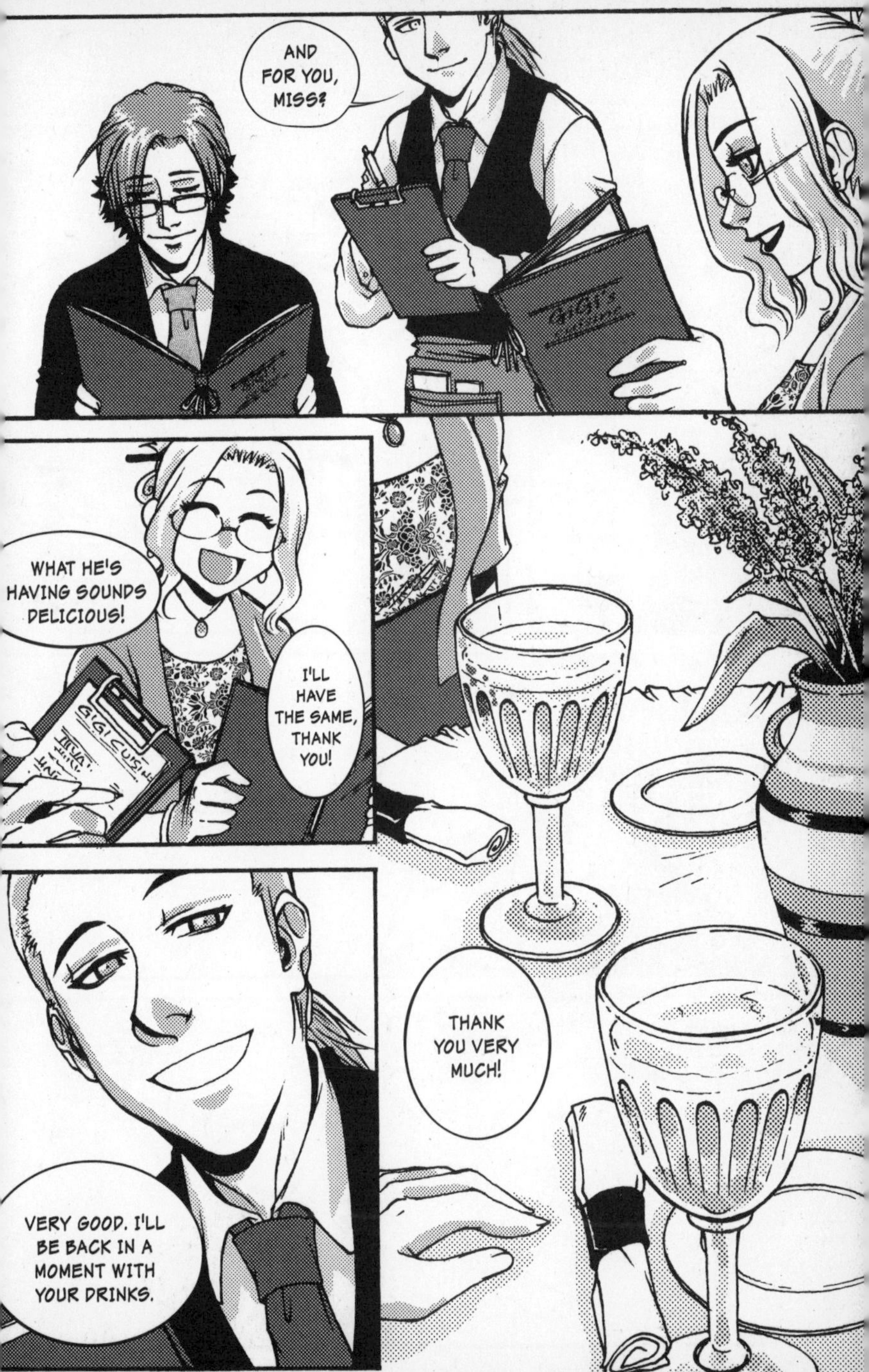

AND FOR YOU, MISS?
WHAT HE'S HAVING SOUNDS DELICIOUS!
I'LL HAVE THE SAME, THANK YOU!
THANK YOU VERY MUCH!
VERY GOOD. I'LL BE BACK IN A MOMENT WITH YOUR DRINKS.

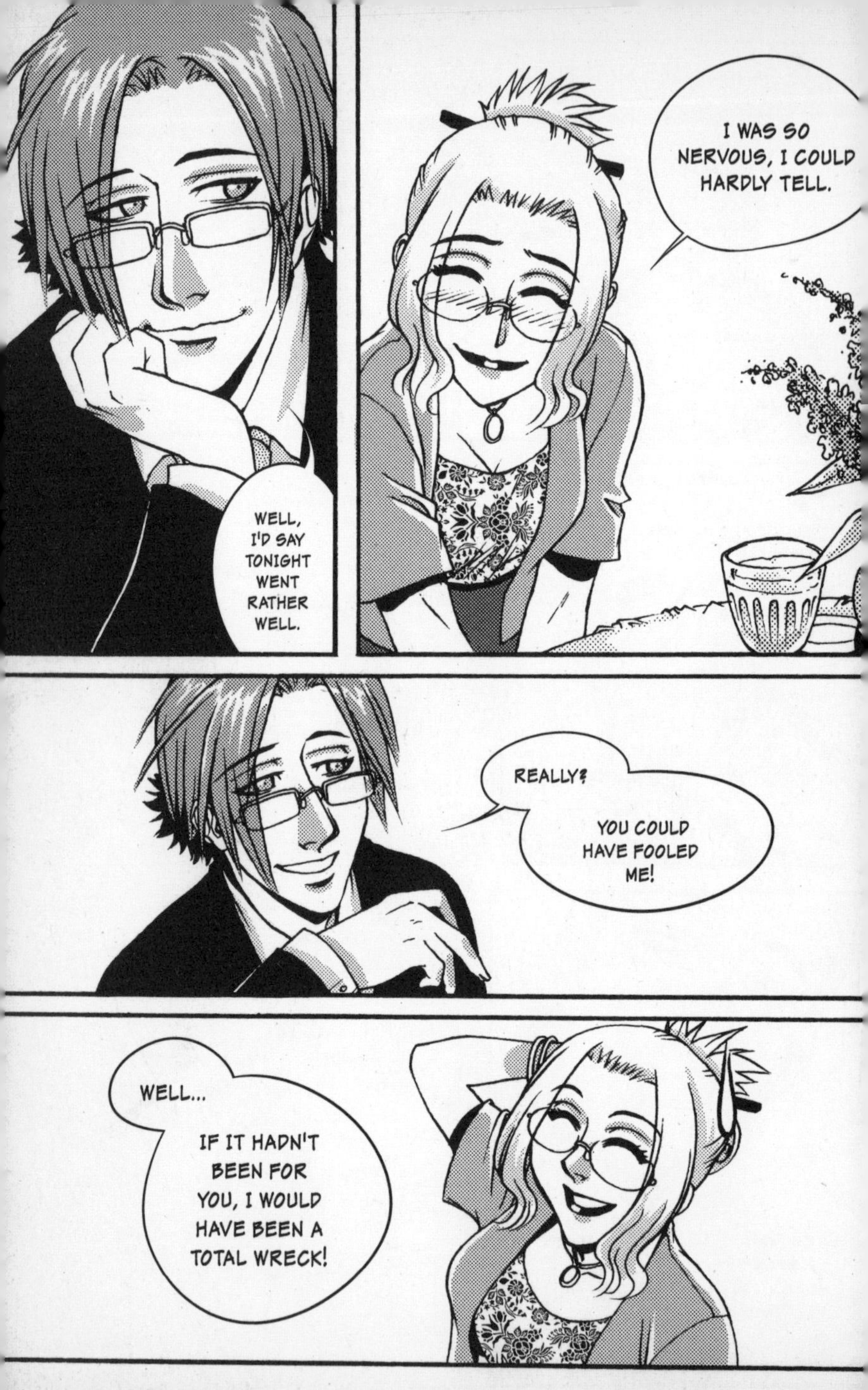
WELL, I'D SAY TONIGHT WENT RATHER WELL.
I WAS SO NERVOUS, I COULD HARDLY TELL.
REALLY?
YOU COULD HAVE FOOLED ME!
WELL...
IF IT HADN'T BEEN FOR YOU, I WOULD HAVE BEEN A TOTAL WRECK!

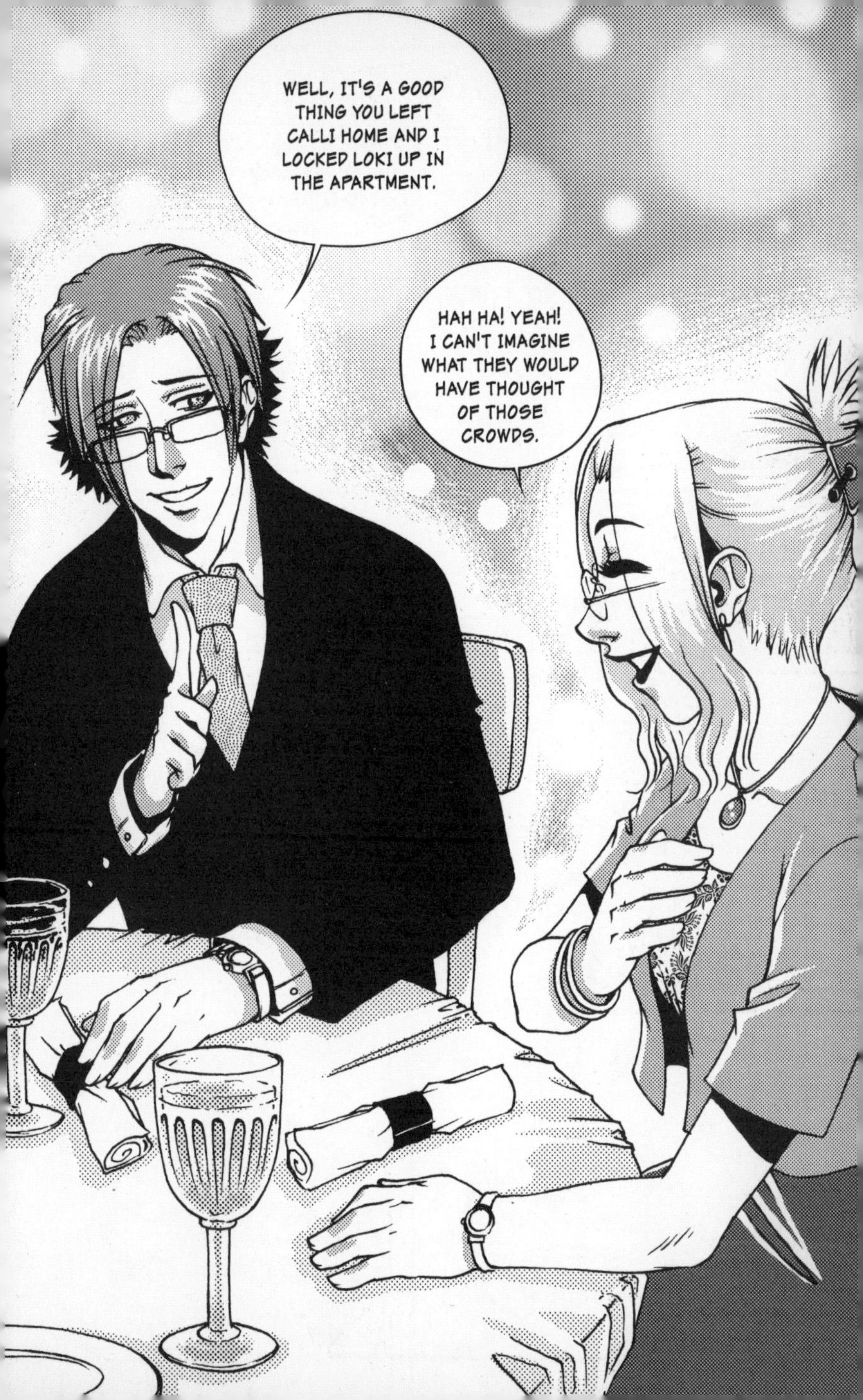
WELL, IT'S A GOOD THING YOU LEFT CALLI HOME AND I LOCKED LOKI UP IN THE APARTMENT.
HAH HA! YEAH! I CAN'T IMAGINE WHAT THEY WOULD HAVE THOUGHT OF THOSE CROWDS.

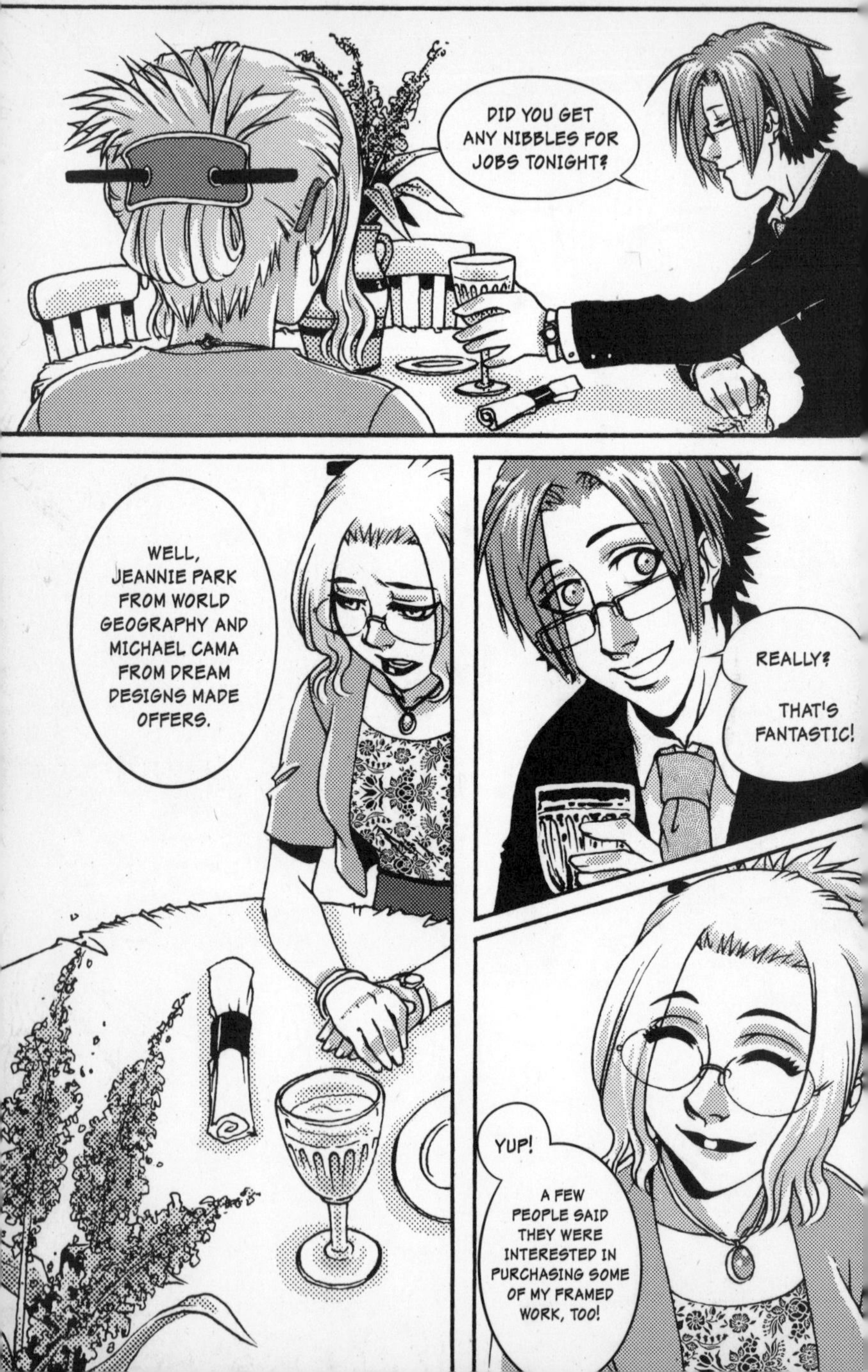
DID YOU GET ANY NIBBLES FOR JOBS TONIGHT?
WELL, JEANNIE PARK FROM WORLD GEOGRAPHY AND MICHAEL CAMA FROM DREAM DESIGNS MADE OFFERS.
REALLY?
THAT'S FANTASTIC!
YUP!
A FEW PEOPLE SAID THEY WERE INTERESTED IN PURCHASING SOME OF MY FRAMED WORK, TOO!

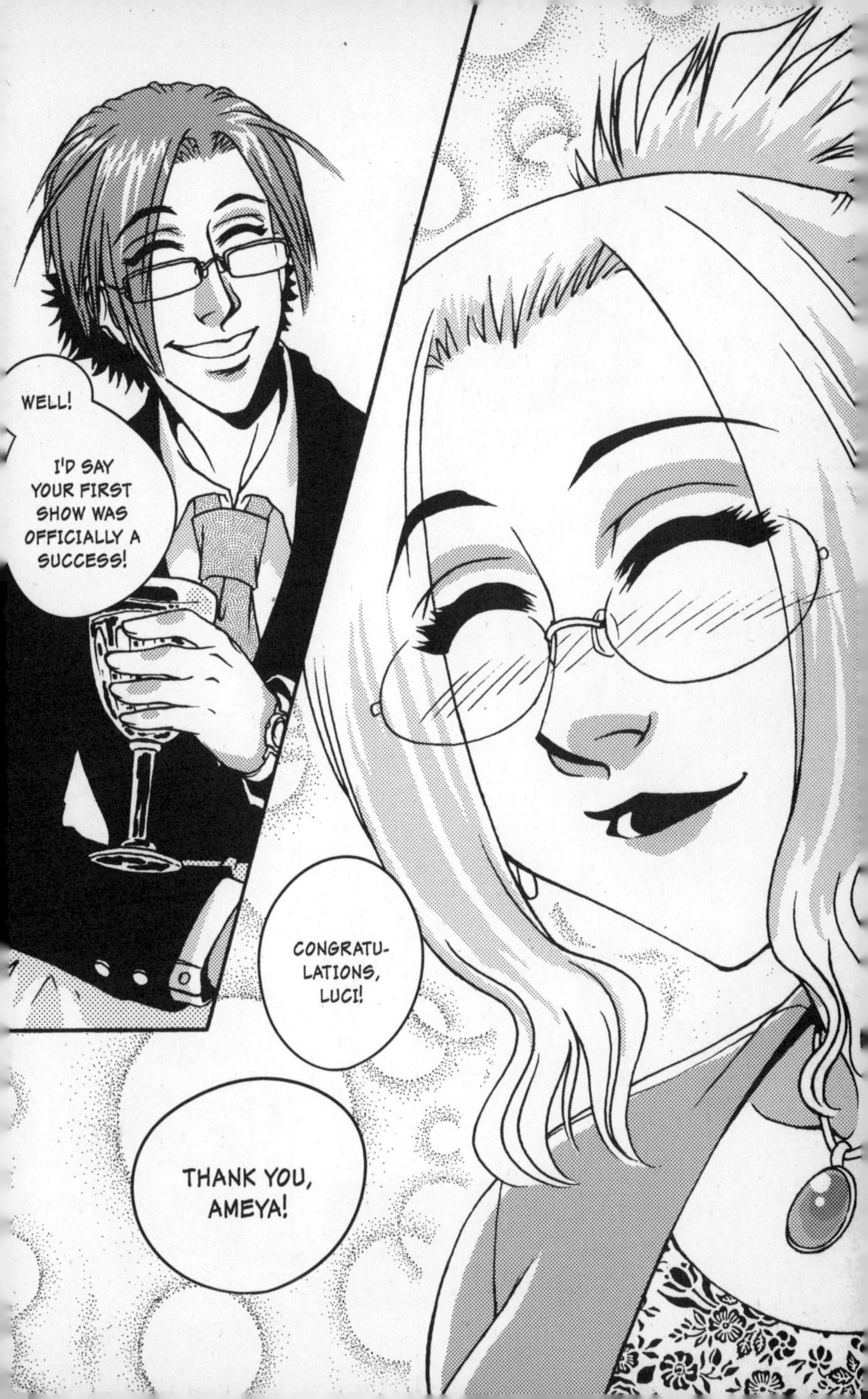
WELL!
I'D SAY YOUR FIRST SHOW WAS OFFICIALLY A SUCCESS!
CONGRATU-LATIONS, LUCI!
THANK YOU, AMEYA!

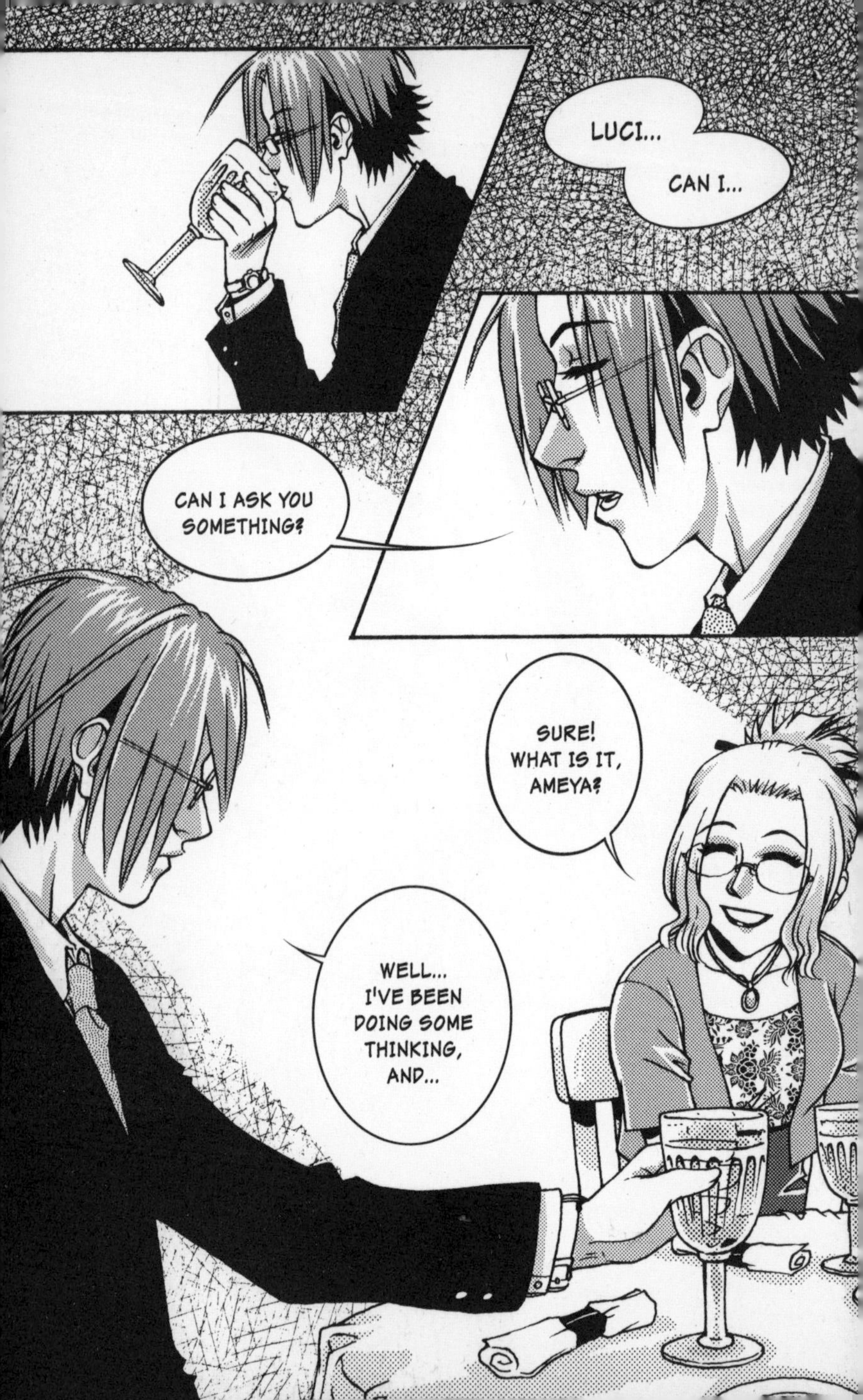
LUCI...
CAN I...
CAN I ASK YOU SOMETHING?
SURE! WHAT IS IT, AMEYA?
WELL... I'VE BEEN DOING SOME THINKING, AND...

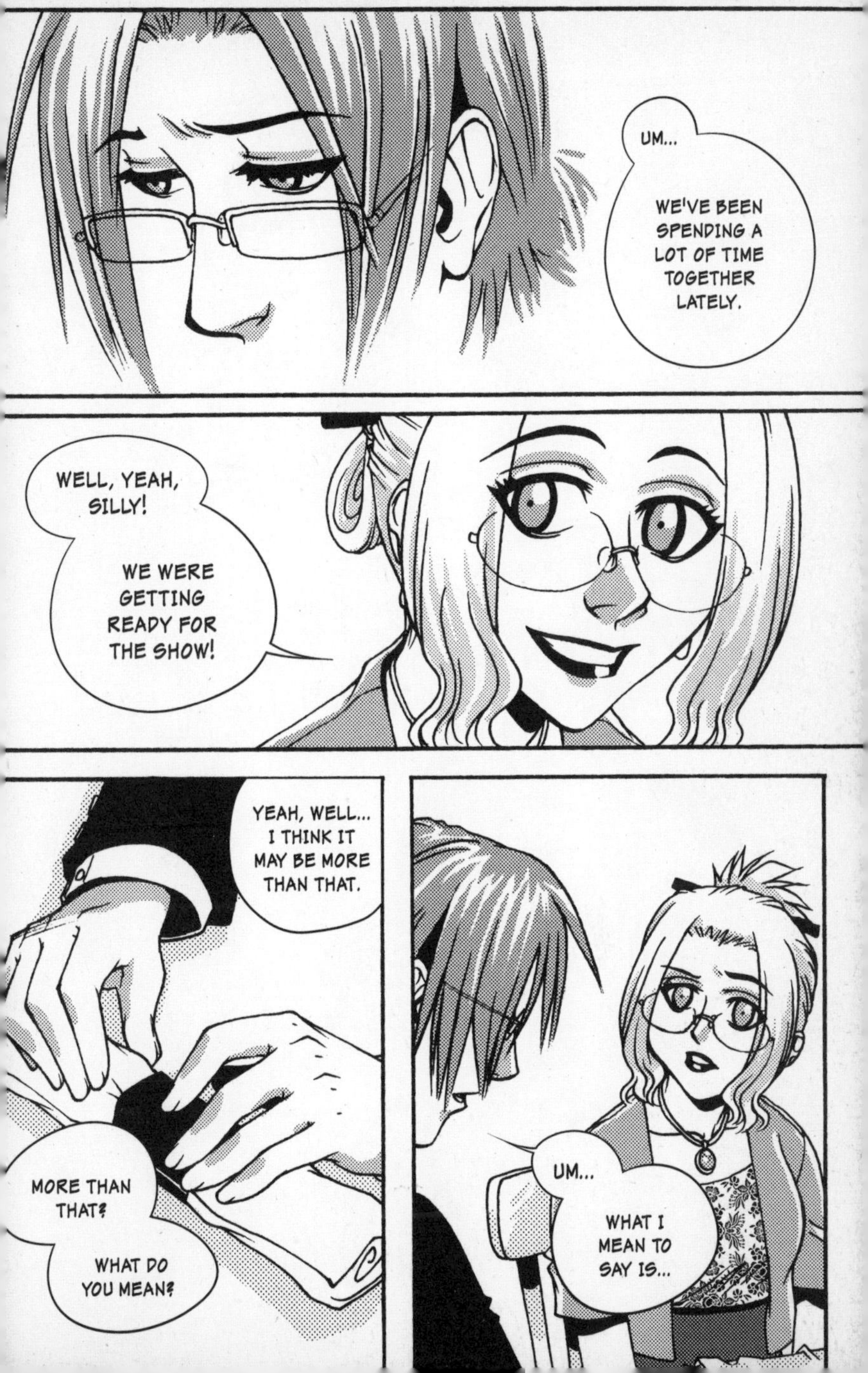
UM...
WE'VE BEEN SPENDING A LOT OF TIME TOGETHER LATELY.
WELL, YEAH, SILLY!
WE WERE GETTING READY FOR THE SHOW!
YEAH, WELL... I THINK IT MAY BE MORE THAN THAT.
MORE THAN THAT?
WHAT DO YOU MEAN?
UM...
WHAT I MEAN TO SAY IS...

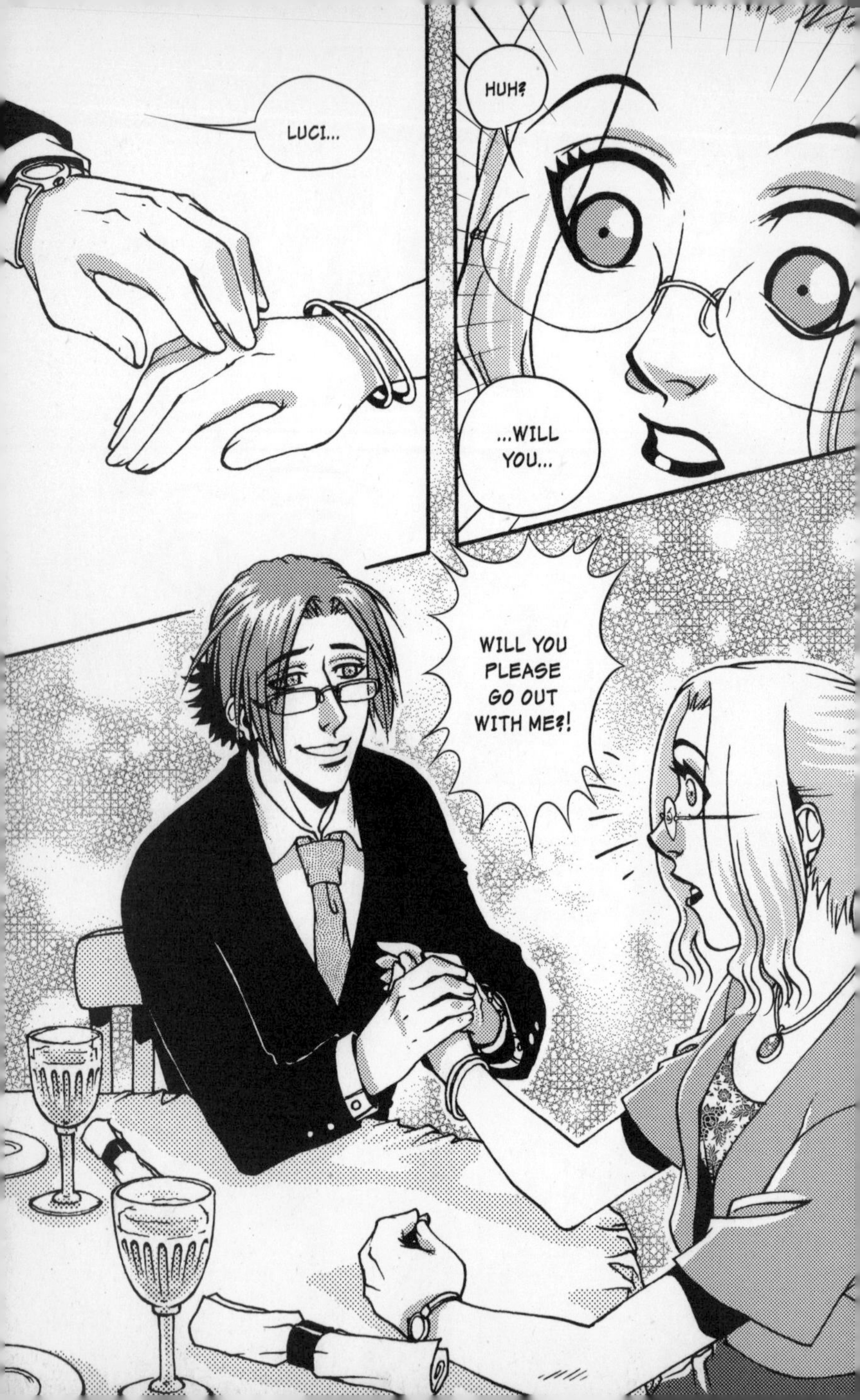
LUCI...
HUH?
...WILL YOU...
WILL YOU PLEASE GO OUT WITH ME?!

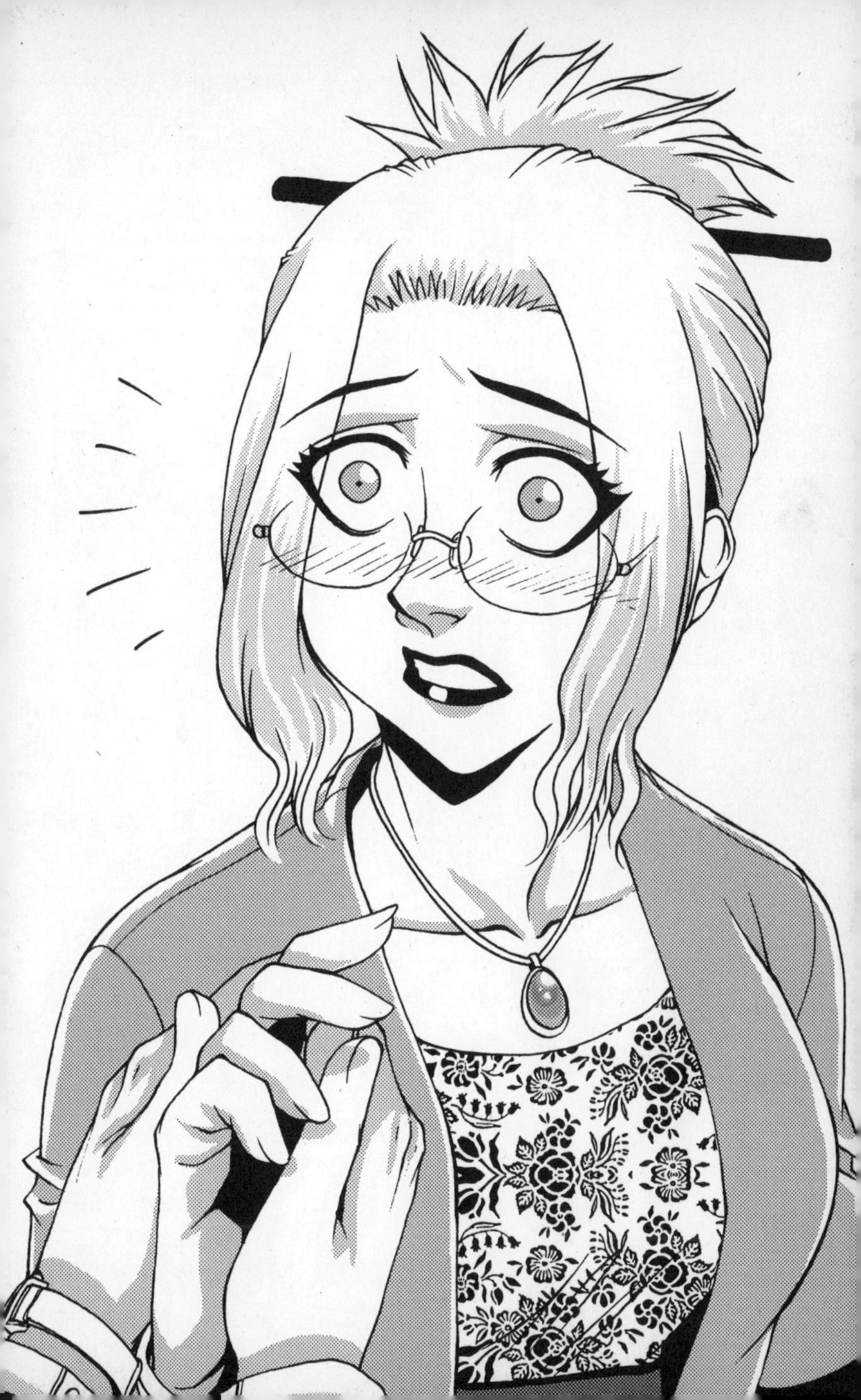

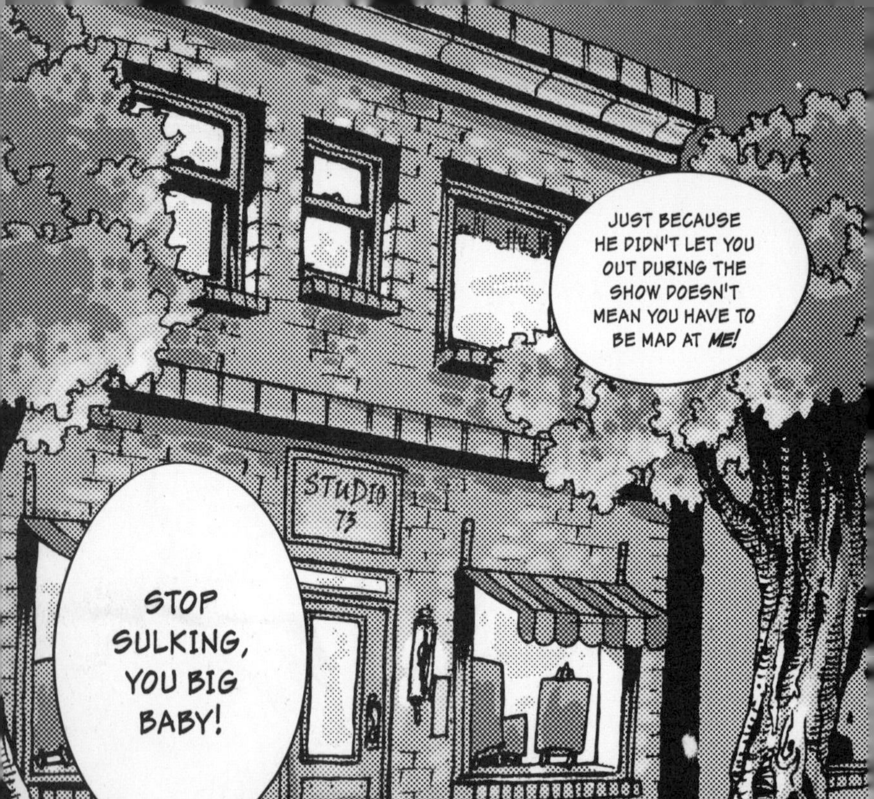
STUDIO 73
STOP SULKING, YOU BIG BABY!
JUST BECAUSE HE DIDN'T LET YOU OUT DURING THE SHOW DOESN'T MEAN YOU HAVE TO BE MAD AT *ME!*

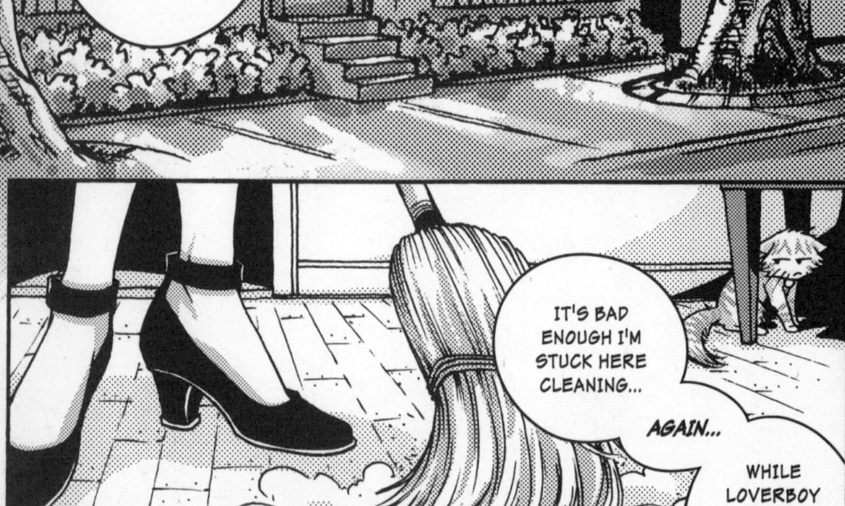
IT'S BAD ENOUGH I'M STUCK HERE CLEANING...
AGAIN...
WHILE LOVERBOY IS OUT ON HIS DATE!

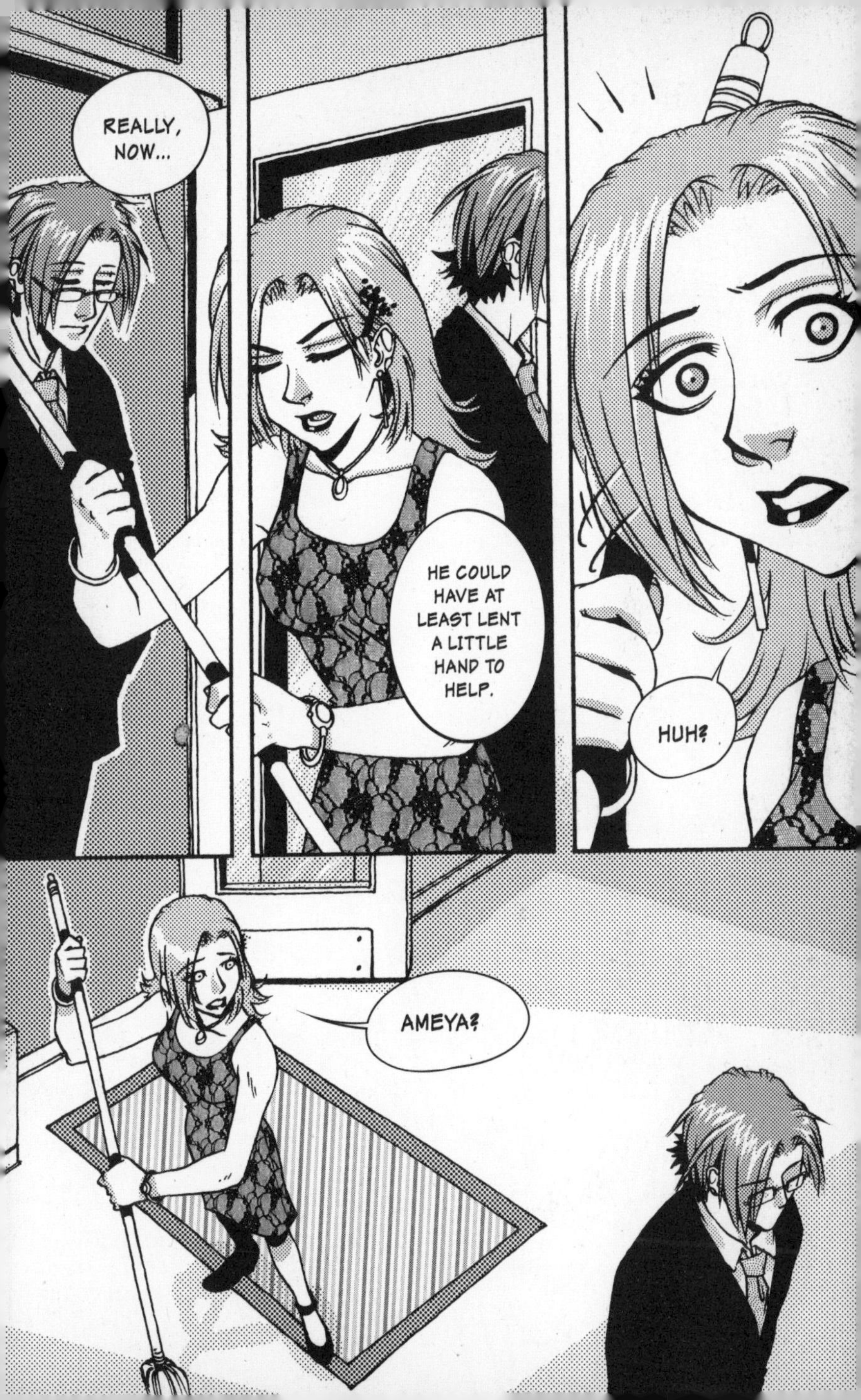
REALLY, NOW...
HE COULD HAVE AT LEAST LENT A LITTLE HAND TO HELP.
HUH?
AMEYA?

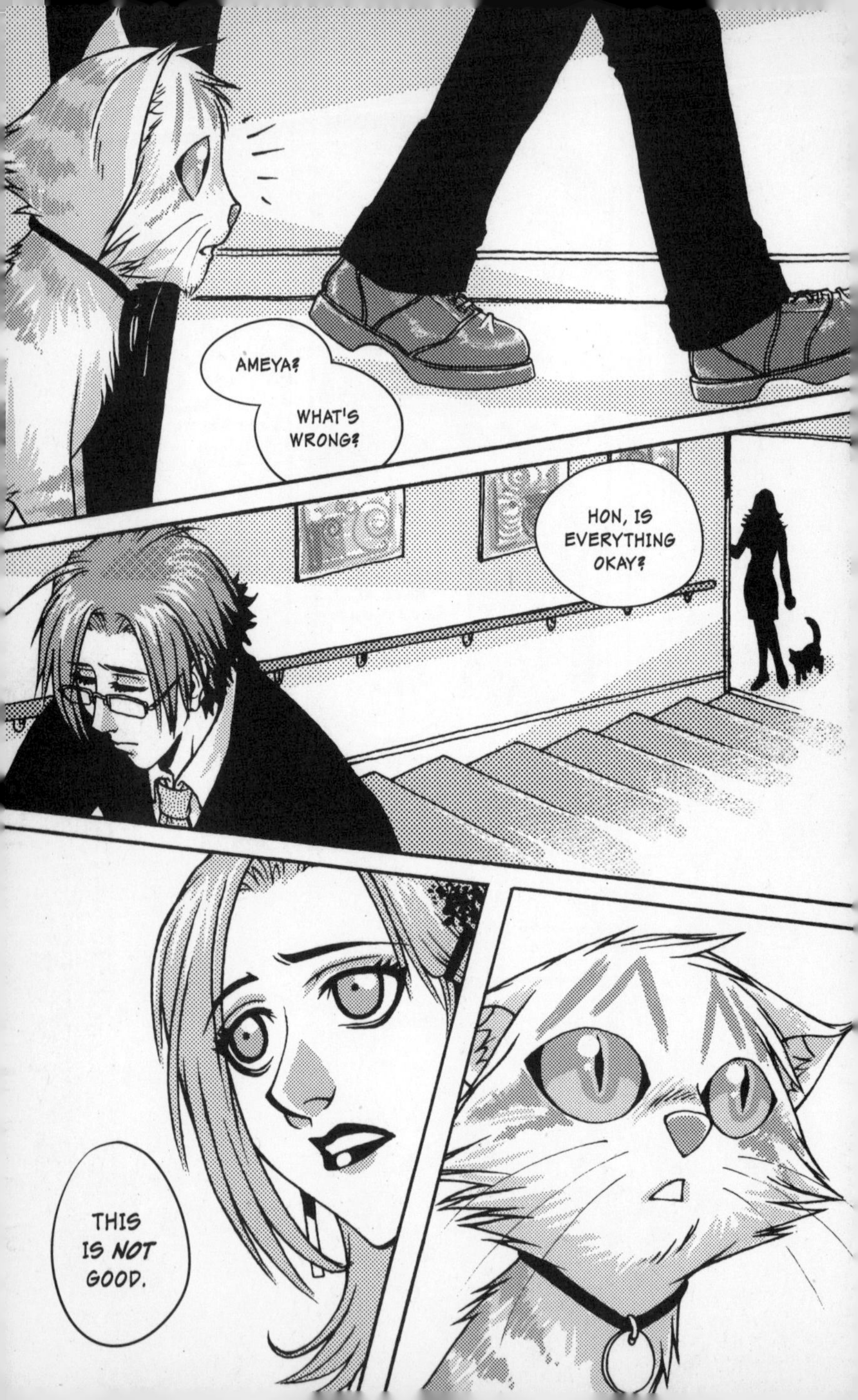
AMEYA? WHAT'S WRONG?
HON, IS EVERYTHING OKAY?
THIS IS *NOT* GOOD.

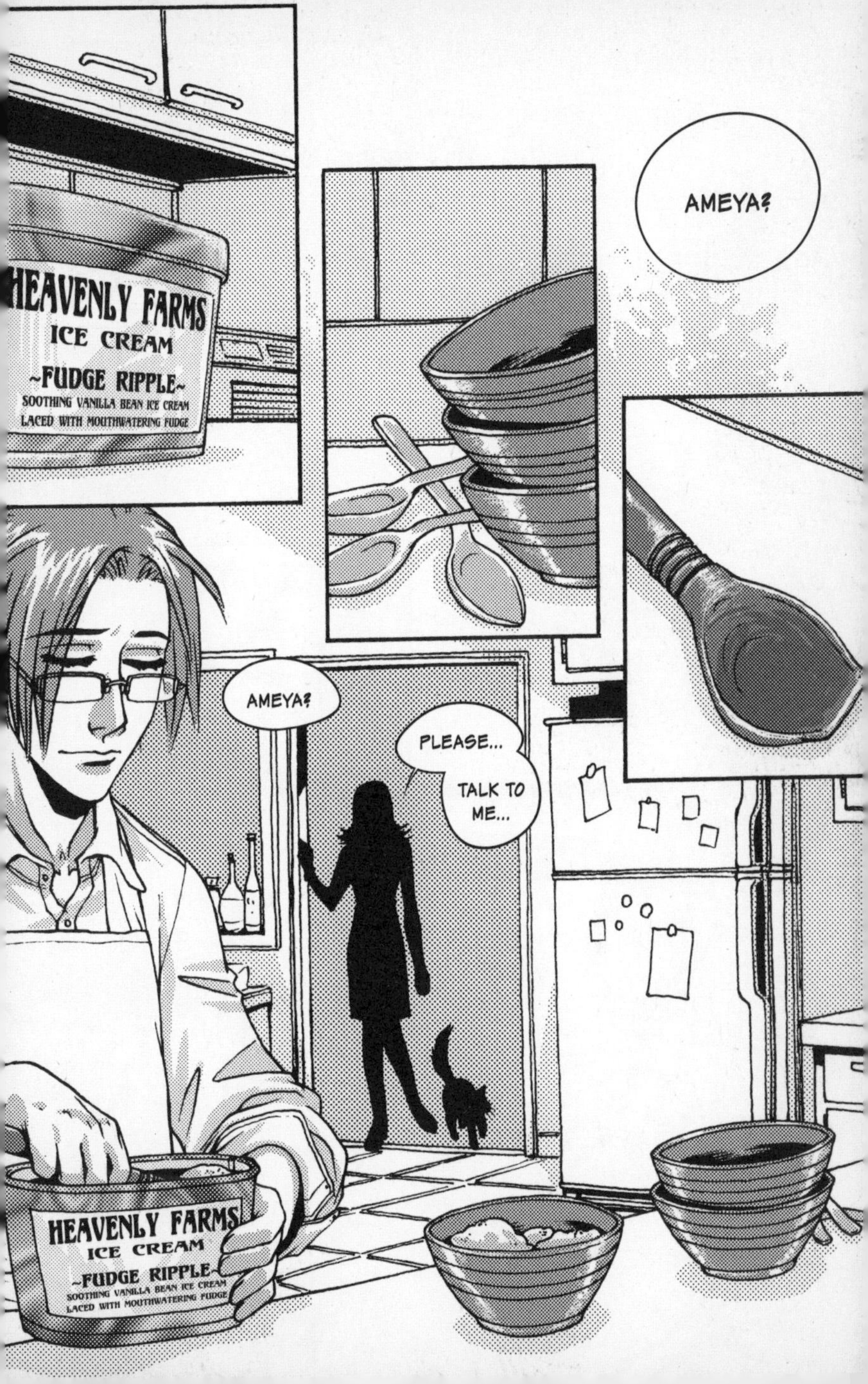
HEAVENLY FARMS
ICE CREAM
~FUDGE RIPPLE~
SOOTHING VANILLA BEAN ICE CREAM
LACED WITH MOUTHWATERING FUDGE
AMEYA?
AMEYA?
PLEASE...
TALK TO ME...
HEAVENLY FARMS
ICE CREAM
~FUDGE RIPPLE~
SOOTHING VANILLA BEAN ICE CREAM
LACED WITH MOUTHWATERING FUDGE

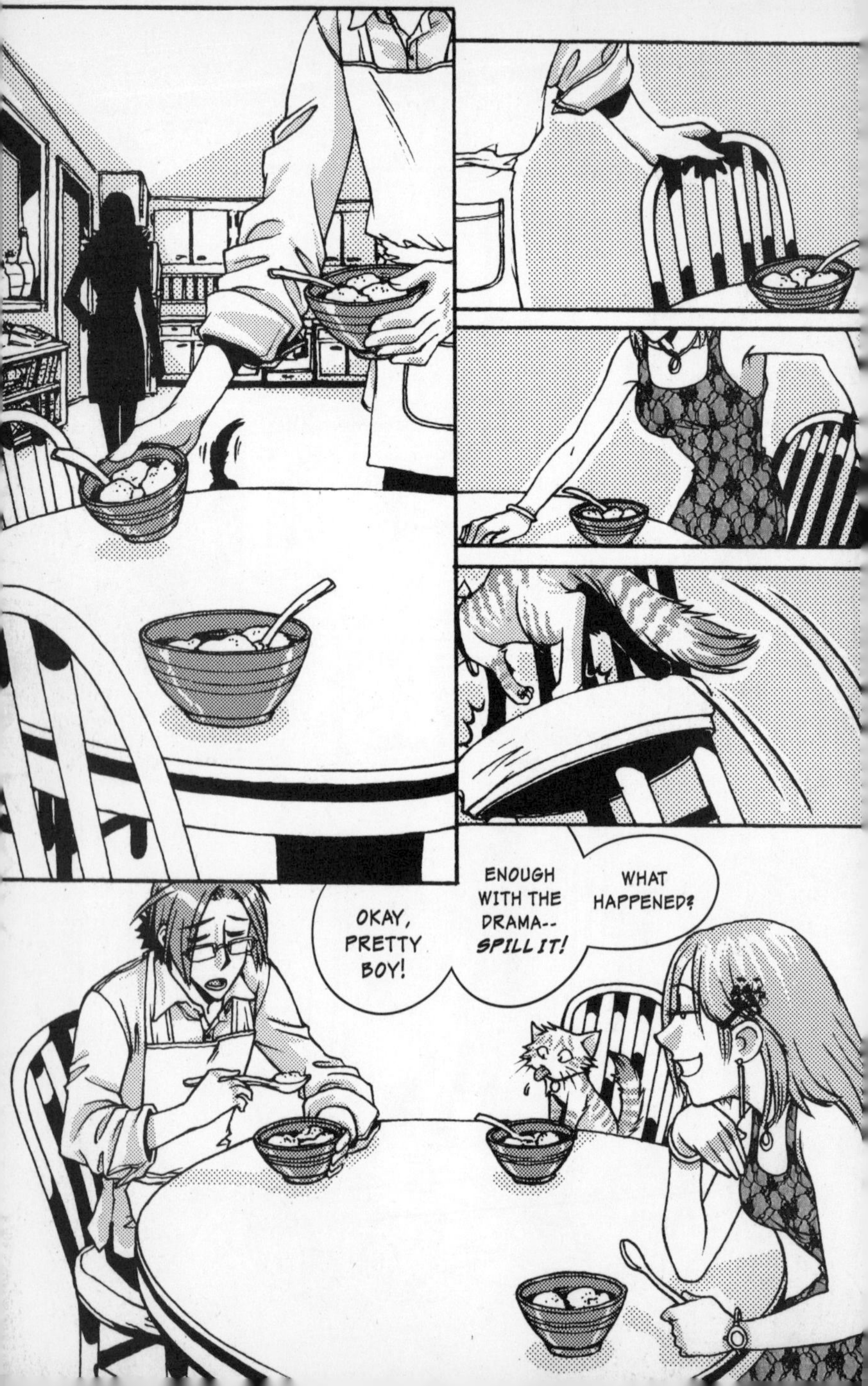
OKAY, PRETTY BOY!
ENOUGH WITH THE DRAMA-- SPILL IT!
WHAT HAPPENED?

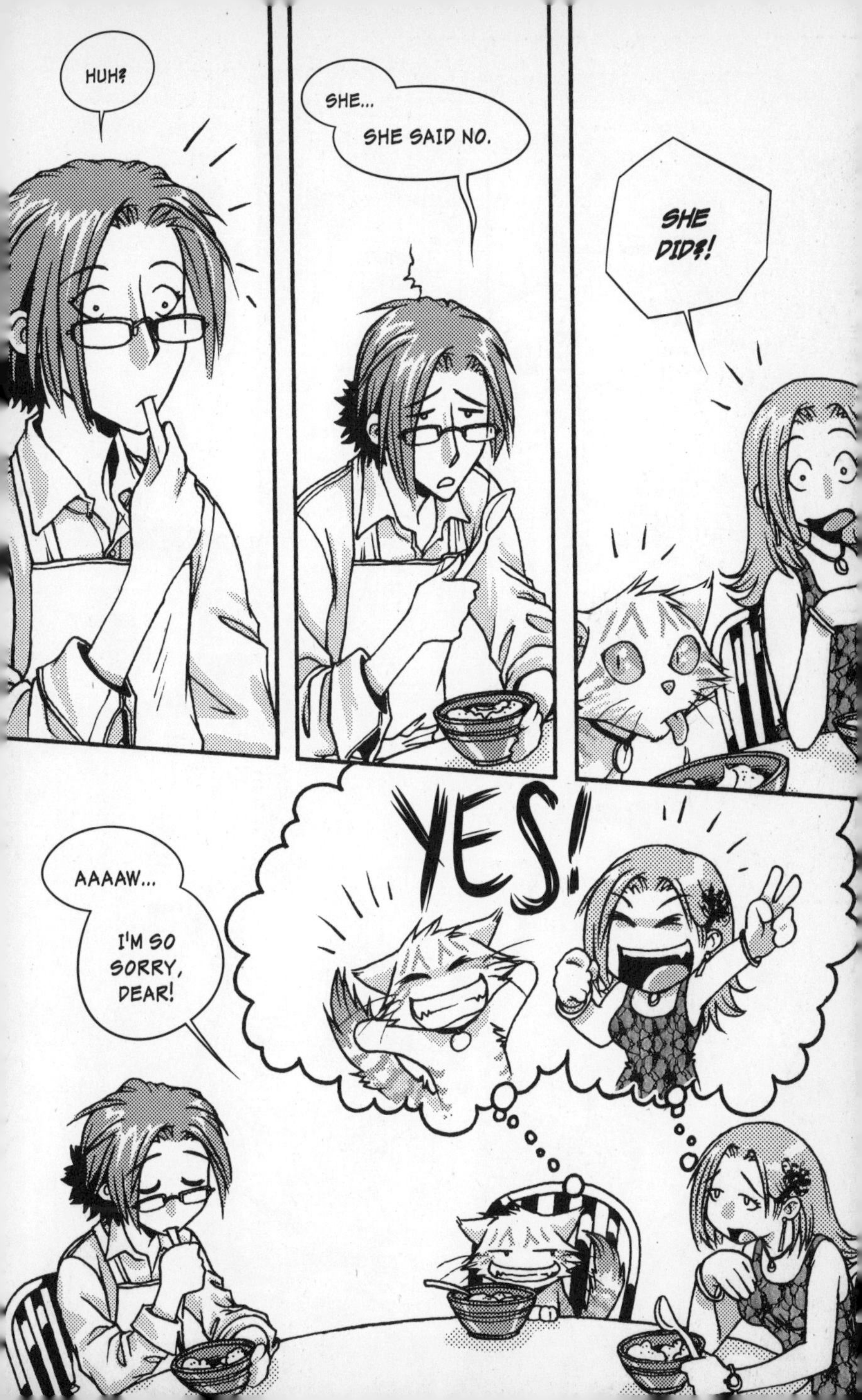
HUH?
SHE...
SHE SAID NO.
SHE DID?!
AAAAW...
I'M SO SORRY, DEAR!
YES!

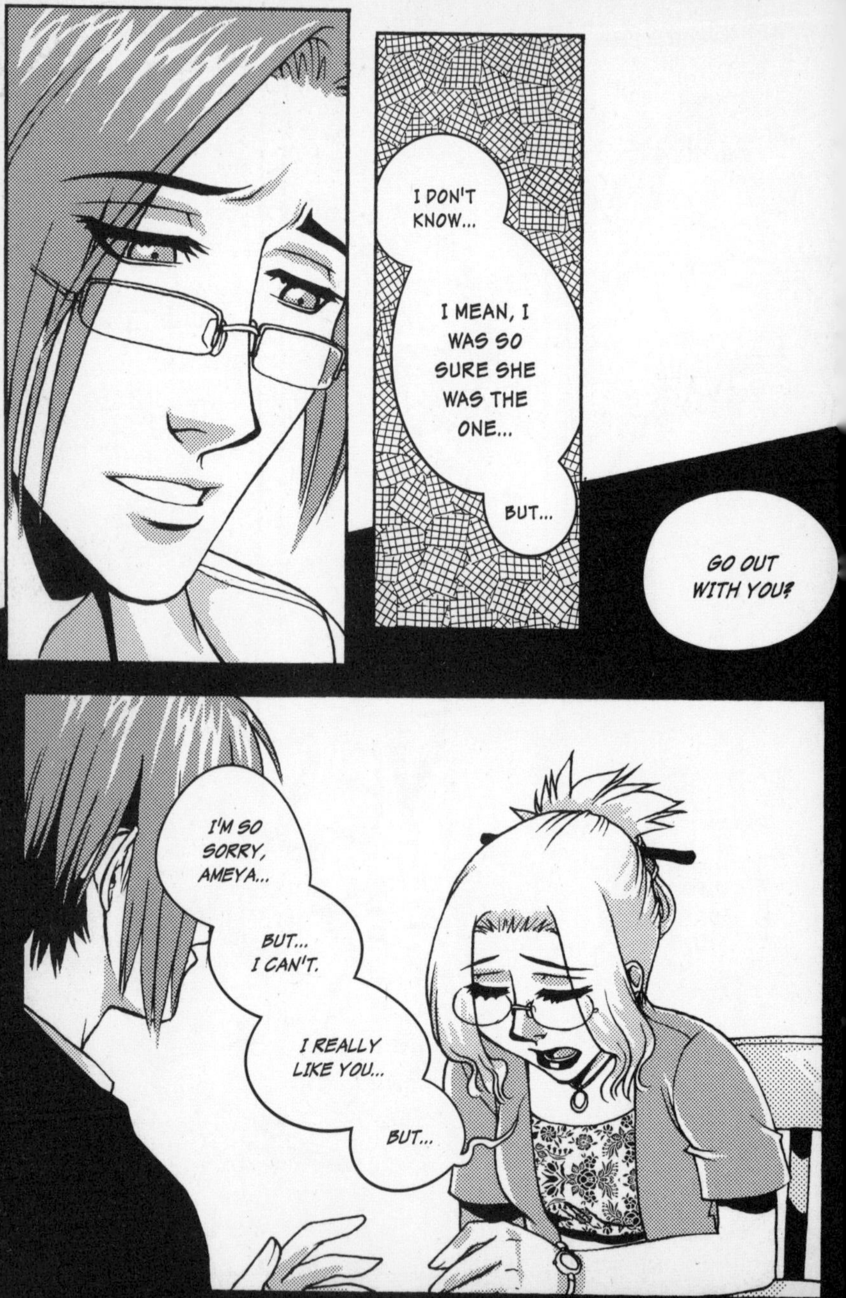
I DON'T KNOW...
I MEAN, I WAS SO SURE SHE WAS THE ONE...
BUT...
GO OUT WITH YOU?
I'M SO SORRY, AMEYA...
BUT... I CAN'T.
I REALLY LIKE YOU...
BUT...

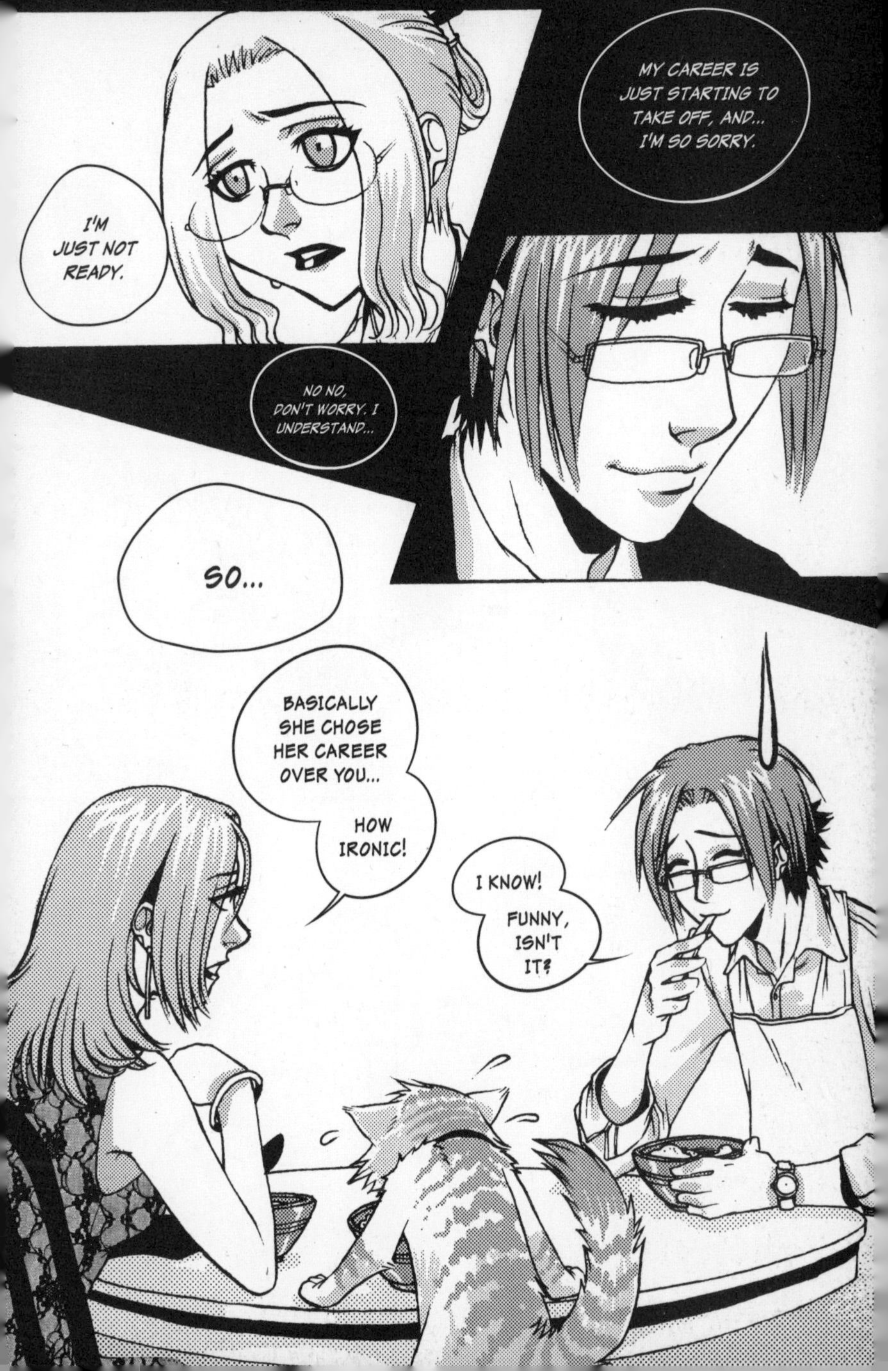
I'M JUST NOT READY.
MY CAREER IS JUST STARTING TO TAKE OFF, AND... I'M SO SORRY.
NO NO, DON'T WORRY. I UNDERSTAND...
SO...
BASICALLY SHE CHOSE HER CAREER OVER YOU...
HOW IRONIC!
I KNOW!
FUNNY, ISN'T IT?

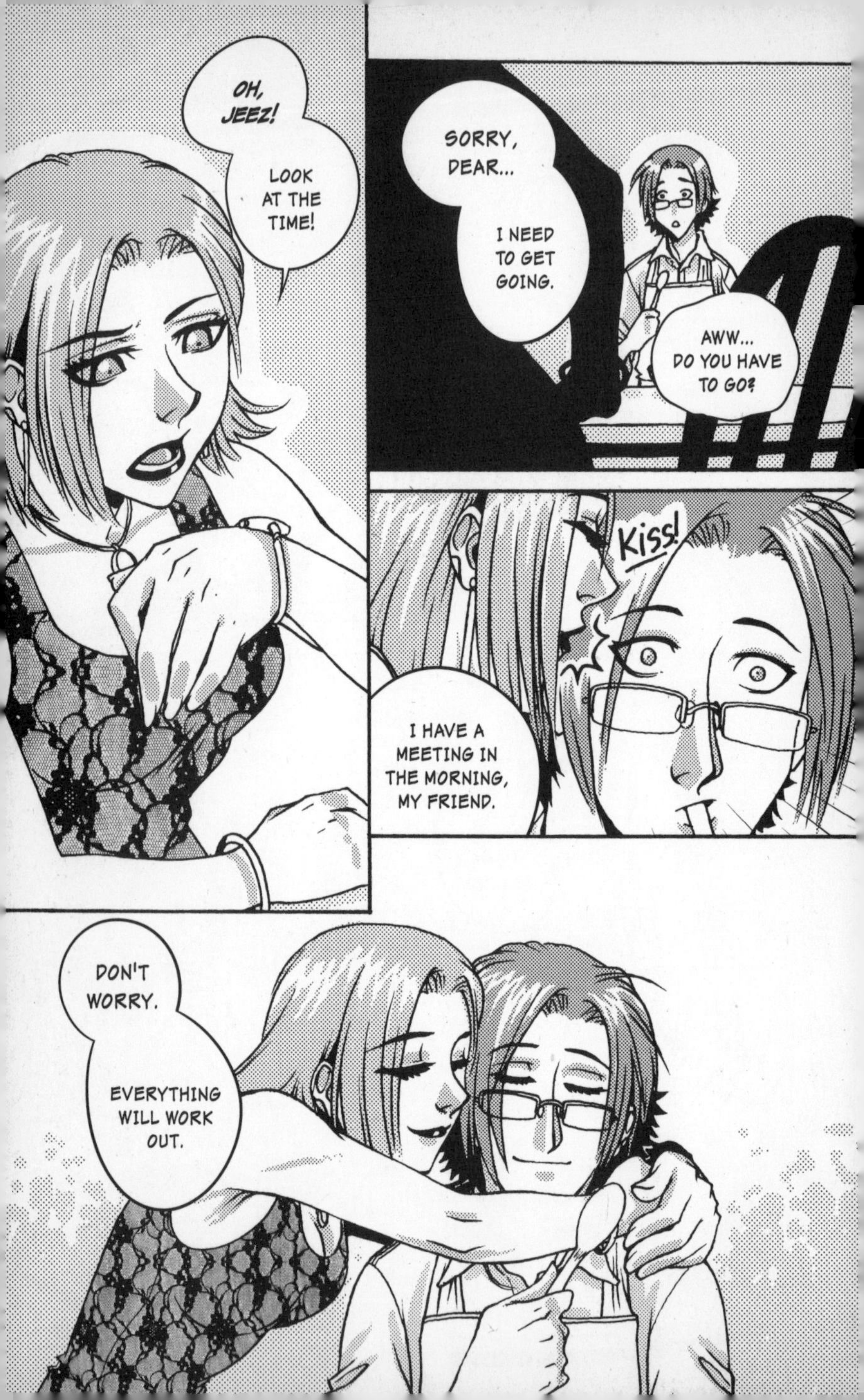
OH, JEEZ!
LOOK AT THE TIME!
SORRY, DEAR...
I NEED TO GET GOING.
AWW... DO YOU HAVE TO GO?
KISS!
I HAVE A MEETING IN THE MORNING, MY FRIEND.
DON'T WORRY.
EVERYTHING WILL WORK OUT.

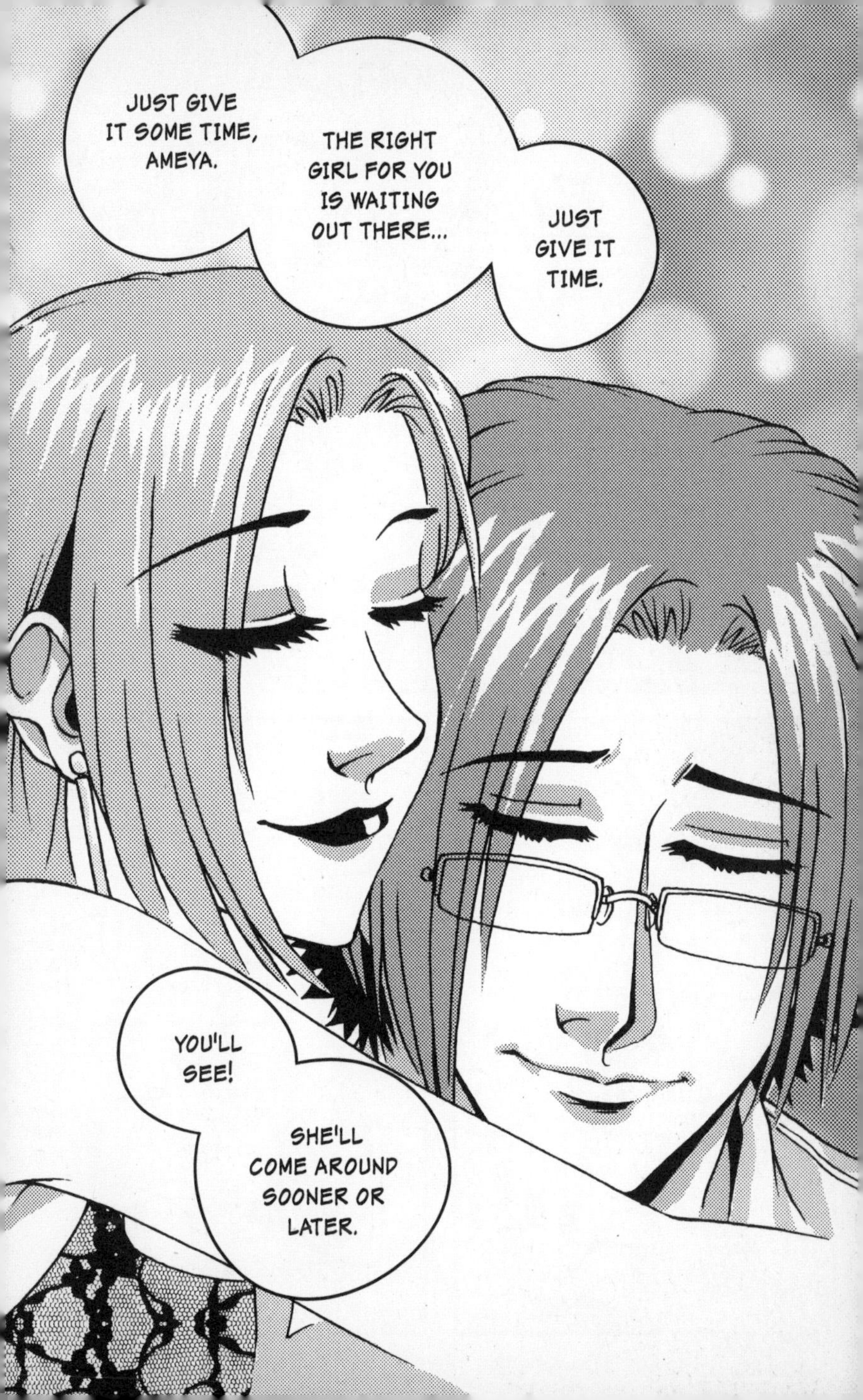
JUST GIVE IT SOME TIME, AMEYA.
THE RIGHT GIRL FOR YOU IS WAITING OUT THERE...
JUST GIVE IT TIME.
YOU'LL SEE!
SHE'LL COME AROUND SOONER OR LATER.

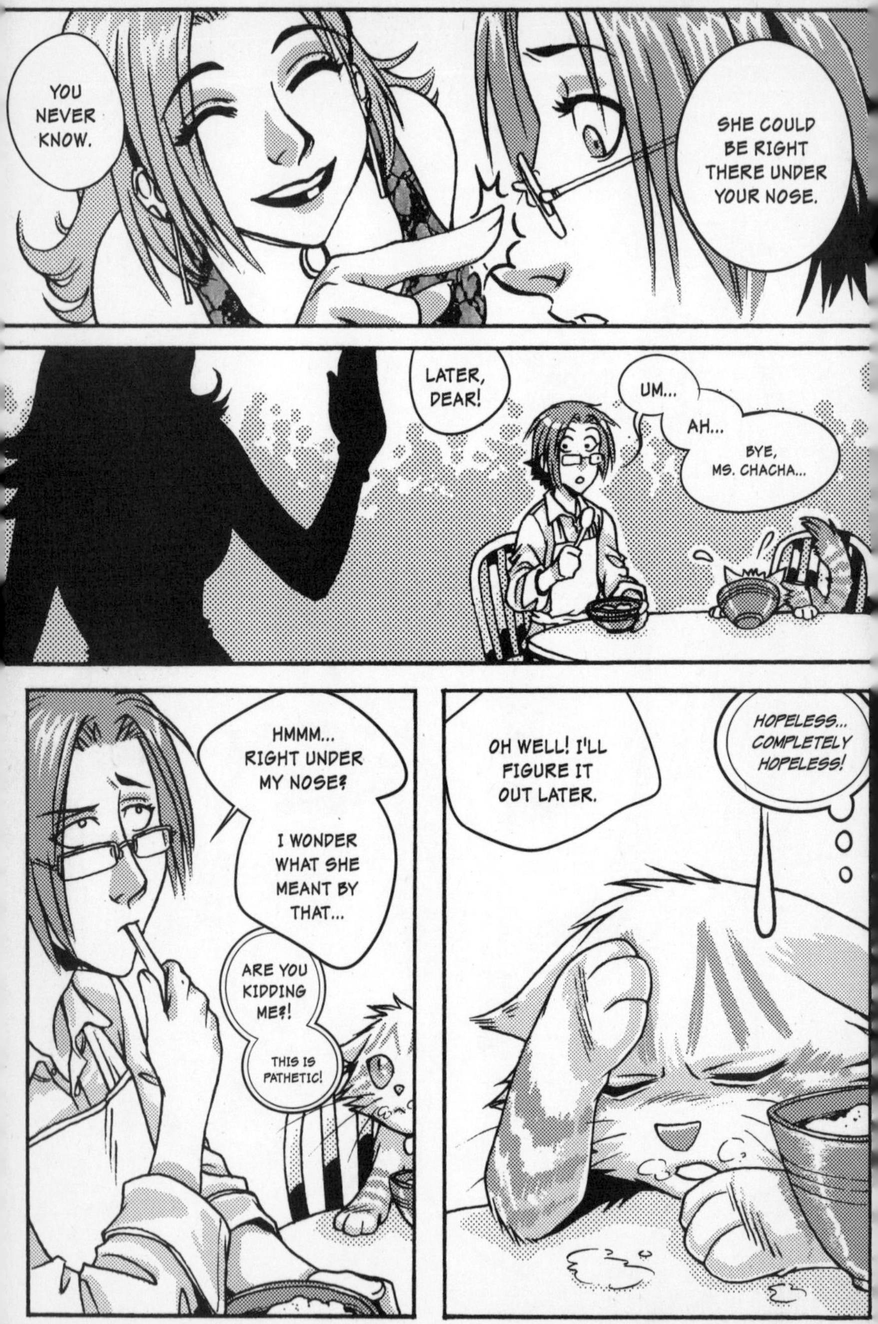
YOU NEVER KNOW.
SHE COULD BE RIGHT THERE UNDER YOUR NOSE.
LATER, DEAR!
UM...
AH...
BYE, MS. CHACHA...
HMMM... RIGHT UNDER MY NOSE?
I WONDER WHAT SHE MEANT BY THAT...
ARE YOU KIDDING ME?!
THIS IS PATHETIC!
OH WELL! I'LL FIGURE IT OUT LATER.
HOPELESS... COMPLETELY HOPELESS!

CHAPTER 6

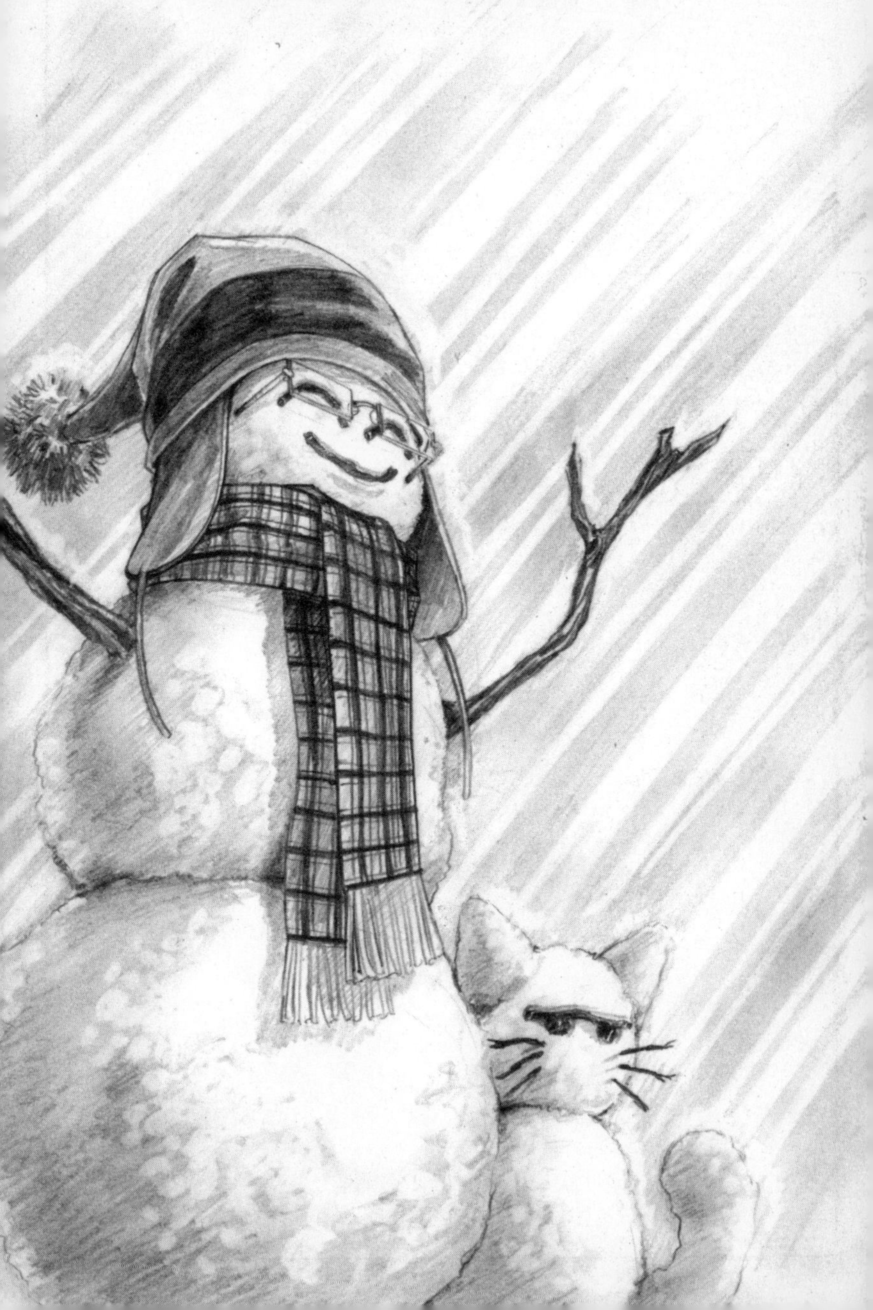

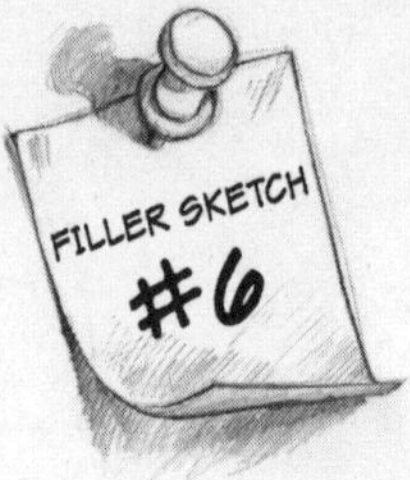
FILLER SKETCH
#6

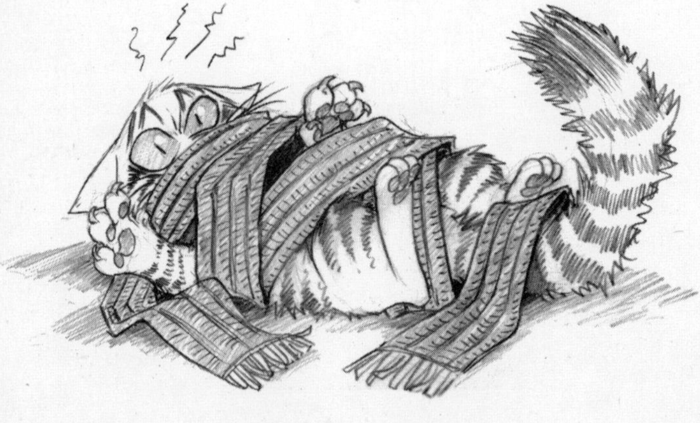

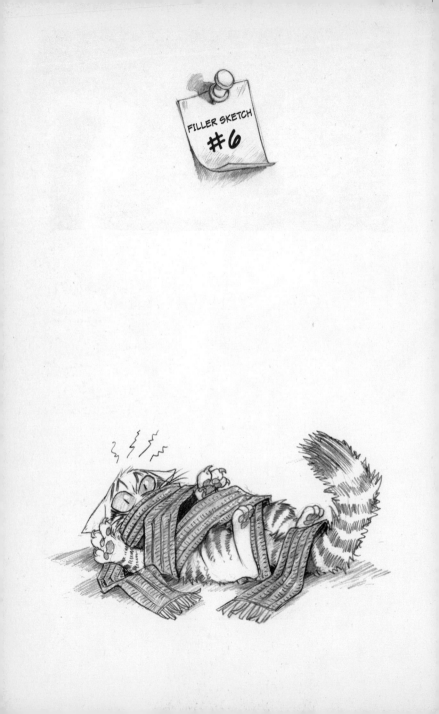

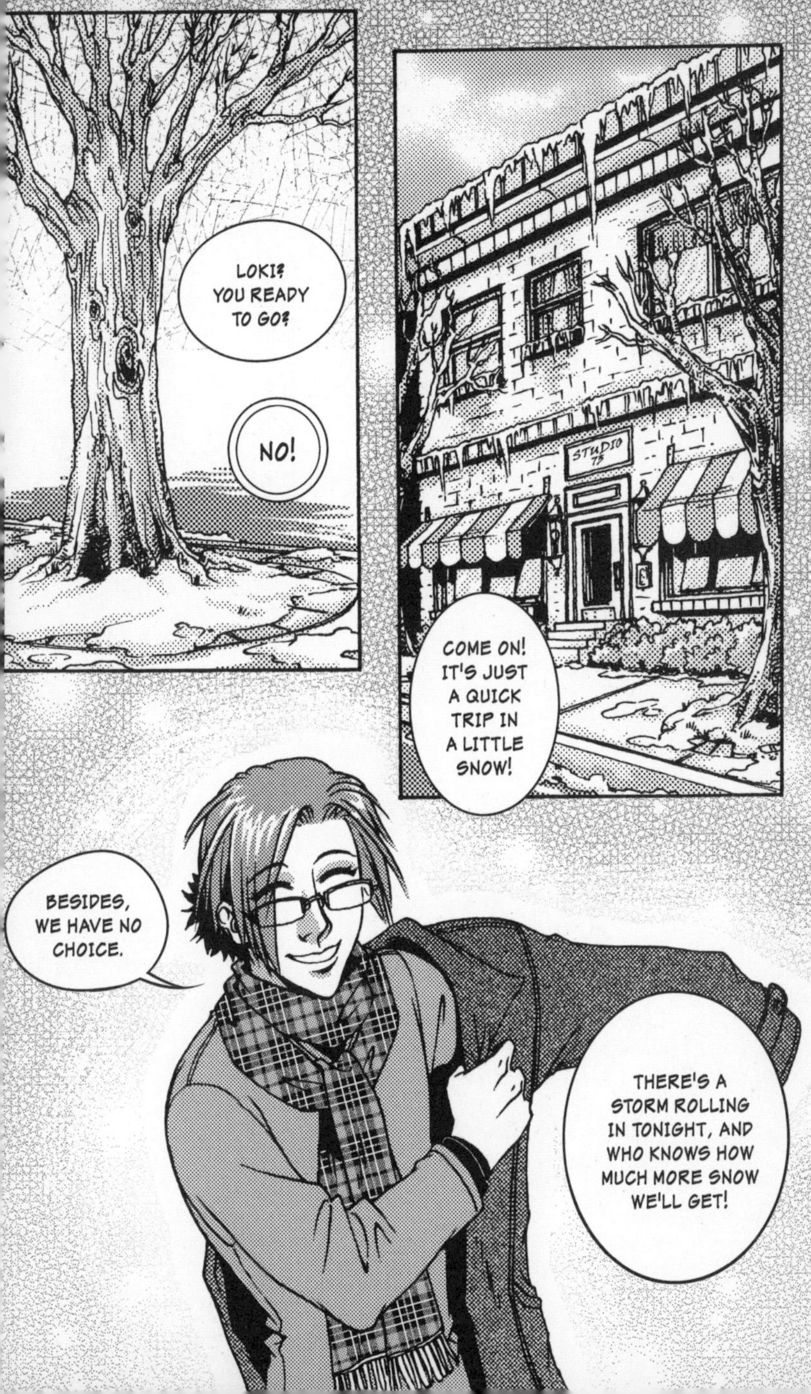
LOKI? YOU READY TO GO?
NO!
STUDIO 73
COME ON! IT'S JUST A QUICK TRIP IN A LITTLE SNOW!
BESIDES, WE HAVE NO CHOICE.
THERE'S A STORM ROLLING IN TONIGHT, AND WHO KNOWS HOW MUCH MORE SNOW WE'LL GET!

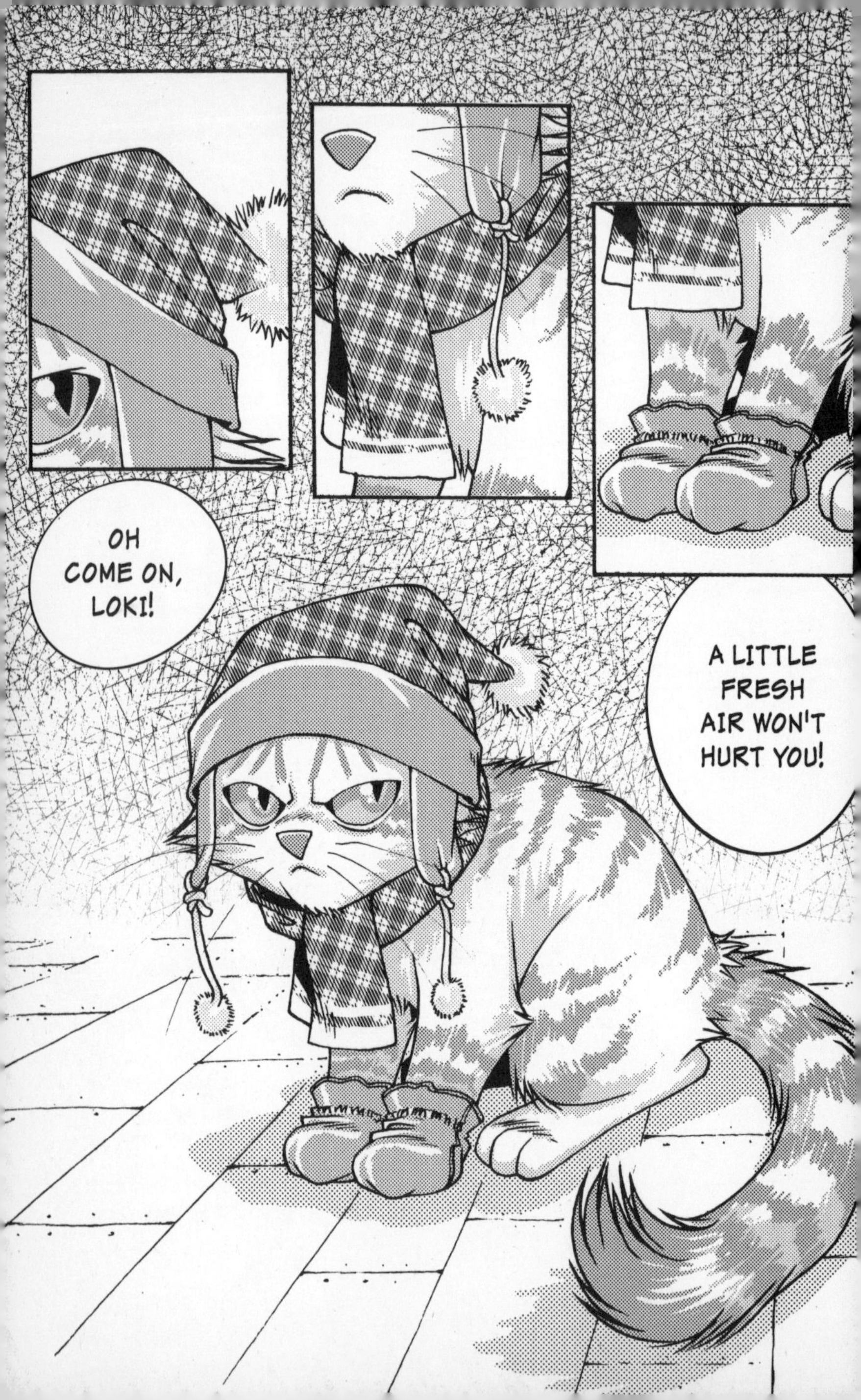
OH COME ON, LOKI!
A LITTLE FRESH AIR WON'T HURT YOU!

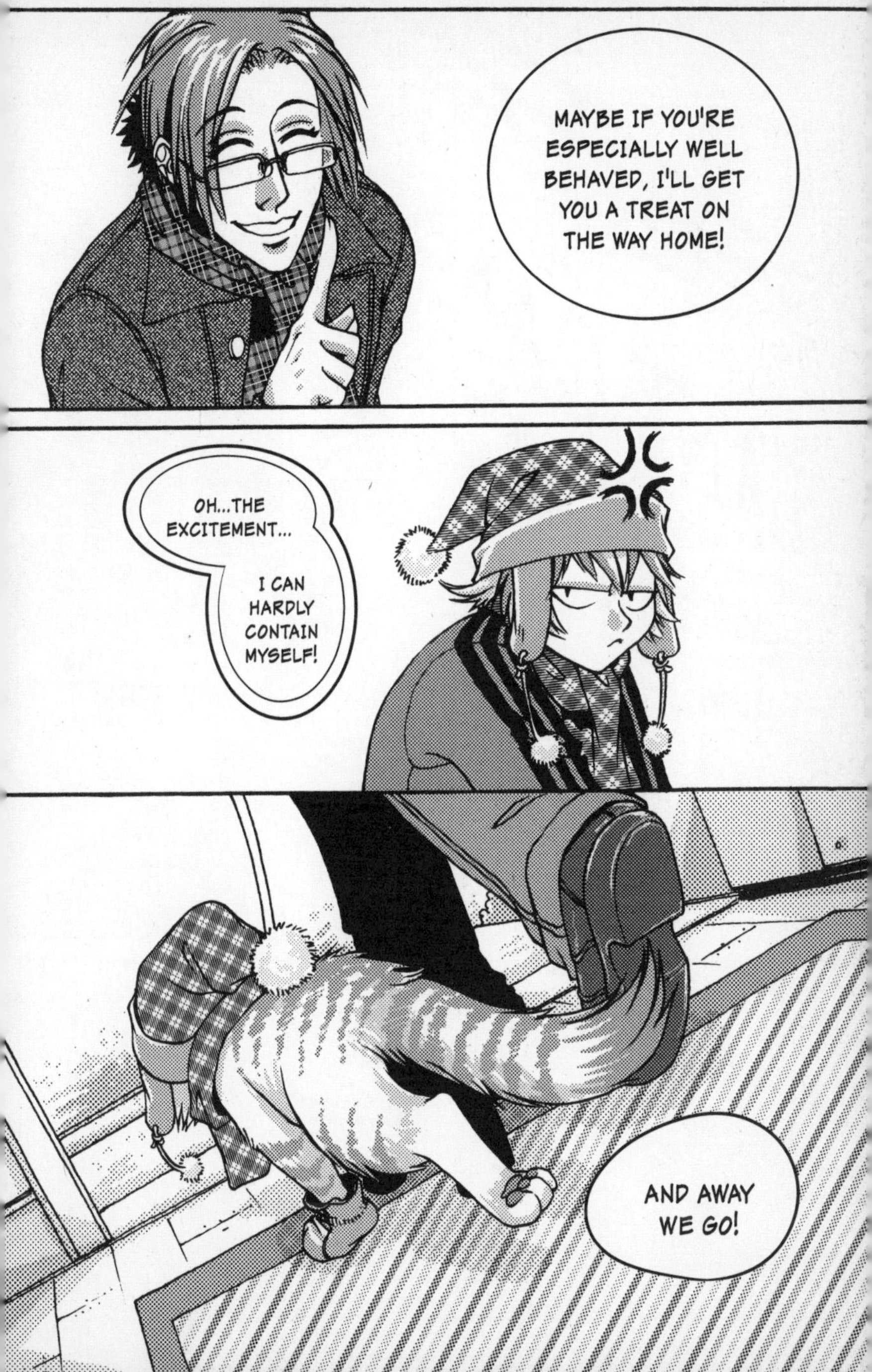
MAYBE IF YOU'RE ESPECIALLY WELL BEHAVED, I'LL GET YOU A TREAT ON THE WAY HOME!
OH...THE EXCITEMENT...
I CAN HARDLY CONTAIN MYSELF!
AND AWAY WE GO!

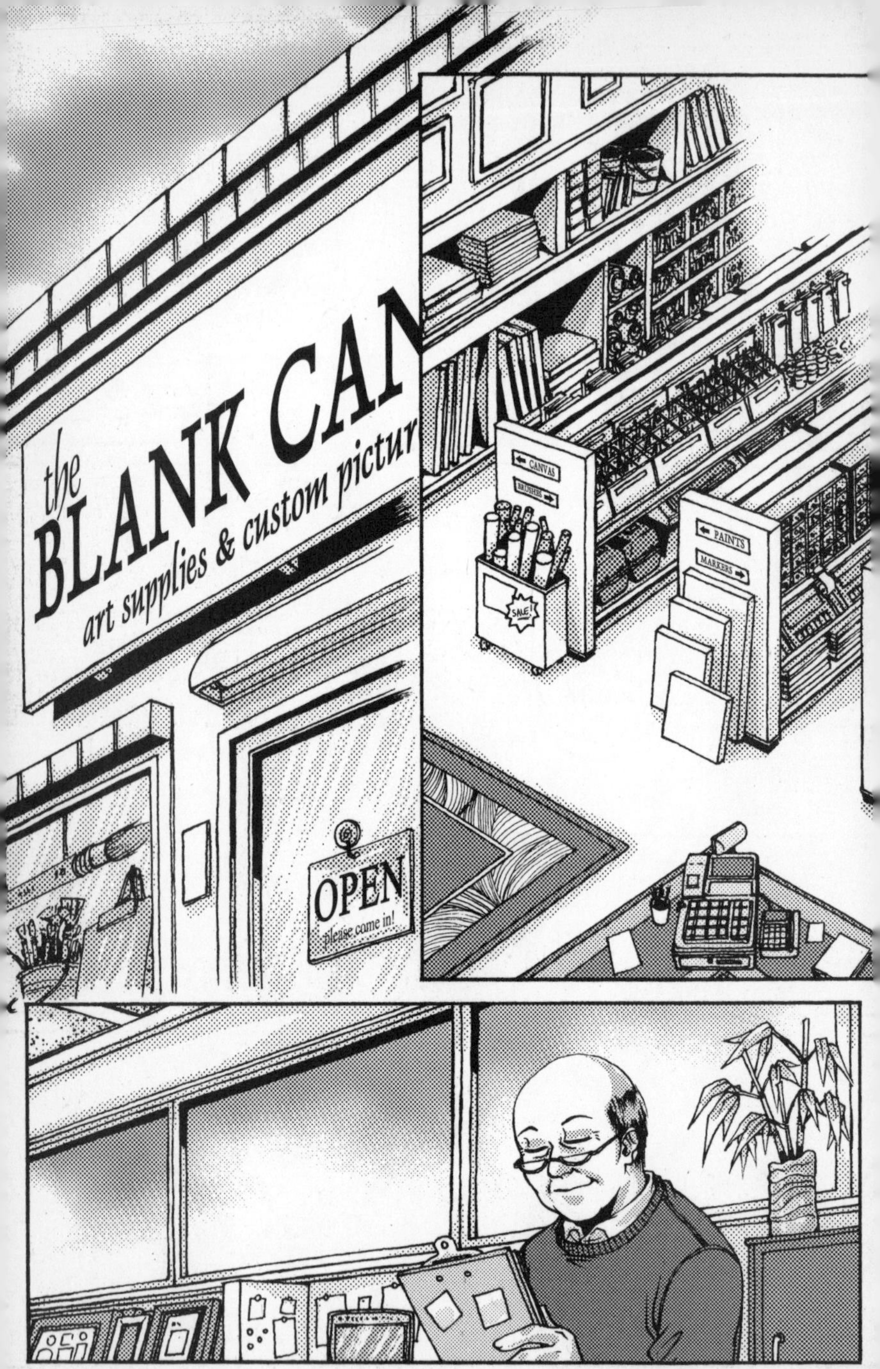
the BLANK CAN
art supplies & custom pictur
OPEN
please come in!
CANVAS
BRUSHES
SALE!
PAINTS
MARKERS

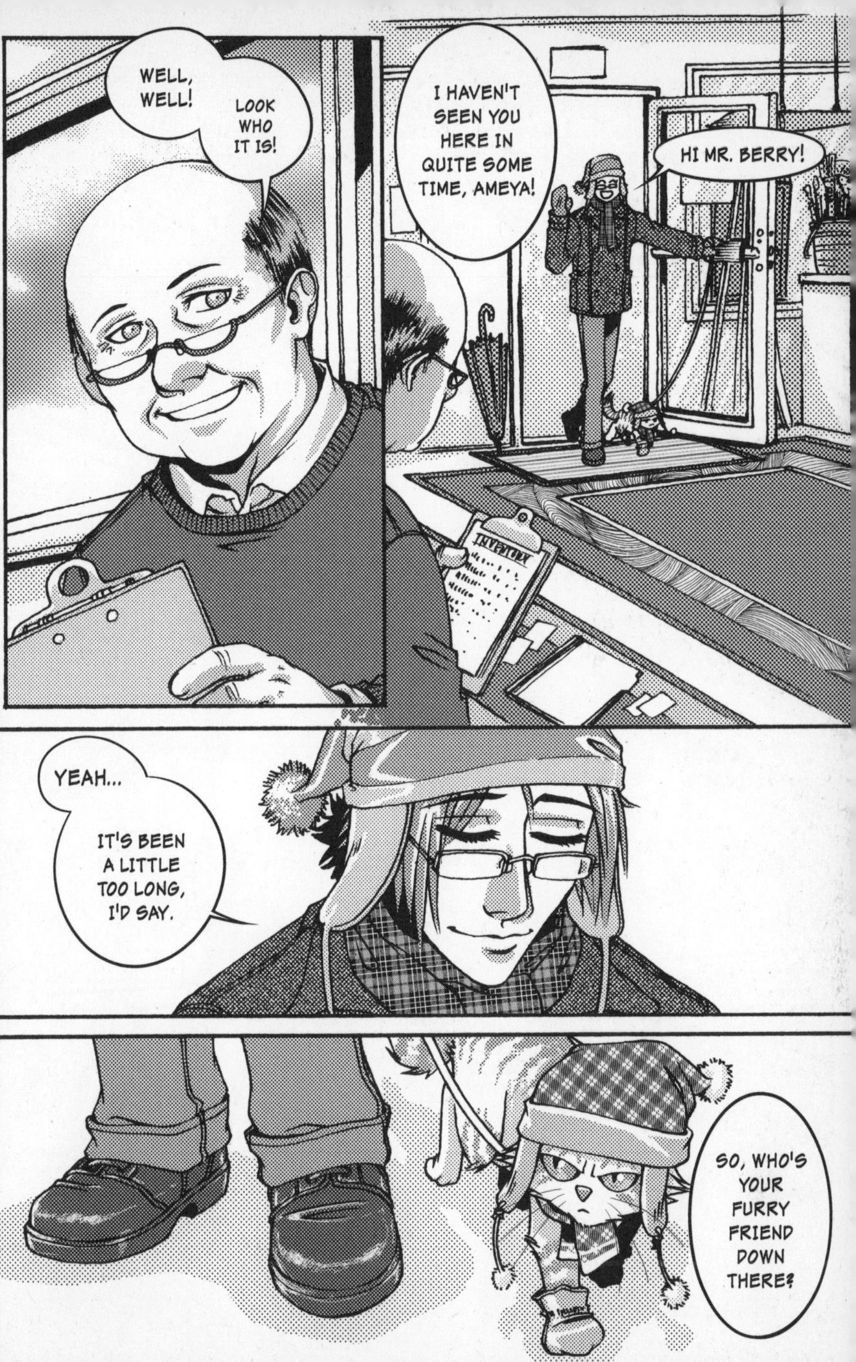
WELL, WELL!
LOOK WHO IT IS!
I HAVEN'T SEEN YOU HERE IN QUITE SOME TIME, AMEYA!
HI MR. BERRY!
YEAH...
IT'S BEEN A LITTLE TOO LONG, I'D SAY.
SO, WHO'S YOUR FURRY FRIEND DOWN THERE?

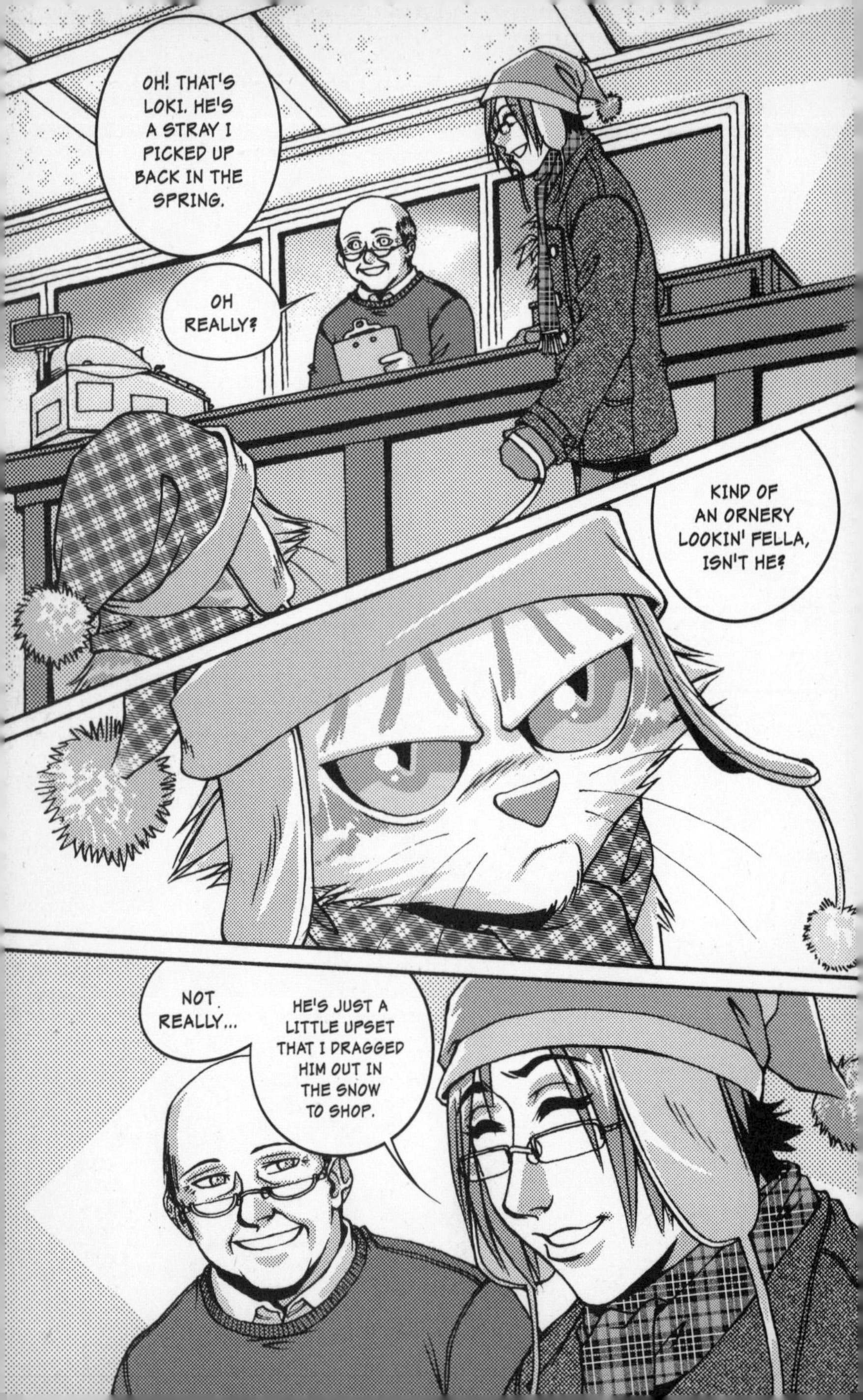
OH! THAT'S LOKI. HE'S A STRAY I PICKED UP BACK IN THE SPRING.
OH REALLY?
KIND OF AN ORNERY LOOKIN' FELLA, ISN'T HE?
NOT. REALLY...
HE'S JUST A LITTLE UPSET THAT I DRAGGED HIM OUT IN THE SNOW TO SHOP.

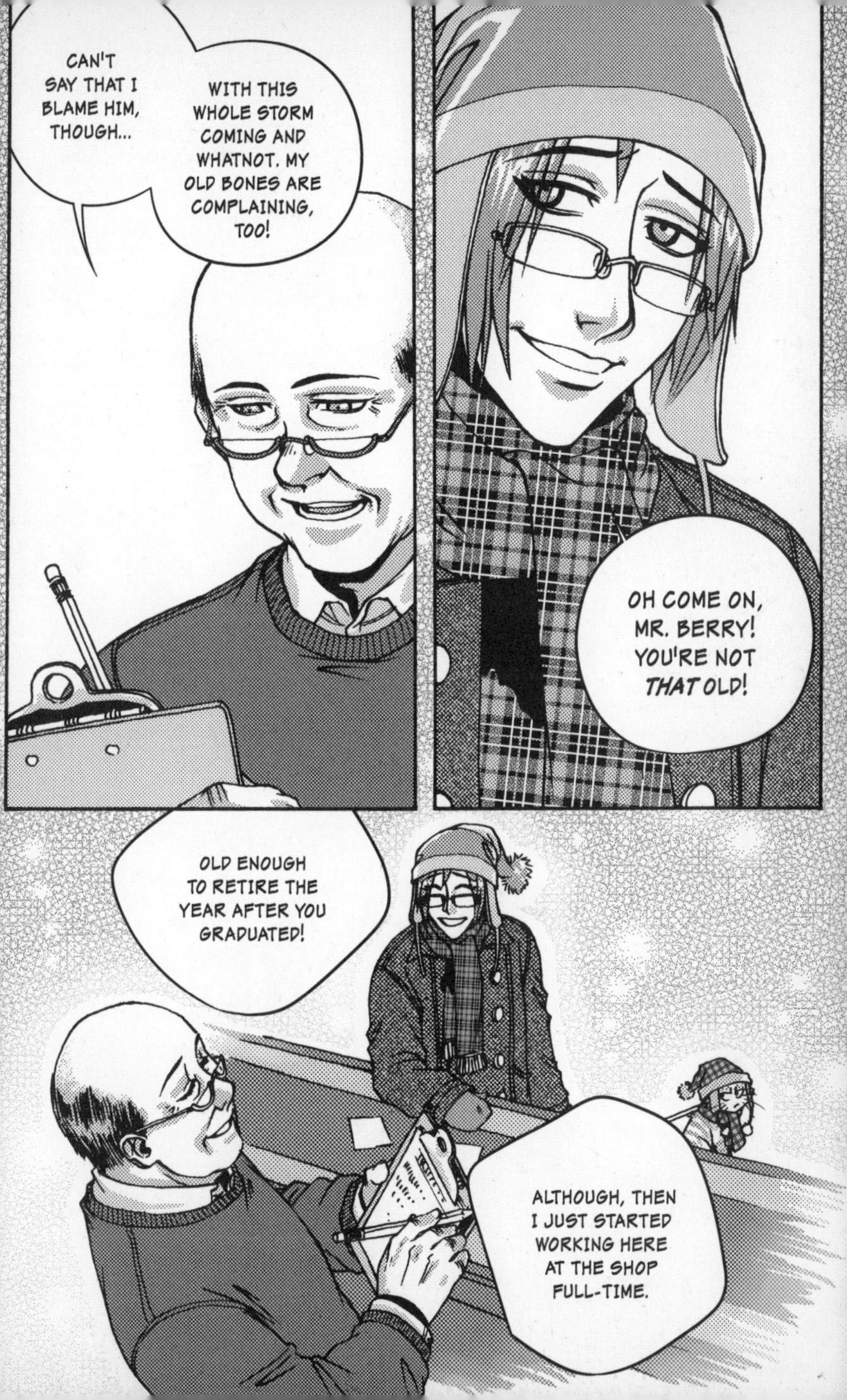
CAN'T SAY THAT I BLAME HIM, THOUGH...
WITH THIS WHOLE STORM COMING AND WHATNOT. MY OLD BONES ARE COMPLAINING, TOO!
OH COME ON, MR. BERRY! YOU'RE NOT *THAT* OLD!
OLD ENOUGH TO RETIRE THE YEAR AFTER YOU GRADUATED!
ALTHOUGH, THEN I JUST STARTED WORKING HERE AT THE SHOP FULL-TIME.

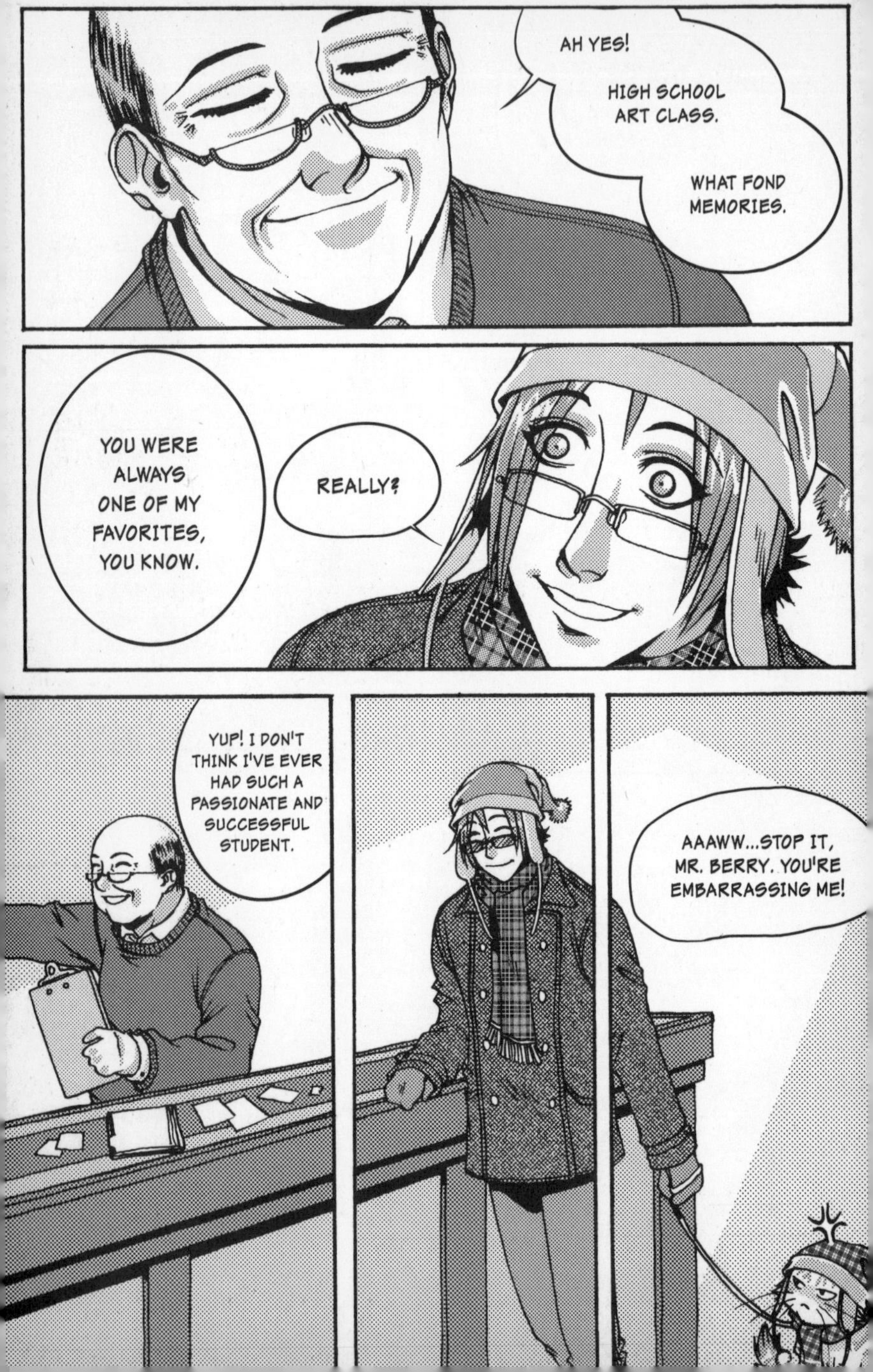
AH YES!
HIGH SCHOOL ART CLASS.
WHAT FOND MEMORIES.
YOU WERE ALWAYS ONE OF MY FAVORITES, YOU KNOW.
REALLY?
YUP! I DON'T THINK I'VE EVER HAD SUCH A PASSIONATE AND SUCCESSFUL STUDENT.
AAAWW...STOP IT, MR. BERRY. YOU'RE EMBARRASSING ME!

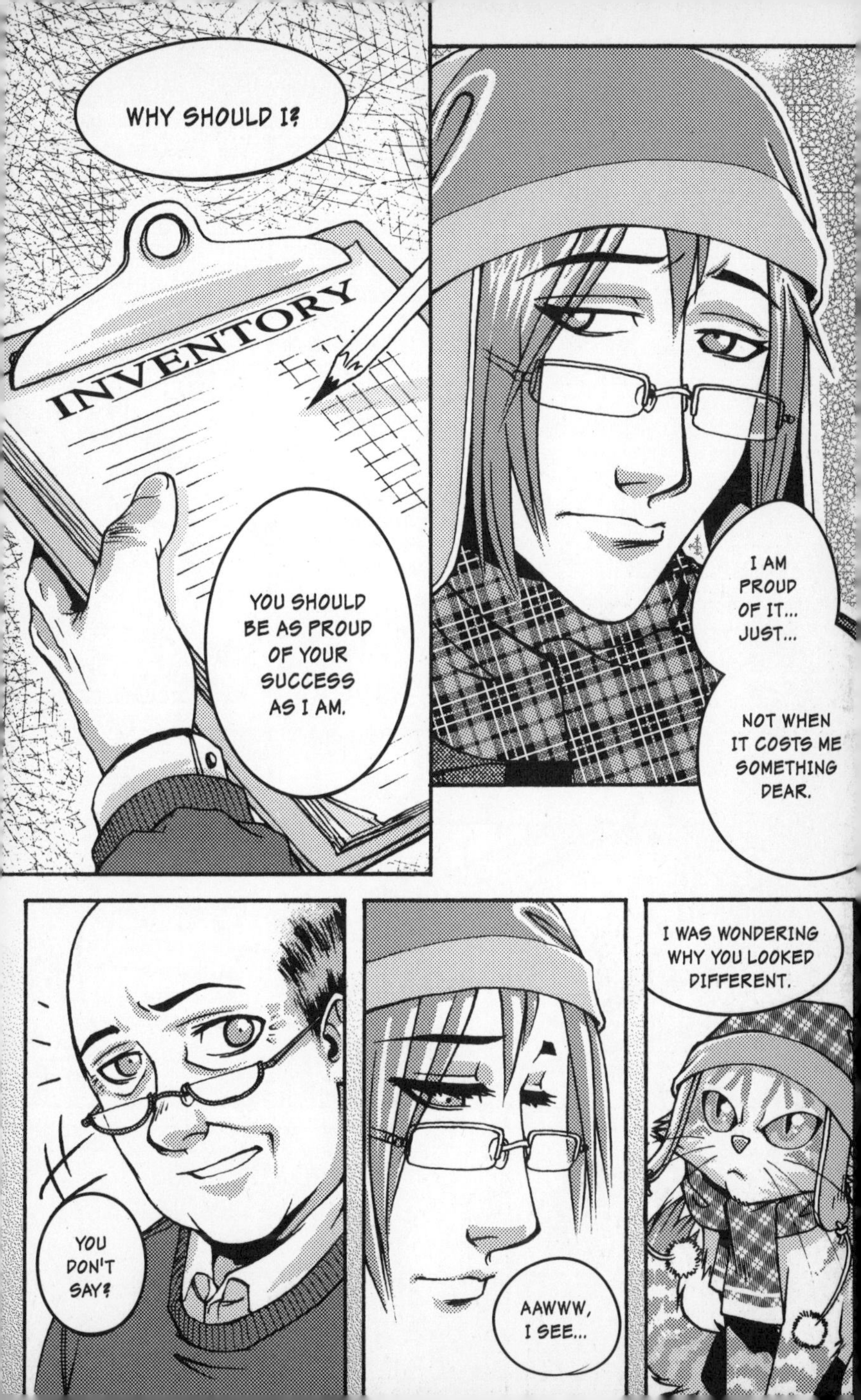
WHY SHOULD I?
INVENTORY
YOU SHOULD BE AS PROUD OF YOUR SUCCESS AS I AM.
I AM PROUD OF IT... JUST...
NOT WHEN IT COSTS ME SOMETHING DEAR.
YOU DON'T SAY?
AAWWW, I SEE...
I WAS WONDERING WHY YOU LOOKED DIFFERENT.

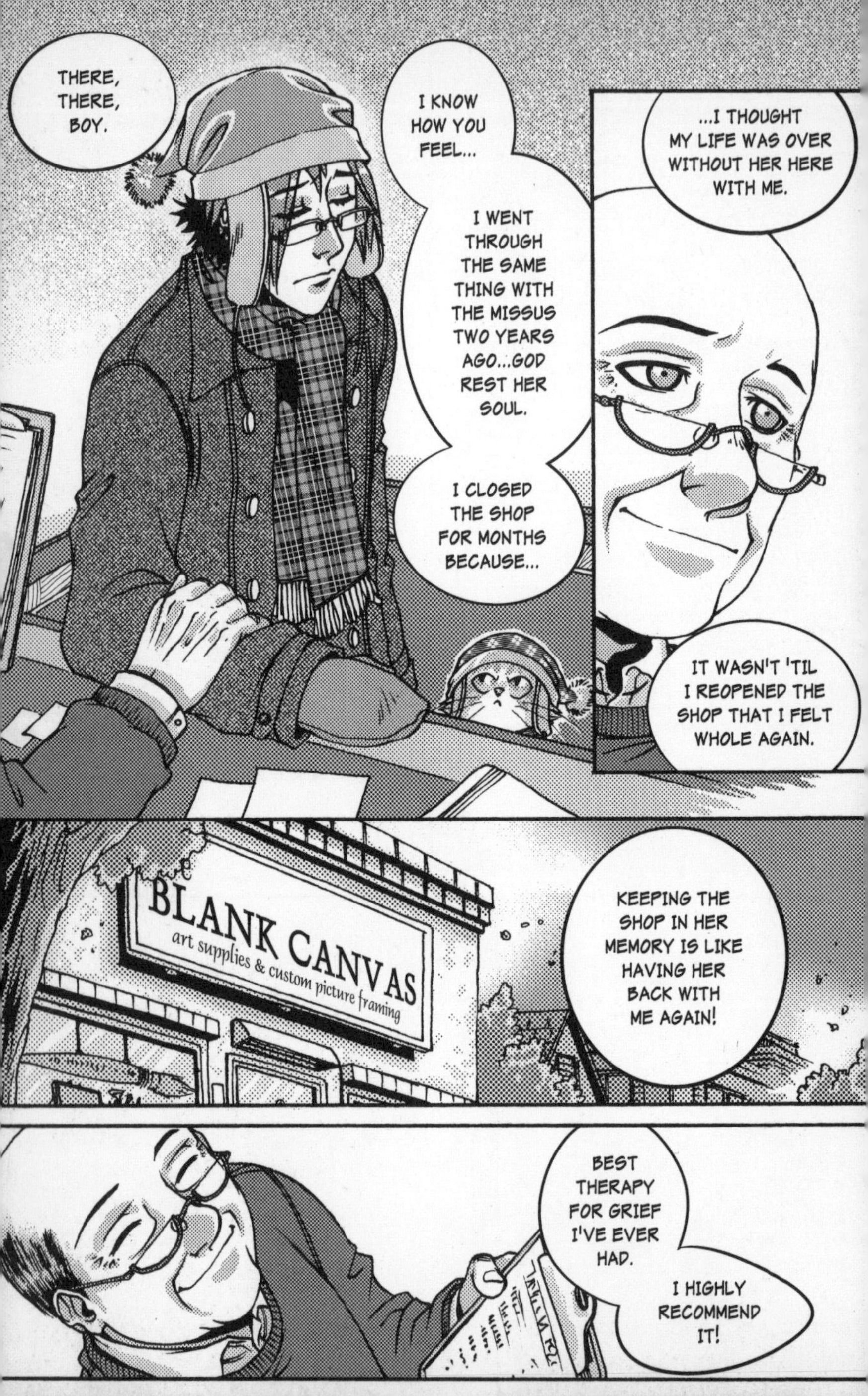
THERE, THERE, BOY.
I KNOW HOW YOU FEEL...
I WENT THROUGH THE SAME THING WITH THE MISSUS TWO YEARS AGO...GOD REST HER SOUL.
I CLOSED THE SHOP FOR MONTHS BECAUSE...
...I THOUGHT MY LIFE WAS OVER WITHOUT HER HERE WITH ME.
IT WASN'T 'TIL I REOPENED THE SHOP THAT I FELT WHOLE AGAIN.
BLANK CANVAS
art supplies & custom picture framing
KEEPING THE SHOP IN HER MEMORY IS LIKE HAVING HER BACK WITH ME AGAIN!
BEST THERAPY FOR GRIEF I'VE EVER HAD.
I HIGHLY RECOMMEND IT!

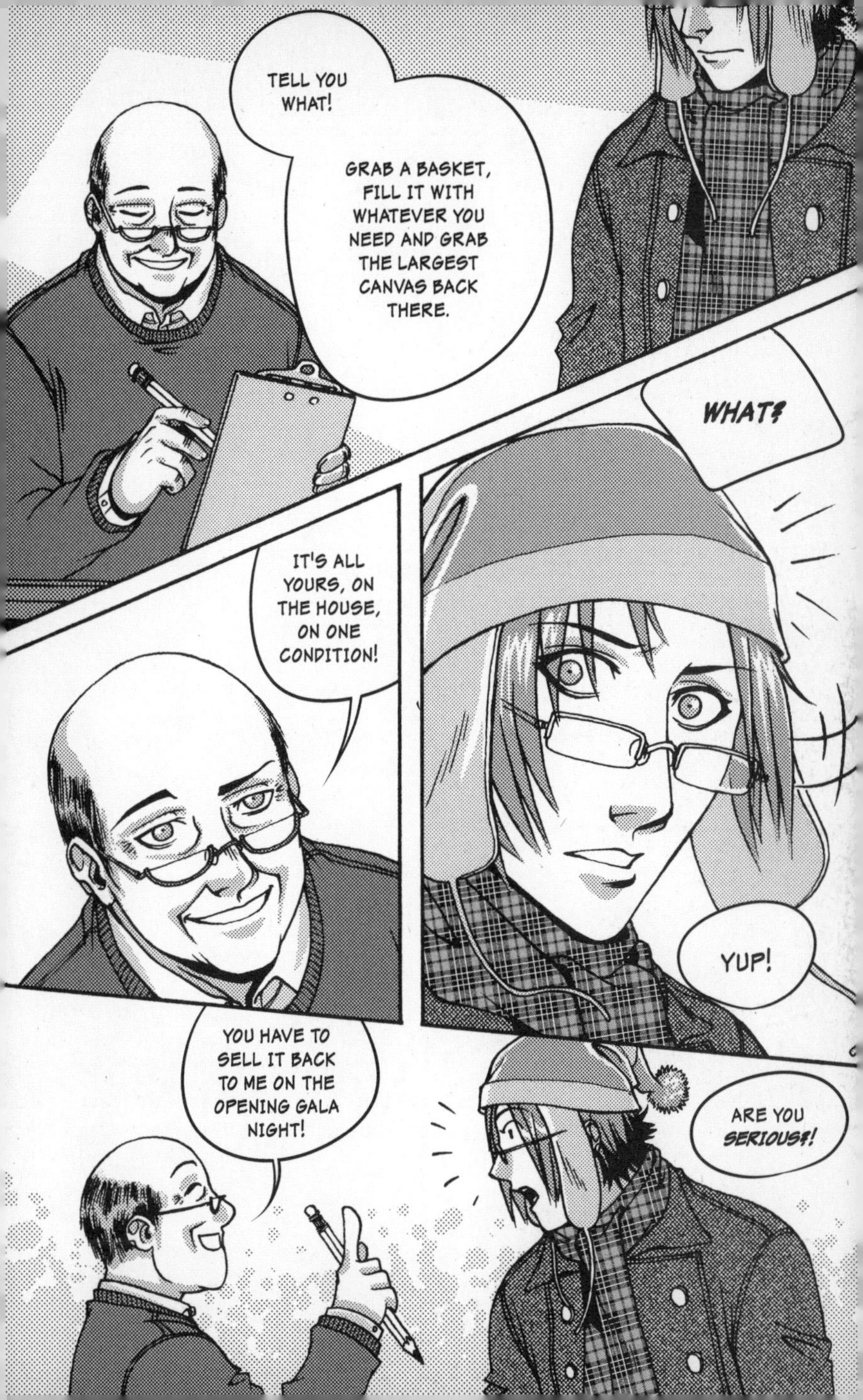
TELL YOU WHAT!
GRAB A BASKET, FILL IT WITH WHATEVER YOU NEED AND GRAB THE LARGEST CANVAS BACK THERE.
IT'S ALL YOURS, ON THE HOUSE, ON ONE CONDITION!
WHAT?
YUP!
YOU HAVE TO SELL IT BACK TO ME ON THE OPENING GALA NIGHT!
ARE YOU *SERIOUS?!*

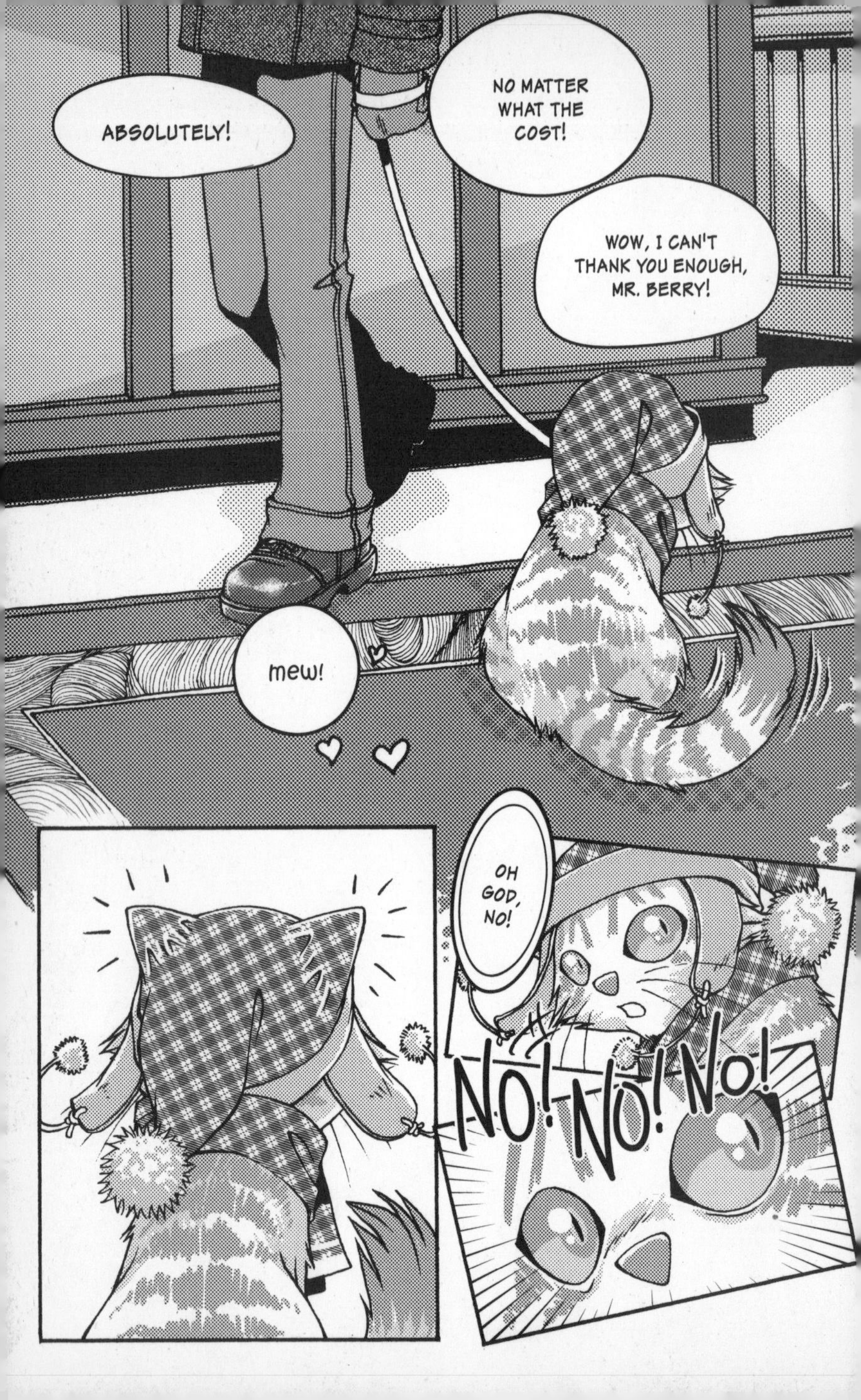
ABSOLUTELY!
NO MATTER WHAT THE COST!
WOW, I CAN'T THANK YOU ENOUGH, MR. BERRY!
mew!
OH GOD, NO!
NO! NO! NO!

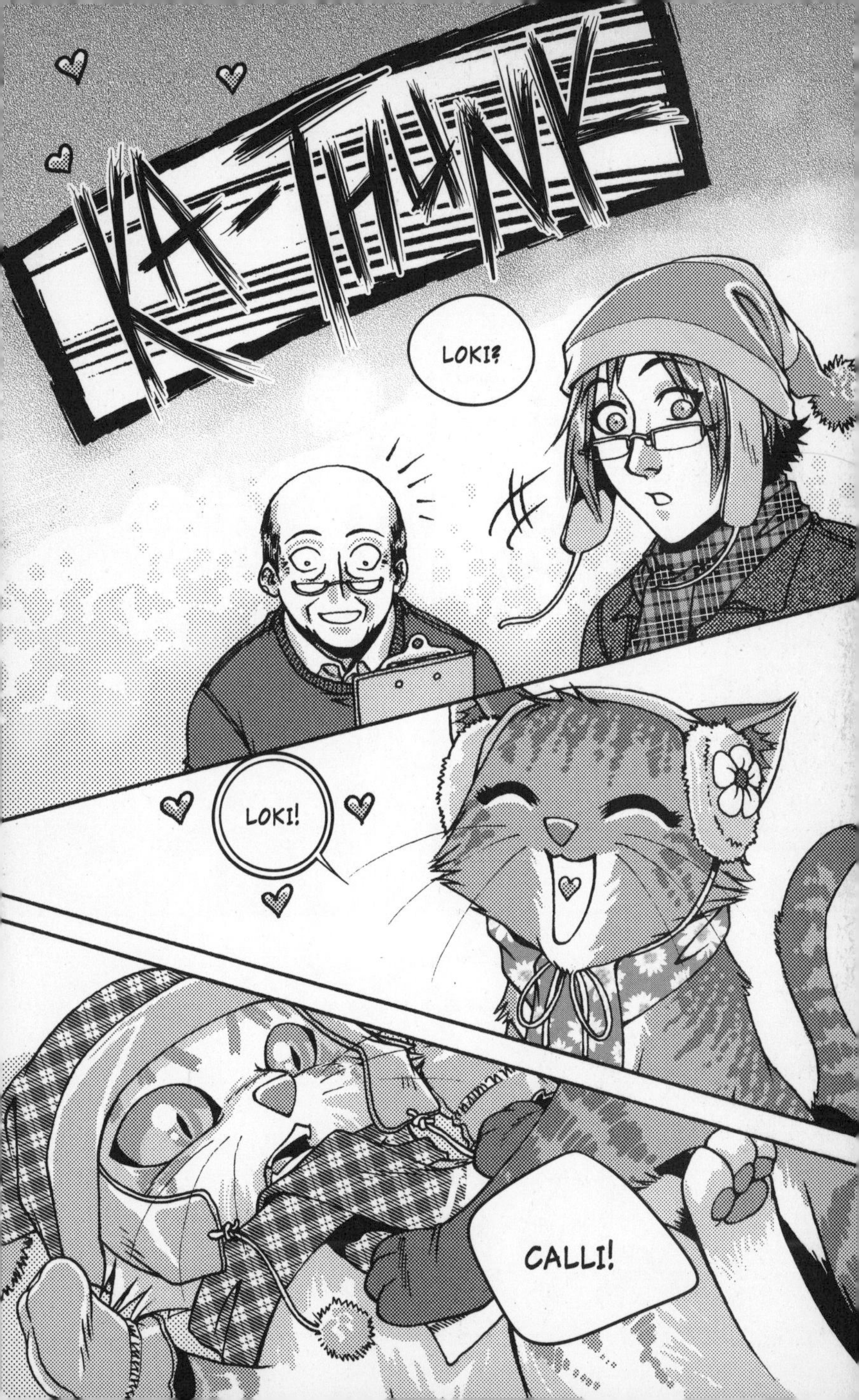
KA-THUNK
LOKI?
LOKI!
CALLI!

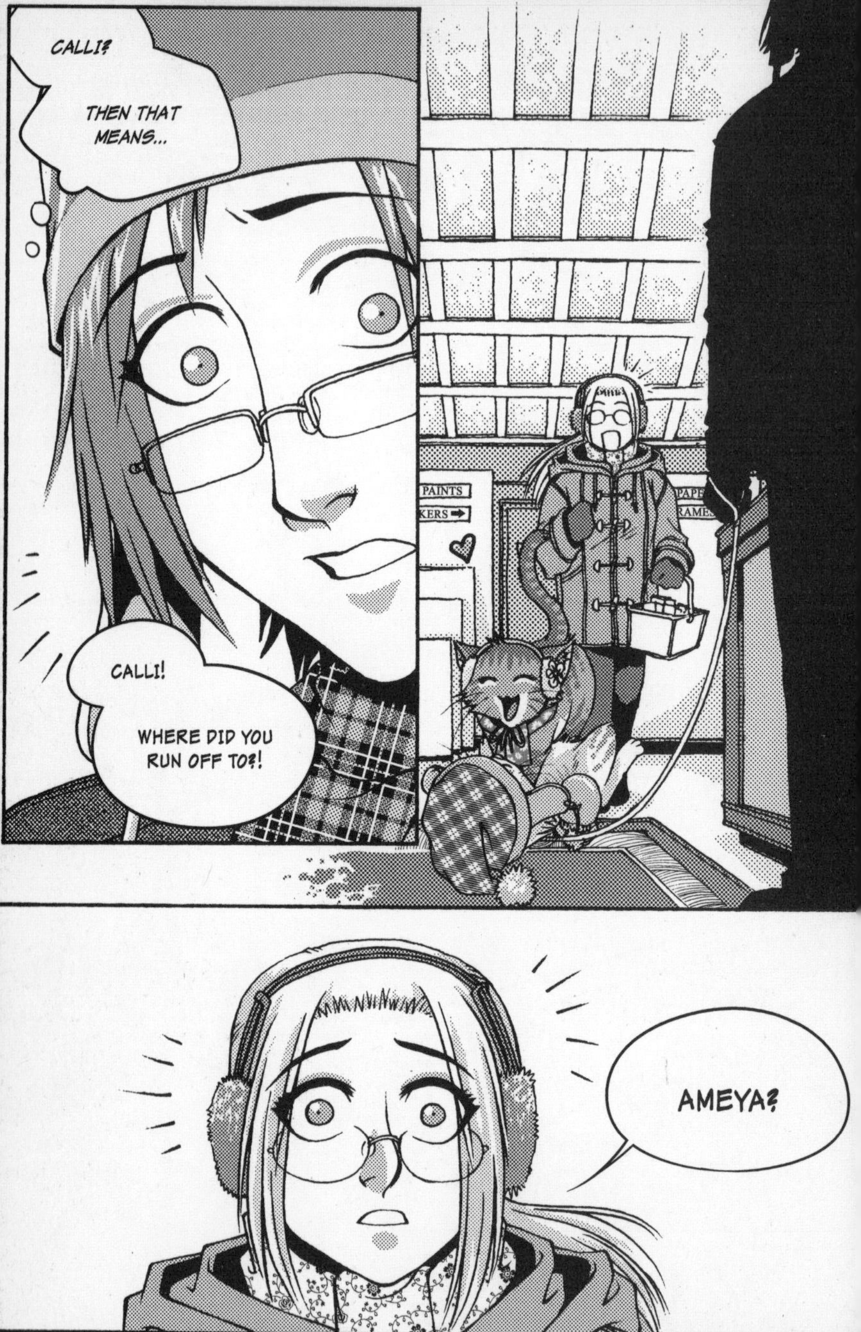
CALLI?
THEN THAT MEANS...
CALLI!
WHERE DID YOU RUN OFF TO?!
PAINTS
AMEYA?

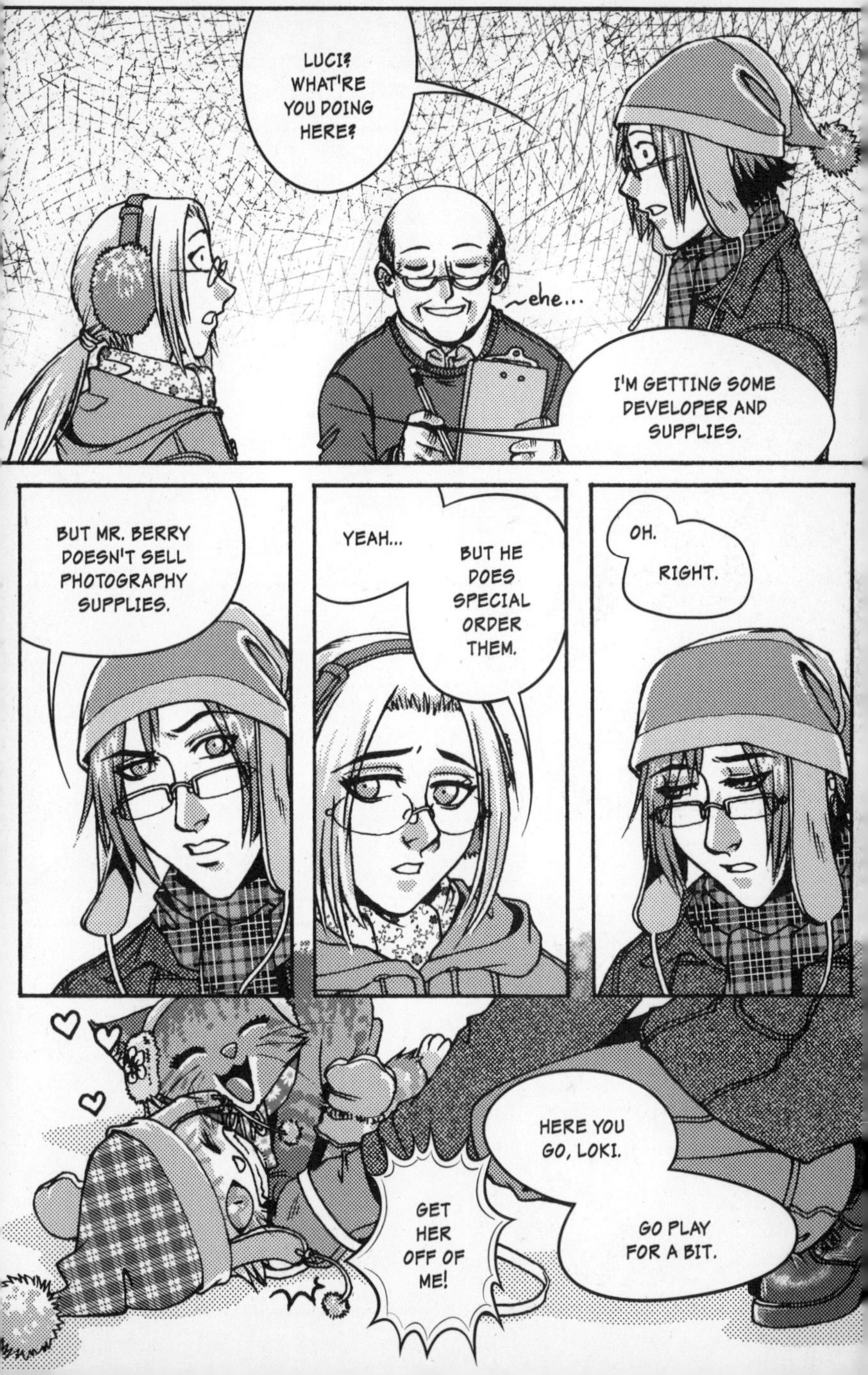
LUCI? WHAT'RE YOU DOING HERE?
~ehe...
I'M GETTING SOME DEVELOPER AND SUPPLIES.
BUT MR. BERRY DOESN'T SELL PHOTOGRAPHY SUPPLIES.
YEAH...
BUT HE DOES SPECIAL ORDER THEM.
OH.
RIGHT.
GET HER OFF OF ME!
HERE YOU GO, LOKI.
GO PLAY FOR A BIT.

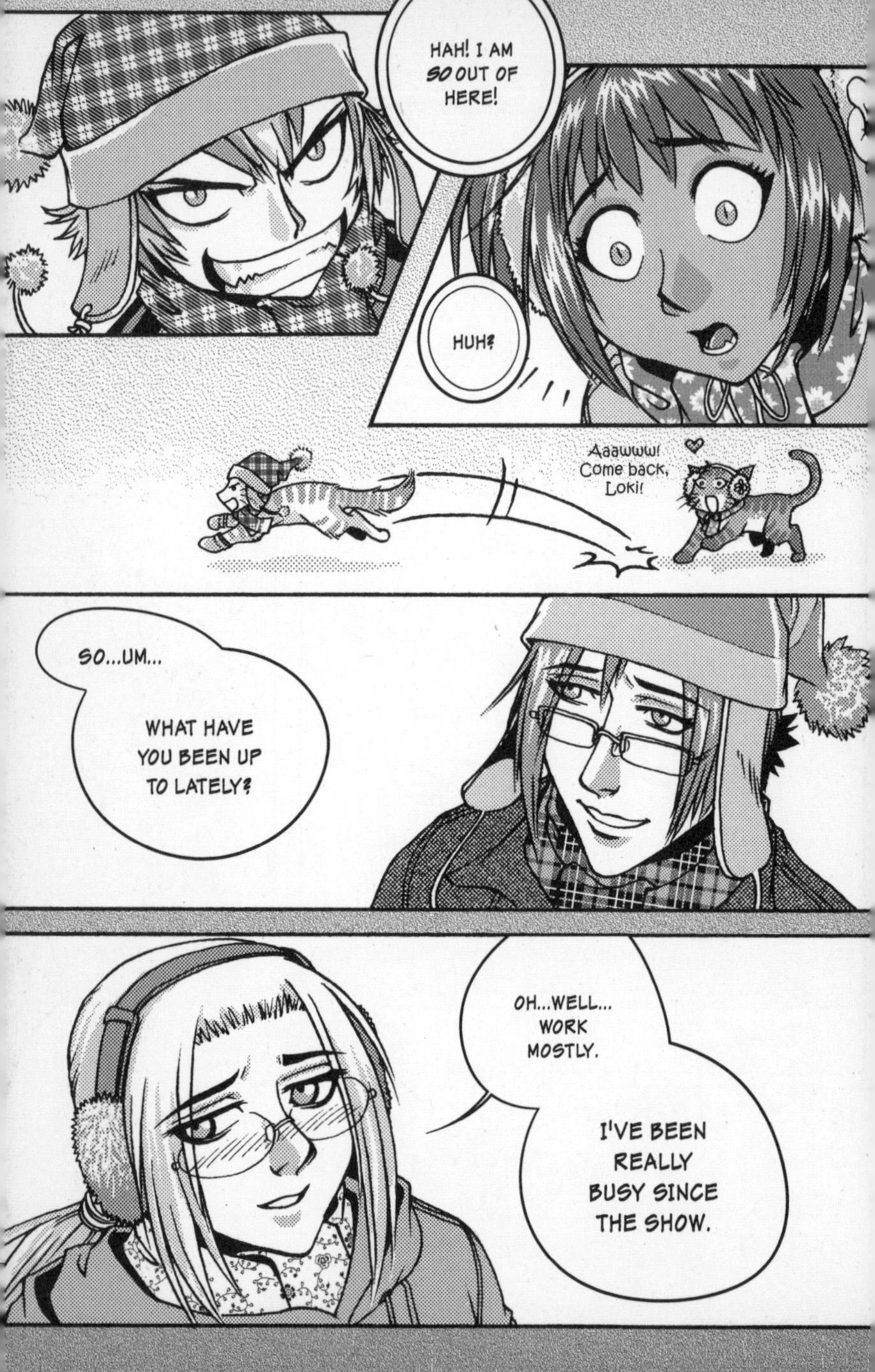
HAH! I AM SO OUT OF HERE!
HUH?
Aaawww! Come back, Loki!
SO...UM...
WHAT HAVE YOU BEEN UP TO LATELY?
OH...WELL... WORK MOSTLY.
I'VE BEEN REALLY BUSY SINCE THE SHOW.

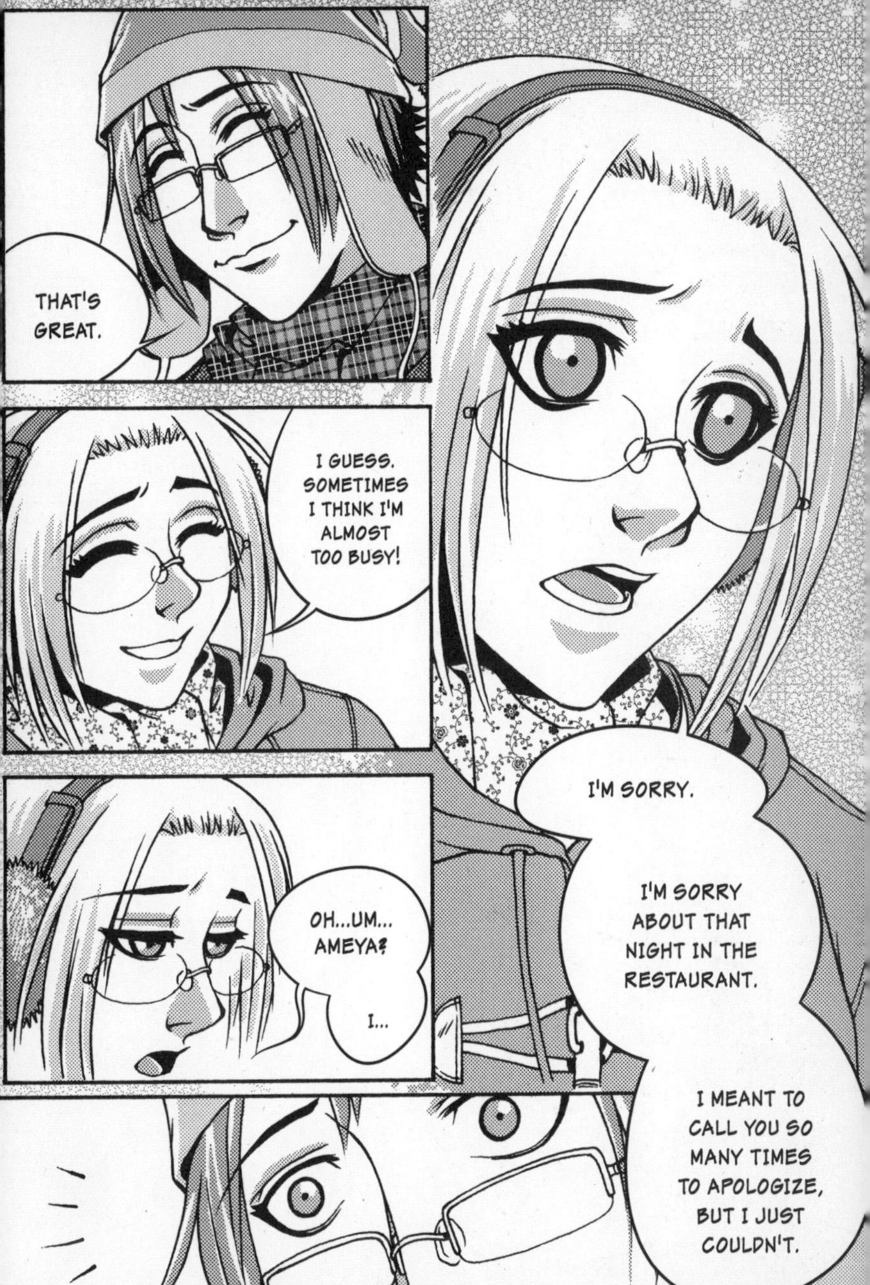
THAT'S GREAT.
I GUESS. SOMETIMES I THINK I'M ALMOST TOO BUSY!
OH...UM... AMEYA?
I...
I'M SORRY.
I'M SORRY ABOUT THAT NIGHT IN THE RESTAURANT.
I MEANT TO CALL YOU SO MANY TIMES TO APOLOGIZE, BUT I JUST COULDN'T.

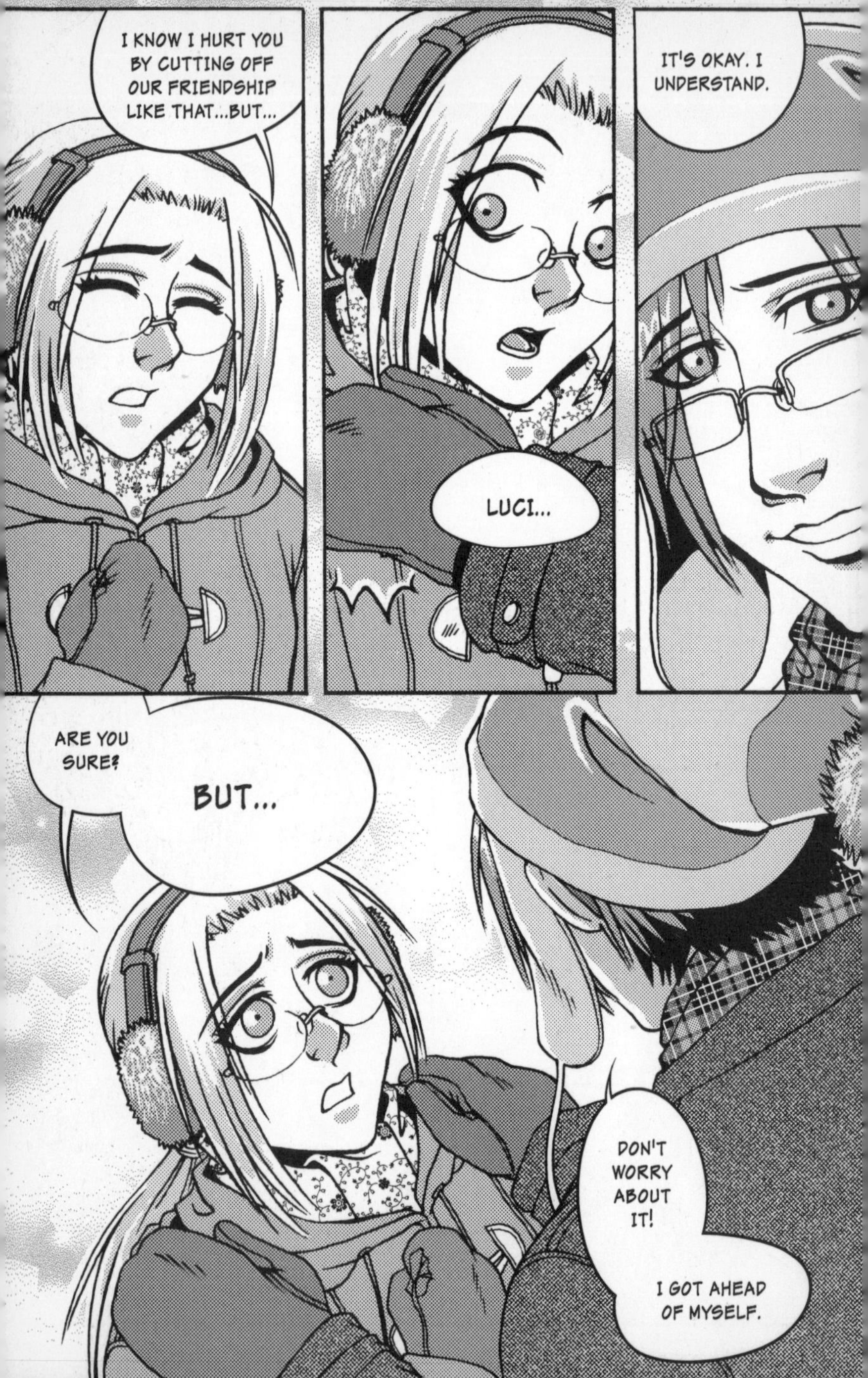
I KNOW I HURT YOU BY CUTTING OFF OUR FRIENDSHIP LIKE THAT...BUT...
LUCI...
IT'S OKAY. I UNDERSTAND.
ARE YOU SURE?
BUT...
DON'T WORRY ABOUT IT!
I GOT AHEAD OF MYSELF.

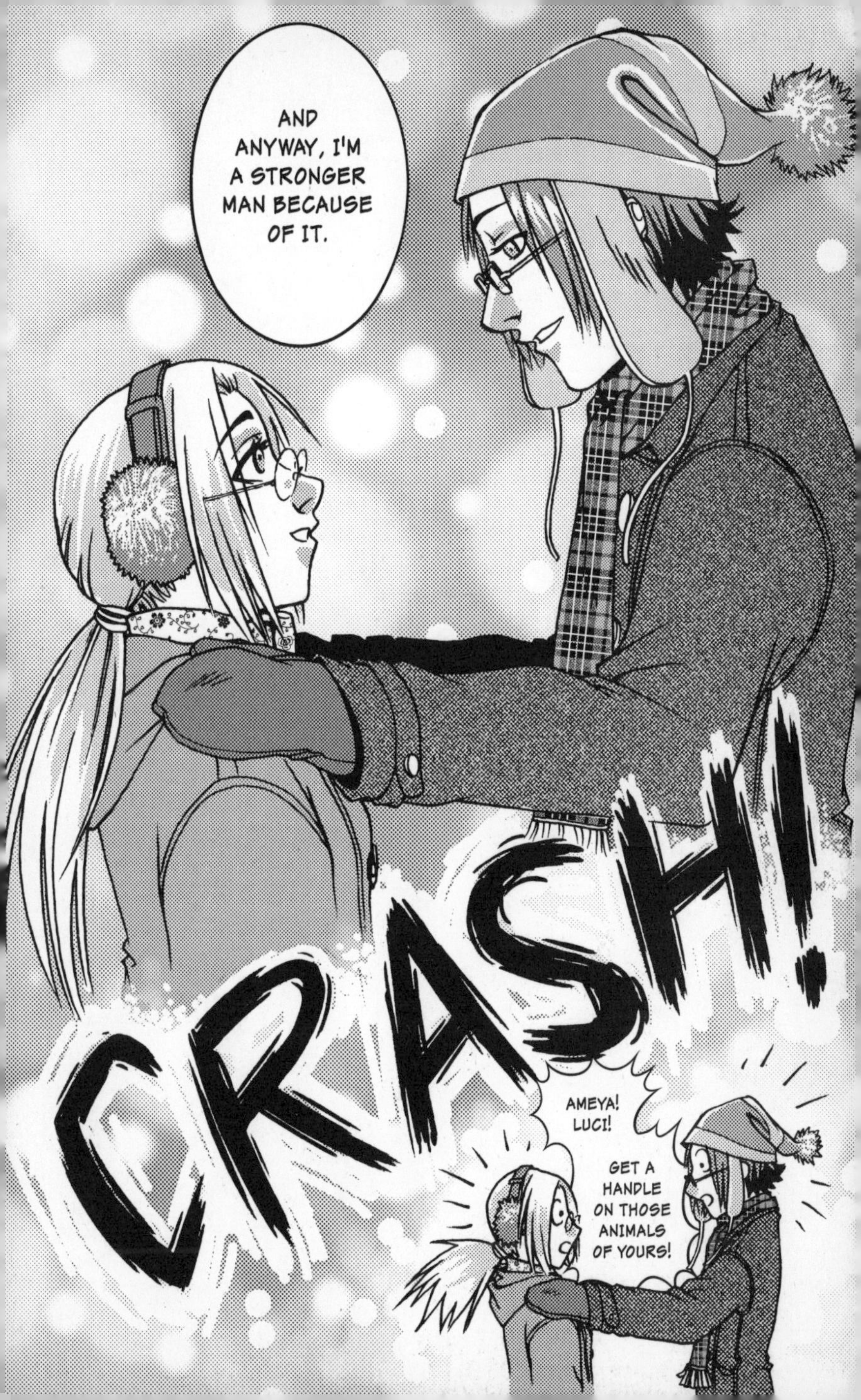
AND ANYWAY, I'M A STRONGER MAN BECAUSE OF IT.
CRASH!
AMEYA! LUCI!
GET A HANDLE ON THOSE ANIMALS OF YOURS!

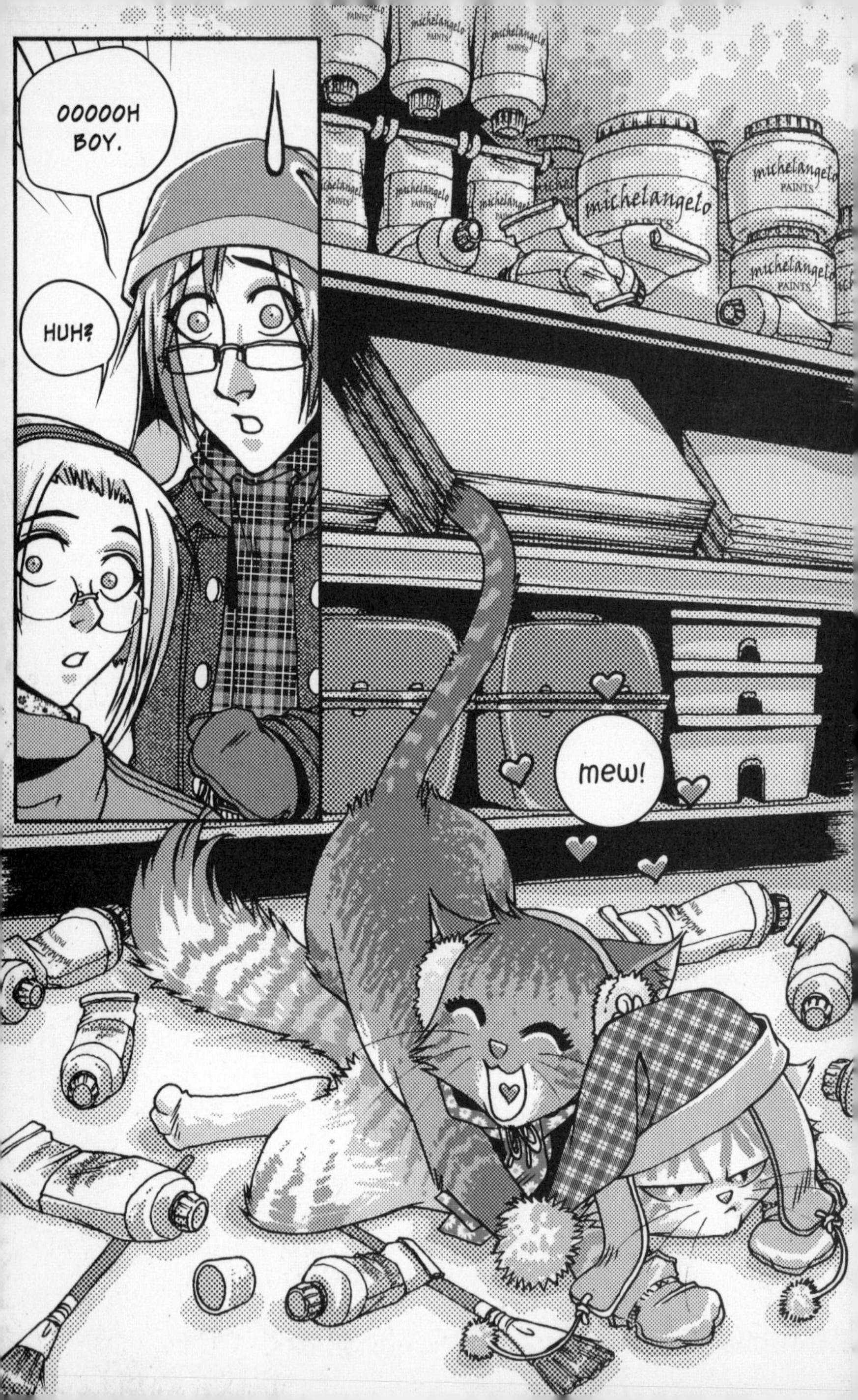
OOOOOH BOY.
HUH?
michelangelo PAINTS
mew!

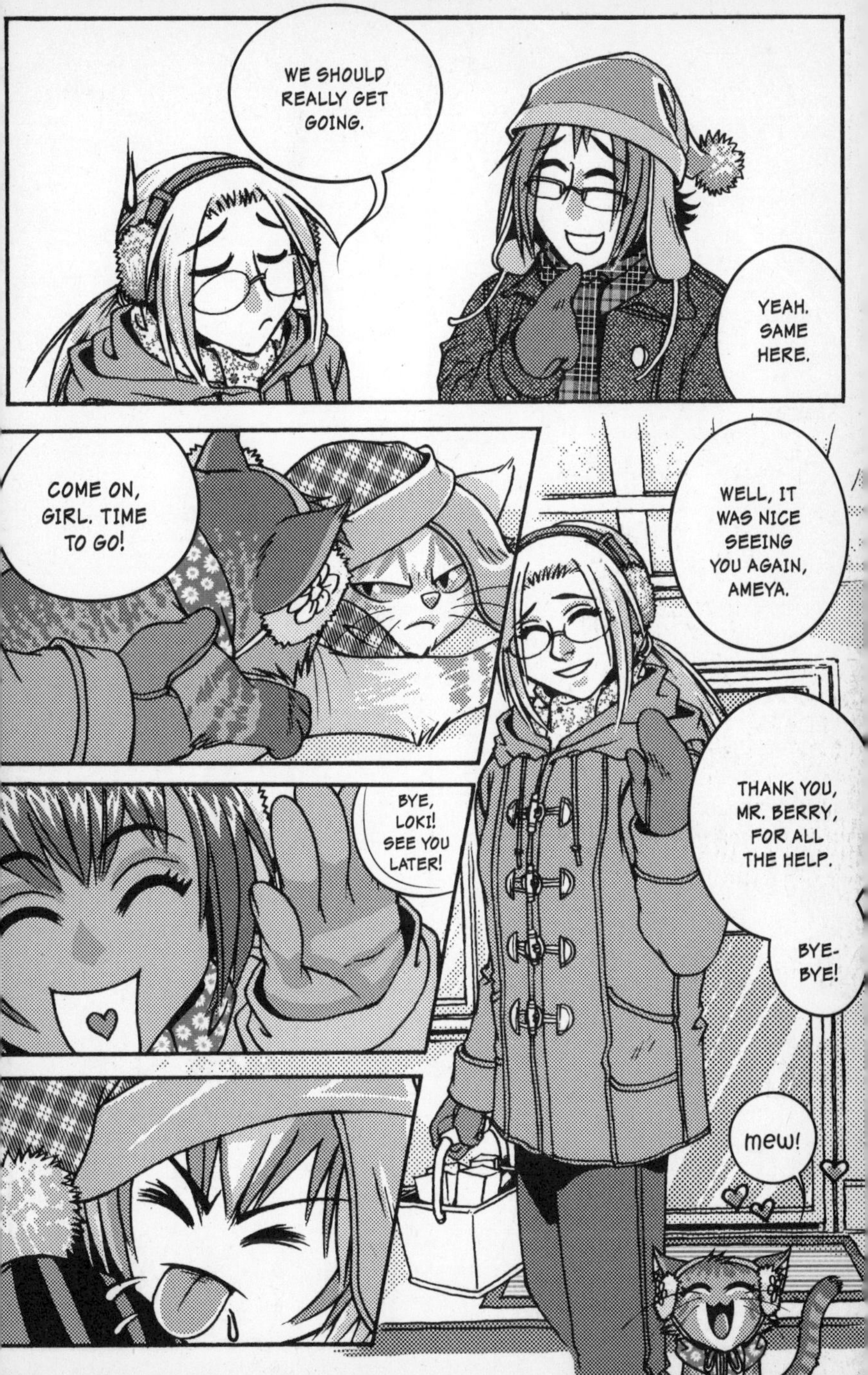
WE SHOULD REALLY GET GOING.
YEAH. SAME HERE.
COME ON, GIRL. TIME TO GO!
BYE, LOKI! SEE YOU LATER!
WELL, IT WAS NICE SEEING YOU AGAIN, AMEYA.
THANK YOU, MR. BERRY, FOR ALL THE HELP.
BYE-BYE!
mew!

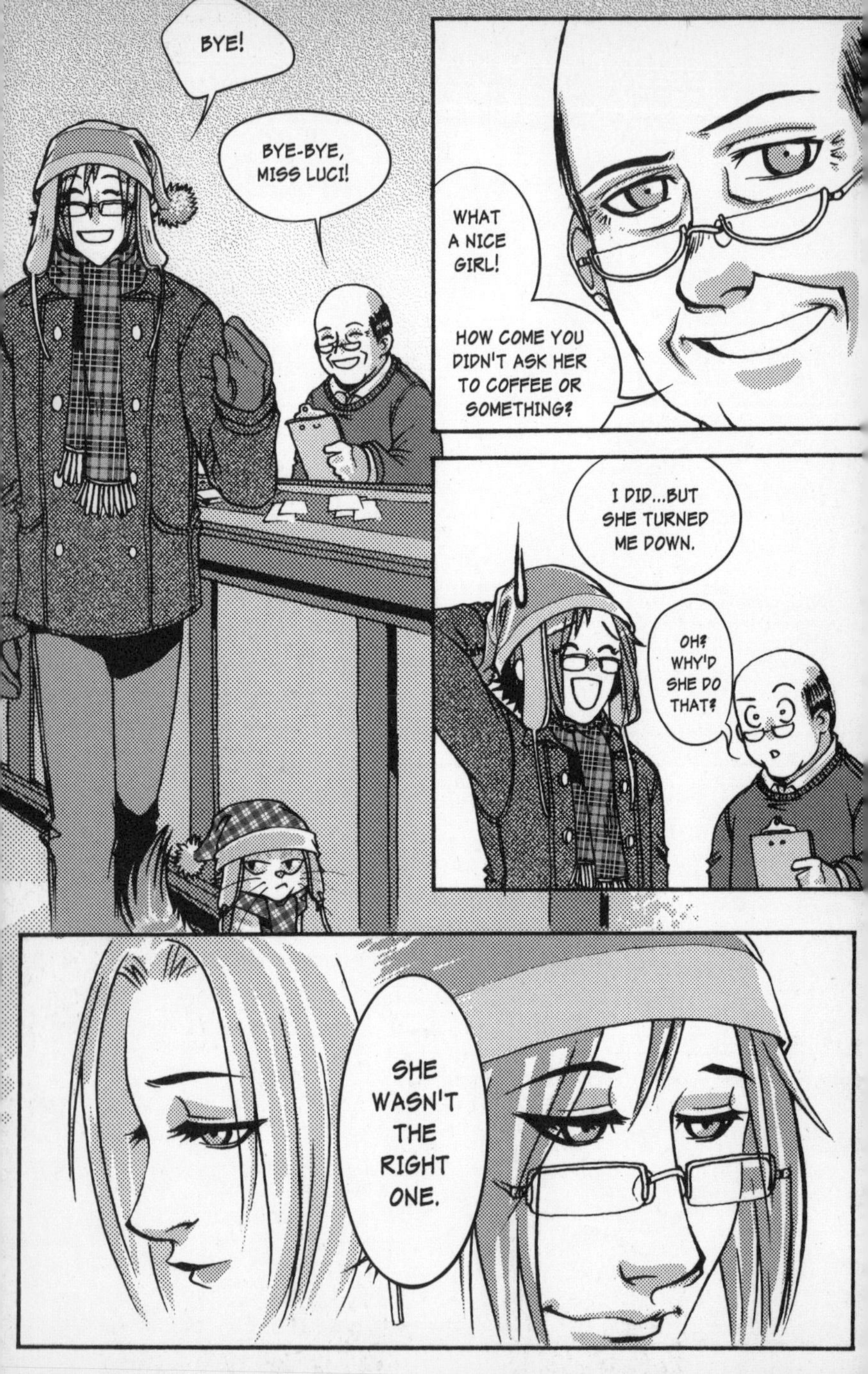
BYE!
BYE-BYE, MISS LUCI!
WHAT A NICE GIRL!
HOW COME YOU DIDN'T ASK HER TO COFFEE OR SOMETHING?
I DID...BUT SHE TURNED ME DOWN.
OH? WHY'D SHE DO THAT?
SHE WASN'T THE RIGHT ONE.

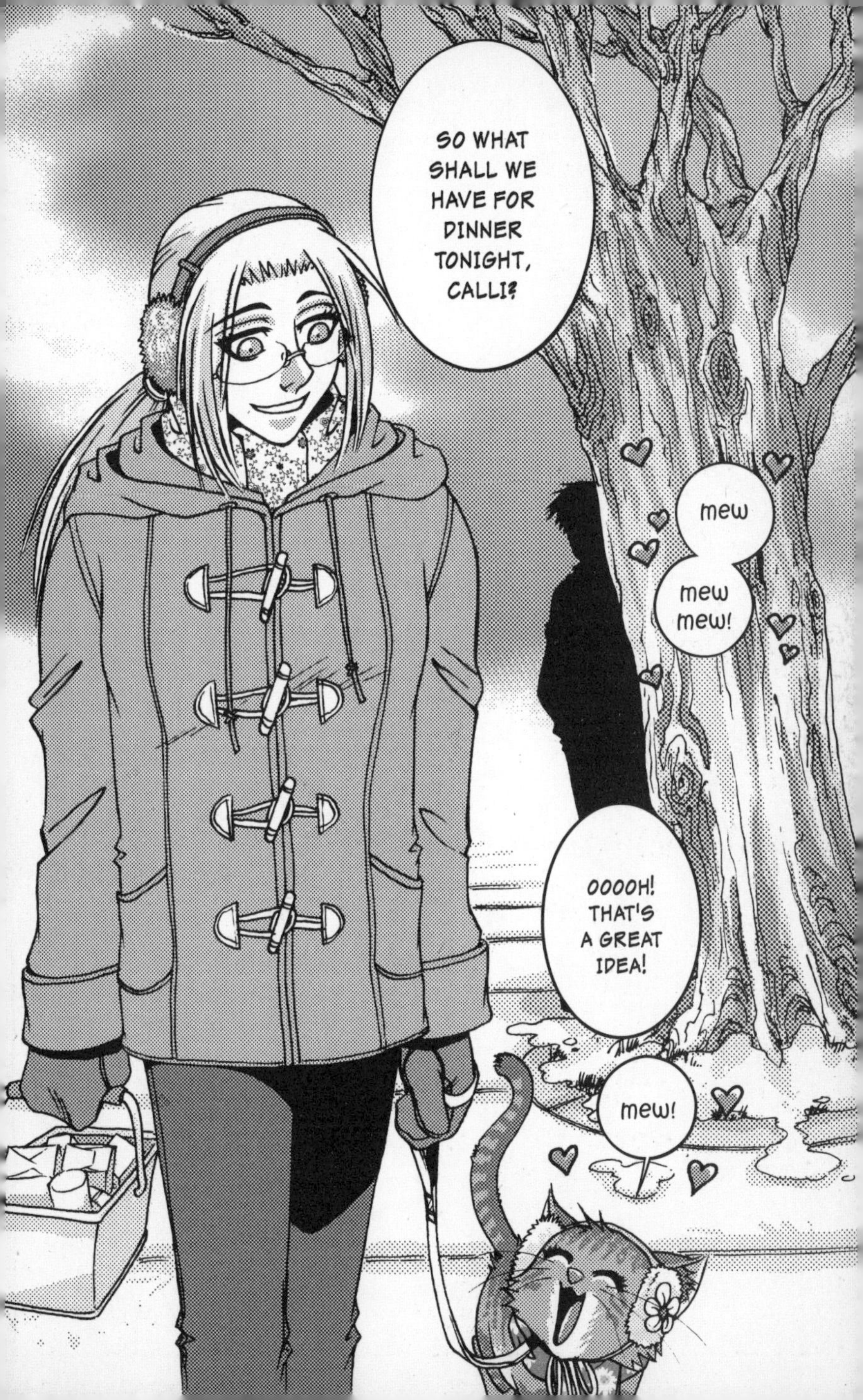
SO WHAT SHALL WE HAVE FOR DINNER TONIGHT, CALLI?
mew
mew mew!
OOOOH! THAT'S A GREAT IDEA!
mew!

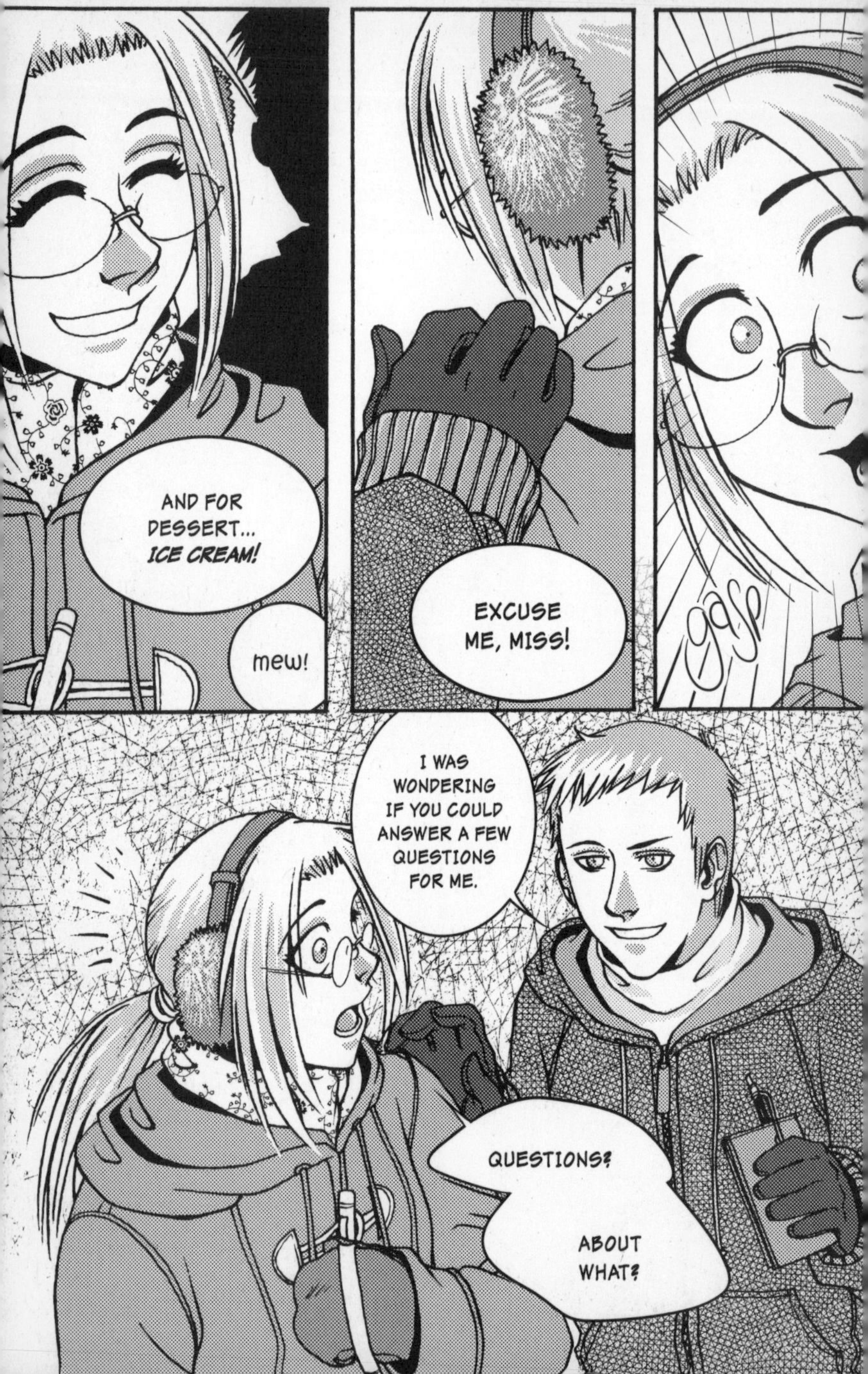
AND FOR DESSERT... *ICE CREAM!*
mew!
EXCUSE ME, MISS!
gasp
I WAS WONDERING IF YOU COULD ANSWER A FEW QUESTIONS FOR ME.
QUESTIONS?
ABOUT WHAT?

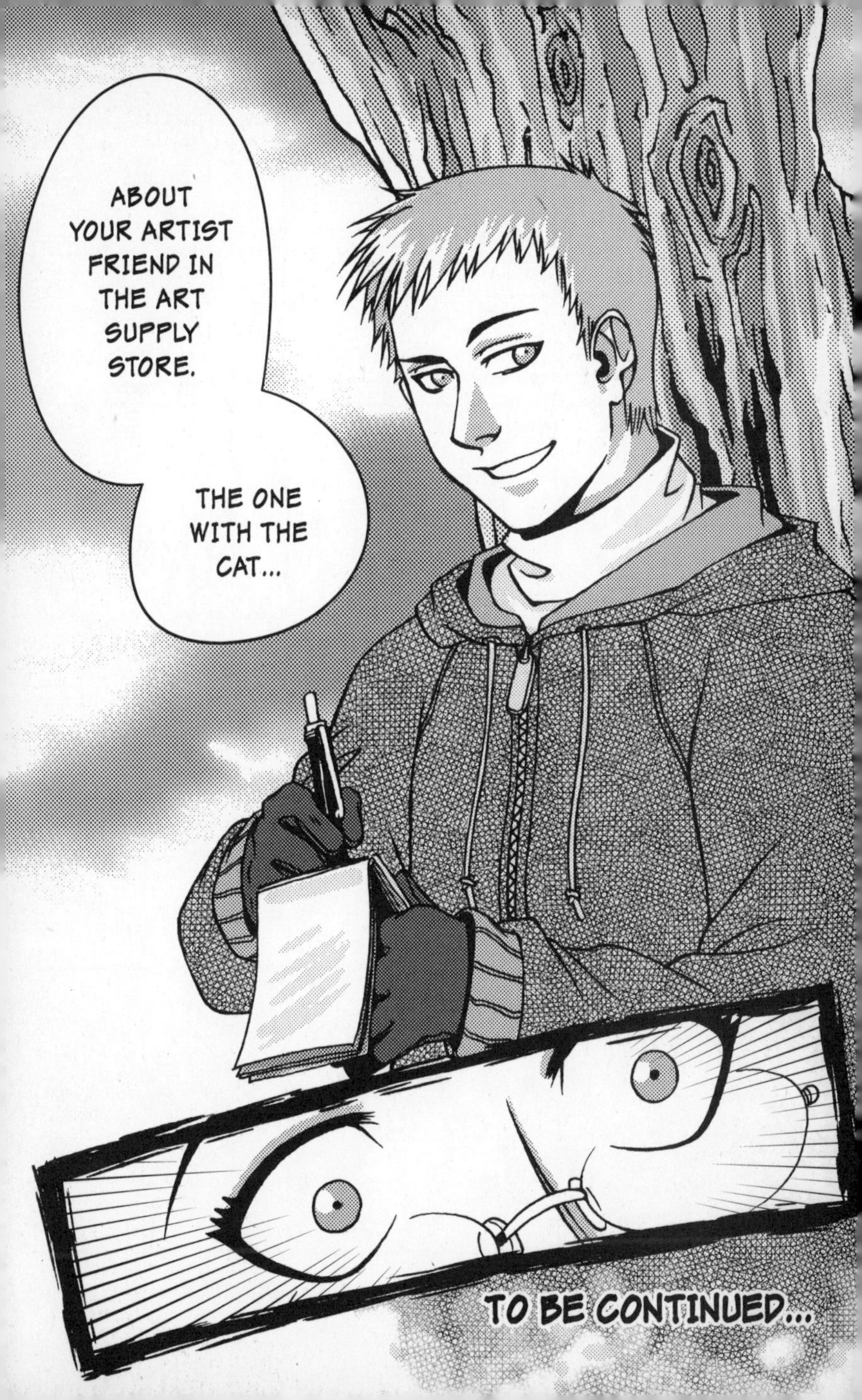
ABOUT YOUR ARTIST FRIEND IN THE ART SUPPLY STORE.
THE ONE WITH THE CAT...
TO BE CONTINUED...

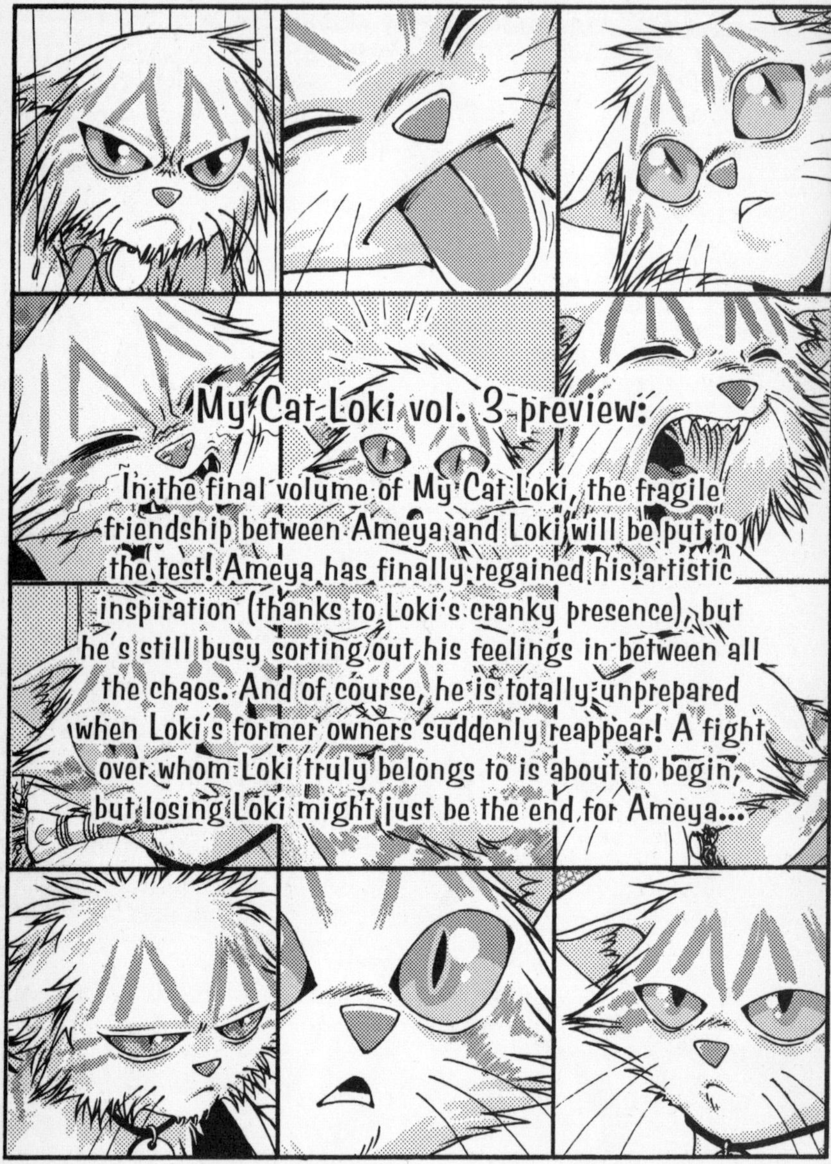
My Cat Loki vol. 3 preview:
In the final volume of My Cat Loki, the fragile friendship between Ameya and Loki will be put to the test! Ameya has finally regained his artistic inspiration (thanks to Loki's cranky presence), but he's still busy sorting out his feelings in between all the chaos. And of course, he is totally unprepared when Loki's former owners suddenly reappear! A fight over whom Loki truly belongs to is about to begin, but losing Loki might just be the end for Ameya...

Notes from the Drawing Board

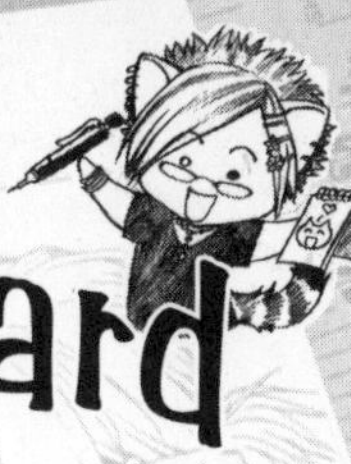

HUZZAH! HUZZAH! HUZZAH!
WELL! Here we are again! The end of another volume of My Cat Loki...and let me tell you...it's been QUITE a ride! Looking back, I'd like to think I've grown as a comicbook artist with the creation of this volume, as I've noticed many improvements in my techniques along the way!^_^V Again, I'm proud of my accomplishments with the completion of this volume. I still can't believe it! TWO WHOLE BOOKS under my belt now! SERIOUSLY! That's a WHOLE lotta work and am VERY happy that I've made it this far!

*Now...only ONE volume to go...and it'll be the BEST by FAR! XD I am DEFINITELY looking forward to working on it!^,^V But before I do that, I cannot forget to acknowledge all those who have had their part in helping make this book possible!^______^*

*LILLIAN ~ You continue to be the BESTEST EDITOR EVER! Am SO honoured to be working under your guidance, kindness and patience. I honestly don't think I'd have made it this far if it weren't for your constant encouragement and support! ^_^ ***BIG LOVIN HUGS!!****
FRIENDS ~ *Both on and off line, for continuing to be there for me thru the thick and thin, again, I seriously can't thank you enough!* ****BIG LOVIN' HUGS TO ALL!****
MY FAMILY ~ *For continuing to believe in my dream to become what I am today, supporting my accomplishments and still help to provide a roof over my head and food for sustenance. Yes, I WILL eventually move out of the house...in the meantime, I'm really learning how to cook well, aren't I?!!* ***:D***
THE FANS ~ *For your continuing support and appreciation of my work. My love and **GREAT** thanks to you all! ^____^*

And last, but certainly NOT least...
My cat Morris- *You will always be my inspiration. I dearly miss you, but your place in my life and heart will always remain and never be forgotten.*
This story is for you! =^_^=

Lots of love, GREAT appreciation and BIG LOVIN' HUGS,

*~Bettina ^_____^*

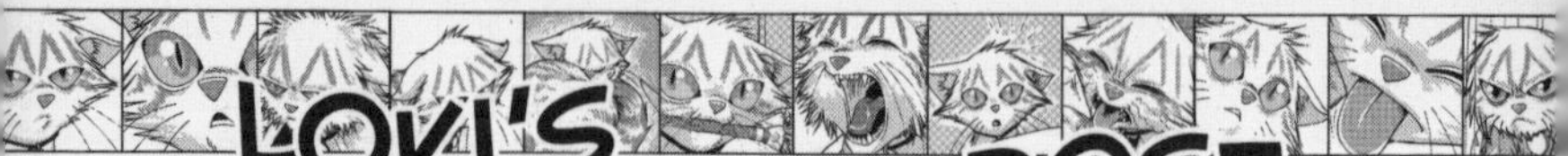

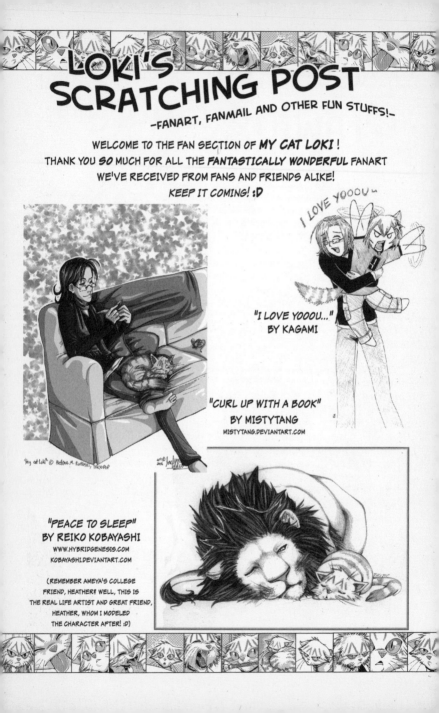

LOKI'S SCRATCHING POST

-FANART, FANMAIL AND OTHER FUN STUFFS!-

WELCOME TO THE FAN SECTION OF **MY CAT LOKI** !
THANK YOU ***SO*** MUCH FOR ALL THE ***FANTASTICALLY WONDERFUL*** FANART
WE'VE RECEIVED FROM FANS AND FRIENDS ALIKE!
KEEP IT COMING! :D

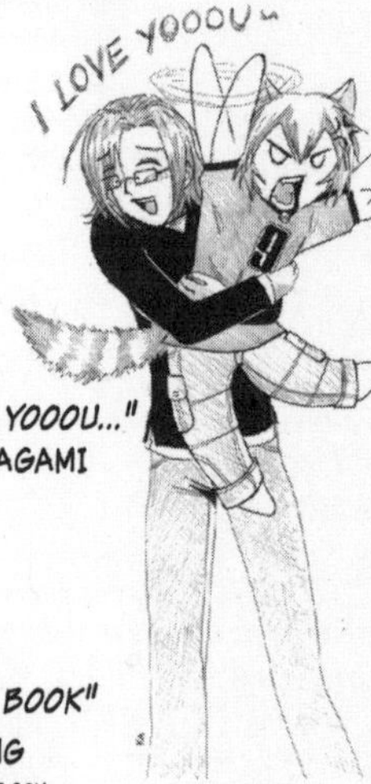
I LOVE YOOOU~

"I LOVE YOOOU..."
BY KAGAMI

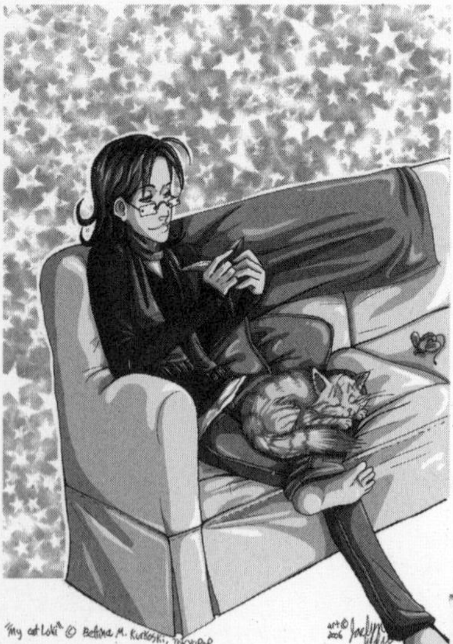
"My cat Loki" © Bettina M. Kurkoski, TOKYOPOP
art © 2006

"CURL UP WITH A BOOK"
BY MISTYTANG
MISTYTANG.DEVIANTART.COM

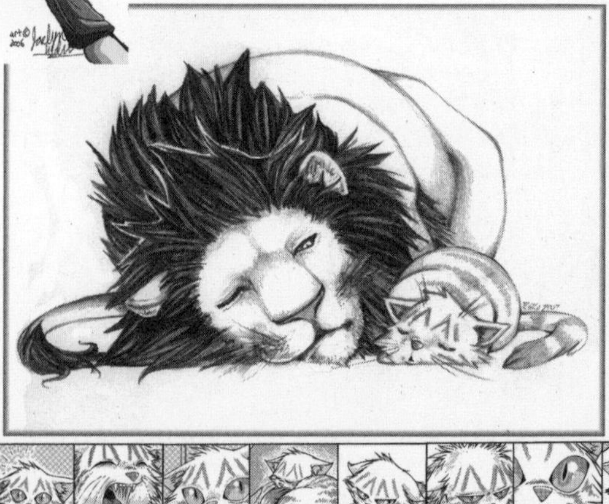

"PEACE TO SLEEP"
BY REIKO KOBAYASHI
WWW.HYBRIDGENESIS.COM
KOBAYASHI.DEVIANTART.COM

(REMEMBER AMEYA'S COLLEGE FRIEND, HEATHER? WELL, THIS IS THE REAL LIFE ARTIST AND GREAT FRIEND, HEATHER, WHOM I MODELED THE CHARACTER AFTER! :D)

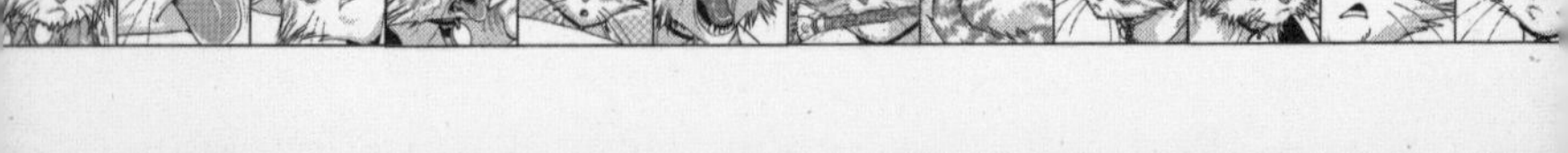

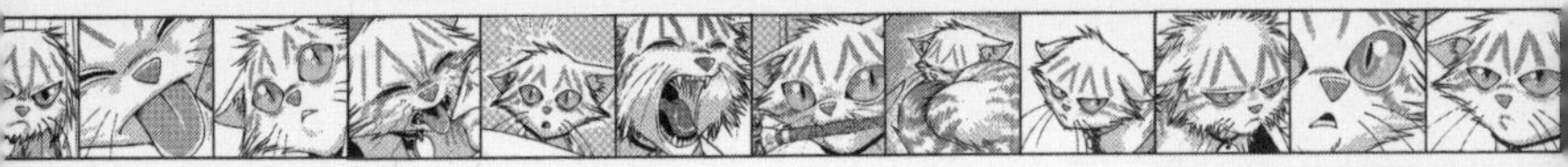

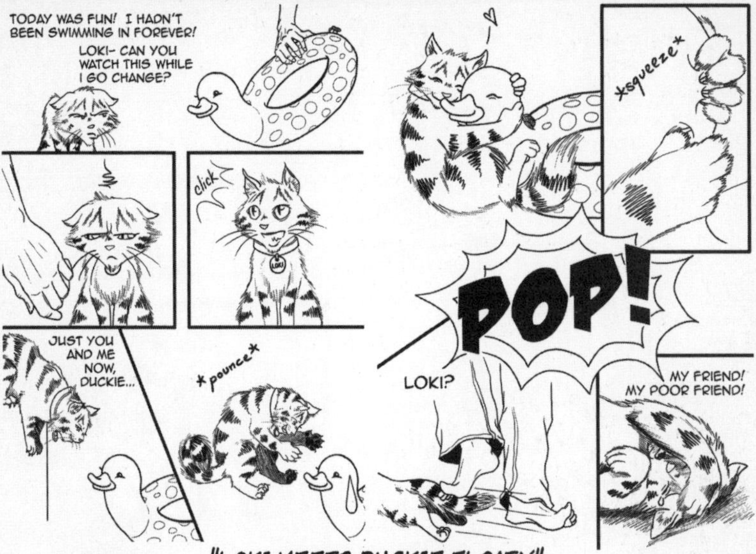
TODAY WAS FUN! I HADN'T BEEN SWIMMING IN FOREVER!
LOKI- CAN YOU WATCH THIS WHILE I GO CHANGE?
squeeze
click
JUST YOU AND ME NOW, DUCKIE...
pounce
POP!
LOKI?
MY FRIEND! MY POOR FRIEND!

"LOKI MEETS DUCKIE FLOATY"
BY PUDDLE
MIZUTAMARI.DEVIANTART.COM

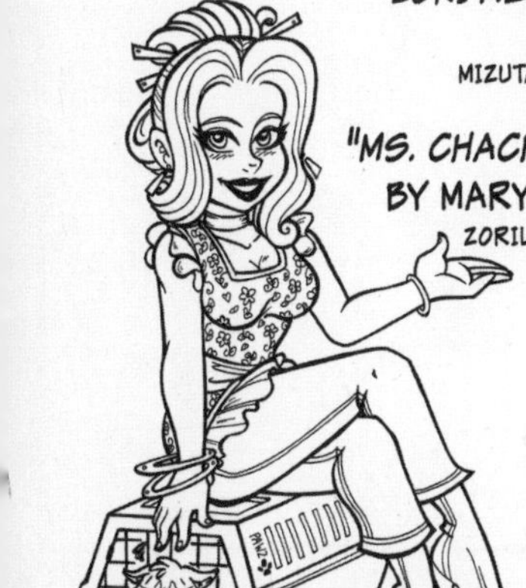

"MS. CHACHA AND LOKI"
BY MARY BELLAMY
ZORILITA.BITTERMAUSE.COM

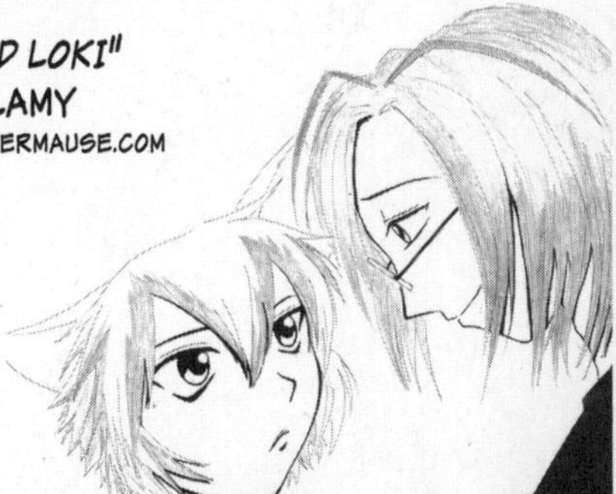
LOKI

"HUMAN LOKI AND AMEYA"
BY KAGAMI

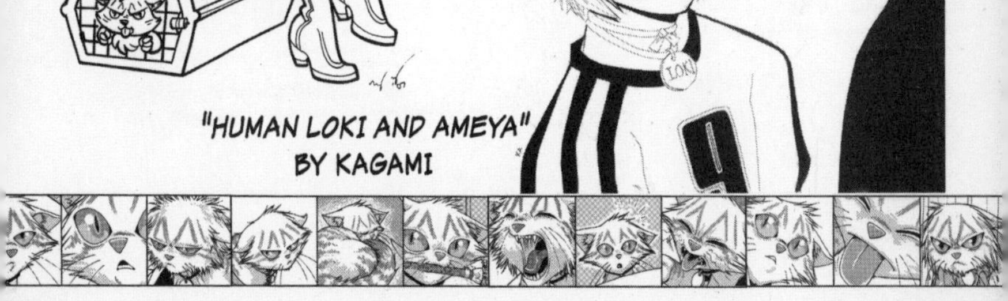

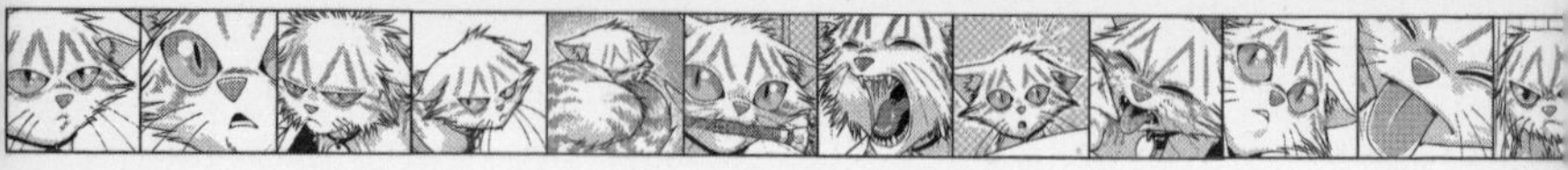

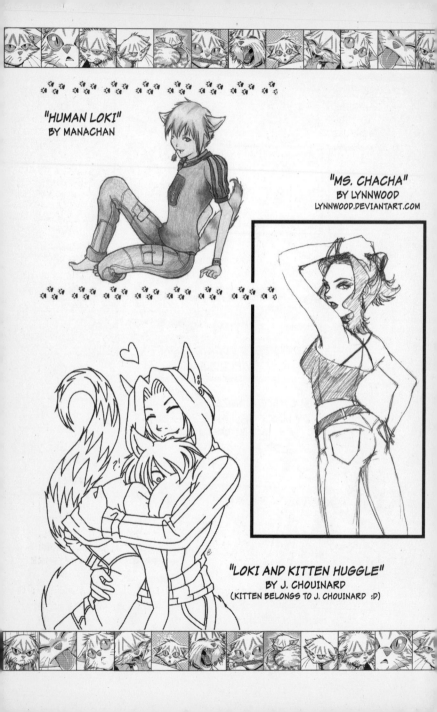

"HUMAN LOKI"
BY MANACHAN

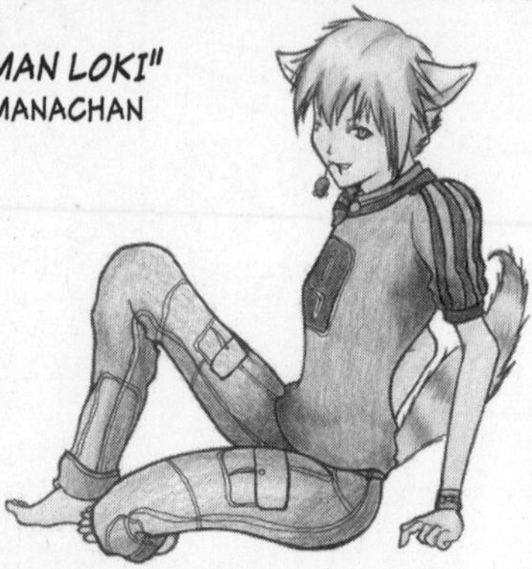

"MS. CHACHA"
BY LYNNWOOD
LYNNWOOD.DEVIANTART.COM

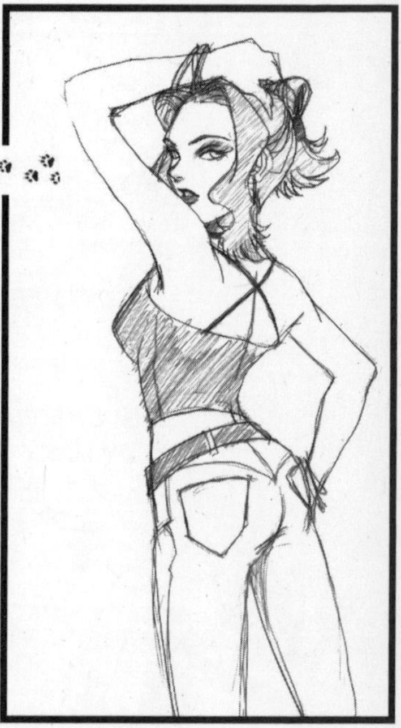

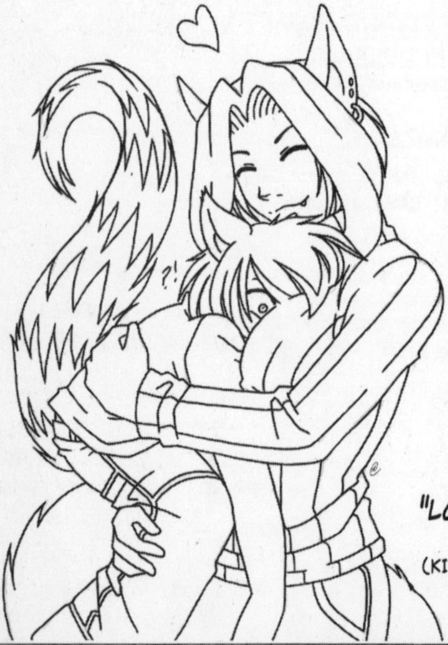
?!

"LOKI AND KITTEN HUGGLE"
BY J. CHOUINARD
(KITTEN BELONGS TO J. CHOUINARD :D)

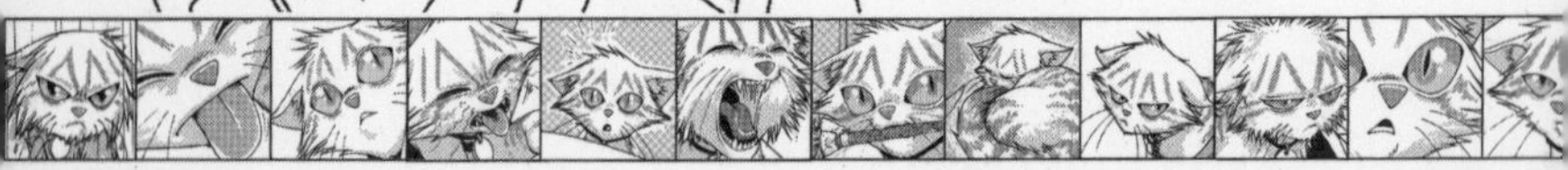

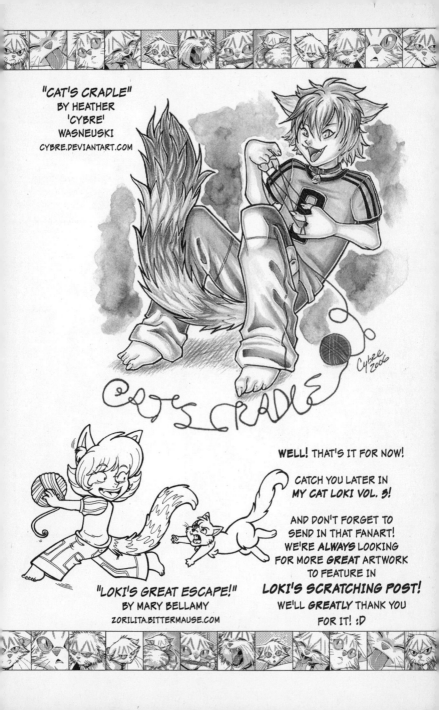

"CAT'S CRADLE"
BY HEATHER
'CYBRE'
WASNEUSKI
CYBRE.DEVIANTART.COM

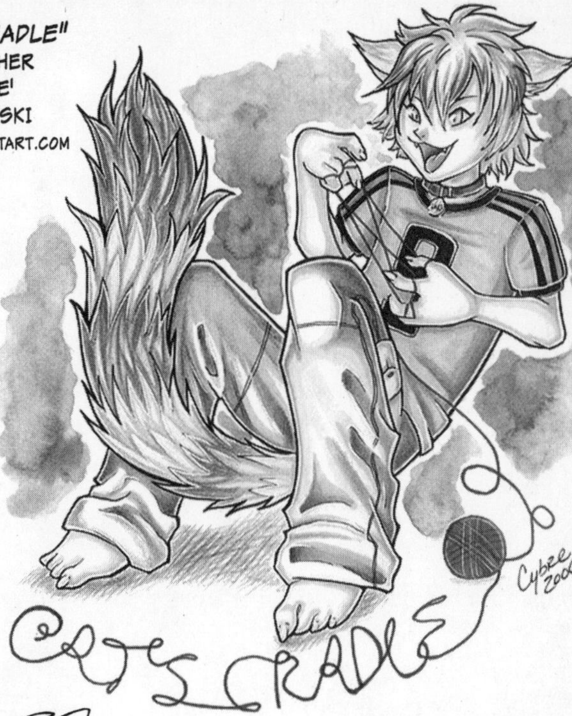
CATS CRADLE
Cybre 2006

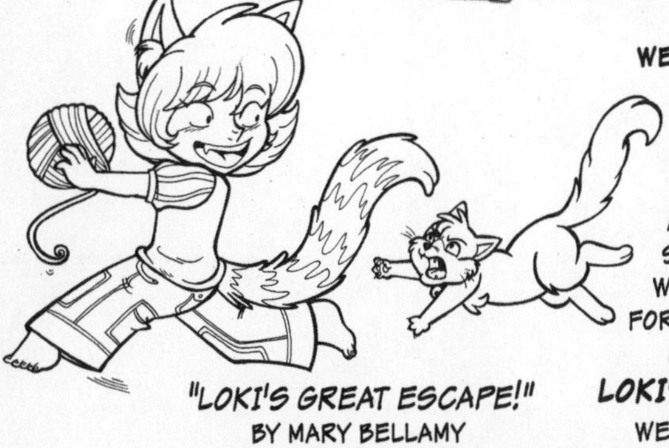

"LOKI'S GREAT ESCAPE!"
BY MARY BELLAMY
ZORILITA.BITTERMAUSE.COM

WELL! THAT'S IT FOR NOW!

CATCH YOU LATER IN
MY CAT LOKI VOL. 3!

AND DON'T FORGET TO
SEND IN THAT FANART!
WE'RE **ALWAYS** LOOKING
FOR MORE **GREAT** ARTWORK
TO FEATURE IN
LOKI'S SCRATCHING POST!
WE'LL **GREATLY** THANK YOU
FOR IT! :D

TOKYOPOP.com

WHERE MANGA LIVES!

JOIN the
TOKYOPOP community:
www.TOKYOPOP.com

LIVE THE MANGA LIFESTYLE!

EXCLUSIVE PREVIEWS...
CREATE...
UPLOAD...
DOWNLOAD...
BLOG...
CHAT...
VOTE...
LIVE!!!!

WWW.TOKYOPOP.COM HAS:
- News
- Columns
- Special Features
- and more...

THE MANGA REVOLUTION • LEADING
漫画
革命
THE MANGA REVOLUTION • LEADING